ALSO BY TJ KLUNE FROM TOR PUBLISHING GROUP

BOOKS FOR ADULTS

The Green Creek Series
Wolfsong
Ravensong
Heartsong
Brothersong

The Cerulean Chronicles
The House in the Cerulean Sea

Standalones
The Bones Beneath My Skin
Under the Whispering Door
In the Lives of Puppets

BOOKS FOR YOUNG ADULTS

The Extraordinaries Series
The Extraordinaries
Flash Fire
Heat Wave

SOMEWHERE BEYOND THE SEA

TJ KLUNE

TOR PUBLISHING GROUP
NEW YORK

This is a work of fiction. All of the characters, organizations, and events portrayed in this novel are either products of the author's imagination or are used fictitiously.

SOMEWHERE BEYOND THE SEA

Copyright © 2024 by Travis Klune

All rights reserved.

Interior art by Shutterstock.com

A Tor Book
Published by Tom Doherty Associates / Tor Publishing Group
120 Broadway
New York, NY 10271

www.torpublishinggroup.com

Tor® is a registered trademark of Macmillan Publishing Group, LLC.

The Library of Congress Cataloging-in-Publication Data is available upon request.

ISBN 978-1-250-88120-5 (hardcover)
ISBN 978-1-250-37504-9 (international, sold outside the U.S., subject to rights availability)
ISBN 978-1-250-88121-2 (ebook)

Our books may be purchased in bulk for promotional, educational, or business use. Please contact your local bookseller or the Macmillan Corporate and Premium Sales Department at 1-800-221-7945, extension 5442, or by email at MacmillanSpecialMarkets@macmillan.com.

First Edition: 2024

Printed in the United States of America

10 9 8 7 6 5 4 3 2

*For the trans community the world over:
I see you, I hear you, I love you.
This story is for you.*

SOMEWHERE BEYOND THE SEA

"We are at a crossroads. The purpose of this hearing—and any that may follow—is to determine what, if any, changes need to be made to the current RULES AND REGULATIONS *that govern the magical community. As has been covered by the press ad nauseum, the Departments in Charge of Magical Youth and Magical Adults have recently come under heavy scrutiny. With the dissolution of Extremely Upper Management, the departments are without permanent leadership."*

Stepping off the ferry and onto the island for the first time in decades, Arthur Parnassus thought he'd burst into flames right then and there. He did not, but it was a close thing: the fire burning within him felt brighter than it had in years. He itched to break out of his skin and spread his wings, to take to the sky and feel the familiar salt-tinged wind in his feathers. But he knew if he did, chances were he'd fly away and leave this place behind forever. And that wouldn't do. He'd come back for a reason.

The owner of the ferry—an ornery fellow with a pockmarked face, stained coveralls, and the charming name of Merle—called down to him from the railing ten feet overhead. "You better be sure about this. Once I leave, you're stuck here. I don't come out here after dark."

Arthur didn't look at the ferry operator, transfixed by the dirt road stretching out before him, winding its way into a wood with a canopy so thick the light from the midday sun barely reached the moss and leaves covering the forest floor. The sound of the sea lapping at the white sandy shores filled his ears, a reminder of his youth: the good, the bad, everything. "Thank you, Merle. Your assistance has proven invaluable." He glanced back at the ferry. "I think I'll be just fine. Should I need to return to the mainland, I'll summon you."

"How? No phones connected on the island. No electricity. No water."

"That will change. Utilities have been scheduled to come out tomorrow morning at ten on the dot. You'll bring them over, won't you?"

He scowled, but Arthur saw the greedy flash in his eyes, there and gone. "Rates will fluctuate," Merle said with a haughty sniff. "Petrol isn't cheap, and running one person back and forth will—"

"Of course," Arthur said. "You deserve to be appropriately compensated for your time."

Merle blinked. "Yes, well. I suppose I do." He looked down at the two suitcases sitting on either side of Arthur. One old, the other new. "Why'd you come here?"

Barely a cloud in the sky. The blue above matched the blue below. The tail end of summer, warm, but then he was always warm. The salt in the air tickled his nose, and he breathed it in until it filled his lungs. "Why not?"

"This is a terrible place," Merle said with a shiver. "Haunted, or so I've heard. No one lives here. Hasn't for a long time." He spat over the side railing. "And when they did, we weren't supposed to talk about it. Hush-hush, you know."

"I know," Arthur murmured. Then, raising his voice, he said, "Merle. You wouldn't happen to know a man named Melvin, would you?"

"What? How did you—he was my father."

"I thought as much," Arthur said. Ouroboros. A snake eating its own tail in an infinite cycle. Maybe this was a mistake. The village they'd come from across the sea looked the same from this vantage as it had years before, buildings in pastels of pink and yellow and green, people in summer wear without a care in the world, safe, because why wouldn't they be? They were human. The world was built for them.

The ferry was the same, though a few upgrades had been made over the years: a fresh coat of paint, new seats to replace the cracked and split ones. Even Merle did not bring a sense of dissonance, looking so much like Melvin, mouth turned down, eyes flat. It was the same. All of it was the same. Except for Arthur. "I knew him once." *You too,* he almost added, remembering the glowering teenager who skulked around the ferry with a mop.

Merle grunted. "Dead now. Ten years."

"I'm sorry for your loss."

Merle waved him off. "How did you know him?"

Arthur smiled. "I'll be in touch." With that, he picked up both suitcases and squared his shoulders. He was here. Finally, at last. It was time to see what he could see and hope this endeavor would not be in vain. "Your kindness will be remembered. I'm off! Cheers, my good man."

The dirt road wound its way through the thickening wood, the sun casting shadows that flickered with the breeze. He wasn't sweating, not yet, but the road proved longer than he remembered. *Such is the folly of youth,* he thought to himself. Boundless energy where a mile could have been six or seven for all it mattered. Nearing forty, Arthur was in mostly good shape, but the days he could run endlessly were long gone.

He rounded a corner and stopped. Trees blocked the way.

Five in total, they'd grown across the road, trunks so close together it would be impossible to slip through. They reached toward the sky, towering over him, looking far older than they should have—a hundred years, if not more. But they couldn't be. The last time he'd walked down this road they hadn't been here, not even tiny saplings.

Which meant it was something else. Rather, it was *someone* else. Not the trees themselves, of course; no, he was being watched.

He set down his suitcases and approached the tree in the middle. The bark was cracked, rough against his skin as he pressed his hand against it. "Are you there?" he asked. "You must be. These are your doing, I expect."

The only answer came in the form of birdsong.

"You know me," Arthur continued. "Or who I used to be." He laughed, though there was no humor in it. "I have returned to this place in hopes of making it more than it was." Closing his eyes, he pressed his forehead against the trunk. "And I'll do it alone if I have to, but not without your permission."

He opened his eyes when the trunk began to vibrate. Moving back slowly, Arthur watched as the trees on the path trembled with a low rumble, roots bursting up through the earth like tentacles. They slithered along the ground, wrapping around trees off the road. Wood groaned as the roots tightened, pulling the trees aside to make an opening.

Only the middle tree remained. It shivered, limbs rattling, leaves shaking. He didn't flinch when a thin branch caressed his cheek, a green leaf tickling the side of his nose. In it, he heard a whisper: *The boy. The boy with the fire has come home.*

"Yes," he whispered back. "I have returned."

The tree twisted, the dirt road cracking and breaking apart. The tree roots rose up through the ground and he grinned when they acted as feet, walking the tree off to the side of the road. Once it found a place to settle, the roots sank beneath the ground once more. Ahead, dirt rose in the divots left behind, filling them in. A moment later, the road ahead was as smooth as the road behind.

"Thank you," Arthur said with a little bow. "If and when you're ready, I'll be here." Picking up his luggage, he moved on.

The moment he stepped out of the wood and saw the house for the first time in twenty-eight years was unremarkable. Set back over a jagged cliff, it loomed above him, backlit by the sun. An empty cement fountain sat out front, the basin streaked with green and black mold. The brickwork appeared to have fallen into disrepair, cracked and broken, pieces half buried in the grass around the house. Shattered windows in white frames were surrounded by crawling ivy half covering the front. The turret—a tower that rose twenty feet from the top of the house—looked as if it would fall over at the slightest nudge. Next to the house was an overgrown garden with flowers in golds and reds and pinks, overtaking the gazebo where, at the age of nine, a boy with fire in his blood had carved his initials into the brick to prove he existed: AFB. Arthur Franklin Parnassus.

Set away from the house was a second building, one he'd never seen before. It hadn't been here when he'd left as a child, crying out against the bright sunlight after having been trapped in darkness for so long, a strong arm wrapped around him, guiding him up the stairs and out to a waiting vehicle. This other building was small, made of similar brick as the house he'd dreamed about time and time again. He knew the so-called orphanage had changed owners a time or two over the years, but as far as he could tell, no one had lived here for quite a while. The guesthouse, for that was what it seemed to be, would do for now. The windows were intact, and the roof looked to be in better shape than the main house, where some of the shingles had been blown off by storms past.

He left his luggage near the porch steps, moving as if in a dream. The path through the garden was difficult to navigate, the plants and shrubbery thick, encroaching. He passed by the gazebo, pushing his way through the wild garden. The path wrapped around the side of the house to the back, and there, affixed to the base of the house, stood a pair of double wooden doors that led underground, streaks of scorched black upon them. The doors were sealed with a rusted padlock. He had the key. He had all the keys.

He didn't go inside. He knew what was down there. Tick marks scratched into the wall. Blackened stone from when he'd burned. Perpetual darkness, aside from his fire.

A ghost, then, rose behind him, wrapping an arm around his throat, holding him captive. "You earned this," it snarled in his ear. "You'll learn your place, mark my words, boy. Say it. What are you? *Say it.*"

"An abomination," Arthur said dully as the arm faded away.

He stared at the wooden cellar doors as the sun drifted across the sky.

He couldn't do this. He didn't know why he'd thought he could. Too much. It was all too much. Arthur fisted his hair as he walked back around to the front of the house. His luggage was where he'd left it.

He bent over, hands brushing against the handles of his suitcases.

A voice said, "Arthur." Loud, clear, as if someone stood on the porch right in front of him.

He lifted his head. He was alone.

Except that wasn't quite true. Because he saw something he'd missed upon his arrival: a tiny yellow flower growing through the warped wood of the first porch step. Barely the size of his thumbnail, the flower had persisted, pushing through the wood until it reached sunlight.

He walked toward it slowly. Reaching the porch, he crouched down in front of the flower, touching the yellow petals gently, sun-warm against his fingertips. Rebirth. Perseverance. Color. Life. Everything important in the smallest packages.

He smiled, and for the first time in a long time, felt something right itself in his chest. "Well," he said, "if you can do it, I suppose I can too."

Summer drifted toward autumn, the leaves changing, the air not quite as warm. Arthur stood on the porch, sanding down the railings so he could repaint them. He was thinking white to match the windowsills he'd already redone. Merle had proven to be an asset of sorts, one who grumbled about all the materials Arthur brought to the island on a weekly basis. To be fair, his grumblings subsided upon receipt of payment. He'd even halfheartedly helped load supplies into the back of a maroon van that Arthur had purchased weeks before.

Arthur had almost finished sanding the last railing, and it was time to check the grout between the kitchen tiles to make sure it was drying correctly. He was about to step back into the house when something fluttered at the back of his mind, the gentle touch of butterfly wings against skin.

He looked at the road.

A woman stood there, wearing a long flowing white dress, her feet bare. Her head was cocked, her white afro like a cloud. In her hair, pink and white flowers, opening and closing in the afternoon sunlight. Her skin was a lovely shade of deep brown. She looked ageless, her youthful face at odds with her dark eyes, ancient and unsure.

Her wings—four appendages growing from her back, each longer than Arthur's arms—fluttered slightly, translucent, the sunlight shining through them and sending a cascade of colors onto the ground. Her bare arms rested at her sides, her delicate fingers shaking slightly.

Arthur walked down the steps slowly. When he reached the bottom, he stopped, more nervous than he expected to be. He wasn't sure what to say, where to begin.

She glanced over his shoulder to the house before looking back at him. "You're here." She sounded like he remembered, soft, melodic, with a tinge of sadness.

"I am," Arthur said.

"Why?"

"Because it's the right thing to do," he said simply.

She nodded as if that were the answer she thought he'd give. She took a step toward him, and beneath her feet, grass sprouted through the dirt. Behind her, he could see similar grassy footsteps showing her path up the road.

"This house," she said. "This place. It should've burned."

"Yes."

"And yet here you are."

He smiled quietly. "Here I am. And here you are. Together again."

She shook her head. "How can you stand to be here? How can you even think of . . ." She sighed, her wings drooping. "I thought about destroying it. After . . . after you all left. I thought about coming here and opening the earth to swallow the house whole." She wiped her eyes with the back of her hand.

"But you didn't."

"No," she said. "I didn't." She looked away off into the trees. "And now I wonder why. Why I didn't do it. Why I waited. Why I even came here today."

"I can't answer that for you," Arthur said. "All I can do is tell you that things will be different this time around. I will give the children what I never had: a place to be whoever they want to be, no matter what they can do or where they come from."

"You can't do this alone."

"I can," he said. "And I will if I have to."

"No," she said. "You won't." She marched by him without so much as a glance in his direction, snatching the sandpaper from his hand. Muttering under her breath, she climbed the steps and frowned down at the railing. She nodded, and then began to sand down where Arthur had left off.

"Your dress," he said. "Do you want to . . . ?"

She paused. "It's fine. It's just a dress."

He watched her for a long while, feet refusing to move. When she eventually looked up at him, he said, "Hello, Zoe."

Zoe Chapelwhite said, "Hello, Arthur." Her bottom lip trembled. "I'm . . ." Then, in a breathy rush, "I'm so sorry for—"

He held up his hand. "I don't need that from you. I never have."

"But I did nothing to stop—"

"Zoe," he said. "You aren't to blame. You never were. You ran the risk of outing yourself. If they'd discovered you, they'd have come for you too."

"We'll never know," she said, eyes on the railing.

"Perhaps," Arthur said. "But you're here, regardless. What does that say about you? Something good, I expect."

Eyes wet, she said, "'Give me your tired, your poor, your huddled masses yearning to breathe free, the wretched refuse of your teeming shore.'"

"Emma Lazarus," Arthur said, pleased. "Yes, Zoe. We will take them all in."

"You mean that," she whispered.

"I do," he said. "I could use all the help I can get, but if this is something you can't do, I understand. I will continue on as I have been. Might take a little longer, but I'll get there."

She did not leave.

It took them the better part of a year to bring the house back up to code. If all went as he'd hoped, there would be inspections of every little detail, and he knew if even *one* thing was amiss, it'd be held against him.

One day, Zoe told him to stop.

"What?" he asked, looking up from the last bit of paint he was putting on the wall in the kitchen. It wasn't exactly needed, but he'd noticed the paint had dried with tiny bubbles in one section—small, about two inches wide and four inches tall—and that wouldn't do. It had to be perfect.

"Come with me," Zoe said.

He shook his head. "I can't. We're busier than ever. We have a mulch delivery tomorrow, and don't even get me started on the gazebo. I found a loose nail in one of the floorboards, and that means I need to go through and check every single nail in the entire house to make sure—"

"Arthur, the work is finished," Zoe said. "It's *been* finished for close to a month. You know it. I know it." She stared at him for a long moment. Then, "Go to your office. You know what needs to be done." She turned to leave, but stopped in the entryway to the kitchen. Without looking back, she said, "The island used to be bigger. Did you know that?"

She left him standing in the kitchen, staring after her.

He did as he was told, and found a typewriter sitting on top of an old desk. A blank piece of white paper had already been fed into the typewriter with more sitting on the desk next to it. The top page had spikey writing on it. Zoe had left him a note.

It's time to bring them home.
Z

He laughed. He cried. "I'm frightened," he whispered. "More than I've ever been in my life."

He began to type. He did not stop until he finished.

> To whom it may concern at the Department in Charge of Magical Youth,
>
> My name is Arthur Parnassus. I write to you with a proposal. I have assumed ownership of a particular house on Marsyas Island. For the last year, I—along with some associates—have renovated the property to make it not only livable, but suitable to serve, once again, as a home for orphaned magical children. Enclosed, you will find photographs documenting the work. . . .

He did then what the ten-year-old version of himself could not: he mailed a letter. As he dropped it in the public mailbox in the village, he caught sight of something he'd never noticed before, and his blood ran cold. There, hanging in the window of the post office, a poster of a family. A boy and a girl, both towheads with bright smiles. On either side of them, figures who appeared to be their parents, holding their hands as they walked through a sun-drenched field of wildflowers. Below them, in stark block lettering, words that Arthur read over and over again in disbelief.

PROTECTING YOUR FAMILY BEGINS WITH YOU!
SEE SOMETHING, SAY SOMETHING!

And below that: SPONSORED BY THE DEPARTMENTS IN CHARGE OF MAGICAL YOUTH AND MAGICAL ADULTS.

He turned and hurried back to the ferry.

A month passed. Then two. Then three and four and five. He did not despair. He knew it was only a matter of time before they got a response.

Then on a cool autumn day, the doorbell chimed.

A man stood on the porch, suitcase in one hand, the other holding a briefcase. He was younger than Arthur expected—thirty or thereabouts, and handsome, too, his wavy dark hair slightly mussed from the trip over on the ferry. His black suit was tailored to his thin frame, his tie a furious shade of red, his dress shoes coated in dust from the road.

He said, "Greetings! I'm looking for a Mr. Arthur Parnassus."

Arthur held out his hand. A minor test. "You've found him."

The man only hesitated briefly before shaking the proffered hand. His grip was solid, skin warm. When they let go, he smiled. "Ah! How wonderful. I come as a representative on behalf of Extremely Upper Management for the Department in Charge of Magical Youth. My name is Charles Werner. I'm here to discuss your proposal, and we have a proposal of our own. It's a bit . . . unorthodox, but I think it's something you'll be interested in."

Bait on a hook. Arthur knew that. And yet, he did the only thing he could: he stepped aside and invited Charles Werner in.

Later, Arthur Parnassus stood on the dock as the ferry approached. On board, a child. The first, but not the last. The sun lowered toward the sea, turning the waves into small, rushing mountains of fire.

Next to him, Zoe asked, "Are you afraid?"

"Ah," he said. "I suppose I am, of many things. But this? No. Never this. I have no reason to be afraid."

And in his head, a seductive whisper: *They're the ones who should be afraid.*

He banished the voice to the depths of his mind, and as the ferry grew closer, Arthur Parnassus began to sing quietly under his breath. "Somewhere . . . beyond the sea . . . somewhere, waiting for me . . ."

*My lover stands on golden sands
and watches the ships that go sailin'.*

SOMEWHERE BEYOND THE SEA

TJ KLUNE

ONE

Years later, on a warm morning in June, Arthur Parnassus opened his eyes and frowned. The sun filtering in through the window was too bright. His sleep-addled mind put forth drowsy, terrifying thoughts that a certain son of the Devil might have something to do with it. Last week, he'd threatened to crash the sun into Earth after he'd gotten in trouble for attempting to give life to a mud man he'd made after a fierce storm. Arthur had discovered him covered head to toe in filth, the mud man half-formed. When Arthur reminded him that it would not do to give sentience to mud, the boy had promised vengeance in the form of planetary annihilation, as per his usual.

So, when Arthur shot up in his bed, he was sure he couldn't be blamed. It wasn't as if he thought Lucy would *really* merge the sun and Earth, but then he'd really seemed fixated on the mud man, who was now nothing more than a mud puddle.

When he glanced at the alarm clock sitting next to the bed, Arthur realized it wasn't the sun bringing the end times: no, it was something far, far worse.

It was eight thirty-two in the morning on a Saturday, and the house was silent.

When one had six children of varying shapes, sizes, and magical abilities, one knew that having a lie-in was nothing more than a fanciful dream. Children—especially *these* children—didn't seem to understand the concept of time. Why, just the day before, an amorphous green blob had entered their bedroom at half past five in the morning, his squishy voice loud with glee, shouting that he'd accidentally squirted ink from his nose, something that he didn't know he could do. "I didn't shove a pen up there or *anything*. Why am I inking all over the place? Oh my goodness, do you think I'm becoming a *man*? Also, how do you get ink off the ceiling?"

This, of course, had led to a discussion in which the ink was decided to be a mark of puberty, something the blobby boy had grimaced over before pivoting to how he'd look with a mustache or a mat of chest hair. By the time he'd settled back down, three more children had wandered in, and it'd been barely six in the morning.

Arthur had noticed—now that he was in his midforties—that six in the morning came far sooner than it used to. Joints grumbled and cracked as he stretched, his light-colored hair (with shots of gray that seemed to spread daily) sticking up every which way. His back popped deliciously as he flexed his bare toes. Muddled thoughts became clearer as the last vestiges of sleep fell away.

Where were the children?

He turned toward the lump in the bed next to him, comforter pulled up high, leaving only a mop of thinning brown hair visible along with the sound of small snores. He shook the lump, glancing toward the door to the small room attached to theirs. It was open. The occupant—the destroyer of suns—was gone, leaving only a half-made bed, discarded socks on the floor (mismatched), and cracked records hanging from the walls.

"Whazzit?" the lump muttered. "No, Grandmother, I don't want to help you find the yams."

"Linus," Arthur said, giving the lump another shake. "Wake up. Something's wrong."

He almost fell out of bed when Linus Baker shot up, pajamas a wrinkled mess, hair and eyes wild as he looked around. "Who is it?" he demanded. "Who stole the yams from Grandmother's cellar?" He blinked. "I don't know why I just said that." He patted the thick slope of his stomach. "Must have been a dream. That's what

I get for having cake before going to bed." His hand dropped as he frowned. "Arthur? Why are you staring at me like that?"

"I adore you," Arthur said, and meant every word.

"Oh," Linus said, face flushing. "Yes, well. I happen to feel the same. Is that why you woke me up? That's lovely, but—why is the sun so bright? What time is it?"

"Half past eight."

Linus's eyes bulged. "In the *morning*? That's impossible! We've never been allowed to sleep this late. The closest we got was six forty-two, but that was only because the children were staying with Zoe. And even then, they *still* came back and woke us up." He hurried toward the door, snatching their matching blue robes that hung from a hook. "What on earth are you still doing in bed? We have to find them!"

Arthur rose and moved swiftly. But instead of taking the robe from Linus, Arthur cupped his face and kissed him soundly, morning breath be damned. Linus blinked slowly, dazed, and Arthur hoped it would always be this way.

"What was that for?" Linus asked.

"Because I could."

"I see. You could do it again if you wanted."

"Could I?" Arthur leaned forward to do just that.

Only to be met with a hand in his face, pushing him back gently. "You *could*," Linus said. "Or we could go and see why we were allowed to sleep so late. I swear, if they've brought home another animal they call a friend, we're going to have words."

"The last one wasn't so bad," Arthur said, taking the robe and sliding it on.

Linus made a face. "It was a lizard the size of Calliope that tried to eat my loafers."

"And you handled it with your usual grace and aplomb by shrieking and calling it a boa constrictor."

"I know you got it in your head at some point that you're funny. And you are, but now is not the time for humor. Now is the time for panicking."

"Perhaps nothing's wrong and we're overreacting," Arthur said, trying to be semi-reasonable.

Linus rolled his eyes. "You know as well as I do that with them, it would not be overreacting. Remember when Talia— Where's Calliope?"

Calliope, the so-called thing of evil. A cat, but unlike any other cat Arthur had seen before. It wasn't just her size—her gorgeous, fluffy hair made her appear far larger than she actually was—or her coloring, mostly black with a small patch of fluffy white on her chest. No, it was her bright green eyes that made her different. Watching, always watching, undoubtedly plotting the demise of anyone she deemed unfit to exist in her presence. Though Arthur knew humans had a tendency to anthropomorphize their pets and extoll their intelligence ("He's so *smart*! He can do what I trained him to do over a period of six months!") Calliope was something else entirely. If Arthur hadn't known any better, he'd have thought she understood them. But, true to her species, she held her own counsel and tended to ignore everything else.

Most nights, she lay curled at the foot of their bed, purring in warning should they even move their legs an inch. But her space was empty, leaving only behind black hairs on a blanket that Sal had knitted for her. When he'd presented it to her, Calliope had meowed her pleasure so loudly, it could be heard throughout the rest of the house.

"She must be with them," Arthur said. "And if she is, I know they're all right. She wouldn't let anything happen to them."

"Too right," Linus said. "I pity anyone who tries to cross them with her around. I expect it's painful to lose your eyes to a cat."

The long hallway was quiet. All the bedroom doors belonging to the children were open and the rooms empty. Sal's room had his desk in front of the window, typewriter tucked away in a monogrammed oak case Arthur and Linus had gifted him for Christmas. Chauncey's room smelled faintly of salt, warm seawater covering the floor, pumped in from the ocean through heated pipes. In Phee's, amidst dozens of plants hanging from the ceiling, a mural covered the walls showing a forest in varying degrees of talent as all the children had helped: Lucy's trees looked like skeletons, while Talia's appeared to be green candy floss on top of brown sticks. Speaking of the garden gnome, Talia's own room was oddly plant free; instead of flowering vines, there were cork boards attached to each wall displaying a magnificent collection of garden tools. And last—but certainly not least—through a hatch in the ceiling up to the attic, where a particular wyvern had built one of several nests. Climbing up the ladder that descended from the hatch, Arthur peered into the semi-dark of the attic. Theodore's nest: blankets, towels, and a brick he'd had a three-week love affair with. But no wyvern.

Arthur didn't want to panic, but not knowing where the children were caused an icy grip to squeeze around his heart. Zoe would have warned them if someone had attempted to come to the island uninvited, but that did little to ease Arthur's worry.

"Anything?" Linus called up from below him.

"No," Arthur said, climbing back down.

"Where could they be? They wouldn't leave without asking, so it's not as if—"

A thump from the first floor, followed by a loud crash.

"Kitchen," Arthur and Linus said at the same time.

They calmed as they neared the stairs that led down to the first floor. Peeking over the railing, Arthur and Linus saw Phee sitting on the bottom step, her fiery red hair pulled back into a loose ponytail, her wings fluttering behind her. The forest sprite wore shorts and a green tank top, her pale shoulders dotted with freckles. Shortly after her twelfth birthday, she'd gone through a bit of a growth spurt, sprouting up like one of her trees.

In front of her stood Chauncey, the amorphous green boy with tentacles for arms, suckers lining both lengths. On top of his head rose thin, foot-long stalks, his eyes at the top, bouncing up and down excitedly. He was wearing a trench coat cinched around what could either be his waist or his chest, and it didn't take long for Arthur and Linus to learn why.

"You think they heard that?" Chauncey asked, voice like a thick, wet sponge being squeezed into a metal bucket.

"Shh," Phee said. "Not so loud."

His stalks shrank until his eyes rested on top of his body, wide and unblinking. "You think they heard that?" he whispered.

"Probably not," Phee said, tugging at the bottom of his coat. "They both snore, so I don't think they heard anything."

Linus huffed next to him, and Arthur did little to hide his smile.

"Oh," Chauncey said. "Do I snore?"

"You're a boy, so probably. What's with the trench coat?"

He puffed up proudly. "We're on a secret mission. Everyone knows when you're on a secret mission, you have to dress like it." He flipped up the collar of his coat. "Secret Agent Chauncey, at your service."

"I thought you wanted to be a bellhop."

"I can do both," he said. "Save the day *and* carry your luggage. It's called going undercover. I read about it in a book." His eyes turned 360 degrees. "Can I tell you something I've never told anyone before?"

"Sure," Phee said. "What is it? You all right?"

He flapped a tentacle at her. "Yeah, I'm good. No, not just good. I'm *prodigious*."

Linus elbowed Arthur gently. "You hear that?" he whispered excitedly. "My vocabulary lessons are working."

"—which means to cause amazement and wonder," Chauncey was saying when they looked back down the stairs.

Phee laughed. "What did you want to tell me?"

"Right," Chauncey said. "Have you ever been walking through the woods, and you see a pine cone on the ground, and no one is there to tell you that you can't eat the pine cone?"

"Well, sure. But—"

"Oh my goodness," Chauncey breathed. "Me too! I thought I was the only one. I feel better now."

"Did . . . did you eat the pine cone?"

"I did," Chauncey said proudly. "Guess what it tasted like."

"I have absolutely no idea."

Chauncey's eyes leaned forward, stopping only a couple of inches from Phee's face. "Do you remember when Talia tried to make pecan pie but we were out of pecans so she used candy corn instead and there was so much sugar in it, Linus said it'd rot our teeth, but we ate it anyway and didn't sleep for three days because we could all smell colors?"

"That's what the pine cone tasted like?" Phee asked with a frown.

"No, I just like that story. The pine cone tasted *bad*, and it took forever to chew."

Phee coughed, sounding like she was trying hard not to laugh. "You . . . you ate the whole thing?"

Chauncey blinked, first the left eye, then the right. "Ye-yes? Why?"

"Female pine cones have edible seeds called pignoli," she explained. "They're a little sweet, a little nutty. In Italy, they make pignoli biscuits."

Chauncey's skin darkened to the color of pine needles. "Are you saying I ate a *girl*? Oh no." He threw his tentacles up in the air, tilting his head back. "I didn't mean to do it! I fell on her and she just . . . went into my mouth?"

"Oh dear," Linus said. Then, "Not a word, Parnassus. Not a single word."

"Not like that," Phee said. "Plants can be male or female, but not in the same way you and I are. They're alive, but it's different. Many plants are hermaphroditic, which means they're both male *and* female. Like roses and lilies. When I say female, I just mean they're the ones you get seeds from."

Chauncey blinked. "Ohhh. I get it. So it's not like eating people when I eat pine cones."

"Uh. No?"

"Oh, thank God." He looked away as his skin changed to a pea green. "They're already scared enough of me as it is."

"Absolutely not," Linus muttered, starting to move toward the stop of the stairs.

Arthur took his wrist gently, pulling him back, shaking his head.

Linus's mouth twisted angrily. "I'm not going to let Chauncey think he's—"

"I know," Arthur said quietly. "But let's give Phee a chance."

Phee reached out and tugged on the trench coat, pulling Chauncey toward her. He wrapped his tentacles around her, laying his eyes on the top of her head. "Did something happen?"

Chauncey sighed. "Maybe."

"Do you want to talk about it?"

"Maybe."

"You don't have to do it right now, especially if you're not ready." She stroked his back.

"It's stupid," he mumbled. "A woman came in. She had, like, *seven* suitcases. And," he continued dreamily, "Mr. Swanson"—the hotel's lead bellhop, his true hero—"was busy with another customer, so I went to help her."

"Sounds like you," Phee said.

"But when I offered to take her bags for her, she screamed that a sea slug was trying to steal her belongings."

"A sea slug?" Phee said. "Please. She should be so lucky."

"Right?" Chauncey said, pulling out of the hug. "Mr. Swanson heard her and came over. I thought he was going to take her bags instead, but you know what he did?"

"What?"

"He told me that people like her aren't welcome in our fine establishment, and then he kicked her out of the hotel!"

"Whoa," Phee said, sounding as impressed as Arthur felt. "I bet that pissed her off."

"I thought she was going to explode," Chauncey said. "Then Mr. Swanson said it was lunchtime, and we ate sandwiches and he told me about all the other bellhops he'd met."

"But," Phee said.

"But," Chauncey said, "I just don't get it. All I want to do is help. I can't control how I look. It's not my fault I'm—"

"Handsome as crap?" Phee said.

Chauncey gaped at her. "What."

"You're handsome," she said. "And even better, unique. I've never seen anyone look like you. Your eyes? Pfft, get out of here. Those are so cool. You think any of us could pull off a trench coat like you do? Remember how funny I looked when I tried on your bellhop cap? But when you put it on, all I want to do is pack a bag just so you can take it from me even though I'm not going anywhere."

"I am pretty good at taking luggage."

"You are," she said. "I can't tell you something like that won't happen again. But all you need to do is remind yourself it's on *them,* not you."

"I'm not a monster," Chauncey said.

"Nope," Phee said. "You're Chauncey. The best Chauncey I've ever known."

"And I'm handsome as crap."

"Hell yes."

"And I can eat all the pine cones I want because they're *not* human."

"Except it probably won't feel good when you have to poop."

"All my poops feel good, so no worries there!"

Another crash from the kitchen, followed by a small devil cursing in colorful language that he absolutely did *not* learn in this house. "Gangrenous *donkey* testicles!"

"Follow my lead," Arthur whispered, pulling Linus partway down the hall. They stopped in front of Sal's room. Winking at Linus, Arthur raised his arms above his head in a stretch, yawning quite ferociously. Raising his voice—so that the sound carried down the hall and stairs—he said, "Oh my, that was such a restful sleep. Wouldn't you agree, dear Linus?"

"Quite!" Linus practically shouted. "I'm not even remotely

concerned about the state of the kitchen and instead am focused on how rested I feel!"

They both had to stifle laughter when Chauncey began to yell, "Battle stations! Battle stations! The chickens are coming home to roost!"

Another din from the kitchen, this time followed by Lucy shouting, "But we're not ready yet! Choke the chickens!"

When Arthur and Linus reached the top of the stairs, Phee and Chauncey smiled up at them as innocent as the day was young.

"Good morning," Arthur said cheerfully as he and Linus descended the stairs. "Phee, Chauncey, did you sleep well?"

"So well," Chauncey warbled. "And even better, we're not doing anything illegal!"

"Yet," Linus said.

Arthur and Linus took turns hugging Phee and Chauncey, both of the children holding on tightly. Once done, Linus glanced at Arthur and said, "Time seems to have slipped away from us this morning. You wouldn't know anything about that, would you?"

"Who, us?" Phee asked, batting her eyelashes.

"We have no idea what you're talking about," Chauncey said.

"Hmm," Arthur said. "Well, I suppose we should start preparing breakfast. Linus, why don't you see where the other children are and I'll just go into the kitchen and—"

Phee and Chauncey hurried toward the kitchen doors, blocking the entrance. "You can't," Phee said. "It's . . . occupied."

Above them, through the porthole windows in the double doors, Arthur saw a flash of reptilian scales fly by, with what looked to be a whisk grasped in his claws. A moment later, a lovely face appeared in one of the portholes, eyes widening. Sal disappeared a second later, followed by Lucy shouting, "What do you mean they're right outside?"

"We're going to be in so much trouble," Talia said, out of sight. "How did you get batter on the ceiling?"

"By aiming," Lucy said. "Duh."

"Oh no!" Chauncey said loudly. "I just remembered that I needed to talk to Arthur and Linus about stuff! And things!"

"Name two," Linus said, folding his arms.

"Potatoes and Portugal," Chauncey said promptly.

"What about them?" Arthur asked.

"I have absolutely no idea," Chauncey said. He deflated. "Sorry, Phee. I did my best."

"You sure did . . . something," Phee said. "Well, our cover's blown, so we might as well get this over with." She glared up at Linus and Arthur. "It was all of our idea, so if we're going to get grounded, you have to ground all of us."

"Sounds serious," Arthur said gravely.

"And more than a little worrying," Linus said.

"Hold, please," Phee said. She grabbed Chauncey by the tentacle, backing them both through the double doors slowly. Though she did her best to keep Arthur and Linus from seeing the kitchen, the doors cracked open enough for herself and Chauncey to slip through, but also to give Arthur and Linus a glimpse of the kitchen itself.

When the doors swung closed, Linus said, "What was that on the walls?"

"It looked like ketchup," Arthur said. "Isn't it wonderful?"

"You and I have very different definitions of the word."

"Perhaps you need to attend a vocabulary lesson then," he teased.

Inside, hushed voices. But since these voices belonged to a group of six children being who they were, "hushed" was, perhaps, a bit of a misnomer.

"They know!" Chauncey whisper-shouted. "They're standing *right there,* and they know *everything.* We're doomed."

"Lucy," Phee said. "What the hell did you do to the counters?"

"I had trouble cracking eggs," Lucy said. "And then Calliope walked in it, and now we have neat sticky paw prints on the floor."

"How'd they get on the ceiling?" Chauncey asked.

"I accidentally reversed gravity when I was trying to measure butter."

"Oh," Chauncey said. "That makes sense. I bet that happens to a lot of people because cooking is hard."

Theodore chirped loudly, and Sal said, "Theodore's right. We should take responsibility for the mess we've made."

"You didn't make any mess," Talia said. "Lucy did. And so did I because it's not fair that he gets to smash all the eggs."

"I *didn't*. I tried to let you do one, and you threw it against the wall!"

"No," Sal said. "We're in this together."

"Yeah," Chauncey said. "Let's *all* get grounded. Who's with me? Why is no one raising their tentacles?"

Theodore clicked in his throat twice, followed by a low growl, and the children burst into laughter. "Yeah, Linus would do that, wouldn't he?" Phee said. "I bet his face would turn red too."

Linus huffed quietly. "Well, I never."

"Your face is a little flushed," Arthur whispered. "Are you ill, dear Linus?"

"They think they're funny because of *you*."

"Phee," Sal said, "you distract them until we're ready. Everyone else, let's clean up as best we can. The quicker we work, the sooner we'll be done."

Phee slipped through the double doors, smiling widely. "Hello!" she said as if they hadn't heard every single word. "Thank you for your patience. It's appreciated."

"Wonderful," Arthur said. "Shall we go into the kitchen right this very second?"

"Uh," Phee said, glancing back over her shoulder. "Not . . . yet? Oh! I just remembered. Linus, I wanted to ask you something very, very important. It's all I've been thinking about for the last minute or so."

"We await with bated breath," Arthur said.

"Right," Phee said. "So. Um." She winced when something fell to the floor in the kitchen. Before Arthur could comment on it, Phee blurted (quite loudly), "Your organs!"

Linus groaned. "This again? How many times do I need to tell

Talia that no matter what she says, I won't sign a 'do not resuscitate' while also granting permission for her to harvest my liver, kidney, and lungs. I don't know where she got the idea my organs would help her roses, but they *won't*."

"That's what I told her," Phee said. "And then I reminded her that it was only a matter of time, so. Win-win!"

Arthur lowered his voice. "We heard you talking to Chauncey."

Phee fidgeted uncomfortably. Out of all the children, Phee was the biggest enigma. She loved her brothers and sisters and supported them completely. Arthur knew her to be compassionate, kind, and more than a little prickly. That being said, she still struggled with being complimented, or having attention placed upon her. It was a tricky line to walk with her: lay it on too thick, and she'd shut down, waving it off and changing the subject. He'd made it his mission to tell her at least once a day how proud he was of her.

"It's not a big deal. Chauncey needed someone to talk to, and I was right there. Anyone would have done the same." She shrugged, averting her gaze.

"Perhaps," Arthur said. "But Chauncey didn't come to me with it. He did not come to Linus, nor any of the others. He came to *you*, Phee. He trusts you with his happiness, but also with his troubles."

"He shouldn't *have* troubles," Phee retorted. "I thought things were supposed to be better. You said they would be." She deflated before they could reply. "Sorry," she muttered. "That isn't fair."

"It's absolutely fair," Linus said, "we did tell you that. And I wish I had a better answer for you other than that these things take time. I'm sorry." He took her hand in his.

Phee looked back up at Linus, and Arthur was struck by the softness in her eyes, a chink in her formidable armor. Every now and then, she'd grace them with a peek of the girl underneath, and he treasured these moments as much as Theodore did his buttons. "Thanks, Linus. You're all right."

He squeezed her hand. "Anything for you. Now, are we going to see the kitchen, or are you—"

But before he could finish, Lucy yelled in unfettered joy, "You can breathe *fire*? Holy crap, Theodore! Let's burn everything!"

"And that's our cue," Arthur said.

"This is what happens when you sleep late," Linus muttered. "Just when you think you're getting extra rest, someone breathes fire."

TWO

Arthur pushed through the kitchen doors so quickly they bounced off the walls. The conversation ceased immediately as everyone froze.

First, there was Lucy, dragging a chair across the kitchen, his tongue stuck out between his teeth in concentration. His eyes were ringed with red (as they often were when he was doing something that might be dangerous), the cowlicks on either side of his head giving the appearance of black horns made of hair. He wore a frilly pink apron over his frayed plaid shorts and billowing white shirt.

Then there was Talia, a short, squat garden gnome holding at least a dozen eggs. Her white, luxurious beard rested on her chest, the end curled into a little loop. Atop her head, a pointy red cap, the end of which crooked to the left, a tuft of her white hair curling out onto her forehead. She wore a blue vest with a black belt around her waist, and brown trousers with black work boots that rose to her knees, spotted with what appeared to be yolk. Her exposed skin—face and hands—was tanned, evidence of the hours she spent out in the garden. Her cherry-red lips turned into an *O* as her blue eyes narrowed.

Next was Sal, their resident shifter, who could turn from a boy into a tiny, fluffy dog in the blink of an eye. At fifteen, Sal was the oldest child on the island, the one the other children looked up to. Coming into his own, the once quiet boy had begun using his voice more and more, an extension of the words he put on a page that never failed to enchant whoever was lucky enough to read them. He was tall—as tall as Linus now, much to their chagrin—and while obviously a teenager (lamenting over spots on his nose and forehead, few though there were), he was an old soul, his dark eyes catching almost everything. He, too, wore shorts—tan—and a short-sleeved collared shirt—a warm yellow—with pearl snap buttons, complimenting his dark brown skin. His hair was longer these days, tightly coiled in a way Zoe had taught him how to manage.

Chauncey sat in a mop bucket on the floor near Sal, a soap bubble resting on top of his head between his eye stalks. Above him, sitting on the counter, a Machiavellian feline: Calliope, near the sink, tail swishing dangerously, licking batter off her right front paw, dismissive gaze trained on Arthur.

And Theodore, maw wide open, rows of sharp wyvern teeth on display. He stood on the floor, wings spread, head cocked back, smoke rising from his slitted nostrils. When he saw Arthur, his jaws snapped closed, and he swallowed down whatever had been about to come out. A moment later, he burped out a black cloud of smoke, frantically using his wings to try to make it dissipate in a poor attempt to hide the evidence.

"Uh," Lucy said. "I can explain?"

"Can you?" Arthur said mildly as Phee and Linus crowded behind him. "Because it sounds as if you're trying to get Theodore to start fires."

"That's exactly what I was doing!" Lucy said. "You know me so well. We don't need this chair, right? It's Linus's, but he told me he likes standing when eating."

Linus snorted. "I said no such thing."

"Theodore?" Arthur said. "Is it true? Can you create fire?"

The wyvern glanced at Sal, who nodded. Theodore began to click and growl, spreading his wings and moving his head up and down. Arthur listened intently as Theodore explained that he'd woken up a few days before with a brightness in his chest he'd never felt before. He ignored it at first, but it made him itchy, like his skin was vibrating. He hadn't said anything because he thought it'd pass on its own.

It wasn't until this very morning when he'd woken up, stretched, yawned, and breathed a small gout of fire. It hadn't hurt, he added, clicking and chirping that it had felt *good*, like stretching a stiff muscle. He chirped a question that Arthur—for all he'd seen and done—didn't have the answer to.

"I don't know," he said, tapping his chin. "I was under the impression that wyverns—though descended from dragons—were incapable of creating fire. Linus? Have you ever heard of a wyvern making fire?"

"No," Linus said from somewhere behind him. "Granted, Theodore's the only wyvern I know, but I thought they hadn't evolved in such a way as to make fire. Something about not having the gland that secretes the oily mixture needed to ignite."

"It's *green*," Chauncey said from his bucket. "Like me."

"Green fire," Arthur said. "Can you control it?"

Theodore hesitated for a moment before nodding.

Arthur took a step back and said, "Show me, if you feel up to it."

Theodore pranced on his two feet, claws clicking on the tile floor as he spun in a circle, obviously eager. He waved his right wing for them to take a step back to give him enough room. Linus, for his part, opined that perhaps indoors wasn't the best place for a demonstration of fire, but he was quickly outvoted when everyone (including Arthur) booed him. Linus then reminded them of the last time an event involving fire had occurred indoors (Talia's birthday; too many candles and not enough fire extinguishers). "And that's the reason I think we should consider going outside to—"

It was about this time that Theodore reared his head back, eyes narrowed. A ripple of iridescent light moved across the black scales along his back toward his head. As Theodore opened his mouth, Arthur smelled the comforting familiarity of smoke and flame, and then a jet of green fire shot from Theodore, stretching at least five feet, the heat immense. It only lasted a few seconds before the fire died out, but Theodore was obviously pleased with himself, puffing out his chest and hopping on either foot as smoke leaked from between his jaws.

Pleased, that is, until the banner hanging above the table caught fire and began to burn. Arthur whirled around, raised his hand, and sucked the fire down into his palm. It formed a crackling sphere that snuffed out when he closed his fingers around it.

"Well done, Theodore," Arthur said, suitably impressed.

"Again!" Lucy yelled, punching his fists in the air. "Again!"

"And *this* is why we don't breathe fire inside the house," Linus said, hands on his hips. "You can't just . . . There's not . . ." He frowned. "Why does the sign above the table say HAPPY BIRT?"

"It's supposed to say 'birthday,'" Sal said, scratching the back of his neck.

"I like 'happy birt' better," Talia said as she tossed the eggs into the mop bucket, causing Chauncey to proclaim he was egg drop soup. "It sounds dumb and amazing, like Lucy."

"Happy birt!" Lucy crowed.

"I knew this was going to blow up in our faces," Phee muttered.

"Oh no," Chauncey whispered as eggs bobbed around him. "What are we supposed to sing now? The happy birthday song doesn't work when it's a happy birt song. Haaaaapppy birt to you. See? It sounds like *nothing*."

Linus shook his head. "It's not someone's birthday. The next is Chauncey's in August."

Arthur closed his eyes, suddenly realizing what all of this was about. The mess in the kitchen—for, yes, there was batter on the walls and ceiling, along with paw prints—was a small price to pay for what the children had done on their own.

He opened his eyes when Sal said, "It's your birthday, Linus."

Linus laughed and said, "What? Of course it isn't. My birthday is in . . ." His mouth moved silently as he ticked off his fingers. "Wait. What day is it?"

"June eighth," Arthur murmured. "Your birthday."

"My . . ." Linus looked around the kitchen. The HAPPY BIRT sign was still smoldering slightly, but below it, on the table, were place settings for each of them. In the middle of the table, a fry-up: platters of burnt sausages, half-burnt bacon, fried eggs (with bits of shell in them), a plate of baked beans that were still in the shape of the can they'd been poured from, tomatoes and mushrooms from Talia's garden, and a stack of toast that appeared to have had each piece gnawed on by a certain child of reptilian persuasion.

"You did this all for me?" Linus whispered, hand at his throat.

"It was my idea," Talia said. "You're welcome."

"But all of us chipped in," Sal said as Theodore climbed up his side to his usual perch on Sal's shoulder. "Everyone had a role."

"Phee and me were the lookouts," Chauncey said, eyes bouncing. "We did amazing, so you're welcome."

"You didn't have to do this," Linus said with a watery smile.

"It's not *just* for your birthday," Talia said, taking him by the hand and leading him toward the table. Lucy shoved the chair against the back of his legs, causing him to sit down roughly.

"What else is there?" Arthur asked, taking the broom from Sal and motioning for the children to take their seats at the table. The mess could wait. Chauncey climbed out of the mop bucket, announcing he was done being soup for the day, but that he'd like to try it again tomorrow.

"It's a going-away party," Phee said.

Arthur paused at the pantry. He took a deep breath, stored the broom away, and turned back around. Everyone was seated: Linus at one end of the long table, Lucy, Phee, and Talia to his right, Chauncey, Sal, and Theodore to his left. Aside from Arthur's spot at the other end of the table, there were two more place settings: one next to Talia, the other next to Theodore.

"Going-away party," he said. "I see." He moved around the table, touching each of them on the shoulder before taking his seat, folding his hands on the table near his empty plate.

"Is it a going-away party if we'll only be gone for a few days?" Linus asked. His voice was light, easy, but Arthur knew him well enough to recognize the undercurrent of worry. He felt similarly, though perhaps not quite for the same reasons. Yes, Linus fretted over the idea of leaving the children—even if it was only for three days. Leave tomorrow, and if all went well, back by Wednesday. But Linus had been on the island for less than a year. It was the only thing Arthur had known for far longer, and it made him uncharacteristically nervous, stepping out into the world beyond the island and the village. What they were—*he* was—about to do had never been done before, at least not with the openness he planned to bring. So many things could go wrong.

"You've never left us alone before," Lucy said, attempting to spear a sausage and somehow making it shoot across the table, snatched out of the air by Theodore. "What if something happens and I have to be evil and take over the world?"

"But you won't be alone," Arthur said. "You'll have—"

"Us," another voice said from the entrance of the kitchen. They turned to see Zoe Chapelwhite leaning against the doorway, the flowers in her hair open, the petals thick and colorful. Her dress was violet with pink blooms along the hem, her hands in the large pockets. She smiled and winked at Arthur.

"Oh my," another voice said. "Happy birt? That's a new one."

Helen Webb appeared in the entryway, stopping to stand on her tiptoes to kiss Zoe on the cheek. The mayor—and owner of Talia's favorite gardening store—had carved out a place for herself in their home. Arthur still remembered the wispy girl with big, pretty eyes who'd served him ice cream when he was a child. Now, she was pleasantly plump and wore her usual: a pair of denim overalls over a wrinkled work shirt, her boots similar to Talia's.

The children all yelled their greetings, and Arthur chuckled at the cacophony. He doubted he could ever go back to the quiet way it'd once been here, when it'd been just him, Zoe, and an unrealized dream.

"We're going to be with you," Zoe said as she took her seat next to Phee and Arthur, Calliope ignoring Helen as she tried to pet her in her spot on the windowsill above the sink. Calliope allowed it to go on for longer than normal before she raised a paw, put it on the back of Helen's hand, and pushed it away as if to say *Thank you, but enough.*

"That's right," Helen said as she took the last empty seat. "And we're going to have so much fun. Anything you need, you just ask. Zoe and I will take care of it."

"Anything?" Lucy asked sweetly.

"Within reason," Arthur said.

"Stupid reason," Lucy muttered, grabbing a piece of toast and munching mutinously.

"Can we stay at your house?" Chauncey asked Zoe. "It's my turn to use the tree hammock."

"No, it's not," Talia said. "You got it last time. It's *my* turn."

Arthur cleared his throat pointedly.

"Or," Talia said, "we can share."

"Heck *yes*," Chauncey said, eyes lowering toward the baked beans and inspecting the sloppy can-shaped tower. "But just remember that I ink now. Lucy called them my nocturnal emissions, which is a funny way of putting it because it doesn't always happen at night."

"Lucy," Linus said sternly.

"Eat, everyone," Arthur said. "We have much to discuss, and I think we'll all feel better about it with full bellies."

"Why is the bacon bleeding?" Zoe asked.

"It's not blood," Sal said. "Lucy wanted to use real blood, but we didn't know where to get any legally so I mixed corn syrup, chocolate syrup, and red food coloring."

Lucy rolled his eyes. "*I* know where to get real blood, but Arthur said I'm not allowed to do that anymore."

"I did," Arthur said simply.

"This meal certainly looks . . . somewhat edible," Linus said. "Arthur, would you like to try the bacon first?"

"Oh, I couldn't," Arthur said. "It's your birt, after all. You should get the first bite."

"I insist."

"Do you? How kind of you. I'm afraid I must insist even more."

"So many people want to eat my food," Lucy said in awe. "This must be what it feels like to be God. Fun fact! Some people go to church and ritually eat Jesus and drink his blood. Isn't that interesting?"

"Oh my goodness," Chauncey whispered. "I'll just stick to eating pine cones, thank you very much."

"So very interesting," Linus said. "I suppose I will have some bacon."

"One bloody entrail coming up!" Talia said, stabbing a piece with her fork and lifting it off the tray. She handed the fork over to Phee, who sniffed the meat and grimaced. She gave it to Lucy, who in turn set it on Linus's plate.

Linus poked at it for a moment until Lucy leaned in and whispered loudly, "I made it with love."

Linus winced, took a deep breath in through his nose and let it out through his mouth, and then brought the wet bacon up to his lips. Lucy tracked every movement, eyes growing wider and wider as Linus bit daintily, breaking off a small chunk. He chewed slowly, myriad emotions crossing his face—horror, disgust, confusion, followed quickly by surprise, disgust again, then something that closely resembled forlorn acceptance.

"Well?" Lucy demanded.

Linus swallowed thickly, throat bobbing. "It was... surprisingly edible." And with that, he took another bite. "Thank you."

"Bloody entrails for all!" Lucy cried, and the birt breakfast was underway.

After the breakfast had been partially consumed, Arthur cleared his throat, causing everyone to look at him—even Calliope, who had settled onto Sal's lap.

Arthur chose his words carefully. "As you know, Linus and I will be traveling over the next few days, and I want to make sure you all understand what we're doing."

"You're testifying," Phee said. "In front of the government."

"Yes, I am. I have been asked to provide an account of my time here on the island when I was a child."

Theodore clicked a question, a single word: *Why?*

"Because..." He paused. Then, "Because, if there is a chance someone will listen and learn from the past, then that's a chance I need to take. You know of my history with the island, how I was brought up in this very house. And how it... ended."

"The cellar," Sal said quietly.

A flash of memory—screaming until his voice was hoarse, fire raging around him, smoke thick and noxious—and he didn't push it away. He let it settle, gave it room to breathe, and though he felt the low thrum of decades-old anger, it smoldered rather than burned. The children didn't know everything about his time on the island, but they knew enough. "Yes, the cellar. However, it wasn't just that. It was this house. The island. The people in charge who thought they knew what was best for the rest of us. They didn't."

"But you still came back here," Talia said.

"I did," Arthur agreed. "Because I believed—and still do—that places, just like people, can hold power over you if you let them. Unearned power that gives them the right to decide how others should be treated simply because of who they are. Do you know what generational trauma is?"

"It's when one group of people goes through something bad," Sal said. "And then it affects the next generations too."

"Yes, Sal. That's correct. Perhaps it's missing a bit of the nuance behind it, but for purposes of this discussion, it's enough." He looked across the table at Linus, who smiled warmly and nodded. "I wasn't treated right when I was a child, but I was far from the only one. You have all experienced it for yourselves, in one form or another. I wish I could take that from you, but I can't. And I don't know if I would have the right, even if I could. You are more than the sum of your parts, but your past is still that: yours. I wouldn't presume to take something from you that you might not want to give up, even if it's painful to think about. I want to do the next best thing: use my voice to bring attention not only to this island, but to others who might not have found their home yet."

"Are you going to talk about us?" Phee asked.

"I am," Arthur said. "Not in too many specifics, but I think it's important for people to hear just how far each of you has come. But take heart, my children, and know that your secrets are safe."

"He wants to brag about you," Helen said. "He's just too modest to call it as such."

Arthur snorted. "Yes, I suppose that's what it is. I *do* want to brag about each of you. Sal's words. Chauncey as a bellhop. Lucy being an expert in all things music. Phee with her trees, and Talia with her garden. I bet no other wyvern has a hoard as magnificent as Theodore's."

"We are pretty amazing," Chauncey agreed. "You have my permission to tell them that I ink now."

"Noted," Arthur said dryly. "But this isn't just about me or even us. It's about the wider magical world, and what we want going forward. The changes that must be made. The laws that must be repealed to make way for a world where anyone and everyone has a chance to be free to do with their lives what they wish."

"That sounds like a lot of work," Talia said, tugging the end of her beard, something she did when she was thinking hard.

"It does," Arthur said. "Because it will be." He looked at each of them in turn. "I won't lie to you. The road ahead will not be smooth. No matter what I—*we* say, there will always be those who refuse to accept the truth. They surround themselves with likeminded people, and it creates an echo chamber that's nigh on impossible to escape. A feedback loop that never ends. We must—"

"Aren't we doing the same?" Sal asked suddenly, causing everyone to look at him. He winced a little, started to slouch in his seat, but stopped before he could get too far. Instead of trying to make himself as small as possible, he sat upright, squaring his shoulders.

"Explain, Sal, if you please."

Sal looked down at his plate, picking up a fork and pushing around the remains of his breakfast. "We're surrounded by likeminded people. We all want the same thing, or something close to it. Isn't that an echo chamber? How does that make us any different?"

"Excellent," Arthur said, and Sal flushed, lips quirking. "I don't think I've told you today how impressed I am by you. You are correct, which is exactly why I need to take our truth out of this house and into the ears of the people we don't trust to hear it yet. Even then, I prefer to think of standing before a vast lake on a windless day: the surface smooth until one of us—say, you, Sal—picks up a stone and tosses it into the water. What happens then?"

"It causes ripples," Phee said.

"Yes," Arthur said. "And what if you, Phee, picked up your own stone and threw it in along with Sal? And the rest of you did the same? The ripples would bounce off each other, spreading in new directions, growing as more people toss their stones in. And if we keep on doing it, who knows how far the ripples could reach in the end?"

Sal nodded. "We keep on throwing stones until someone listens."

"I don't know why we just don't throw stones at *them*," Talia muttered. "Seems to be a waste of a good rock if you ask me."

"Because violence is never the answer," Arthur said.

Talia smiled sweetly. "But it can be the question."

"It can," Arthur allowed. "But I believe the greatest weapon we have at our disposal is our voices. And I am going to use my voice for you, and for me. Hate is loud. We are louder."

"What if they don't listen?" Phee asked. "What if they don't care what you have to say? What if they come here and try and take us away again?"

"They wouldn't get very far," Zoe said, the flowers in her hair opening and closing. "The island belongs to me as much as I belong to it. Should anyone try and come here with the thought of removing anyone from their home, they're going to have a rude awakening."

Arthur nodded. "And we have to try because if we don't, no one else will."

He did not miss the surreptitious glance exchanged between Helen and Zoe.

Theodore clicked and growled, tongue snaking out across his lips, eyes bright.

Arthur closed his eyes and took a deep breath, letting it out slowly. When he opened his eyes again, he found everyone watching him, waiting for his answer. He smiled gently and said, "No, Theodore. I don't believe it will affect the petition for adoption."

"Because you want to be our dad," Chauncey said.

Out of the mouths of babes. "I do," Arthur said. "More than anything in the world."

"It's going to be on the radio?" Phee asked.

"It is," Arthur said. "And I know you'll want to listen, but I'm not so sure that's a good idea."

"Why?" Talia asked. "If you're going to talk about us, we should probably listen to make sure you describe my garden right. Make sure you mention my begonias. I'm awfully proud of them."

"As you should be," Linus said, glancing at Arthur, who nodded. "But these things can be . . . complicated. Some of the questions Arthur will be asked might seem unfair, or even rude. While Arthur and I are expecting this, it won't make things any easier." He smiled. "And if all goes well, we'll bring someone back with us."

"David," Sal said.

Talia rolled her eyes. "Of course it's another boy. So many penises in this house."

"I don't have a penis," Chauncey said. "It's more like a cloaca."

"What's that?" Phee asked.

"Oh! It's this thing where—"

"I don't know that we need to talk about our genitals at the table where we eat," Linus said.

"I don't mind," Chauncey said. "I like my body. It's squishy."

Helen to the rescue. "Yes, David. I hope you're as excited as I am for you to meet him. From what I've been told, he's . . . blossomed, in the care of the people he's with. Let's just say I think he'll fit right in here with the rest of you."

"That sounds suspiciously like a threat," Linus mumbled.

Theodore chirped a question, bobbing his head up and down.

"I don't know," Arthur said. "For now, he's not being included on the adoption petition because we don't know if he'll want to stay. This could be just one stop on his journey, and if that's the case, we will welcome him just the same and make his time here a peaceful one. It's why we've worked so hard over the last weeks to get his room ready for him. Having a place to call your own is an important first step. The best I can say is that we'll need to take it one day at a time."

The timer on the oven dinged, and Lucy's face lit up. "My sticky buns! Yay, yay, *yay!*" He pushed back from the table, knocking his chair over as he skipped toward the oven.

And that was the end of that.

After they made quick work of cleaning up the kitchen, the children made Linus promise he would close his eyes and keep them closed in preparation for receiving his birt gift. He made a big show of it, bending over to allow Lucy to wave his hands in front of Linus's face to prove he couldn't see. Lucy asked Arthur to do the same.

The children led the way, followed by Zoe, Linus's hand in hers, Arthur bringing up the rear, holding on to Linus's hips.

When they stood in the sitting room, eyes closed, Zoe—under instructions from Sal—positioned them to face what Arthur thought was the fireplace. In the darkness, Linus's hand gripping his, he heard Lucy and Talia arguing over how long the countdown should be before he and Linus could open their eyes. Lucy wanted to start at three. Talia wanted to start at five million. They compromised and decided seven would be good.

"Okay," Talia said. "Seven. Six."

The others joined in.

"Five. Four—"

"*Threetwoone!*" Lucy shouted.

Arthur waited a beat to allow Linus to open his eyes first. It was his birt, after all. And he knew he'd done the right thing when Linus gasped, squeezing Arthur's hand tightly. He opened his own eyes, and there, hanging above the fireplace, was the gift.

Curved picture frames formed what appeared to be a perfect circle. The frames themselves were made of wood, each white with blue and yellow and pink flowers painted onto it. The right and left sides of the circle were made up of three photographs each: Linus with each of the children. Sal and Linus reading together. Lucy and Linus in their pajamas, hands above their heads as they danced to Bessie Smith. Talia and Linus in the garden on their hands and knees, a pile of weeds beside them. Chauncey and Linus standing in front of the hotel in the village, Chauncey's bellhop cap sitting at a jaunty angle atop his head. Theodore and Linus with their heads underneath the couch, their rears pointed up, Theodore's tail caught mid-swing. Phee and Linus walking hand in hand through the forest, Linus wearing his explorer's outfit.

The bottom of the circle seemed a little off compared to the rest; it was as if a frame was missing, especially seeing as how the photograph across the top was longer. The bottom frame held a picture of Zoe, standing with the children in front of the house, all of them smiling widely. The photograph at the top of the circle had Linus and Arthur center frame, dancing in Zoe's home with the children watching in the background.

Lovely, this, lovely in ways Arthur wasn't sure he could articulate with any clarity. How could anyone look upon these or any children and only know fear?

Especially when he saw what sat in the middle of the circle. Another frame, this one square. Instead of a photograph, however, the frame held words upon a crisp white page.

See me.
See me for who I am. I am magic. I am human. I am inhuman.
See me.
I am a boy. I am a girl. I am everything and nothing in
    between.

See me.
You do. You see me. You recoil in fear. You scream in anger.
See me.
I bleed. I ache. You see me, and you wish you hadn't. You wish I was invisible.
Out of sight, out of mind. Unseen, faded, muted. You want my color. You want my joy. You want a monochrome world with monochrome beliefs. You see me, and you want to take it all away. But you can't.
You want me lost, but I am found in the breaths I take, in the spaces between heartbeats.
I am found because I refuse to be in black and white, or any shade of gray.
I am color. I am fire.
I am the sun, and I will burn away the shadows until only light remains.
And then you will have no choice but to see me.

"Do you like it?" Chauncey asked. "We worked really hard on it. Zoe helped with the photographs, but we did everything else." Theodore chirped loudly, and Chauncey added, "Except for the poem. Sal wrote that."

Arthur couldn't speak; the lump in his throat was far too large.

Linus managed for the both of them. In a strangled voice, he said, "You did this for me?"

Talia frowned. "Yes? It's your birt." She squinted up at him. "Oh no. Are you going senile again? I *knew* forty-one in human years was old as crap. We'll have to put him into a home where we'll promise to visit but then we don't."

"But he already has a home," Chauncey said, confused. "Why would he live somewhere else?"

Helen, standing off to the side, sniffled as she pulled a handkerchief from one of the pockets on her overalls.

"They wanted to show you that you belong," Zoe said.

"I can see that," Linus said, wiping his eyes with the back of his hand. He laughed, and it felt like the sun coming out after the rain. "I . . . when I lived in the city, I dreamed in color, of places where the sea stretched on for miles and miles." He looked at each of the children in turn. "But what I didn't expect was that the color didn't come from the ocean, or the trees, or even the island itself. It came from all of you." He blinked rapidly, throat working. "This has been the best birt. Thank you. You've made me the happiest I've ever been."

Linus dropped Arthur's hand and rushed forward, scooping up as many of the children as he could manage (three!) while the others held on tightly to various limbs.

Arthur waited until they began to pull away before speaking in a hoarse voice that he'd never heard come from himself before. "At the bottom. Is there a photograph missing?"

Sal looked at him and said, "That's for David, in case he wants to be up there too. We didn't want him to feel left out when he got here."

Arthur closed his eyes and breathed.

THREE

The train arrived right on schedule, early on a Sunday morning, a black steam engine with half a dozen blue-and-green carriages in tow. The sky looked angry, the sun's rays casting the thin clouds in a furious shade of red. It appeared a storm was brewing as the children gathered before Arthur and Linus to say their goodbyes.

"You'll listen to Zoe, yes?" he said with an undercurrent of nervousness unlike anything he'd ever felt before. "You won't give her any trouble?"

Lucy smiled prettily. "Oh, we wouldn't dream of it. Cross our hearts, hope to die."

"That's what we're concerned about," Linus said. "No death. No destruction. And I'd better not hear from Zoe that there were explosions of any kind."

"I'll make sure nothing blows up," Sal said, Theodore on his shoulder, nipping at his ear. "Shouldn't be too hard, now that Talia doesn't have grenades anymore."

"I still haven't forgiven you for that," Talia said, glaring up at them.

"You have to miss us," Lucy demanded. "And you have to call me every hour so I can tell you what I did the previous hour. In *great* detail."

"You have to bring us back presents," Talia said. "And if one of the presents—say, for a beautiful, talented gnome—happens to be twice as expensive as the others, then we'll just have to deal with that."

Theodore growled, and Linus assured him if he found any discarded buttons, he'd bring them back for the wyvern's hoard. Theodore was so pleased he took to the sky, wings spread wide as he circled above them, his shadow stretching along the ground.

While the others continued to tell Linus what he and Arthur could and could not do, Sal looked at Arthur and jerked his head. They stepped off to the side of the platform, near an orange courtesy phone that hung from a post.

"What is it?" Arthur asked. "Did something happen?"

Sal shrugged. "No, it's not like that. It's . . ." He looked away out onto the rolling dunes rising beyond the platform, thin reeds bending in the warm breeze. "I just . . . I wanted to talk to you about something."

"Anything," Arthur said with a nod. "Always."

Sal took a deep breath, and said, "We're going to listen to your testimony. On the radio. We talked about it—"

"Did you?" Arthur asked. "All of you?"

"Yes."

He should've expected this, and though a prickle of unease danced along the back of his neck at the idea of them listening, it was no match for how proud he felt. He knew how hard this must be for Sal. For all the progress he'd made, Sal still had moments of extreme doubt.

"And you're all in agreement?"

"We are," Sal said firmly, even as he shifted his weight from one foot to the other. He sighed. "You confuse me sometimes."

Arthur chuckled dryly. "It's not the first time I've heard that."

Sal arched an eyebrow. "Might want to work on that, then."

"Cheeky."

"You want to protect us from the people who don't like us, and I get it. I do. But then in the next breath, you tell us we need to use our voices because those same people should know who we are."

"A conundrum," Arthur agreed.

"You can't protect us forever," Sal said, and the sorrow Arthur felt was sharp, a dagger through the heart. "I know you want to, but how else are we supposed to learn? How am I supposed to help you fix what's broken if you shield us from everything?"

"You are a *child*," Arthur said, that unease changing from a prickle to a full-on thrum. "All of you are."

"I'm fifteen," Sal reminded him. "If that's a child, fine. But even then, I—*we* won't be for long. You say you trust us. Doesn't that mean you should trust us to make some decisions for ourselves?" He glanced over Arthur's shoulder at the others, Chauncey's vibrant voice echoing across the platform. "This is *about* us, Arthur. Don't we have the right to know what's being said?"

"You do," Arthur said quietly. "Sal, I . . ." He shook his head. "Yes, you do have the right." He laid his hands on Sal's shoulders. "If this is what you want, then I'll support it. All I ask is that you allow Zoe and Helen to be present to help you all make sense of it. And any questions you have for me or Linus, we'll answer them upon our return."

Sal nodded, obviously relieved.

"Is that all?" Arthur asked carefully.

Sal cleared his throat, gaze darting around. "I know . . . we talk about it. About you adopting the kids." He winced. "And I know I'm probably too old for—"

"It wouldn't matter if you were one or one hundred," Arthur said. "You would still be mine as much as I am yours. Nothing will ever change that."

Sal exhaled sharply as he sagged. When he looked back at Arthur (*at*, not up, seeing as how he was almost as tall as Arthur now) his vision was clear, sure, and he said, "I didn't know my parents. They were gone before I could remember anything about them. But you're here. You said you would be, and you've kept your word."

"And I meant it," Arthur said.

The train whistled sharply, signaling an imminent departure. Arthur turned toward it, only to jerk his head back when Sal blurted, "We love you, you know? We don't say it very much, but we do."

Arthur pulled Sal toward him, wrapping his arms around the boy as tightly as he could. Sal gripped his back, forehead on Arthur's shoulder. "I know," he whispered. "And I—"

An attendant—a burly fellow in a snappy uniform with two rows of gold buttons down the front—leaned out from the train and called, "All aboard! Final call for those leaving Marsyas!"

They hugged the children for the last time and lifted their luggage—two suitcases between them—as they headed for the train to find their seats.

But as the train began to pull away, Arthur did not sit. He hurried from carriage car to carriage car as the train picked up speed, waving frantically to the children as they ran next to the tracks, Theodore coasting on the wind. Soon, the train proved to be too fast, and the children stopped. He leaned out the window and shouted, "I love you! All of you!"

Whatever they said in reply was lost to the sounds of the train and the warm wind.

Bowing his head, he struggled to control his breathing. He looked up when a gentle hand squeezed his shoulder. He didn't have to turn around to know who it was. "I've never left them before," Arthur whispered. "I didn't expect it to be so hard."

"Leaving is never easy," Linus said, laying his forehead against Arthur's back. "But knowing they'll be waiting for us to come back will make it that much sweeter when we do."

Arthur turned and gathered Linus up in his arms. "It's as if I've left my heart behind."

He felt Linus smile against his throat. "I've never seen you so out of sorts before. You delightful man, they will be well because *you* taught them how to be. Come, now. Calm, even breaths. The sooner we arrive, the sooner we can return home."

Midway through their journey, the first raindrops began to fall.

The city was as Arthur remembered from his youth: extraordinarily loud, cars trapped in gridlocked streets, people bustling on the sidewalk, umbrellas up against the rain that fell in droves, the black and gray of the metal buildings gloomy under a darkened sky. Stepping off the train, Arthur entered a different world, one where he was a stranger. He couldn't smell the salt of the ocean, couldn't hear the crashing of waves against rocky cliffs. The stench of petrol and rubber mingled with the sounds of honking horns, and part of him—the child trapped in the cellar—screamed at him to get back on the train.

Linus bumped into him from behind, grumbling under his breath about the never-ending rain. "Remembered my umbrella for once." He glanced up at the clock hanging against the far wall of the train platform. Arthur did the same and saw it was the middle of the afternoon.

"The hotel, then?" Arthur asked, taking Linus's suitcase so he could open the umbrella.

With the umbrella sorted, Linus took his suitcase back. He looked at Arthur, that funny little wrinkle in his forehead making an appearance. "I . . . I have something to show you first. Will you come with me? We'll have to take the bus."

Arthur would follow him anywhere and told him as much. Linus rolled his eyes (though he couldn't hide his smile) and said, "Besotted fool. Come on."

The trip on the bus took almost forty minutes. Linus promised the journey to the hotel wouldn't take half as long after. Arthur, for his part, didn't mind, fascinated by the way everyone standing swayed each time the bus came to a stop at a light. They were, for a brief moment, all the same. The farther they went, the more the bus emptied, and though they had seats available to them, Arthur told Linus he preferred to stand after the long train ride, for some reason enjoying the simple act of being on a bus, something he hadn't done in years.

"We're approaching our stop," Linus said, reaching up to pull the cord hanging from the ceiling. A bell sounded from somewhere near the front of the bus, which began to slow, turning into a pullout off the road next to a small stand.

The rain hadn't lessened. Linus and Arthur had to jump from the last step on the bus to the sidewalk to avoid a large puddle. As the bus pulled away, Arthur waved. No one waved back.

"They don't care," Linus said.

"Perhaps," Arthur replied. "Still, it's only polite." He took in their new surroundings. The buildings of the city rose in the distance, hulking giants reaching toward a slate-colored sky. Around them, a neighborhood of middle-class housing, single-story homes made of brick and wooden paneling. It was much quieter here, the traffic nowhere near as severe as it'd been closer to the city center. The only sound came from the splatter of rain and a dog barking somewhere.

"This way," Linus said, the umbrella open. They began to move down the sidewalk, Linus quiet, tension making his shoulders stiff.

Arthur wanted to ask where they were going but got distracted by the trees that lined either side of the road. They didn't look like the trees back on the island. Even though it was summer, the leaves were dull, dark, as if all the color had been sapped from them. It was off-putting in ways he couldn't describe, and he was about to tell Linus as much. But before he could, he saw a street sign that led farther into the neighborhood. HERMES WAY, it read.

"This is where you lived," he said.

"It is," Linus said in a clipped voice, as they turned onto Hermes Way, a boxlike lorry driving past, splashing water near their feet. Arthur found it odd that no lights seemed to be on in the darkened houses. Even if people were at work, wouldn't they want to come home to brightness rather than shadows?

It didn't take long for them to reach their destination. Linus stopped in front of a house. Eighty-six Hermes Way. It wasn't much: small, brick at its base, with paneling in a dark shade of blue. A porch with white railings, complete with a rocking chair tucked away safely out of the rain. And there were flower beds, but they held no flowers, just misshapen bushes that could use a trim.

"This is it," Linus said quietly, but he didn't look at Arthur. He stared at the house with an expression Arthur didn't like, a tinge of sadness that made him look older than he was.

"It's . . . lovely," Arthur decided.

"Is it?"

"It's small," Arthur admitted, looking back at the house. "I don't know how it could contain all that you are."

Linus was startled into laughter, eyes bright. "I'll have you know I've lost half a stone."

"I didn't mean it that way, and you know it. I happen to love those stones, lost or found. It's just . . . it's not you."

"It was," Linus said. "Perhaps no longer, but this was my home."

"You're still the owner."

"I am." He nodded toward the house next door. "Mrs. Klapper lives there. Her nephew is in the process of purchasing the property, but he and his new husband went abroad, and we're waiting for him to get back to finalize everything. We don't need to go inside, but there's something I need to do."

"What's that?" Arthur asked as they made their way up the walkway toward the house.

Linus ducked his head. "I made a promise."

"We do that, don't we? Make promises."

"We do," Linus said as they stopped in front of the porch, the rain tick, tick, ticking against the umbrella. "Could you set our luggage on the porch out of the rain? According to Talia and Phee, this shouldn't take long."

"And a promise to those two is one to keep," Arthur said, having an idea of where this was going. He took Linus's suitcase from him and climbed the steps, setting it near the door. When he went down the steps, Linus held a small cloth pouch in his left hand, the other gripping the umbrella. He looked up at the house, shook his head, and stepped off the walkway into the overgrown grass. Arthur followed him, stopping when he did in front of the empty flower beds.

Linus handed Arthur the umbrella and pulled the green string that held the pouch closed. Inside, Arthur could see a pile of seeds, some oval in shape, others square, all black with speckles of white on them.

"Okay," Linus said. "Phee and Talia told me that I don't even need to plant them." He poured a handful of seeds into his hand, bouncing them once, twice, before sprinkling them along the flower beds. After emptying the pouch, Linus stepped back from the flower beds with a frown, forehead lined. "They said it should only take a minute or two."

"What should?" Arthur asked with great interest. He peered down at the seeds lying in wet soil. They rested where they'd fallen, and if anything was supposed to happen, he couldn't see what it was.

Until, that is, one of the seeds began to wiggle. As Arthur looked on in amazement, he was reminded of sand fleas the children dug up on the shores, little gray crustaceans with tiny legs scrabbling for purchase. The first seed burrowed into the ground, followed by another and another until all of them were digging in near silence. When the last one disappeared, a little bubble appeared above the hole it had created. It grew and grew until it was the size of an apple. Then it popped, and in this insignificant explosion, Arthur felt a familiar rush of magic, a mixture of Gnomish and sprite, so green it felt like the birth of life.

The ground rolled beneath their feet, a low tremor that rattled the railings on the porch. Linus grabbed Arthur's hand, pulling him back as the soil where the first seed had disappeared parted, a small stalk pushing through, a shade of green that was startling in this colorless place. He heard a groaning sound, and his eyes widened when more plants burst through the soil.

When all was said and done, it took less than a minute. Where once was a barren, muddy nothing now grew dozens of flowers in pink and blue and white and orange, the leaves and stalks so green, they looked plastic. The flowers rushed toward the sky, bursting open, soaking up the rain. The centerpiece was a large sunflower at least seven feet tall, the bloom wide. It was unexpected, stunning in its simplicity for something that was undoubtedly a complex piece of magic. He knew the children were powerful—wasn't that why they'd been sent to him to begin with?—but having such evidence never failed to knock the breath from his lungs.

"I'm nervous," Arthur said quietly.

Linus smiled as if he were expecting the confession. "You're doing the right thing." He leaned against Arthur, a warm, comforting weight. "Be nervous, Arthur. Be frightened. I am too."

Knowing what they were to face the next day, Arthur and Linus decided to make it an early night. The return bus trip was mostly uneventful, with one particular exception: a newspaper, discarded on a cracked seat. Arthur's own face stared back at him in black and white, though decades younger, his straw-colored hair longer, a cocky twist to his smile. Above the picture, stark words in black type: WHO IS ARTHUR PARNASSUS? Below that, in smaller type: LANDMARK TESTIMONY FROM A MAGICAL BEING.

"Who indeed?" Arthur said to no one at all.

"All right?" Linus asked, coming up behind him.

Arthur turned, blocking the newspaper. "Let's sit farther back."

By the time they were back in the city, darkness had fallen. The rain had lessened to a miserable drizzle, and even though it was summer, the air had a chill to it that reminded Arthur of winter on the island.

They picked up takeaway, Linus shuddering when Arthur asked for extra brown sauce. "No accounting for taste," Linus said with a sniff, as if he hadn't gotten more ketchup than was necessary.

They took their meal to the hotel a couple of blocks down from the restaurant. The hotel—The Rose & Thorne—was an old thing. On a busy street corner, it loomed above, a white stone building with a black facade inlaid with gold designs of a rose surrounded by prickly thorns. The bellhop—a young lad with a unibrow and a crooked smile—opened the door for them, bowing as he welcomed them to the hotel.

They had chosen The Rose & Thorne for its proximity to Bandycross, the governmental building where Arthur would be giving testimony. It would make for an easy trip come morning.

Making quick work of getting checked in—tipping their young

bellhop handsomely—they hurried to their room, laughing when both reached for the phone as soon as they'd set down their luggage. The call home lasted thirty minutes, given that each of the children wanted to give a complete accounting of how they'd spent their Sunday. Though heartened to hear their voices, Arthur felt a desperate urge to flee this place, to spread his wings and fly until the rain had stopped and the air smelled of the sea, especially when Chauncey asked if they'd met David yet, and if he was tall. The reason Chauncey asked, he explained, was because he'd read yetis could grow upward of ten feet, and he thought that would be extremely helpful when something was on the top shelf in the kitchen. Arthur replied that he would report back just as soon as he'd met David himself.

When they hung up—with promises to call again in the morning and again in the afternoon and *again* at night—Arthur sat on the edge of the bed, staring off into nothing, his meal half-eaten and now cold. Regardless, he didn't have the stomach to finish it.

Linus went into the loo after the call, and when he came out he had a funny look on his face, button-down shirt half-open, revealing sparse hair on pale skin.

Arthur frowned. "What is it?"

Linus shook his head, bringing a finger to his lips. Moving quickly, he went to the radio sitting on the desk across from the bed. He flipped it on and spun the dial across the stations until he found Little Anthony singing about the tears on his pillow, the pain in his heart. Turning the volume up as loud as it would go, he motioned for Arthur to follow him. Arthur rose from the bed without question, Linus leading him to the hall closet. Opening the door, Linus shoved him inside, pulling the door closed behind him. He could barely make out Linus's face in the darkness.

"A little light, if you please," Linus whispered loudly.

Arthur brought up his hand, and a small bloom of fire rose from the tip of his index finger, flickering as if a wick had been lit. Linus's face was illuminated as he leaned forward.

"Who knew we were staying at this hotel?"

Arthur blinked. "Zoe and Helen. The children. Why?"

"One of the lightbulbs over the sink was out. I thought it was dead until I saw that it wasn't screwed in all the way. I tried to fix it, but it wouldn't go in any farther. I figured something was blocking it, so I poked around in the fixture and found this." He lifted his hand, turning it over so the palm faced the ceiling. Sitting in his hand were shards of black plastic mixed with silver, none bigger than the half-moon crescents on his fingernails. Next to the shards, a green wire, detached.

"What is it?" Arthur asked, peering down at Linus's hand.

"A bug," Linus muttered. "Or it was until I destroyed it. Someone wants to listen in to whatever we say."

"Truly?" Arthur asked, shocked into a bright bark of incredulous laughter. "That's a little much, don't you think?"

"You don't know the government like I do. I wouldn't put it past them to do something insidious to try and get a leg up on tomorrow." He bounced the plastic in his hand. "The reservation was in my name. They could easily have found out where we were staying. Which means—"

"That we were put into this room for a reason," Arthur finished for him. He leaned back against the closet wall, mind whirring. "Could there be more?"

"I have no doubt," Linus said. "We need to change rooms. No, we need to change *hotels*."

"Or," Arthur said thoughtfully, pushing himself off the wall, "we could give them a show."

Linus's eyebrows rose. "What did you have in mind?"

They stepped out back into the room, Little Anthony having given way to Patsy Cline. Perfect.

He took the pieces of the broken device from Linus, setting them aside on the desk. He turned slowly, right foot dragging along the floor in an arc before he snapped to attention, one arm across his chest, the other at his back. He bowed, never taking his eyes from Linus. When he rose, he asked, "May I have this dance, my good man?" He held out his hand in invitation just as Patsy began to sing about seeing the pyramids along the Nile, watching the sunrise on a tropical isle.

Linus rolled his eyes in exasperation, but his lips quirked. "Now? Really? But what about—"

"We can worry about tomorrow, or we can dance. I know what I want."

Linus watched him for a moment. Then, "Who am I to refuse such an offer?"

Arthur pulled him close, hands on Linus's hips. Linus put his own hands over Arthur's shoulders, fingers in the back of his hair. They began to sway back and forth, feet shuffling on green carpet. Leaning his forehead against Linus's, Arthur whispered, "Let them listen to what joy sounds like. Maybe they'll learn a thing or two."

FOUR

Bandycross stood ominously before them, a Gothic revival building made of darkened stone and constructed in the latter part of the eighteenth century. Two towers rose on either side of the pointed gable, and a layered archivolt sat above the massive double doors. The rose window above the archivolt was made of stained glass, a five-pointed star at its center. The building was beautiful and menacing at once, low curls of fog crawling along the streets and sidewalks.

Arthur and Linus stood opposite Bandycross, watching the gaggle of reporters gathering on the front steps, most of them holding either a camera or a microphone in addition to an umbrella. There were at least two dozen of them, but they were outnumbered by something Arthur did not expect.

In the streets, blocking traffic, a crowd of people from all walks of life. The old, the young, magical and human. They held signs lambasting the proceedings, and as Arthur and Linus looked on, a chant picked up. "Magical rights are human rights! Magical rights are human rights!" Cameras clicked and flashed, reporters shouted questions that went unanswered as the crowd yelled and marched in a wide circle. Beyond them, rows of barricades lined with police holding back counter-protesters spewing filth in the form of jeers, teeth bared in furious snarls. They, too, held signs, some displaying that old chestnut SEE SOMETHING, SAY SOMETHING.

"We could try and get in through the back," Linus said, sounding worried. "We have time."

Arthur shook his head. "I won't hide, Linus. To do so might give the notion that I'm ashamed. I am anything but. No. We will walk in through the front doors with our heads held high and prove to them that we will not be intimidated."

"But what if someone means you harm?"

"Then they will see what I'm capable of," Arthur said in a hardened voice. "I am a child no longer. I can handle myself."

"I know," Linus said, sounding rather helpless. "But I don't want anything to happen to you."

Arthur said, "Shortly after you came to the island, you rightly took me to task for keeping the children from the village. You said something I've never forgotten: that the longer the children stay hidden away on the island, the harder it would become for them. That the island wasn't forever, and that world outside was waiting."

"That certainly sounds like me," Linus said begrudgingly. "And I assume you're taking the point I was making about the children and applying it to yourself."

"I am," Arthur agreed. "When we live in fear, it controls us. Every decision we make is smothered by it. I refuse to live like that any longer. I have every right to walk in through those front doors, same as anyone else."

"You do," Linus said. "And I wouldn't dream of taking that away from you. My apologies if it sounded like that's what I meant. I'm just . . ."

"Worried."

"Yes."

Arthur reached over and straightened Linus's tie, smoothing it down the front of his chest. He had on a black suit—the first time he'd worn one since leaving DICOMY permanently. His tie was a lovely shade of reddish-orange, the color of fire. It was not lost on Arthur the reason Linus had picked that tie in particular: a little sign, a burst of flame in the muted gray of this rain-drenched city.

Arthur, too, wore a suit. His coat and trousers were navy blue, his dress shirt covered in blooms that reminded him of Talia's garden. The top plastic button at his throat had been replaced by a brass one, sewn on with care. His tie was a wonderful shade of green, not unlike a certain bellhop. His shortened trousers revealed gray socks with little fluffy Pomeranians on them. Pinned to his shirt, a small gold leaf plucked from a tree on the island grown by a forest sprite. On his jacket, a pocket square, black with little red devil horns on it.

"Just . . . be careful," Linus said. "Listen. Watch. Don't give more away than you get in return. And for the love of all that's holy, do *not* mention the animal skulls Lucy collects, especially to the reporters. Professionalism, Arthur. It's all about professionalism, even if we have to fudge the truth a bit."

Arthur kissed his forehead. "Noted. Come. The sooner we arrive, the sooner we'll be finished."

With Linus at his side, Arthur held his head high as he crossed the street, stepping around the standing puddles on the road, fastening the buttons of his suit coat. A heavyset man with curly hair and crooked teeth saw them first. He stood on the third step, an ancient camera hanging around his neck by a leather strap. His gaze moved around the crowd, landed on Arthur, stuttered, then moved swiftly to Linus. His eyes widened as he looked back at Arthur. "Arthur Parnassus!" he yelled, nearly falling as he stumbled down the steps. His camera came out, and *flash, flash, flash.* "Sir! Is there any truth to the rumors that the Antichrist is plotting the end of the world?"

The effect on the crowd was instantaneous. A brief moment of silence—as if all the world held its breath—and then an explosion of noise as *everyone* turned toward them—reporters, protestors, counter-protestors, all shouting at once, microphones and signs raised.

Arthur and Linus were swarmed, people reaching out, touching Arthur's shoulders, his arms, his hands, his back. Linus squawked angrily as someone bumped into him hard, knocking him forward. Arthur managed to keep him upright as they pushed their way toward Bandycross, questions being shouted at them from all directions. Beyond them, the counter-protestors hurled vitriol, screaming *"SEE SOMETHING, SAY SOMETHING!"* over and over again.

They managed to reach the steps of Bandycross, climbing halfway before Arthur stopped, turning around. He held up his hands as cameras flashed. Linus stood next to him, their arms brushing together.

"I'll keep this brief," Arthur said, raising his voice. "I am honored to have been invited to Bandycross today to speak of my history with the Department in Charge of Magical—"

"Where is the Antichrist?" someone shouted. Though he couldn't see who it was, it sounded like the man who'd spotted them first. "Can you promise he's not going to split the planet open like an egg?"

"Oh," Arthur said. "I highly doubt it. You see, he's still learning how to crack chicken eggs properly, so I expect it'll be quite some time before he's ready for planetary destruction."

Every face stared up at him in shock.

"Remember what I told you about your sense of humor?" Linus hissed at him. "Now is *not the time* to try and be funny!"

"Try," Arthur huffed. "Ouch." He raised his voice once more. "That was a poor attempt at humor. My apologies. To answer your question, Earth will not be destroyed today."

"*Or* anytime in the future," Linus added loudly.

"Too right," Arthur said. He saw a girl of perhaps ten or eleven standing in the crowd between a man and a woman who appeared to be her parents. In her hands, she held a glittery sign that read MAGIC MAKES THE WORLD BEAUTIFUL. She waved shyly at him, and he winked in return, causing her to grin widely.

"Dana Jergins," a woman said, stretching her microphone toward him, her perfect teeth on full display in a shark's grin. "*The Daily View*. Mr. Parnassus, why are you here today?"

He leaned forward until his mouth was inches from the microphone. "I was invited."

The skin under her right eye twitched, but the skilled facade held. "And why were you invited? Out of everyone in the world, why you?"

"That's a question for those sending the invitation, don't you think?"

She wasn't to be deterred. Even as the other reporters began to shout their questions, her voice rose above them, pointed, unignorable. "Is it because you're a phoenix who has found himself in possession of some of the most dangerous children ever known?"

The other reporters fell silent.

"Possession?" Arthur repeated, eyes narrowing. "They aren't *things*. They are people, just like you and me. And they are no more a danger than any other child in the world."

"That's not quite true, though, is it?" Dana said. "Other children can't do what those in your care can. Our readers deserve to know what you're doing to keep the magical youth contained."

"Contained?" Linus said. "*Contained?* Do you hear yourself? My God, what is *wrong* with all of you?" He puffed out his chest, glaring down at the reporters. "You should thank your lucky stars that Arthur Parnassus agreed to even be here. He's already done more than you ever will. And you can quote me on *that*. Good day." He began to turn toward the Bandycross entrance.

The reporters instantly shouted more questions.

He looked over his shoulder, mouth curved in a bland smile, and said, "Good. *Day.*" Then he pulled Arthur up the stairs, muttering under his breath about nosy busybodies who knew nothing about anything.

"Ah, professionalism," Arthur teased, trying to settle his nerves. "A lost art."

"Shut it, you," Linus grumbled. "They were frothing at the mouth. It's only going to get worse from here."

The interior of Bandycross was just as impressive as the exterior had proven to be. The vaulted ceilings of the lobby were high, thick wooden beams crisscrossing at least fifty feet above a cream stone-tiled floor. Rain pattered against stained glass, and Arthur wondered what it would look like in sunlight, a kaleidoscope of fractured color. It felt impressive, but artificially so, as if anyone who stepped into this great hall was *supposed* to be intimidated by all the pomp and circumstance. Instead, it left Arthur as cold as the walls and floors appeared.

Rows of people in suits and dresses and fancy hats stood in lines before security guards situated behind high wooden desks that set them at least a foot and a half above those whose credentials they were inspecting. The lines appeared to be moving at a good clip with a mixture of reporters and the public, all of whom had earned a place at the hearing by lottery. According to Linus, there was great interest in the proceedings, and they'd supposedly had tens of thousands of entries into the lottery. All told, Linus expected an audience of hundreds, a mixture of the public, the press, and those with official government positions. Arthur understood why; it wasn't every day that a magical being was invited to speak *against* government programs designed *for* magical beings.

They were deciding which line to stand in—Linus saying they couldn't wait long, as time was already growing short—when a nervous-looking Desi woman appeared before them wearing a plaid skirt and a black blazer, her inky-black hair pulled back into a loose ponytail. She held thick folders in her arms, papers sticking out, the edges bent. "Arthur Parnassus? Linus Baker?"

"Yes?" Linus asked warily.

"My name is Larmina," she said. "I've been asked to bring you inside."

Linus frowned. "And who's doing the asking?"

She glanced around, head turning as if on a swivel before she leaned forward, dropping her voice. "A friend."

"Interesting," Arthur said. "I would have thought us without friends here."

Larmina blanched. "Not all of us are . . ." She shook her head.

"It doesn't matter. Please. If you'll follow me, I'll take you to where you're supposed to be."

Arthur studied her for a moment. For her part, she didn't look away. "Your lead, then."

Relieved, she said, "Thank you. I promise it'll be worth your time." With that, she spun on her flats and marched toward a security guard near the far right wall. The young guard had no one in his line, with a sign before his desk that read: VIP ONLY.

They reached the desk right as Larmina said, "They're with me."

The guard's eyes widened, his bushy eyebrows rising to his hairline as he leaned forward over the desk. "Is that . . ."

"Yes."

The man seemed to have a hard time tearing his gaze away from Arthur. "Are you sure about this, Lar? If they find out, it's both our arses on the line."

"Duncan," Larmina said. "We talked about this. They won't. Let us in. We don't have much time."

"I know, I know." He waved them through. "You may pass. Stay with Larmina. She'll show you where you need to be."

Larmina led them farther into Bandycross, up a set of stairs, through an open doorway into a long hall with burnt-orange carpet and doors lining the walls. Nameplates sat next to each of the doors, bearing names Arthur recognized from the papers, politicians who made lofty promises without follow-through.

She stopped in front of a pair of golden elevator doors with guards on either side. She nodded at them as she pressed the button. Glancing down at the small gold watch on her wrist, she said, "Shouldn't be long now." She looked to Arthur, then, making sure he was watching, turned her gaze toward the guards, then back to Arthur. He touched the side of his nose in response.

A moment later, the doors opened with a flat chime. Larmina stepped inside, motioning for Arthur and Linus to follow. Once inside the elevator, Larmina pulled a chain from her blouse. Attached to the end was a small silver key, two inches in length, its teeth serrated. She put the key into a lock on the panel, twisting it before pressing a button without a number on it.

The elevator began to rise. The second floor, the third, the fourth, and Arthur was about to demand Larmina explain herself when she reached out again, this time slapping her hand against the large red button to the left of the panel. The elevator shuddered around them before groaning to a stop between the fourth and fifth floors.

Larmina said, "This is one of the few places in the entire building where we can speak without the risk of being overheard. Everything—including most elevators—is under surveillance. Cameras everywhere."

"But not here?" Arthur asked, looking up at the ceiling. No cameras as far as he could tell.

"No," she said. "This one is different. It goes to the Floor of Enigmatic Situations. No cameras, no listening devices. Hush-hush meetings occur there, out of sight, away from prying eyes. Privileged information, need to know only."

"And yet here we are, stuck in an elevator," Linus said.

"Because they would know," Larmina said. "At least this way, we can pretend the elevator malfunctioned, and no one will be the wiser."

Linus folded his arms. "I appreciate your . . . sensitivity to certain matters, but the fact remains, we don't know you. You could be working for—"

"My wife is magic," Larmina blurted, cheeks splotchy. "She can . . . It doesn't matter what she can do." A fierce pride filled her voice. "There's no one like her. I would do anything for her."

"Even work in a place like this," Linus murmured.

"*Especially* work in a place like this," Larmina retorted. She blanched. "Apologies. I'm—"

"No apologies necessary," Linus said. "It wasn't a slight against you, merely an observation." He chuckled dryly. "One I know quite a bit about."

"What is your wife's name?" Arthur asked.

"Minnie," Larmina said.

"She must be someone special to have earned such devotion."

"She is," Larmina said. "And I— Oh, blast it, the *time*. Please, just listen. I have to get this right. She trusted me to—"

"Who?" Linus asked.

"Ms. Doreen Blodwell," Larmina said.

Linus startled. "*What?* The secretary for EUM? That Doreen?"

The one Linus had once referred to as Ms. Bubblegum, Arthur realized.

Looking relieved, she said, "Yes, her. She would've been here to greet you herself, but there were . . . other matters that required her attention. She's since been reassigned. I'm not at liberty to say to what department, but you should know that things aren't always what they seem. Ms. Blodwell came across certain . . . information about what you can expect during the hearing. She felt that sharing it might even the pitch."

"Why should we trust you?" Linus asked. "Or her? For all we know, you're working with the government to find out what we know."

"She thought you'd say that," Larmina said. "Which is why she wanted me to give you this." She folded back the pages on her clipboard and pulled out a small, square piece of fabric. She held it out to Linus.

Huffing in exasperation, Linus snatched the proffered gift out of Larmina's hand. He looked down at it and froze.

"What is it?" Arthur asked.

Linus turned toward him with a stunned expression. He held up the object, and it took Arthur only a moment to recognize it.

A mousepad, the picture creased and worn, showing a white, sandy beach with ocean waters so blue, they seemed impossible. Or they would, at least, if Arthur hadn't seen such an ocean only yesterday. And across the top in stylish cursive lettering, a question: *Don't you wish you were here?*

He did, and desperately so.

"You spoke of this," Arthur said as Linus's bottom lip wobbled. "You said it was a little escape."

"Yes," Linus said hoarsely. "It was one of the few things I had that made DICOMY bearable." He looked down at the mousepad, tracing the whitecaps of the waves with a finger. "It felt like a dream." He turned back toward Larmina. "We're listening."

"The hearing has been upgraded," Larmina said as the elevator creaked and groaned around them. "You will be facing four parliamentary members." She paused. "In the Council of Utmost Importance."

The blood drained from Linus's face. "Surely you jest."

"I wish I was," Larmina said solemnly. "Word came down early this morning."

"What is that?" Arthur asked. He'd never heard of such a thing, but then he wasn't as versed in government nomenclature as Linus was.

Linus began to pace in the small confines. "It's *ridiculous*, is what it is. There are levels of councils, depending upon the situation. Council of Insignificant Propositions. Council of Moderate Ideas. Council of Serious Inquiries."

"Ah," Arthur said. "Clear as mud."

"Yes, yes," Linus said, distracted. "It's the government. What do you expect? Transparency is a fanciful lie they tell constituents to distract them from the truth. The Council of Utmost Importance is reserved for the direst circumstances. It's one step below terrorism investigations."

"It's not *all* bad," Larmina said, as if she felt guilty for relaying the information. "Two of the council members have signaled their support for repealing some of the laws pertaining to the magical community—"

"Some," Linus said. "But not all."

Larmina laughed without humor. "You were an employee of the government not too long ago. Have you already forgotten how things work?"

"I haven't," Linus replied. "But that's why we're here. To light a fire under them."

"Figuratively or literally?"

"You haven't told us anything we didn't already know," Arthur said.

"Jeanine Rowder."

The name was familiar, but Arthur couldn't place the name to a face.

Linus didn't have that problem. "The minister of education? What does she have to do with anything?" Sensing Arthur's confusion, he added, "Former teacher. One of the youngest ever elected. Moved up quickly, amassing powerful friends." He made a face. "I had no dealings with her myself, but I heard things about her that left me cold. Though it didn't get very far, for a time she supported legislation that would have made it illegal for children who come from queer families to talk about them, saying that it would only confuse children who came from *proper* families. There were even rumblings about coming down hard on parents of transgender children seeking medical care."

"So everyone in the government is mostly terrible," Arthur said.

"Mostly," Larmina said. "But it's gotten worse with her. She's going all in on the so-called *issue of the day*. Some are of the opinion that she's been radicalized, but that implies an external force played a role. Ms. Blodwell doesn't believe that to be true. She thinks Rowder's sudden interest in all things magic has another end game in mind. Rumor has it that she has her eyes set on the ultimate prize."

"Which is?" Arthur asked.

"Prime minister," Larmina said gravely. "And all the power that comes with it."

"And why are you helping us?" Arthur asked, curiosity winning out over his growing discomfort. "Same with Ms. Blodwell."

"Because something has to give before it's too late," Larmina snapped, and this time, she did not apologize. Arthur's opinion of her rose swiftly. "I fear we're on the cusp of either salvation or destruction. And if I don't do everything I can to make things right, then how can I go home and look at my wife? How can I stand before her and know that I failed her? I refuse to let that happen." By the time she finished, she was panting, but she did not back down.

Linus hesitated. Then, "If what you're saying is true, how has DICOMY not discovered you? Or Doreen?"

Larmina laughed bitterly. "Because we understand how the minds of men work. Give them a little smile, touch their arm, hang on their every word, and they believe they're God's gift to women." Her face suddenly changed, going from a flat mask to big eyes and pouty lips. When she spoke again, her voice was in a higher register. "And that's all we are. Pretty girls without a thought in our heads." The facade melted, replaced by steel. "That's the funny thing about those in power. They underestimate everyone beneath them, even knowing their secrets are heard by *someone*."

"It's still quite the risk," Linus said.

"A time will come," she said, "when all of us will have to make a choice between what is right and what is wrong. I worry that time is closer than we think. And I don't know that we're prepared. If Rowder continues on the path she's on, then no one—not you, not your children, *no one*—is safe. This hearing isn't meant to be a condemnation of DICOMY, DICOMA, Extremely Upper Management, or the practices of said departments, past, present, or future. It's a PR campaign."

"To what end?" Linus asked.

"The complete and total annihilation of the reputation of one Arthur Parnassus."

Arthur and Linus exchanged a glance. When Arthur looked back at Larmina, he said one word, and one word only: "Why?"

FIVE

"Please state your name for the record."

"Arthur Franklin Parnassus."

"Mr. Parnassus, do you affirm that the testimony you have agreed to provide today will be truthful?"

"Yes."

"And to confirm, you are without a representative."

"Yes."

"Do you understand that you are entitled to have a representative present?"

"Yes."

"And you are choosing to continue, knowing what you say is being broadcast live around the country."

"Yes."

The man settled against his high-backed chair, hands folded on the table in front of him. The other committee members—two women, one man—sat in similar chairs on a raised stone dais, putting them at least three feet above Arthur, each under a powerful spotlight shining down from above. Arthur sat at a smaller table in the dim light of the rest of the courtroom with a single microphone set before him next to a glass of water and a half-empty pitcher. Behind them and attached to the wall, an electronic reader with red words moving from the right to the left, reminding everyone in attendance that there were to be no outbursts, no interruptions, and that such things if they occurred would lead to the immediate dismissal of the person with no questions asked, regardless of their intent.

The chambers—called Netherwicke—were enormous, made of dark wood and stone. It was as if the absence of color that engulfed the city had leached its way into these hallowed halls, leaving behind only the dreary brown-black of coffee dregs at the bottom of a mug. The floors creaked, the walls groaned. The ceiling was a dome-like structure made entirely of glass, revealing a dark, windswept sky, the clouds heavy, rain falling in sheets. The smell of the downpour had seeped its way into Netherwicke, thick and wet, mingling with the scents of old wood and parchment.

It was strangely quiet, given the hundreds of people sitting in the hall. Behind Arthur were rows and rows of reporters, the public, and more than a few elected officials. Though he didn't turn around, Arthur knew Linus was sitting directly behind him, a wooden railing separating them. Above them—to the right and left—a second-floor gallery opened up to the hall below. This, too, was filled with people, representatives of the government, their faces mostly hidden by shadows, gesturing as they leaned over and whispered to one another.

Arthur ignored them all, his focus firmly on the four people sitting before him. The man who'd spoken first was older, his face lined with canyons. His white hair appeared to have migrated from his head to his ears, curly tufts sticking out. He—like his colleagues—wore a black robe, the arms of which were a tad too long, falling over the backs of his hands. The nameplate before him declared him to simply be BURTON.

Next to him, a grandmotherly figure, her hair a pile of pink candy floss, a pair of gold spectacles sitting on the bridge of her nose attached to a beaded chain around her neck. Her painted-on eyebrows gave her an appearance of perpetual surprise. Her nameplate read HAVERSFORD.

The third person was a young man who looked as if he would still get asked to verify his age when he went to a pub. He was a fidgety sort, and his black hair was slicked back and shone wetly in the overhead lights. He had a nervous habit of chewing on his fingernails and seemed a bit ill at the sight of so many people before him. The plate named him as SALLOW.

And then there was the last: Jeanine Rowder. At ease in front of the audience, barely giving them any notice aside from the flick of her cool gaze toward the second floor. Roughly Arthur's age, she was a tall woman with robes that billowed as she took her seat, smiling widely before sitting down. Her shoulder-length hair was a soft shade of reddish-brown, her teeth perfect little squares of white. She looked like anyone Arthur would pass in the street, but there was something off about her, something that chilled Arthur to the bone. Perhaps it was the way she held herself: shoulders squared, posture perfect. Or perhaps it was the way she barely acknowledged his presence, glancing dismissively in his direction once or twice, her focus mostly on the stack of folders she had sitting before her. Burton, Haversford, and Sallow, too, had folders, though nowhere near the number Rowder had. And hers appeared to have dozens of tabs, marking what, Arthur didn't know.

Burton appeared to have seniority, as he spoke for the rest of them. "The Council of Utmost Importance is gathered here today, facing a question that never seems to have a satisfactory answer, at least not one that can be agreed upon by a majority. What is to be made of the magical community? This has—"

Arthur leaned forward and cleared his throat pointedly into the microphone.

A low titter rolled through the crowd.

Burton frowned. "Yes?"

"Apologies, sir," Arthur said. "But you have made it a point to ensure my honesty, which I appreciate. To keep things fair, I ask that you do the same."

The titter turned into a rumble.

"I beg your pardon?" Burton snapped.

Arthur adjusted the microphone. "You said that no answer has been agreed upon by a majority. Hopefully you're aware of the government-sponsored poll from six years ago that showed fifty-one percent of those asked believed that any and all magical beings should have the same rights as their human counterparts. Though this poll declined to invite anyone magical to participate, I believe fifty-one percent of respondents is still a majority. Again, my apologies for the interruption, but it's important that the record show there *is* a majority." He smiled. "Granted, the government's response to the findings was to launch the 'see something, say something' campaign, so I can understand how there might be some confusion."

"Mr. Parnassus," Burton said sternly. "There is an order to these proceedings. Please refrain from speaking unless it is your time to, or you have been asked a direct question. Understood?"

Arthur nodded.

Burton waited a beat and then resumed. "We are at a crossroads. The purpose of this hearing—and any that may follow—is to determine what, if any, changes need to be made to the current RULES AND REGULATIONS that govern the magical community. As has been covered by the press ad nauseum, the Departments in Charge of Magical Youth and Magical Adults have recently come under heavy scrutiny. With the dissolution of Extremely Upper Management, the departments are without permanent leadership." He folded his hands. "To that end, Mr. Parnassus has been invited to give evidence as he finds himself in a unique position: not only did he live in one of the government-sanctioned orphanages in his youth, he is currently the master of the same orphanage, located on Marsyas Island." He looked down at the folders before him, lifting one of the pages. "As of today's date, there are six children occupying this—"

"Living," Arthur said.

Burton pinched the bridge of his nose. "What was that?"

Arthur leaned toward his microphone. "You said occupying as if they were some sort of invading force. They don't *occupy* their— our home. They live there. Perhaps that's semantics, but I believe words matter."

"Mr. Parnassus, I'll warn you one last time. I do not like being interrupted."

"Understood, sir. But if we're going to determine the best path forward, I'm sure you would agree to avoid language that some might consider offensive."

Burton gaped at him. "And who might be offended?"

"I take offense," Arthur said. "Sir. And, as a reminder, the children have names. Hello, Lucy. Hello, Chauncey. Hello, Talia. Hello, Theodore. Hello, Sal. Hello, Phee." In his head, he added, *And to you, David; I haven't forgotten.* "They're listening," he explained as whispers swept through the audience. "It's not every day that a child gets to hear their name spoken aloud on the radio. And I highly doubt they're the only magical people listening, so yes, words matter, especially now."

"We understand things are volatile in your community," Haversford said, speaking for the first time, her voice deeper than Arthur expected. She pushed her glasses up the bridge of her nose. "It's one of the purposes of this hearing, to hopefully cool the fires burning. But we are not the enemy, Mr. Parnassus. Surely you know that."

"Ah," Arthur said. "Hoisted on my own petard. I'm afraid I must amend my earlier statement. Words matter, yes, but actions matter even more. Anyone can say anything they wish, but it's the follow-through that's important. Correct?"

"Of course," Burton said with a sour expression.

He closed the trap. "Then surely you can see why I—and I am only speaking for myself here—might have a different definition of the word 'enemy,' given the actions of the government with regard to the magical community."

Burton sputtered, Sallow appeared as his name suggested, Haversford sighed, and Rowder did absolutely nothing, sitting stock-still, back straight, gaze never leaving Arthur. The rain lashed against the dome above, an ever-present reminder of the dark sky overhead.

"Mr. Parnassus," Haversford said, not unkindly, "you have every right to feel as you do. I won't tell you I can understand what you went through, because that would be a falsehood built upon privilege."

He nodded. "Thank you for recognizing that."

"That being said, we'll never get anywhere if we can't even move beyond the introduction. If my colleagues will agree, perhaps we should save any speechifying until after we've heard from Mr. Parnassus. It would seem he is eager to speak, and isn't that what we're here for?"

"There is procedure to follow," Burton retorted.

"There is," Haversford agreed, "but we find ourselves in uncharted territory and procedure can only take us so far. I know I'd prefer to hear what we came to hear rather than talking over each other." She looked to Sallow and Rowder. "In favor?"

"Aye," Sallow said, voice cracking. "Yes. That would be beneficial."

Rowder merely nodded, tapping her fingers impatiently against the folders in front of her.

Burton seemed irritated. "Fine. But I won't let this devolve into baseless accusations being flung about willy-nilly."

"I assure you," Arthur said, "that any accusations I intend to make aren't baseless. Instead, they are factual, given that I was present for all of them."

Burton snorted derisively. "So you say. Very well, then. Mr. Parnassus, the floor is yours. Use your time wisely."

Behind him, he heard Linus mutter, "I'll show *you* wisely, you pretentious git."

Arthur pretended to cough so he could cover his smile with his hand. "Thank you." Though he knew all eyes were on him—not just here, but around the country and perhaps the world—he focused his attention on the man behind him, the four in front of him, and the group of children who no doubt surrounded the radio at home.

How long had he waited for this moment? Months since Linus arrived? Or did it go back further than that? He thought it did. Years and years, back to the boy who had written a letter in hopes of salvation—not just for himself, but the other children, too—only to be imprisoned for having the audacity to believe in freedom. Yes, this moment felt as if it had been a lifetime in the making, and though extraordinarily nervous, he refused to let Burton, Haversford, Sallow, or Rowder see it.

He began.

"When I was a child, I was abused at the hands of an employee of the Department in Charge of Magical Youth. The abuse wasn't just physical violence. It was also psychological, as the master made it his mission—as he often said—to put us in our places, a reminder that as magical beings, we were intrinsically lesser. The violation of our basic rights as people escalated unchecked until I—with the wisdom and boldness only found in youth—decided that something must change, that we—as *people*—should not be made to suffer. So I wrote everything down and attempted to mail it to the people I believed would help. The result of daring to ask for help from the very government whose representatives sit before me today? Imprisonment. Six months in a cellar with no windows and no lights. I was fed once a day and forced to use a bucket as a toilet. There was a metal bed with an old mattress that was riddled with mold. Cracks in the walls that I memorized by the light of my own flames because I had nothing else to occupy me. No books. No schoolwork. No visitors, and I wasn't allowed to leave.

"For the first three days, I screamed. The week after, I burned. The week after that, I was beaten so thoroughly, I couldn't breathe right for what felt like years. Like many who have suffered abuse, I was told it was my fault. That I deserved it. That I had it coming to me simply because I wouldn't *listen*. He knew what was best, after all. He was an adult. A government employee. And I was just a child. I began to believe him.

"Time became slippery, elastic, and it stretched in ways I can't even begin to describe with any clarity. For my own sanity, I kept track of the days with tick marks scratched into the walls. It was the only thing I had to keep me occupied, counting the days one by one. By the end, I was so delirious I'd convinced myself it'd been years rather than months.

"But I'm getting ahead of myself. I arrived at Marsyas Island when I was seven years old. I had nothing and no one...."

All told, he spoke uninterrupted for two hours and forty-six minutes. Along with the rain, the only other sounds in the deathly quiet of Netherwicke aside from Arthur were audible gasps and the odd sniffle or three from the audience. By the end, Arthur's voice was hoarse, throat burning, cooled only by a sip of water. He felt hollowed out, soft, and though the anger still burned, it was a negligible thing that sparked weakly.

Through his entire testimony, he kept his gaze forward and locked on the four before him. Burton gave nothing away, his default setting appearing to be a scowl. Sallow and Haversford took copious notes throughout the time Arthur spoke, the scratch of their pens a soothing metronome. For her part, Rowder did nothing aside from listen, ignoring the folders stacked before her. Though he didn't expect it, he half hoped Larmina had been wrong about her, that she was nothing more than an elected official blinded by the idea of power.

"Thank you, Mr. Parnassus," Haversford said after he'd finished. "That was . . . illuminating in ways I did not expect. I can't imagine how difficult it was for you to come here and speak as honestly as you have, and you are to be commended. Before we continue, would you like to take a break to collect yourself?"

"No, thank you," he said before clearing his throat. "I'm able to continue if you are."

"So be it," Burton said, sitting forward and riffling through the papers he had before him. "Mr. Parnassus, you testified against this former master, did you not?"

"I did."

"He was censured, sacked, and found guilty, was he not?"

Arthur could see where Burton was heading, and more than willingly rose to the challenge. "Yes, but not in that order. He was found guilty, censured, and *then* sacked. From what I understand, he was on paid leave through DICOMY's internal investigation and his sentencing, after which he was put on probation for three years. Only then was he no longer an employee of DICOMY, and therefore, not entitled to a further salary."

"And your testimony was sealed given that you were a minor. Nothing has been released publicly."

"That is correct, though I believe it had little to do with the fact that I was a minor, and more to do with DICOMY saving face."

"Do you have proof of this?" Burton asked.

"Consider it a well-informed assumption."

"So, no, then," Burton said. "Mr. Parnassus, you reached a settlement with the government after an inquiry found negligence on the part of the Department in Charge of Magical Youth. How much was the settlement agreement for?"

"It sounds as if you already know."

"Answer the question, Mr. Parnassus."

Arthur smiled. "One million pounds."

The crowd murmured around him.

"One million pounds," Burton announced grandly, as if he'd scored a point in his favor, whatever that might be. "A godly sum, wouldn't you agree? Especially to a child. Though I do empathize with your plight, Mr. Parnassus, I can't help but think you've been adequately compensated. And now, instead of financial gain, you appear to be after a pound of flesh."

"That's one way of looking at it," Arthur said. "Another might be that I was paid a settlement as penance for years of government-sanctioned abuse."

"Now, see here," Sallow said, eyes bulging. "There has *never* been sanctioned abuse. Why, the very idea is as preposterous as it is sickening. The *RULES AND REGULATIONS* clearly states that a child should *not* come to any harm, regardless if they're magical or not."

"Strange," Arthur said. "Because according to public records from the three decades since I was taken from the island, DICOMY has had seventy-six masters accused of some form of abuse toward minors in their care. Twenty-seven were sacked. Five quit of their own accord, though they were given severance. The remaining masters were relocated after going through what was called *sensitivity training*. More than half of *that* group went on to have further allegations levied against them. As of today's date, twelve are still active masters in orphanages around the country." He looked from Burton to Haversford to Sallow to Rowder. Her eyes matched the stormy sky above: gray and flat. "If it wasn't sanctioned by the government, that would suggest DICOMY has the unfortunate luck of recruiting people who feel physical abuse is necessary when dealing with children."

"And how did you come by this knowledge?" Burton asked, a sour expression on his face. "I highly doubt public records were that specific."

Secreted out by one Linus Baker, of course, before he left DICOMY. But Arthur wasn't about to tell them that. "Do you deny it?"

Sallow puffed out his chest. "We are not the ones being interrogated here, Mr. Parnassus. You are."

As the crowd began to murmur from above and behind him, Arthur watched as Haversford frowned, glancing at Sallow. She said nothing as she looked back at Arthur.

He arched an eyebrow. "I wasn't aware we'd moved on from voluntary testimony to interrogation. I might have prepared differently had I known that was going to be the case, especially in light of being in front of the Council of Utmost Importance."

Sallow said, "It wasn't . . . that's not what I mean! I'm merely trying to—"

"You claim abuse," Burton said.

Arthur nodded. "More than claim, but yes. While I won't speak for others who have found themselves in a similar position, I can and will speak to my own experiences. That sort of abuse—the pain it causes—is cumulative. Whether physical or psychological, each new blow lands upon a wound not yet given time to heal. It builds until something has to give."

"You were paid an exorbitant sum because of it."

"Blood money," Arthur said, voice clipped. "If you think for one moment I'd take the payment over my innocence, you'd be gravely mistaken. And since I know you're all arbiters of truth and justice, I will add that, when cross-examined, my former abuser suggested that not only did DICOMY *know* about the abuse at the hands of the masters, it turned a blind eye."

"Even *if* that were true," Sallow said, "it was never meant to be permission or endorsement of that sort of conduct."

"Do any of you have children?" Arthur asked. Then, without waiting for an answer, he said, "I have six. Children, especially while young, begin to learn the difference between what is right and what's wrong. Many times, you must tell them no. And I dare you to find any child who won't follow the word 'no' with the word 'why'?"

A few in the crowd chuckled. Maybe even more than a few. Encouraging, but then people could be extremely fickle.

"And that's to be expected," Arthur continued. "Because their wonderful brains are growing just as they are. When you tell them no, you must explain the why of it, so as to provide them with context, boundaries. That's how children learn. If you say nothing at all when a child does something they shouldn't, to the child, it could imply permission. So I ask that you, as members of the government, explain why telling a child no is something we all agree is necessary for their growth—as discussed in the seminal tome *RULES AND REGULATIONS*, chapter four, from pages two fifty-seven to three forty-three, written by a former member of EUM—but you can't do the same for adults who take advantage of the power dynamic. Are you concerned with them asking *why*? You shouldn't be. They're adults. They should know better."

"I was punished as a child when I was wrong," Burton said, eyes narrowed. "My father took a switch upside my rear when I stepped out of line, and I turned out just fine."

I wouldn't go that far, Arthur thought but didn't say. He knew he was already walking a tightrope, and it wasn't as taut as he'd hoped. "I'm sorry for that. I truly am. A child—human or otherwise—should never be struck as a form of punishment. It's understood that one should never strike a pet such as a dog because it's cruel, but when it comes to children, we're supposed to think that it's for their own good and they'll turn out just fine?" He shook his head. "I refuse to believe that."

Burton scoffed, waving his hand in dismissal. "You aren't here to tell other people how to parent those in their care."

"You're right, I'm not. I'm here to provide evidence that children are *suffering*. That alone should give you pause. Do any of you know what it means to be unloved? How it feels?"

No answer, only silence. Thick, electric.

"Of course you don't. You have friends. Family. You can never know the terrible feeling of having no one to love you. I know. I *remember* how that felt. No child should ever have to feel that way. They are our *future*. And yet, countless children go to bed every night in DICOMY-sanctioned orphanages, never knowing a kind word or a gentle hand." Arthur shook his head. "How can you claim that it's the *children* who are dangerous when you've done everything you can to back them into a corner?"

Sallow cleared his throat, looking wan. "Speaking of children. You have in your possession six children who—"

" 'Possession' implies ownership," Arthur said evenly. "I do not own anyone. Again, words matter, sir."

"The fact remains that they are some of the most powerful beings in existence. Children capable of—"

"Being children?" Arthur asked. "Yes, they are."

"Be that as it may, they are still children who can tap into an as yet unknown level of magic." Sallow looked down at a folder in front of him. "Chauncey, for instance. What is he?"

Arthur shrugged. "We don't know exactly. Isn't that wonderful? But since you're asking for something specific, Chauncey is a bellhop, and one of the very best."

"What hotel would hire him?" Burton asked. "His appearance is . . . unsettling."

"What hotel wouldn't?" Arthur said. "They'd be lucky to have him, should there be an opening. And I think you meant to say 'unique' rather than 'unsettling' because I have it on good authority he's handsome as crap."

"Talia," Sallow said. "A garden gnome."

"Yes," Arthur said. "But she's so much more than that. She's fierce, funny, and protective, and she digs some of the most perfect graves I've ever seen. Oh, and her begonias are the best in any garden."

A familiar chuckle from behind him, and Arthur's lips quirked.

"Theodore," Haversford said. "A wyvern."

"One of the smartest children I've ever had the pleasure to know. His hoard is unparalleled, and he's recently learned how to land without tipping over. Quite impressive."

Haversford chuckled. "And Sal?"

"A gifted writer who has grown before my eyes, both figuratively and literally. He's coming into his own. I can't wait to see the man he'll become. I expect great things from him."

Sallow tapped the folder in front of him. "Who can also pass on his . . . condition, in the form of a bite."

"He can," Arthur said. "And he did, once, in fear after an adult struck him while he was trying to get *food*. Who would you like to ask about next? Phee? She is a forest sprite who can already grow trees even though she isn't yet a teenager, and who has taken to her role as an empathetic sister with gusto." He grinned razor sharp. "No, I think you're working your way toward one child in particular, aren't you? You want to know about Lucy." Larmina—and in turn, Doreen—had been right. This had never been about Arthur, or the wrongs of DICOMY. It was a fact-finding mission, and he'd played right into their hands, believing that some good could come from this.

Oppressive silence, leaving only the creaks and groans of Netherwicke.

"The Antichrist," Burton finally said, grimacing as he did so.

"We don't use that word," Arthur said. "Not because *we* feel it's wrong, but because everyone else seems to think that word means the end of all we know. I won't have this child—or any other, for that matter—believing in such tripe."

"Tripe?" Sallow asked. "There has never been one such as him before. What is he going to be capable of when he gets older? What if the world doesn't twist to his every want and whim?"

"Since you're speaking as if you know my son personally instead of only what's written in his DICOMY file, I assume you have a point. What do these children have to do with my experiences under the rule of DICOMY?"

"Oh, he does have a point," a sweet, musical voice said, causing Arthur to turn his head. Jeanine Rowder smiled, cocking her head. Her nose wrinkled slightly, as if she'd caught an unpleasant smell. "Perhaps it was a little artless, but what I believe my colleague is trying to say is something firmly in your wheelhouse, Mr. Parnassus. At least from what I understand."

"And what would that be?" Arthur asked.

"A philosophical quandary. And since you brought up the Anti . . . Lucy, as you call him, I think the line of questioning is relevant, as it relates to their master." She frowned, but it felt like an act. "Oh, that word just won't do either, will it? The connotations! Let's call you what you are. As the *guardian* of potentially dangerous magical youth, do you have a moral duty to act if you have knowledge that could potentially put innocent people at risk?".

Oh, this one, Arthur thought. *This one is going to be trouble.* "That depends on if you believe in utilitarianism or deontology. Utilitarianism revolves around the concept of the ends justifying the means, the belief that outcomes as the result of an action have greater value than the actual action itself. It is a consequence-oriented philosophy. Take, for instance, DICOMY and DICOMA."

Burton began to sputter angrily, but Rowder held up her hand and he snapped his mouth closed.

Arthur continued. "I tend to adhere to the theory of deontology, the principles of Immanuel Kant which state that both the actions *and* the outcome must be ethical. Greater weight is placed upon the action's morality, but it also says that a *wrong* action does not make its outcome the same."

"That could also describe DICOMY, don't you think?" Rowder asked, steepling her hands under her chin, never looking away from Arthur even as she smiled prettily. She didn't give him a chance to respond. "But that's a topic for another day. It seems to me we're going about this all wrong. After all, this isn't about the children, but Arthur Parnassus. He has graciously provided a harrowing account of his time under DICOMY's purview, and I, for one, applaud his bravery." Her smile melted into a mien of sticky sympathy. "It can't have been easy, coming here."

His skin thrummed, and he forced himself to take calm, even breaths. "It was not, but as I said before, it's important."

"Quite," Rowder said. "And while I think there is relevance to hearing about your wards—especially since you have petitioned to adopt them all, haven't you?—the fact remains they are, as you eloquently stated, just children."

"In that, we agree."

"Whose real parents are all . . . deceased."

Tightening the screws. She knew the children were listening. "Seeing as how the word 'orphan' is part of 'orphanage,' yes, that is the case."

"Why these children?"

Arthur blinked in surprise. "I don't know what you—"

"Out of all the children in the world that fall under the watch of the Department in Charge of Magical Youth, why these six?"

"Because they needed a home."

"I suppose that's one reason," she said. "But what about *you*, Mr. Parnassus? You are not a child. And, as much as it pains me to say, after everything you've been through, you should, by rights, be extraordinarily upset with DICOMY and DICOMA. From what I've heard in your testimony today, you are, and with good reason."

"Once again, we are in agreement. Though I feel 'upset' is, perhaps, a euphemism."

"Of course you do," she said with a chuckle. "Let's turn the focus back where it belongs, shall we?" Without waiting for an answer, she leaned forward quickly, a pair of violet half-moon glasses appearing as if by magic on the bridge of her nose as she looked down at the open file before her. "Dead parents. No siblings. No other family. Into a department orphanage at the age of seven." She *tsk*ed, shaking her head. "How terribly sad, that. Positively awful. You have my sympathies. You are a phoenix, yes?"

Conversational whiplash, but that was her point, wasn't it? To keep the ground rolling beneath his feet. "Yes. I am."

She nodded. "Wonderful. Prove it."

A murmur rolled through the crowd, a low sigh like the wind off the sea under a steel sky. "I beg your pardon?"

She looked surprised. "Oh, silly me. I thought I was being clear. Let me try again, and please let me know if there is still any misunderstanding. I am asking, Mr. Parnassus, that you prove you are what you say you are. I don't think it's asking too much. After all, no one at DICOMY or DICOMA has seen evidence since you were a child, and even then, it's mostly secondhand reports."

Haversford cleared her throat. "Councilwoman, I don't think that—"

Rowder ignored her. "Mr. Parnassus?"

He hesitated only a moment before lifting his hand, palm raised toward the ceiling. He could hear the others shifting around him, all craning to see what he would do. Arthur paid them no mind. A small fire appeared above his hand, no bigger than the flame of a candle. It danced above his skin before he closed his fingers around it, snuffing it out, a small cloud of smoke rising from between his fingers.

Rowder blinked. "Is that . . . is that it? That's what you can do?" She *tsk*ed again. "I must admit to being a little disappointed. From your files, I understood that not only can you take the shape of a phoenix, but it can act as an extension of yourself as well, independent, though under your control. What you just showed us is a parlor trick." She sighed, sitting back in her chair.

Arthur bristled, knowing she wanted to get a rise out of him, but unable to do much to stop it. "I will not be made to dance for you. You think yourself better than me, and I—"

Her eyes widened. "Mr. Parnassus, I pride myself on being accepting of *everyone*, no matter their background or lot in life. Any suggestion to the contrary is not only false but slanderous, and I won't stand for it. That being said, I have a job to do, one I don't take lightly. Perhaps the files were wrong? As much as I hate to admit it, DICOMY and DICOMA have indeed made their share of mistakes. Extremely Upper Management, for one. Speaking of, Mr. Parnassus, do you know why EUM approved the Marsyas Island orphanage remaining open?"

"I'm afraid my powers do not extend to reading minds."

"For which we're all grateful," Rowder said. "I must admit to finding it strange that EUM just . . . rolled over when it came to you." Her eyes lit up as if a new thought had entered her head. "Unless it had to do with Charles Werner. You knew him, didn't you? And to avoid any confusion, when I say you *knew* Mr. Werner, I mean intimately."

"What does any of this have to do with—"

"Do you deny it, Mr. Parnassus?" she asked.

"Mr. Werner and I were involved for a time, yes. But unbeknownst to me, he was using me to further his own career with—"

"I'm not finished," Rowder said, her voice still light, easy, as if this were a conversation over brunch. "Because then there's one Linus Baker, a former employee of the Department in Charge of Magical Youth. You are currently in a romantic relationship with him, correct?"

"Yes, but—"

Rowder sat back in her chair. "You seem to have a habit of collecting our employees for your own pleasure. I do hope we don't lose any more good men to you. Employee retention is important, and a revolving door of paramours isn't something children should be exposed to. It does raise an interesting question, however: Did Lawrence Baker, oh, excuse me"—she looked down at the folder once more, though Arthur knew it was all for show—"*Linus* Baker, falsify reports from Marsyas Island in order to appease you, Arthur Parnassus?"

Haversford looked stunned. "This has *never* been brought to our attention before, nor have we seen or heard any evidence that even remotely suggests such a thing. Councilwoman, what are you accusing Mr. Parnassus of, exactly?"

Rowder held up a piece of paper covered in black lettering that Arthur couldn't make out. "I have in my possession a sworn, signed affidavit from Charles Werner, a former member of Extremely Upper Management. After the dissolution of EUM last year, Mr. Werner took it upon himself to offer on record his keen insight into Arthur Parnassus. In addition to saying he felt threatened by Arthur Parnassus and Linus Baker—which is why, he claims, he and the other members of EUM agreed to keep the Marsyas Island orphanage open—it was his not-so-inconsiderable opinion that Mr. Parnassus is, for all intents and purposes, training magical youth to be soldiers."

An explosion from all corners of Netherwicke: the crowd around Arthur rose to their feet, shouting, fists raised in the air. Cameras clicked and flashed, and people shouted over one another, their words lost in a wall of noise. Those in the second-floor gallery stomped their feet, beating their hands against the railing before them.

"*SILENCE!*" Burton bellowed, the word a whipcrack. Most everyone blinked rapidly as if awaking from a fuzzy dream. "We will not allow such outbursts during these proceedings. Anyone who speaks out of turn again will be removed immediately. Do I make myself clear?"

The crowd returned to their seats, the tension so thick Arthur practically choked on it.

"Mr. Parnassus?" Rowder asked sweetly. "Would you care to respond to these allegations?"

"Allegations," Arthur repeated.

"Yes. About the children. Are you training them?"

"Beg pardon, but I think you meant to use the word 'raising.'"

"But that's not what I said, is it?" Rowder said, smiling once more. "Again, are you training them?"

"For what? Life? To be good people? To show love and acceptance even in the face of institutionalized bigotry? If that's what you mean, then yes. I'm training them."

Sallow shifted uncomfortably. "I think what she's asking is if you're training these children to go to war for you."

"I wouldn't dream of going to war with any of you," Arthur said mildly. "It would be a battle of wits for which you are wholly unarmed."

A resounding gasp from the observers, followed by furious mutterings, the rain plinking against the windows.

"Now, see here," Burton started. "I will invite you to watch your tone, as—"

"Mr. Parnassus," Rowder said, and Burton subsided, muttering under his breath. "You should know I sympathize with you greatly. And I don't think I'm alone in that regard. Anyone who has heard your testimony today has most likely found themselves irrevocably changed. You have a way with words, sir, and we are all better off for it. That being said, another question, if I may." She opened another folder, this one red like blood. "After your removal from Marsyas, you were placed in no less than seven different orphanages. At the age of eighteen, you were allowed to leave on your own—"

"I was kicked out first thing that morning," Arthur said. "But not before the master attempted to extort me out of the blood money DICOMY paid me. Unfortunately for him, the money was in a trust until my twenty-first birthday."

"You poor dear," Rowder said. "That must have been part of the reason you didn't register with the Department in Charge of Magical Adults as you were legally required to do. Per the records provided from the time, you failed to attend twenty-four different scheduled meetings with a department representative. My question is this: Where were you from the ages of twenty-one to approximately forty when you returned to Marsyas?"

He should've seen this coming. He hadn't, but he should have. Of course they'd do whatever they could to make him appear the fool, and a dangerous one at that. He'd thought himself better, smarter, and some small part of him—optimistic to a fault—had hoped this would be the start of something different, that people would actually listen. His own hubris would be his undoing, and he had no one to blame but himself. No one knew what he'd done during those years, not even Zoe or Linus. It wasn't as if he were ashamed; if he'd had to do it over again, he would have made all the same choices.

He chose his words carefully. "I traveled extensively. I'd never been able to see much beyond the walls of the homes in which I was placed."

"And during your . . . travels, did you ever come across another magical being?"

"Of course I did."

She nodded, pleased. "And did you assist them in any way?"

"Define 'assist.'"

Her mouth dropped open, another practiced move. "Are you *hedging* in front of the Council of Utmost Importance? Mr. Parnassus, surely you understand how unacceptable that is."

He spread his hands as if to say *What can you do?* "If you're going to accuse me of something, do it."

"As you wish. Mr. Parnassus, did you illegally move magical persons to help them avoid detection by DICOMY and DICOMA, thus enabling them to live as unregistered beings?"

"Yes."

A burst of noise that he ignored, though he could feel Linus's gaze boring into the back of his head.

"And you did this knowing it was against the law?"

"Yes."

"And if you were not here today, and if you hadn't found yourself returning to Marsyas Island, is it fair to say that you would have continued helping the magical community flout the laws of this great country?"

"Yes."

Then she asked a question he didn't expect. "During this period, or any time after, did you ever help another phoenix?"

"I wouldn't answer that even if I had."

The low mutterings behind him grew louder.

Rowder sighed. "Mr. Parnassus, how can we help if you won't be honest with us? We aren't the evil masterminds you seem bent on making us out to be. According to the official record, you are the only known phoenix in the entire world. Did you know that?"

"Yes."

"That must be very lonely for you. I don't think you can be blamed, then, for seeking out others like you, to find strength in purpose and solidarity." She grew stern, a mother scolding an unruly child. "However, that doesn't give you the right to act as a vigilante, especially when it seeks to undermine everything we stand for. Have you ever considered the fact that you caused more harm than good?"

"Not once," Arthur replied.

Her forehead wrinkled. "Not . . . once? No twinges of guilt? Nothing deep inside your captivating brain that screamed at you to stop and *think* for once in your life?"

"Never," Arthur said. "Offering food, clothing, and shelter to people who had none seemed like the best way to spend the government's money. Pardon me. *My* money."

Rowder's eyes flashed, but when she spoke, her voice was even. "And sometimes that meant moving people."

"Yes."

"Unregistered people."

"Yes."

"To keep them from following the letter of the law."

"Laws meant to control them," Arthur snapped, his anger finally getting the best of him. "To never let them forget that a government built with the idea of *helping* people only includes those society deems *normal*. I've seen firsthand what your letter of the law entails. Or have you forgotten the reason I'm here?"

"We haven't," Rowder said. "And I'll be the first to say that mistakes were made, mistakes that I wouldn't wish upon anyone. I'm sure the others will agree."

Sallow nodded furiously, Haversford eyed Rowder warily, and Burton looked as if he wished he were anywhere but here in Netherwicke.

"See?" Rowder asked. "So, yes, I think—"

Arthur leaned forward, mouth inches from the microphone. "Then apologize."

That caught Rowder off guard. For a brief moment, the countenance of sympathy failed, replaced by a flash of black rage so severe it knocked the breath from Arthur's chest. It lasted only a second or two before a bland expression of the unperturbed took root, spreading across her face. "You were compensated one million pounds," she said lightly.

"I was," Arthur said. "But I failed to hear a single apology from anyone: not from the master who abused me and others. Nor from any member of a governing body, including DICOMY and DICOMA. You consider optics in everything you do, yes? Of course you do. You're part of the government. So, for your consideration, I not only ask for an apology from you for the way I was treated, but also an apology to every single magical person who has been harmed—physically, emotionally, psychologically—by your rules. By your regulations. By your *laws*. You want to talk about the children? They're listening, along with countless others from our community. Give them a reason to believe you care about us. Give them a reason to believe, after hearing what you have, that you have their best interests in mind, and that you will not fail them as you have failed so many others. Apologize for the harm *you* have caused."

"Mr. Parnassus," Haversford said. "I hear you. I do. I think it's time for a break—"

But Rowder was having none of it. "Did you—at *any* point—train those you helped to fight?"

Keeping his expression neutral was getting harder. "I taught them to protect themselves."

"For the record, please make note of the fact that Mr. Parnassus did not answer the question asked. Mr. Parnassus, are you training an army of the most dangerous magical children this world has ever known? Children you are now attempting to own outright through adoption, along with Linus Baker, a former employee of DICOMY?"

Who did she think she was? "*Own?* I refuse to—"

Rowder spoke over him, raising her voice. "Did Linus Baker reveal classified information to you, either during his month-long inspection of the island or after?"

"I resent the implication. You don't—"

"And Zoe Chapelwhite. An unregistered island sprite who, by Mr. Baker's own reports, is extraordinarily powerful and not only has *contact* with the children of Marsyas Island, but actively contributes to their education. Is that correct?"

"Yes, and she—"

"Which, of course, brings me back to the Antichrist. Lucy. A wonderful name for a boy. But let's call him by his actual given name, shall we? Lucifer. The purported scion of the Devil himself. A boy who—"

"Is only seven years old," Arthur retorted, his anger a molten ball of lead sitting in his stomach. "A boy who loves music and baking. A boy who has chosen to be good because *he* wants to be."

"For how long?" Rowder asked. "What if something—say, your adoption application—doesn't come to fruition? What would he do then in retaliation? Enforce his will upon the population? Level cities? Bring about an age of darkness where he installs himself as ruler of—"

Arthur stood abruptly, his chair scraping the floor. "He is a *child*. They all are. Do you hear yourselves? Any of you? Why are you attempting to influence public opinion by making baseless accusations, ones *we* will have to deal with for the rest of our lives? You don't get to—"

"I think you'll find that I *do* get to," Rowder said. "I am aware they are children, Mr. Parnassus. But even children can travel a dangerous road when led by a man who has decided he is above the law."

"How dare you," Arthur said coldly. "I came here as a show of good faith to—"

"You came here because *we* allowed it," Rowder said as if they were discussing the weather. "I think we've learned all there is to know. Thank you, Mr. Parnassus. Your testimony today has proven enlightening. We will take everything we've heard into consideration while we decide the best course of action." She smiled again, and Arthur's blood turned to ice. "Though it has yet to be announced, I doubt Herman—pardon me, Prime Minister Carmine—would mind if I let the cat out of the bag." Her smile widened, revealing perfect white teeth. "As of last week, I have been appointed interim head of the Departments in Charge of Magical Youth and Magical Adults while the investigation into EUM continues. I am honored the prime minister has placed so much faith in me. As such, I am ready to make my first decree. A new inspector will travel to Marsyas Island to provide a complete accounting as to the goings-on there. Unlike past inspectors who were unable to file reports without subjective commentary, this new inspector will have no such problems." She chuckled. "And no, Mr. Parnassus, this inspector will *not* be male, given your . . . propensities for distraction when it comes to DICOMY employees."

"What is *wrong* with you?" someone yelled, and Arthur turned his head to find Linus Baker standing, gripping the railing in front of him so tightly, his knuckles were bloodless. He was shaking with barely restrained rage. "The lack of decorum and common decency is absolutely appalling. This farce will *not* be forgotten. Everyone will see exactly the kind of people you are."

"Quiet in the gallery!" Burton barked into his microphone, even as reporters began shouting questions over one another, their words combining into unintelligible nonsense.

Rowder ignored them all, raising her voice. "The point of this inspection will be to determine if the children—Talia and Phee and Lucy and Sal and Theodore and Chauncey and David—are safe at Marsyas island, or if they need to be removed for their own well-being and relocated. The safety of these children—and all children, magical or not—is paramount to DICOMY. If they are found to be abused or imprisoned or worse, being *trained,* it's vital that we protect them before it's too late. After all, studies have shown that the circle of violence *must* be broken. For all we know, Mr. Parnassus has locked them away just as was done to him, and I will invite our guest one more time to show me. The. *Bird.*"

He knew he was playing into her hands. She was trying to get a rise out of him, to make him lose control and prove he was as dangerous as she'd not so subtly hinted. He knew what she wanted, and though he tried his damnedest to fight it, the implication that he was a threat against the children—*his children*—proved to be too much. They wanted to see what he was capable of? He'd show them. He'd show them all.

Someone in the gallery above screamed when bright blooms of fire raced down Arthur's arms, engulfing the sleeves of his suit coat. The fire reached his hands—his palms, his knuckles, his fingertips all crackling, a white-hot center that looked like a miniature sun— and in his head, the phoenix awakened from its slumber, fiery eyes blinking slowly as it shifted within. They were not independent of each other, not like Rowder had implied. The man was the monster, the monster the man. They were one and the same, and when Arthur's wings began to take form—orange-red feathers that burned bright, fierce—the relief he felt was all-consuming, vast, tinged with more than a little anger. His vision sharpened, his blood ran boiling hot. Each wing was at least ten feet in length, little droplets of fire falling from them onto the floor, splashing in sparks of blue before dissipating. He saw through his own eyes, but it *doubled* as he was in two places at once: man standing and beast rising. Arthur spread his arms and the phoenix shrieked, a piercing cry that shook the windows of the dome above. Its large fan of tail feathers rattled together like bones.

He thought about giving in to the phoenix, letting it swallow him whole. Already, his thoughts were changing, becoming less complex, guided by instinct rather than the cold calculation of human logic and strategy. *Fly,* he thought as Arthur Parnassus. *Fly,* he thought as a phoenix, but instead of the word itself, it came as a series of images soaked in fire: wings spread wide, pumping up and down, lifting them (*him*) off the floor. Up and up. Sizzling heat shattering the dome, glass melting in crystalline clumps. Freedom in a slate sky, rain hissing the moment it touched the bird's feathers.

Just as he was about to succumb to the phoenix and fly out—after all, hadn't they all but demanded a performance?—something struck the side of his face. It fell onto the table, and he looked down. There, with its edges curled, smoldering, was a mousepad. On it, the words *Don't you wish you were here?*

He jerked his head over his shoulder.

The crowd behind him had risen from their seats, climbing over one another to get away from the heat of the fire. No one had reached the doors quite yet, but not for lack of trying. Chairs were overturned, people shouted, hands raised above them as if to ward off the phoenix. They were scared, they were *frightened,* and for a moment, didn't Arthur revel in it? Didn't the phoenix scream again, only this time in pleasure at the sight of humans fleeing?

He did. *It* did.

Until he saw the one man who wasn't running, the one man who stood with his hair whipping around his head, his shoulders squared. His eyes were wide, unsure as he looked up at the towering creature before him, but he did not back away, did not try to run. Instead, he stood his ground, his tie flapping against his chest.

Arthur turned around, facing him, in what was only the second time Linus had seen the fiery bird since his arrival on the island the previous year. The phoenix lowered its massive head toward him. When it was eye level, it chirped, cocking its head as it blinked rapidly. Linus raised a steady hand, and the phoenix clicked its beak before nuzzling his palm, eyes fluttering.

"There, there," Linus said quietly. "All this fuss, and for what? You are good, Arthur, no matter what form you choose to take."

"Linus," both Arthur and the phoenix said at the same time, the man's voice clear, the phoenix's like a guttural exhalation.

"Come back," Linus said as the phoenix bumped its head against his hand. "You've proven your point. It's time, Arthur."

He closed his eyes, and the bird shrieked once more—pointed, sharp, a reminder of his power to everyone within earshot—before it folded in on itself, head pointed at the top of Arthur's head. It shot down, and he felt his body burn as the phoenix slammed back into him, his arms and legs jerking. It was over in a bright flash of light, leaving only the stench of smoke behind.

He took a stumbling step toward Linus, his knees weak as they usually were when he pulled the phoenix back. Grabbing his arm, Linus pulled him into a hug, the railing between them. Arthur sighed, bowing his head against Linus's shoulder. "You with me?" Linus whispered.

"Yes."

"Good. Then you must listen. Rowder made a mistake."

He tensed but didn't raise his head. "Tell me."

"The children," Linus said. "She mentioned them all by name."

Arthur pulled back with a frown, ignoring the eyes of everyone upon them as they slowly realized there wasn't a threat any longer, shuffling back toward discarded seats. "What do you mean?"

"David," Linus said. "She mentioned *David*."

For a moment, Arthur still didn't understand. They'd mentioned all the children at one point or another, Arthur included. What did David have to—

When it hit him, it hit him hard. She couldn't know about David because anyone who did was either on the island or in a halfway house waiting for Linus and Arthur to arrive. And the only time *they* had said David's name in the city had been last night at the hotel, before finding the surveillance bug.

Arthur whirled around, Linus's hand sliding down his arm, their fingers catching for a quick moment. It took Arthur only a few seconds to stand in front of the table once more, but by the time he did, he was back in control.

Sallow had fallen over the back of his chair and was now crouched behind his desk, only the top of his head visible as he peeked over. Burton was pale, mouth hanging open, eyes wide and filled with shock. Haversford's face was in her hands, her shoulders shaking.

Rowder hadn't moved. She sat where she had before, hands folded in front of her, thumbs pressed together. The gleam in her eyes could only be described as *hungry*, and Arthur cursed silently for giving her what she so obviously wanted.

People scrambling up in the gallery and in the rows of seats behind Arthur froze when she spoke. "That was . . . quite the display." She sounded breathless, the feedback from her microphone causing it to squeal. "Now, hopefully everyone can see why we're so concerned about the safety and well-being of the children under Arthur Parnassus's care. Given how powerful he appears to be and how quick to anger he is, is it any wonder we'd question his intentions?" She stood abruptly, her chair wobbling back on two legs. It didn't tip over. "We've seen quite enough. Mr. Parnassus, the Council of Utmost Importance thanks you for your testimony, and we will take what we learned today into consideration. You will be contacted shortly with the details of your home inspection. Any subterfuge will be considered an act against the government, and we will respond accordingly, up to and including removing the children from the orphanage and dismissing you from your post. Have a pleasant afternoon."

With that, she began to move off the dais, immediately surrounded by a group of muttering staffers. Burton rose slowly, his lips pulled down. Sallow righted his chair and slumped back into it, looking dazed. Haversford looked off into nothing, eyes vacant as she brushed her fingers against the files in front of her.

"Madam," Arthur called, voice carrying.

Rowder turned toward him. Everyone did. No one spoke, all waiting.

Arthur reached into the pocket of his coat. Making sure Rowder was watching, he pulled his hand out and held it over the table. He opened his fingers, turning his palm over. Bits of plastic and green wiring fell onto the table with a clatter. "I think this is yours."

She cocked her head, her politician's smile on full display. "I assure you, I have no idea what—"

"The listening device you had planted in my hotel room," Arthur said, and as one, Haversford, Burton, and Sallow all turned slowly to look at Rowder.

Rowder laughed. "More baseless accusations, Mr. Parnassus? How expected. You should really consider—"

"I'm not convinced you're in any position to tell me what I should or shouldn't consider. Have a pleasant afternoon."

He turned, pushing his way through the wooden gate. Linus fell in step beside him, and as everyone looked on, cameras flashing, reporters shouting questions, they strode down the aisle and left Netherwicke behind.

SIX

Not wanting to take the chance of additional listening devices or reporters finding out where they were staying, Linus decided they needed to change hotels. Arthur agreed tiredly, lost in his own head. They packed their suitcases with little conversation between them and left the hotel behind. Linus herded them onto a city bus, the rain falling steadily. Hands clasped tightly between them, the pair traveled for nearly an hour, Arthur staring out the window at the city passing by.

He startled out of a semi-doze when Linus said, "This is our stop. We need to find a phone. I bet the children are driving Zoe and Helen up the walls."

"You have questions. I can see them in your eyes."

Linus shook his head as the bus slowed, brakes wheezing. "There will be time for that later. Phone first, then room. We can talk after we've settled."

Arthur nodded and followed Linus off the bus. They hurried across the sidewalk toward a hotel nowhere near as nice as the first. No bellhop, no grand sign hanging above the doors. Instead, it was a short, squat building nestled between a department store and a pub where loud music shook the walls.

A courtesy phone sat just inside the entryway. Linus picked up the handset and dialed a familiar number. Arthur leaned against the nearest wall, their luggage at their feet as he heard the tinny ringing of the phone.

Zoe answered on the third ring, and Arthur laughed quietly at her immediate outrage, her voice carrying through the line as Linus winced, pulling the phone away from his ear. "The absolute *gall*," she snarled. "They're lucky they haven't yet showed their faces on my island. The moment they do, I'm going to turn them inside *out* and— No, Lucy. *Lucy.* That was a figure of speech. We're not *actually* going to turn people inside out. Lucy, that was *not permission for murder*." She sighed. "Yes, I probably shouldn't have said that, but we really need to have a discussion about how quickly Lucy agrees to a plan whenever murder is mentioned."

"It sounds like it's going well, then," Linus said dryly. "Did they listen to the entire thing?"

"We all did," Zoe said. She lowered her voice. "Helen and I tried to distract them when Rowder started jabbering on, but they wouldn't hear of it. How's Arthur?"

He pushed himself off the wall, crowding against Linus, heads close together as Linus lifted the phone between them. "I'm fine, Zoe. A little tired, but nothing a good night's sleep won't fix."

"Linus?" she asked.

"He's all right," Linus said.

"And you?"

"Angry. Frustrated. Worried."

"To be expected. Rowder is a piece of work."

"The children?" Arthur asked.

"They had . . . a few choice words about the proceedings that they absolutely did *not* learn from me. Talia called them all mudguzzlers? I'm not quite sure what that means, but she was very forceful when she said it."

Arthur chuckled. "It's a Gnomish insult, one of the worst. A mud-guzzler is someone foul who eats the soil rather than growing things from it. I don't think I've ever heard her say that before. I feel terrible I missed her first time. It must have been delightful."

"That's one word for it," Zoe said. "To be honest, it pretty much went downhill from there. Even Sal said some things that— Lucy.

Talia. That had better not be grave-digging equipment I see. I said no murdering!"

Arthur missed them all terribly.

"Can you put us on speakerphone?" Linus asked. "We won't take long. It'll be better to explain everything when we return home the day after tomorrow."

"Hold on. Kids! Arthur and Linus want to talk to you. Theodore, just because Arthur made fire indoors does *not* mean you can do the same. Sal, would you help him— Chauncey. Where did you . . . Are you eating a *pine cone*?"

"Phee says it's not cannibalism, and it makes my poops an adventure!"

"I said you could eat the *seeds,* not the whole thing!"

"These are definitely your children," Zoe muttered, and Linus and Arthur grinned at each other like a pair of fools. "Okay. You're on speaker."

"Linus?" Talia asked.

"Yes?"

"The man on the radio said you threw something at Arthur's head."

Linus looked at Arthur helplessly, who shrugged and arched an eyebrow. "Yes, I did," Linus said, glaring at Arthur. "But only because—"

"Violence is acceptable when you need to get people to pay attention to you. Got it."

Linus groaned.

"Children," Arthur said. "You undoubtedly have questions, and I look forward to answering them as best I can upon our return. For now, I think it's important to—"

"We do have questions," Sal said, voice crackling through the line. "But they can wait, except for one."

"And what's that?" Arthur asked.

"Are you all right?"

"I'm fine," he said, blinking against the burn in his eyes. "Much better now that I get to speak with you. But fear not; Linus is with me, and woe to anyone who tries to get in his way."

"Damn right," Linus said fiercely.

They ate a quiet meal—takeaway again, the hotel nowhere near fancy enough for room service—and after, Arthur stood in the shower for a long time, the water scalding as he tried to put his thoughts in order. Once he saw to his evening ablutions, he went back out into the room, dressed in a pair of sleep shorts and an old shirt.

Linus had turned off the lights, the only illumination coming from the blinking neon sign across the street for a pharmacy, flashes of blue, blue, blue. Sitting up against the headboard, Linus pulled back the comforter and patted the bed beside him. "Sleep," he said. "Tomorrow is another day, and one we need to be prepared for."

"David," Arthur said as he climbed into bed next to Linus, who pulled the blankets up and over them, cocooning them in darkness. Through the blanket, a pale pulse of neon blue. For a moment, he could pretend it was the sea.

Linus gathered him up, pulling him over, letting Arthur's head rest against his chest. His heartbeat was slow, steady. Listening to the pleasant *thump, thump, thump,* Arthur took a deep breath, letting it out slow.

"David," Linus said. "They know about him. Or, they think they do."

"It doesn't change anything."

"Doesn't it?" Linus asked, hands in Arthur's hair, scratching his scalp. "Not because I don't want him to come with us, but if they're sending another DICOMY inspector, he could be in danger. Should we put him in such a position?"

"He can't stay where he is," Arthur murmured, stretching his legs, tangling them with Linus's. "You know that. Helen said it was always meant to be temporary. He needs space. Room to grow. We may have to hide him when the inspector arrives, but I've done more with less."

Linus stiffened slightly underneath him, but his heartbeat remained calm. "You have." It was not a question.

"Yes."

Linus hesitated, and when he spoke again, it sounded as if he were picking and choosing his words carefully. "Before you came back to the island I'd heard rumors of someone or someones moving people around, but it was right when I started working at DICOMY, and then it was swallowed up by the machine of bureaucracy, much like I was."

Arthur didn't know where to start. "I was . . . young. Cynical. Angry. No one would listen to us. No one would protect us. And on top of that, there were increasing sweeps of towns and cities, hunting unregistered people, forcing them into the limelight so they could be documented, tracked."

"I remember those," Linus whispered with a shiver. "It proved to be an unpopular action, which is why they shut down the program after a few years."

"Unpopular to a slim majority of non-magical people," Arthur said bitterly. "They didn't give a damn about what *we* said."

"So you took it upon yourself."

"Yes."

"How many people did you help?"

Arthur blinked. "I . . . don't know. I didn't keep count."

"More than one?"

"Oh, yes. Many more."

"And you moved them from place to place, to keep them safe."

"I tried."

"Why did you stop?" Linus asked. "There must have been a reason you decided to return to the island."

Arthur said, "I was tired. Tired of never having a place to call home. Tired of being on my own. I tried to keep the loneliness at bay for as long as I could, but eventually, it began to eat away at me until all I felt was hollow, empty."

"Fires can't burn forever," Linus murmured.

"It felt as if I was chipping away at a mountain with a pickax. I could see evidence of my work, but . . ."

"It felt like diminishing returns. For what it's worth, I think I'd feel the same way."

"It's worth more than you know," Arthur whispered. "I couldn't keep up with it. And the worse off I was, the more room there was for error. I didn't want anyone to suffer because of me."

"So you went back to the island," Linus said, his hand in Arthur's hair. "The place where it all began."

"*Sic parvis magna.*"

"Greatness from small beginnings," Linus said.

Arthur nodded. "That's what I hoped and continue to hope. I'm not a perfect man, Linus. I'm riddled with faults. I don't have all the answers, even if I seem like I do. I'm brash, obstinate. I make mistakes. And I worry! I worry *all the time* about the children. I worry about them when they sleep. When they wake up. When they run, when they eat, when they laugh or cry or sneeze. When they ask questions or when they *answer* questions. What does that make me?"

Linus snorted. "That makes you a father."

Arthur blinked, lifting his head to look at Linus. "What?"

"It makes you their father," Linus said again. "And they are so very lucky to have you."

"You mean that," Arthur said with no small amount of wonder.

"Of course I do," Linus said. "Because I happen to love those things you call faults. They're *part* of you. And they have served you well. Arthur, in the eyes of those who love you, those who *know* you, you've done what you always have: your best. That might not mean much to ridiculous councils, but I happen to know six children who would go to the ends of the earth for you. And if anyone faults you for that, I'll have a few choice words for them, believe you me."

Amused, Arthur said, "Then I suppose I should listen to you."

"You should. I sometimes know what I'm talking about."

"So I've gathered. Now you know. Now you know all there is to know about me. I have nothing left to give."

Linus said, "You do, actually. One last thing."

Arthur frowned. "What would that be?"

Linus slid out from underneath Arthur, climbing off the bed and going to the closet where they'd stored their luggage. Arthur watched as Linus opened the closet door and began to dig around in his suitcase. When he found what he was looking for, he stood upright, closing the closet door. He hesitated a moment, hand on the doorknob.

"Linus?" Arthur asked.

Linus jumped, as if he'd forgotten Arthur was there. When he faced the bed, he looked nervous, jittery. One hand was behind his back, clutching whatever he'd pulled from the suitcase. He approached the bed slowly. "I've thought about this," Linus said. "For a while now. You put the idea in my head, so whatever happens next, remember: this is your fault."

"And I accept full responsibility for whatever it is," Arthur assured him. He didn't know why Linus was so nervous. It should have worried him. But for some reason, he felt as if he could float away in the slightest breeze.

Linus stopped next to the bed, thighs against the mattress. He fidgeted from one foot to the other, and right when Arthur was about to ask if he was all right, a change overcame Linus. His breathing slowed, his shoulders squared, and he smiled, a bright, warm thing that made Arthur's heart stumble in his chest. "I love you," Linus said. "You have given my life color in ways I did not expect. You and the children and Zoe."

"You already had it in you to—"

"Perhaps," Linus said. "But it took kindness and patience to bring it out. It took a home where one should not exist. But it does. It does exist, and that's because of you." He brought his hand out from behind his back, and there, sitting on his palm, was a small black box. As Arthur looked on, Linus opened the box to reveal a silver ring with a line of tiny cerulean-blue gemstones across the top, seven in all.

Arthur reached a shaking hand toward the ring. "After all you've heard today? Still, even now?"

"Even now," Linus said firmly. "And tomorrow. And the day after. And the day after that. All the days we have left. You, Arthur. I choose you." He looked away. "If you'll have me, that is. I know I'm not much, but I do try my best. I come with a ridiculous cat, and I can be a little fussy—"

"Is that what we're calling it now?"

Linus scowled. "Hush, you. I'll have you know that *some* people appreciate—"

"Me," Arthur said. "I'm one of those people. In fact, I might appreciate you more than they do. Is that ring for me? I'd quite like to try it on, if you don't mind." He extended his hand, wiggling his fingers.

Though he almost dropped the box while fumbling it, Linus managed to pull the ring from the box without loss of limb or life. He slid the ring onto Arthur's finger. There was a little pressure at his knuckle that gave way when the ring slid past. It fit perfectly.

He remembered. "Talia."

Last month, Talia had invited Arthur to tour her garden as the end of spring approached. He'd exclaimed over every flower, every leaf, telling Talia this year's garden was her best yet. To which Talia replied that of course it was. In her opinion, it was the best garden in existence, and anyone who disagreed would—in her words—meet her favorite shovel face to face.

Before they had finished up, she had done something she'd never done before: taking a blade of grass, she'd tied it around his ring finger, saying it was a Gnomish custom to say so long to spring as summer approached. Though he considered himself a bit of an expert in all things Gnomish, he hadn't heard of such a ritual before. Even more curiously, Talia had removed it almost immediately, careful not to let it break. When he'd asked what she was going to do next with it, he'd been told in no uncertain terms to mind his own business.

"Talia," Linus agreed. "Said you believed her."

"That sneak," Arthur said, suitably impressed.

"So."

"So," Arthur said, having more than a little fun.

Linus threw up his hands. "Well? I asked you a question!"

"Actually," Arthur said, extending his hand to look at the ring, "you didn't."

"What? Of course I—I said—I gave you the *ring*—I didn't even *ask*?" He groaned, putting his face in his hands. "Well, old boy, you've gone and done it now."

"Linus?"

He sighed and dropped his hands.

"Yes."

"Yes?"

Arthur said, "Yes. Yes to you. Yes to us. Yes to all of it."

When Linus smiled, Arthur was reminded of the sun, of a blinding light coming to chase the darkness away. Such a lovely fellow, with his sturdy heart and fierce loyalty. Arthur hoped he would be enough for such a man. When Linus crawled back onto the bed, Arthur kissed him thoroughly, cupping his face, the ring near his ear.

"Yes," he said again. "Yes, yes, yes."

At precisely half past eleven the following morning, Arthur and Linus knocked on the red wooden door of 349 Chesterhill Lane, a firm shave-and-a-haircut, followed by two bits.

The house itself was a plain thing. While not ramshackle, it looked old, the off-white siding cracked, the porch in need of a fresh coat of paint. Ivy hung from hooks in the ceiling, tendrils spilling over the chipped pottery, stretching toward the floor of the porch. From inside, the sounds of people moving about, voices muffled, followed by a loud burst of laughter.

The house sat apart from the others in the neighborhood, the driveway long and winding through sparse trees, knee-high grasses lining either side. When standing on the porch like they were now, it was nigh impossible to see any other home, which must have been the reason it was chosen. Behind the house, a tall fence surrounded what Arthur assumed was the backyard, keeping away anyone with prying eyes.

As soon as Arthur knocked on the door, the voices inside fell instantly silent. When nearly a full minute had passed and no one had answered, Linus said, "Are you sure that was correct? You knocked like Helen said?"

"I did," Arthur said, head cocked as he stared at the door.

"Perhaps we should—"

A panel near the top of the door slid open, revealing green eyes the color of moss and a pair of enormous eyebrows that looked like lines of rust. "Didja see the sign?" A deep, gruff voice with a thick brogue that brooked no arguments.

Next to the door, a placard with black letters: NO SOLICITATIONS.

"We did," Arthur said. "And we've chosen to ignore it."

The eyes crinkled. "Is that so? Then I'll invite you to feck off. Whatever you're sellin', we've no need of it."

Linus bristled. "I assure you we're not going to *feck off*. And we're not selling anything."

"Coulda fooled me," the man said. "You look like a salesman."

"My name is Linus Baker," he said sternly. "And this is Arthur Parnassus. You should be expecting us."

The panel slammed shut.

Linus took a step back from the door. "Well, that was rude. Did we get the address wrong? I thought we triple-checked to make sure—"

The door swung open, revealing the largest man Arthur had ever seen. He towered above them, his mass filling the doorway, as wide as he was tall. He wore a pair of joggers and a shirt covered in old, faded stains that stretched against his sloping gut. His curly hair matched his rust-colored eyebrows, big and wild. He grinned at them, face lighting up under dozens of freckles. He looked to be in his thirties or thereabouts, and a jovial fellow.

"I'm only messin' around," he boomed. "Know who you are. Course I do." He extended a massive hand toward them, Arthur taking it first. His grip was like steel, but Arthur didn't react. Neither did Linus. "Heard ya on the radio." He leaned back into the house and called, "We're good, B! False alarm."

A moment later, voices again in the house. The man stepped out and closed the door behind him. He pushed through Linus and Arthur, stopping at the edge of the porch, looking out at the rain. "Bucketing down, eh? Been a donkey's year since we've seen the sun."

"You're Jason," Linus said, repeating the name Helen had given them.

He nodded. "Aye. And you're here for the boyo."

"David." Arthur looked toward the door. "Is he inside?"

Jason turned to face them, the smile gone, replaced by a wary expression. "Helen said you're good people."

"She's too kind," Arthur said.

"And that you've got . . . others."

"We do," Linus said. "If you listened to the hearing as you say, then you'll know that to be true."

Jason scrubbed a hand over his face. "I heard. Did it go as you thought? B was pretty pissed over it."

"Who's B?" Linus asked.

"My partner," Jason said. "Byron. Uses they/them pronouns, so if that's going to be a problem, you can leave now. Won't have anyone coming after B, not in our home."

"That won't be an issue," Arthur assured him. "We're welcoming of everyone."

Jason stared at him a long moment before nodding. For his part, Arthur didn't look away. "Good to know. Figured as much but can't be too careful." He glanced at the door. "Bad business, yesterday. Seems as if EUM is alive and well, just with different people. Ya seen the papers?"

"We ignored them on purpose," Linus said.

"Don't blame ya for that," Jason said. "Most made your fella out to be something dark. Conveniently ignored everything he said and focused on that little display at the end. Pictures and all. Some are running with your accusations of bugging your hotel room, but . . ." He shrugged. "Woulda done the same, yeah? Show them what's what." He grinned suddenly. "But don't tell B I said that. They're already on the war path, and woe to anyone who gets in their way, me included."

Arthur chuckled at the fondness in Jason's voice. "Sounds as if they are formidable."

"How many people are here?" Linus asked as the sound of laughter came through the open door.

Jason narrowed his eyes, and Arthur felt in him a kindred spirit. "You're not here for them." He held up his hand as Linus started to splutter. "That's how it is. Helen vouched for you, said you were both good men, but trust is in short supply these days, especially for someone who used to work for DICOMY."

Linus nodded stiffly. "I did."

Jason looked surprised, as if he hadn't expected Linus to admit it so readily. "Huh. I see." He sighed, picking dirt from underneath his fingernails as he leaned against the porch railing. "Look, lads. This is delicate work. Probably don't need to tell you that, but I figure it doesn't hurt to be reminded. Not just about us. About the people, yeah? Anything for them. It's why B and me do what we do. Help people that need it. But we help *adults*. Kids are so much harder to explain when an inspector comes around, especially since none of them are registered." He spat over the side of the railing, wiping his mouth with the back of his hand before glancing at Arthur. "But we made an exception for an old friend."

"Helen," Arthur said.

Jason nodded. "Aye, fine lass. Got a fire lit under her some months back." He jerked his head toward Linus. "Said you had something to do with it."

"She popped my bubble," Linus said.

Jason's eyebrows rose. "I don't know about all that, but she's proven herself time and time again. Said her village is more accepting than it once was."

"It is," Arthur said. "Work still needs to be done, but it's getting there."

"Good to know. Helen came to us and asked us to look after a wee boy. Said it was temporary while she, in her words, 'convinced a pair of lovebirds they had room for one more.'" He waggled his eyebrows. "That be you?"

Linus groaned as Arthur held up his hand, the stones of his ring catching the gloomy light.

Jason whistled, bending over until his face was inches from the ring. "Would you look at that! Warms my heart, it does. Love, lads. It's what makes the world go round." He stepped back as Arthur dropped his hand. "So, she right? You have room for another?"

"We do," Arthur said. "More than enough. And our children are just as excited as we are to have David come stay with us."

"He knows we're coming?" Linus asked.

Jason snorted. "Aye, he does. Worked himself up into a right state over it. Excited, nervous, everything in between. Wish we could keep him, but we've got our hands full as it is. Not enough room. Needs more than B and I can give right now. Kids need kids. Simple as that." He sighed. "Doesn't help that we've got our own inspection coming up for the adults we house. I'd rather him be far away from here than run the risk of getting noticed by the government."

"But," Arthur said, because he knew it was there.

"But," Jason said, drawing the word out. "You heard it same as me. Rowder knows his name." He glared at Arthur and Linus as if he thought it was their doing. "Doesn't sit right with me. You're in the same boat, only the inspector is going to be *looking* for children. How's that going to work?"

"We know," Linus said. "And we have contingency plans in place."

"Such as?" Jason asked.

"The island has many secrets," Arthur said. "Trust me when I say David's safety and well-being are a priority to the both of us."

Jason nodded slowly. "I'll hold you to that, Mr. Parnassus. Anything happens to him, you'll answer to me. May not be magic like you and B, but I can hold my own."

A pointed threat, and one Arthur believed.

"How has he adapted?" Linus asked. "Given how quiet Helen said he is, this place must have been a bit of a shock."

Jason laughed loudly, bending over and slapping his knee. "Quiet? For the first couple of days, sure. Now, though? *Quiet* and *David* are at opposite ends of the spectrum." He moved toward the door, stopping with his hand on the doorknob. He looked back over his shoulder at them, wearing an odd smile. "He can be a bit . . . theatrical."

"Theatrical," Linus repeated with that funny little wrinkle between his eyes, the one Arthur recognized well. He was puzzled. "I thought—it's just that Helen told us he's quiet and shy."

"He was," Jason agreed. "And now he's not. Word of advice? Let him do what needs to be done."

"Which is?" Linus asked slowly.

Jason grinned at them. "Oh, are *you* in for a treat."

The interior of the house was much better than the exterior. Cluttered—bookshelves overflowing, random chairs placed all around—but clean, the surfaces without dust, the floors freshly swept and mopped, the faint scent of lemon in the air.

Linus and Arthur followed Jason down a short hallway. To their right, a kitchen with industrial-sized appliances, and a long oak dining table with benches for seats sitting on cracked linoleum. Two adults sat at the table, one with his head bowed over a mug of steaming liquid, the other rubbing his back and whispering quietly. The figure lifted their head, and Arthur saw long white hair pulled into a messy bun, held together by a thick green ribbon. They wore high-waisted slacks and a teal Ship'n Shore blouse over a narrow chest.

"That's B," Jason whispered. "Aren't they a sight?"

As Arthur and Linus looked on, Byron lifted their hand from the man's back and held it up, palm toward the ceiling, fingers curled. Lights began to glow from their fingertips, dripping down onto the palm, forming a ball of shimmering colors. The ball collapsed, and from it rose a butterfly with golden wings. It flew across the kitchen, fluttering in front of Jason, wings brushing against his right cheek. Then, in a furious burst of glitter, it exploded with a low *pop*!

"Butterfly kiss," Jason said, winking at B. "My favorite."

Byron smiled, then went back to the man sitting next to them, rubbing his back in soothing circles once more.

To their right, a sitting room with overstuffed chairs and the biggest sofa Arthur had ever seen, able to seat at least ten comfortably, if one didn't mind close quarters. A few more people—two older women and a young man—sat on the couches, the women with open books in their laps, the man leaning his head back and staring at the ceiling.

"Have a bit more in common than you thought, yeah?" Jason whispered, elbowing Linus in the gut. "Funny how that works out, eh?"

He led them farther into the house, down a long hallway. Muffled sound from behind a closed door on the right, like singing. Arthur felt a strange pull toward it, was about to knock on the door when Jason gently pulled his hand back. "Siren," he said quietly. "She's newer. Still working a few things out."

Jason led them to the door at the end of the hall and stopped before opening it. "David's been bunking with us. Offered him his own room, but he wanted to be near B in case . . . well. He just wanted someone near. We gave him his own bed and a privacy screen. You ready?" Without waiting for an answer, he pushed open the door.

It was dark in the room. Heavy curtains had been pulled over the large windows against the wall to the right, with only a sliver of gray light peeking through. Arthur could make out a massive bed at the other end of the room, piled high with blankets and pillows. To the left, a pair of large double doors that led to a walk-in closet, the light on. Next to the closet, a wooden partition, with the name DAVID written in black ink on a white page hanging crooked from the front.

And there, lying on the scarred wooden floor in a daring pink dress covered in blood, a pile of thick white strings.

Or, at least, that was what Arthur thought when he first saw the yeti known as David.

The boy's eyes were closed, his black lashes like soot against snow-white hair on his face. His gray tongue lolled from between ice-blue lips. He was as big as Arthur had expected. Like Chauncey, Arthur had done his research and knew that yetis could grow to ten feet tall or more, though it was more common for them to top out at around eight feet. David appeared to be—at age ten—already over five feet.

And that was to say nothing about his glorious hair. From tip to toe, David was covered in long white hair, corded together and hanging in thick strands. His hands and feet—though similar to a human's with five digits on each appendage—were tipped with black claws, short and sharp. Atop his head, a messy blond wig, the hair spread out on the floor around him.

But it was the blood that concerned Arthur most. It was splashed against the dress, and the hair on David's chest. Even a bit in the wig.

Linus gasped, looking as if he were about to rush to the child when Jason grabbed him by the arm, shaking his head. He brought a finger to his lips and then cleared his throat pointedly.

The boy on the floor twitched. Then, out of the corner of his mouth, he hissed, "Jason. *Jason*," without opening his eyes. His voice was—for lack of a better word—frosty, brittle, like crackling ice.

"Yes, David?"

"Are they ready?"

"Ready as they'll ever be."

"Good."

Jason reached behind him to the wall, flipping a switch. A light burst from the ceiling, shining down directly on David, almost like a spotlight. The blood—which Arthur could see now was likely a concoction similar to the one made for Linus's birt—glistened wetly on his dress and chest.

Jason cleared his throat and said, "PI Dirk Dasher knew she was trouble the moment she walked through his door. Dame like her, looking like she did, brought back memories of his beloved Agatha, four years gone, taken too soon by a killer only known as the Beast. And now, three days later, finding the dame's body like this, same as Agatha's was, Dirk Dasher knew only two things: the taste of the bottom of a bottle, and the desire for revenge."

"What," Linus said.

"Flashback," Jason said, and David shot to his feet, ignoring them all as he rushed toward the closet, slamming the doors shut behind him. A moment later, the sound of clothes being tossed around, along with David muttering, "Where is my *fedora*? I—*aha*!"

The doors burst open. Gone was the dress (though a little bit of "blood" remained on the hairs on his chin and chest), replaced by a wide-brimmed hat cocked at an angle that meant danger, and a long brown coat, cinched at the waist, the bottom dragging along the floor. In his fingers, what appeared to be a piece of chalk that he brought up to his lips and sucked on, then blew out a puff of air that formed into a crystalline cloud in front of his face.

He hurried across the room, nearly tripping over his coat. Once he reached the desk, David sat in the chair and propped his hairy feet up on the desk. He took another drag from the chalk, blowing cold steam from his mouth and nose, a black oval twice the size of one of Theodore's buttons.

"It was a day like any other," he said, affecting a low, guttural voice that cracked. "Headache like a pulse in my head after another night spent drowning nightmares in cheap whiskey. There I was, up to my eyeballs in debt given my gambling addiction. A pile of bills, all stamped PAST DUE, sat in a drawer, waiting for me to get my shit together."

"David," Jason said sternly.

David ignored him. "The bottle in the cabinet called to me. *Hair of the dog,* it said. And just as I was about to answer that call, *she* walked in."

He jumped from the chair and ran past them again to the closet, slamming the doors.

When the doors burst open again, David wore the dress once more, the blond wig askew on his head. His blue eyes shifted from Linus to Arthur, and settled on Jason. Then he changed his posture, legs slightly bent, hip cocked. When he spoke, his voice took on a breathy quality, though it still sounded distinctly David. "Are you Dirk Dasher, private investigator extraordinaire? My name is Jacqueline St. Bartholomew. I am very wealthy. And seductive, and I'm a widow."

Linus coughed roughly into his hands.

"I need to hire you," Jacqueline St. Bartholomew said, "to find the monster who murdered my husband, Count Deveraux St. Bartholomew. I hear you're hunting the same thing. The Beast."

Back into the closet. A shout, followed by a rattling crash. When David returned, he wore the trench coat over the dress, the wig bunched up messily under the fedora. He looked a little harried, but determined. As it often did with children, this back and forth went on for some time, though Arthur didn't once consider interrupting. Not when David seemed to be in his element.

David stopped, then, head in his hands. When nothing happened, out of the corner of his mouth, he whispered, "*You forgot your line.*"

"Yep, sorry, boyo," Jason said. "I got you. Ring-ring. Ring-ring."

"The sound of the ringing phone startled me from my thoughts," Dirk Dasher said, sitting back up. "It'd been three days since she darkened my doorway, and I was no closer to solving the crime. I needed a break in the case." He brought his hand up to his head, thumb and pinky extended. "Dirk Dasher."

"Mr. Dasher!" Jacqueline cried from the other end of the line. "The Beast, it's *here*! Eek, save me! Eeeeeeek!"

Given the severity of the situation and the art of telling a good story, Arthur was unsurprised when the necessary racing-against-the-clock montage lasted a further ten minutes. David (Dirk) then froze when he stumbled upon a most horrifying sight: the body of Jacqueline St. Bartholomew, a victim of the Beast.

Dirk raised his fists to the sky and shouted, "*Nooooo!*"

Jason rattled the doorknob.

Dirk's head jerked toward the closet, eyes narrowed under his fedora. "Someone's here. Is it the Beast?" He stood upright, crooked fangs bared. "Face me, Beast! I'll make you pay for what you did to Agatha and Jacqueline!"

David rushed to the closet, pulling off the hat and trench coat. A moment later, a doll slid out dressed in Dirk Dasher's clothes. Jason picked it up and set it in the middle of the room. Arthur raised an eyebrow when Jason came back to them.

Jason shrugged. "It's an independent production."

"There I stood," David called from the closet as Dirk. "Ready to face the monster who had stolen so much from me. My lady. My sobriety. My purpose. It was either going to be him or me. One of us wouldn't be walking out of here. *Alive.*"

And then David burst from the closet. He wasn't wearing anything now, his thick hair bouncing around him as he stomped into the room, claws on display, growling ferociously. "Dirk Dasher," he growled, spittle coating his lips. "I knew you'd come here. We all have monsters inside of us. The difference between us is that I let *mine* come out to play."

Arthur frowned slightly, cocking his head to the side.

David pounced on the doll, claws out and shredding the coat. He reared his head back, teeth bared, before he bit down on the fedora, jerking it off and furiously shaking his head. The doll fell over with David on top of it. The mauling of Dirk Dasher was a sight to behold, and by the time the yeti was finished, Dirk's head had been flung across the room, his body falling to the floor.

David stood slowly, standing in the middle of the spotlight. "The monster," he whispered, "is me. Fin."

He bowed.

Jason clapped hard. Arthur followed suit, Linus joining in. It was then that Arthur noticed a change come over David. As the sound of applause went on, he slumped in on himself, brushing the thick hair off his forehead so it wouldn't cover his eyes. He didn't meet their gazes, fidgeting from one foot to the other.

"Fair play, lad," Jason said, going over to him and clapping him on the shoulder. "Best performance yet."

David shrugged, surreptitiously glancing at Arthur and Linus before looking away. "Messed up a couple of times," he muttered.

"Didn't even notice," Jason assured him. "And even if you did, what do we say?"

David rolled his eyes in a way that reminded Arthur of Phee. "As long as I did my best, the rest doesn't matter."

"Exactly," Jason said, beaming down at him. "Gotta admit, the dress was a nice touch. B get that for you?"

David nodded. "Said a dame like Jacqueline needed a killer dress." He tugged on Jason's hand, pulling him down. Jason leaned over, and David whispered in his ear.

Jason nodded along. "Right. Right. You don't say. Interesting. Well, I suppose you should ask him that, yeah? Don't think he'd mind in the slightest."

David looked panicked, shaking his head furiously.

Jason said, "Hey. You got this, okay?" He stood upright. "David, this is Arthur Parnassus. Other one is Linus Baker. Go ahead, boyo. Mind your manners, but always, *always* ask questions if you have them. Good people don't mind questions."

David sighed, still holding on to Jason's hand. He stared down at his feet. He mumbled something that Arthur couldn't make out.

"Could you repeat that, please?" Linus asked gently. "I'm afraid my hearing isn't what it used to be."

David scowled at the floor. "I *said*, was that good enough to get into your school? I know it's not . . . *normal*, but I worked really hard on it."

Linus frowned as Arthur cocked his head. "I beg your pardon?"

Jason laid a hand on David's shoulder. "Boyo here got it into his head that he needed to perform for admission into your school. Thought you would need to see how talented he is before you'd consider him." His tone suggested that anything other than effusive praise wouldn't be tolerated.

Arthur rubbed his chin thoughtfully. "I'm afraid we've gone about this all wrong."

David's head shot up, his anxiety clear. "I'm sorry! I can do something different to—"

Arthur smiled. "No, David. You don't have a single thing to apologize for. It is I who should be apologizing to you."

David blinked, glancing up at Jason before looking at Arthur again. "Um. O . . . kay?"

Arthur nodded. "You see, I think there might have been some miscommunication. We are not here to have you perform for us, though I adored every single second of it. No, we're here for something else entirely: to make our case as to why we'd like for *you* to choose *us*."

David's mouth dropped open. It closed a moment later with an audible *click*. Then, sounding baffled, he said, "I get to choose?"

"Yes," Linus said. "You get to choose. Think of this not as us interviewing you, but rather you interviewing *us*. Ask us whatever questions you wish. If we can answer, we will." As Linus spoke, Arthur moved through the room, stopping in front of the desk. He turned the chair, sat down on it, and folded one leg over the other. Linus joined him after a moment, hand on his shoulder.

David eyed them with suspicion, Jason still standing guard above him. "What time would I have to go to bed?"

"Nine," Arthur said. "Growing boys need rest."

"Will I have homework?"

"You will, but it's not extensive," Linus said. "We're currently on a short summer holiday, so we have time to catch you up in case your schooling has been neglected."

David made a face. "Is there enough food for everyone?"

"There is," Arthur said. The reason for the question seemed

clear, and he mourned that this child—or any other—would know food insecurity. "More than enough, though we try not to let anything go to waste, minus some eggs every now and then. Thankfully, we have Phee who likes to grow fruit trees, and Talia is considering planting vegetables in her garden."

"Oh," David said. "The sprite and gnome?"

Arthur nodded, waiting. David was obviously building himself up to something, but knowing children as well as he did, Arthur figured the yeti's mind was a mess of discordant thoughts that swirled as if caught in a storm. He needed to get there on his own, or he might not listen to what they had to say.

Arthur didn't have to wait long. David looked at the floor, shuffling his feet, his toe claws scraping against hardwood. "The other kids. I've . . . they're . . ." He blew out a breath, the strands of hair hanging on his face billowing up as he twisted his body from side to side. "I've never had friends before. Well, Jason and B and maybe Helen because I've met her a few times, but not, like, you know. Kids." He scowled. "I *could* have had friends. I'm not a loser. I even tried once."

"Tried to make friends?" Arthur asked lightly.

David nodded. "Yeah. It . . ." He winced. "It didn't go very well. They were playing monsters, and I wanted to play too. Stomp around on stuff and growl and eat pretend people."

"Oh my," Arthur said, hand going to his throat. "How many people would you eat?"

"At least ten," David said, blowing on his knuckles and rubbing them against his chest. "My record is twenty-four, but I didn't want to brag."

"Of course not," Linus said. "Confidence is silent. Insecurities are loud."

"Does he always talk like that?" David whisper-shouted to Arthur.

"Yes," Arthur said as Linus jabbed him with an elbow. "I happen to admire it when he does, but then I'm very partial when it comes to Linus Baker, including his pearls of wisdom."

"I'm like an oyster," Linus said proudly. "Might not look like much, but open me up and there's hidden treasure within." He frowned. "Is it me, or did that not sound as complimentary as I thought it would?"

"I would care for you even if you were an oyster," Arthur promised him.

"Ew," David said. "Anyway, I tried to play with them because if they wanted to be monsters, they could learn from someone who is an *actual* monster."

Arthur didn't want to interrupt, so he stored that particular nugget for later. He'd never heard a child use that word so freely to describe themself: "monster." To Chauncey, it was an insult because he didn't see himself that way, even if others might base their opinions upon appearance alone. But David seemed to *like* that word; it made him happy. Arthur had spent so long attempting to disabuse the other children of such an idea. How would David's joy mix with what Arthur had been trying to teach them?

"What happened?" Linus asked after David fell quiet, Jason listening to each and every word.

David wouldn't look at them when he said, "One of the boys said I wasn't scary, I was gross and dirty and probably had fleas. I tried to tell him that I've *never* had fleas because I take good care of my hair." He laughed hollowly. "I have to. It gets messy if I don't. But then he started pulling on my hair, and I didn't like it."

"I don't expect you would," Arthur said. "No one should touch anyone else without express permission to do so. Your hair is part of you, and that's unacceptable."

"Whatever," David muttered. "I growled at them and they screamed and ran away. Who needed them? I didn't. And I don't. I can do things just fine on my own."

Arthur didn't believe that for a moment. He could hear the confusion, the hurt. David's story was just that, David's, but in it, familiarity. The circumstances might have been different—the players, the setting, the event itself—but hadn't all the children at one point or another experienced what David had? Decried, mocked, *touched* as if they were on display.

Arthur said, "I think you'll find Marsyas is a bit different. If you want to eat pretend people while crushing a city of blocks or stone, then you will. And I have a feeling there might be a few other children who would be very happy to join you."

"Really?" David asked, and Arthur's heart ached at the hopefulness in his voice.

"Really."

David gnawed on his bottom lip. "Have you ever . . . have you . . ."

"We're listening, David," Arthur said. "Take all the time you need."

David's eyes flashed angrily. "Have you ever hit a kid?"

"No," Arthur said.

"Put their fingers in a drawer and then closed it so hard, it . . . it . . ."

"Never," Arthur said.

David looked at him with cold eyes. "Your trousers are too short." Mean, meant to lash out, to hurt, but Arthur took it in stride. David was in the process of opening up to them, but he was still wary. Arthur couldn't fault him for that; they were strangers, after all.

He said, "Yes, I do seem to have that problem quite often. Do you like my socks?" Today, Arthur wore sky-blue socks with silver snowflakes of varying shapes and sizes printed on them.

David scowled. "Did you wear those because of me? That won't make me like you."

"David," Jason said, the warning clear in his voice.

He shrugged before muttering an apology, picking up the doll's head off the floor.

"I've never heard of anyone liking someone else just because of their socks," Arthur said. "I think it takes a little more than that. But rest easy, David. These socks are not for you. They're for me. They help to illustrate what I like to think of as the *sock problem*."

"What's that?" David asked, trying to act uninterested but failing spectacularly.

"It's quite the conundrum. These days, socks aren't like what we wore at your age. Many of them have little designs, but our trousers are far too long to show them off."

"And removing your shoes without invitation is quite rude," Linus added.

"Indeed," Arthur said. "Can you imagine?"

"I shudder to think. Even *if* there is a decorative sock, one must remember decorum."

David's head whipped back and forth between them, as if watching a rather vigorous game of tennis.

Looking at David, Linus said, "Arthur prefers to keep the length of his trousers shorter so that his socks may be enjoyed by all."

"Too right," Arthur said, laughing silently at himself for still being so smitten with Linus. Though he had never allowed himself to think on it much—he was always far too busy—before Linus, he had found himself succumbing to encroaching cold, the sharp, frozen needle of loneliness digging into his skin. It wasn't until Linus that the last of the cold had melted away. "It's not unlike what we face on a daily basis when we interact with people."

Confused, David asked, "Their trousers are too long?"

"Precisely," Arthur said. "And by trousers, I mean their staunchly set ways. All they need is to pull their trousers up to find a little color hidden underneath." He did exactly that, showing the snow socks. "But *these,* David, these socks are special. You see, they can only be worn rarely. Otherwise, I'll run afoul of a supremely terrible curse."

That caught David's attention, and he was a second or three late in covering up his excitement. "Yeah, right. Who would curse socks?"

Arthur chuckled. "Interesting question, and one I have pondered longer than you've been alive. Unfortunately, I'm no closer to solving the mystery. All I know for certain is that if I wear these socks on a Thursday, a Sunday, an odd-numbered day, or after three in the afternoon in the month of November, the socks will disappear."

David frowned. "That's not so bad."

"Along with my feet."

Linus sighed. "And before you think he's having you on, trust me when I say he's not. We won't soon forget Thursday, November twenty-third."

David's mouth dropped open and stayed that way, the doll's head falling to the floor, bouncing and rolling under the bed.

"Yes," Arthur said gravely, "so I wear them not to manipulate you into feeling a certain way about this introduction, but because today is not Thursday, Sunday, an odd-numbered day, nor is it November."

David's gaze drifted down to Arthur's socks. "That's *crazy*. I wish I could be cursed. That sounds like so much fun."

"It does, doesn't it? But let's be thankful instead that we both get to keep our feet, at least for the time being. Now, on to your question. Before I answer, might I show you something?"

David looked at him warily. "What?"

"Fire," Arthur said. He held out his hand, palm raised toward the ceiling. With a little push, a bloom erupted from his hand, twin strands of flickering red-orange that twisted, forming a rotating double helix of flame.

David's eyes were wide, reflecting the firelight. Cold blue and hot orange, and for a moment, Arthur felt an icy chill race down his spine. David said, "I think I can do that."

"Do what, David?" Linus asked quietly.

David stood slowly, the doll slumping to the floor. He wouldn't look at them, his gaze darting around the room, but he, too, lifted his hand, mirroring Arthur's. Linus sucked in a sharp breath when blueish ice crystals rose from David's palm, his face scrunched up in concentration. The ice split into two strands, and after a minute of David grunting through gritted teeth, the crystals formed a double helix, spinning rapidly. Even through the small fire in front of him, Arthur could feel the coldness seeping in.

It didn't last long. The ice collapsed in on itself, and a puff of tiny snowflakes drifted toward the floor. David startled and pulled his hand back, gnawing on his bottom lip. "You did it, too, so you can't be mad at me for trying."

Arthur closed his fist, snuffing out the fire, black smoke leaking between his fingers. "I did do it, and I'm pleased you showed me you could too. " He lowered his hand and waited.

Eventually, David said, "It's my choice. It's up to me."

"It is," Arthur agreed. "Though we hope you will decide to visit Marsyas for however long you wish, I know there is a lot to consider. Rest assured, David, whatever you decide won't be held against you. I know how it feels to have the ability to make your own decisions taken from you. You have my word we will never do that to you, and you will not be punished for being you. But you should know that I expect honesty, even if you think it might hurt our feelings."

David hesitated. "Yesterday."

"The hearing."

David winced but pushed through it. "That woman said you were the only phoenix left."

"I am."

"So, your parents, they . . . they're . . ."

"Dead," Arthur said gently. "But not forgotten. My mother was a good woman. Kind, patient. My father was gruff, but I knew he loved me, in his own way. They live on in my memories, kept tucked away for the days I need to be reminded that my history, while difficult, began with people who loved me. While it doesn't negate all that followed, it can be a balm to a weary soul."

"You *are* like me," David whispered with no small amount of awe. "My parents . . ." His bottom lip wobbled. "I don't really remember Dad, but Mom, she smelled like cinnamon. And she would sing to me." He blinked rapidly, little ice crystals forming around his eyes. "I can still remember the last thing she told me."

"Do you?" Arthur asked. "That must be a treasured memory."

With haunted eyes, David said, "No, it's not. She told me to run."

That night, just before midnight, the phone in their new hotel room rang. Linus and Arthur—both of whom had been on the cusp of sleep, legs tangled—shot up immediately. Linus reached the phone first, snatching up the handset and bringing it to his ear. "Zoe?" he said. "Is everything all right?"

Arthur joined him, leaning in to hear. It wasn't Zoe.

Jason said, "David's made his decision."

SEVEN

David, as it turned out, had never been on a train before, and though he tried to contain his excitement, it spilled over when he saw the locomotive sitting next to the station, people milling about around them, hugging and saying farewell to those who would be departing. They caught a few odd looks, but that was to be expected, given David's idea of a disguise.

Since he was unregistered, Arthur and Linus were concerned that if anyone saw him, they might ask questions, especially with Arthur's face splashed across every major newspaper in the country. They had changed tickets for an earlier train, in case Rowder and DICOMY were attempting to follow them.

It was David who'd figured out how he'd go incognito. Granted, he might not have fully understood the meaning of the word, seeing as how he was now six feet tall, walking on blocks of ice that he grew from his feet. Each step he took left a square wet print behind, but thankfully, the rain had continued, and it wasn't noticeable so long as they stayed on damp ground. It probably didn't help that David had donned another trench coat, this one sized for an extremely tall adult. To top it off, he wore an off-white fedora with a pink band above the brim, mirror shades, and a fake black handlebar mustache that was wider than his face, the ends curled up.

It was ridiculous, of course, but David was proud of what

he'd come up with, and Arthur couldn't help but admire his ingenuity.

"We get to go on *that*?" David breathed, stumbling forward, the blocks under his feet making an odd sound on the ground: *thonk, thonk, thonk.*

"We do," Arthur said. "All the way to the end of the line. It'll be a long trip, but I think you'll find the journey worth it."

"To the tropical island," David said dubiously, still looking at the train. "Where it's always sunny and warm. Perfect place for a yeti."

Linus startled. "I suppose that's true, but rest assured, we've made every effort to—"

David twirled his mustache. "Yes, quite. Indeed. Indubitably." The train whistled loudly, and David dropped the mocking, lighting up. "It's so *loud*. How fast does it go? Could you jump off it while it's moving and not die? Would someone explode if they stood on the train tracks and let it hit them? I bet the blood and guts would go on for *miles*."

A woman passing them harrumphed, hand on a little girl's shoulder as she glared at David. "Excuse me, there are *children* present."

David looked left, then right, head on a swivel. "Children, you say? Where? I heard they were extinct. Someone call the papers before—"

"Yes, ma'am," Linus said, stepping in front of David. "You are absolutely correct. Thank you for bringing that to our attention. Have a nice day."

The girl giggled as the woman steered her away.

"You can't bring attention to yourself," Linus said sternly. "Not here. Not now."

David folded his arms, a grumpy expression on his face. "So all that back at Jason's house about me being myself was—"

"We meant every word," Arthur said. "That's all we want for you, David. But you have to remember that not everyone thinks like we do. There are plenty of people out there who don't want you to succeed. Don't give them a reason to—"

"That's not *my* fault," David retorted. "Why should I give a crap what they think about me? If they're scared of me, maybe I should give them reasons *to* be scared."

"To what end?" Arthur asked carefully.

David shrugged. "Fear makes people do things they might not have before. It might even make them a little braver than they thought they could be. Being scared doesn't always have to be bad." He scuffed a block of ice against the ground. "At least, that's how I think it should be."

"That's certainly one way of looking at it," Linus said. "Plenty to discuss, and trust me when I say we'll be having many conversations over the next few weeks. We'll listen, David. I promise. The only thing we ask for in return is that you do the same. Deal?"

David hesitated for a long moment. Eventually, he muttered, "Okay."

"Good," Arthur said, picking up David's suitcase along with his own. It was lighter than Arthur had expected when Jason handed it to him that morning. David didn't have much. It was always the same, wasn't it? Talia. Lucy. Sal. Phee. Chauncey. Theodore. Coming with the bare minimum as if that were all they needed to survive. "I think you'll find the interior of the train just as fascinating as the exterior. Though, I must admit, it's no bus. Have you ever ridden the bus before? I took a bus trip a couple of days ago. They have this delightful line you can pull that'll signal to the driver—" Something caught his eye. "Excuse me for a moment. Linus, be a dear, would you? Get David to the train."

"All right?"

"Yes," Arthur said. "I'll follow momentarily."

Linus looked like he wanted to argue but took David by the hand, pulling him toward the train. "What about him?" Arthur heard David ask.

"Arthur can handle himself," Linus replied. "Here is your ticket. Do not lose this. It's—"

"I get my own *ticket*?"

Without hesitating, Arthur stalked toward a stone pillar. Affixed to the front, a poster. A notice. Big block lettering.

**WHAT WILL YOU DO TO PROTECT YOUR FAMILY?
SEE SOMETHING, SAY SOMETHING.**

Making sure no one was watching, Arthur tore the poster from the pillar, balling it up in his hand. Smoke leaked between his fingers, and when he spread them, ash sprinkled down to the ground. Without looking back, he made his way to the train.

For the first hour of the trip, David didn't move, face plastered against the window as trees and houses and fields of rain-soaked grass passed them by in a blur. He pointed out everything he saw: a strange pile of rocks, an elderly man waving from the rocking chair on his porch. When the conductor came round to punch their tickets, David all but demanded he get to hand over all three, given that he now considered himself to be a bit of an expert when it came to riding a train. The conductor, for his part, barely blinked, taking each of the tickets from David.

"Going on vacation?" the conductor asked.

"Something like that," Linus said.

"They're certainly not kidnapping me," David told the conductor. "Because I'm an adult who does adult things, like taxes and laundry and being sad for no reason."

Unfazed, the conductor said, "How wonderful! I, too, am filled with an encroaching dread over my own mortality. I've always thought that being aware of one's impending demise makes for a more interesting life, but I have yet to prove this particular hypothesis. Have a pleasant trip, and do let us know if there's anything we can do to make your journey as comfortable as possible. Ta!"

"I'll never understand humans," David said after the conductor had moved on. He sat across from Arthur and Linus, the train rumbling around them, the gray world streaking by, water trailing against the glass windows in complicated rivulets that looked like a map from an inebriated mapmaker.

"I doubt anyone can," Linus said.

David grew quieter after that, sitting with his hands folded in his lap, staring out the window.

The third hour, David slumped in his seat, his hat askew on his head. Little puddles appeared on the floor as his ice blocks began to melt. Linus pulled out a handkerchief from his coat pocket, dropping it onto the puddles. David didn't seem to notice.

The fourth hour, David began to fidget, legs bouncing, popping his knuckles over and over. He jumped whenever someone laughed, jerking his head around as if he thought someone was coming for him.

"It's okay to be nervous," Arthur said, and David whirled back around, almost falling out of his seat.

"Nervous?" he exclaimed. "I'm not nervous. I'm aces." He went for a smile, but his mouth must not have gotten the message.

"My mistake," Arthur said, tipping his head slightly. "I thought perhaps you were worried about what awaits us."

"Ha," David said, waving him off with a trembling hand. "I wasn't even thinking about that." He picked at a crack in the plastic armrest of the chair. "But if I *was*, it's only because I was wondering what's going to happen if the other kids don't like me."

"Ah," Arthur said. "A serious concern. What makes you think they won't like you?"

"I don't know," David said. He looked down at himself. "I'm a little . . . me. Not that there's anything wrong with that!" he added quickly, popping his knuckles again. It sounded like ice cracking.

"There isn't," Linus said firmly. "You're exactly as you're supposed to be."

"Oh. That's . . . that's good. I thought so too." He folded his hands in his lap. Arthur began to count in his head. *One. Two.*

Three. Four. "What happens if they don't like me?" David laughed as if he couldn't believe something so ridiculous had come from his mouth. "I mean, that'd be . . . something, right?"

"Who?" Linus asked. Then, "The other children? My goodness, of all the things for you to worry about, that shouldn't be one of them. They are just as excited to meet you as we were."

David scoffed. "They don't even know me."

"They don't," Linus agreed. "But then we didn't know you either and yet, here you are. If you go into a situation expecting the worst, it may cloud your ability to see what good can come from it."

David nodded and looked back out the window. The rain had stopped, and for the first time in what felt like years, Arthur could see bits of blue behind all the gray.

"But what if— Holy crap, what's *that*?" One moment he was in his seat, and the next, his face was plastered against the train window, looking out onto the passing landscape. Arthur leaned over with Linus to see what David had discovered.

A flock of birds flew next to the train, heading east. There had to be at least two dozen of them, white bodies with tanned heads and black-tipped wings. They coasted on the wind, their beaks open in cries that couldn't be heard from inside the train.

"Northern gannets," Linus said. "Usually don't see them so far inland. They typically make their homes in cliffsides. You'll get your fill of them soon enough. They're in abundance on the island."

"Oh," David whispered, watching the birds climb higher and higher until they blotted out the sun.

A line of vehicles waited next to the train platform: a small bus for the hotel, a few shiny rental cars filled with vacationers picking up friends and family. Those who exited the train did so with unrestrained excitement, their sun hats large and colorful, removing their shoes and digging their toes in the white sand around the platform. Parents and grandparents helped children with their plastic buckets and shovels, trying to get them to hold still, *You've got a spot of jam on your forehead, how on earth did you do* that?

David, Arthur, and Linus were the last to exit the train, Arthur carrying David's suitcase. He stepped off the train first into warm sunlight, looking for the familiar sight of Helen's old truck. Linus followed, standing next to him, face turned up toward the sky. "Ah," he said. "Much better. Now, David, if you'll . . . David?"

They turned to find David still on the train, standing on the last step, hands gripping the railings on either side of him. One leg was raised as if he were about to take another step, but he didn't lower it.

"All right?" Linus asked.

"I'm working my way up to it," David muttered. "Give me a second."

It took at least four minutes, but eventually, David lowered the ice-blocked foot to the ground.

It immediately began to sizzle, steam rising up around the ice.

"Uh-oh," David said.

"It's all right," Linus said. "You don't have to worry. We're almost to—"

David jumped off the step, landing on the platform with a heavy *thunk*. The ice beneath his feet sizzled once again, beads of water forming a small puddle on the cement. "There," he said proudly. "I knew I could do it. Also, I think I'm shrinking? It's almost as if ice melts in heat. But that's crazy, right? Almost like bringing a yeti to an island. At least my sunglasses make me look cool." He went to the edge of the platform, crouching down and watching a small crab moving rocks from one pile to another.

"Quiet," Linus murmured. "Shy. Barely talks at all."

Arthur bumped Linus's shoulder with his own. "Any regrets?"

"Oh, many, I expect. But none that have to do with him."

"The children are going to adore him."

Linus shivered despite the summer heat. "That's what worries me. Lucy's going to love him." He sighed, undoubtedly imagining explosions or blood splatter on the walls. "I'm already losing my hair as it is."

Before Arthur could respond, an old truck with whitewall tires pulled up next to the platform. The door creaked open, and the mayor of Marsyas grinned at them as she rounded the front of the truck. "Well, well, well," she said cheerfully. "Look what we have here!"

David lifted his head, and a wide smile blossomed. "Helen!" he yelled, standing up and running toward her. He didn't bother with the steps, launching himself off the platform. He hit the ground hard, the ice blocks shattering and dropping him half a foot in height. The coat tangled around him, but he managed to stay upright as Helen spread her arms wide. He jumped the last few feet, crashing into her. Spinning him in a circle, Helen laughed as David babbled about the train, the birds, the ocean. She set him down, winking at Linus and Arthur as they walked down the steps.

"—and *then* I got to give the man our tickets, and he used this little machine to punch a hole in them to show we were allowed on the train!" He beamed at Helen. "No one could tell me to get off because I had the *right*."

"You absolutely did," Helen said. "I'm so pleased to hear you enjoyed your trip. And just look at you. I swear you've grown since the last time I saw you."

"Half an *inch*," David said proudly, puffing out his little chest. "Maybe even three-quarters."

"I'm impressed," Helen said. She lifted her head. "Linus, Arthur. Welcome home. To say you were missed is an understatement." She raised a hand as Linus started to speak. "And yes, the house still stands, and no one is missing any limbs. Or eyes."

"Fingers?" Linus asked. "Toes?"

"All present and accounted for," Helen said. "Talia did want me to remind you that if you did not, in fact, buy her a present, you should get back on the train and not come back until you have."

Linus grinned. "I bet she did."

Squeezing into the truck proved to be a tight fit, but they made it work: Helen behind the steering wheel, Arthur next to her, his long legs bent up almost to his chest. Linus sat beside him, and David took up the remainder of the bench seat, face plastered against the window, rattling off everything he saw, mixed with questions he didn't seem to want the answers to.

"Look! There's an umbrella. It's so *big*. What's that? Are they *sledding* on sand hills? I didn't know you could do that. How do you— Why is the ocean so huge? Do you think there are monsters in it? I bet there are. With big teeth and glowing red eyes which glow when— Oh my freaking *God*, what are those heathens eating?"

Linus said, "Snow cones. Ice with flavored syrup as a topping."

David turned toward him with wide eyes. "They ruined *ice*? The most perfect thing in all the world?" He bared his teeth. "I'll kill them. I'll kill them *all*. Ha, ha, just kidding." Then, under his breath, "Mostly."

"No snow cones, then," Arthur said. "Noted."

They pulled into the village, turning on the main road that led toward the docks. The sidewalks were packed with people, some in swim clothes, others in shorts and flowery shirts. They stopped in front of store windows, looking at colorful pottery, mosaics created from sea glass, square blocks of freshly made fudge. Kids dug through bins of saltwater taffy, skin pink and crusty from the sun and surf. Others sat at tables in front of restaurants that sold fresh seafood, sipping from clear drinks with sprigs of mint floating on top.

Arthur was about to ask what David thought when the yeti stiffened, back straight, shoulders rigid. "How?" he said, sounding stunned.

"What is it?" Linus asked.

"Those people," he said. "They're..."

Arthur followed his gaze as the truck came to a stop at one of two traffic lights in all of Marsyas. There, standing on the corner, was a family. Two burly women, hands clasped between them. Three children, all appearing under the age of ten. Each of them—children included—had a single large eye in the center of their forehead.

"Cyclopes," Helen said. "I had a chance to meet them yesterday." The light changed, and she drove through the intersection, the truck rumbling around them. "Lovely family. Heard about our little town from some friends and decided to see it for themselves."

David turned toward her slowly. "But... they're just... walking around. Like everyone else."

"Why shouldn't they?" Helen asked, not unkindly. "They are entitled to go on vacation, same as anyone."

David shook his head. "That's not what I meant. They're *here*. And no one is yelling at them to cover up and hide. No one is telling them they don't belong."

"Because they do," Linus said. "This place is different, David. It's unlike anywhere else you've been. Why, a few weeks ago, we had a lovely family of dryads come to the village. Tree people, wouldn't you know. They came and toured the island, wanting to see what Phee had grown in her time there."

"The forest sprite?" David asked.

"Yes," Linus said with a chuckle. "Never seen Phee so excited. She tried to act aloof, but we could all see she was proud people wanted to come and see her trees, especially beings as important as dryads." He cleared his throat. "But we won't have you thinking it's always been like this."

"He's right," Helen said, tapping her fingers on the steering wheel. "A year ago, Marsyas was no different from anywhere else. Awash in propaganda, and people either too afraid to speak up, or who actually believed what they were being told. Myself included."

"But you're not like that anymore," David said.

"No. I'm not." She glanced slyly at Linus and Arthur. "You could say I had my bubble popped. I'm grateful for it, because as mayor, I want Marsyas to be a place for all, no matter who you are. Some people didn't like it—oh, would you look at that? Seems as if the new owner of the ice cream parlor has changed the sign—but I reminded them that there was a great, wide world out there, and I invited them to go see it."

"I think you told Norman to take a long walk off a short pier," Linus reminded her. "Though in much more colorful language."

"And I regret nothing," Helen said. "Good riddance to bad rubbish."

"We're building something, David," Arthur said. "The more people—magical and not—who hear that this town will welcome them with open arms, the better off we'll all be."

I dream of such a place, he thought as they drove toward the sea.

"How do we get there?" David asked as they came to a stop near a long dock stretching out onto the water. In the distance, the island rose, the trees thick and reaching toward the sky. Arthur felt the pull of it, knowing who and what awaited them. Though it had only been three days, it was the longest he'd been away since coming back. He itched to feel the sand beneath his feet, the cacophonous sound of a house filled with wild youth.

"Could take the ferry," Linus said. "I'm sure Merle would be delighted to see us."

"That's one way of putting it," Helen said. "But no, no ferry. Why inflict Merle on someone if we don't have to? I figured we could give David a different sort of experience in traveling to the island."

And with that, she gunned the engine.

Linus gripped Arthur's hand tightly. "I was afraid you were going to say that."

"What are we doing?" David asked. "How are we—"

The truck shot forward, jumping a small curb, Arthur nearly biting his tongue. David shrieked, and for a moment, Arthur thought he was afraid. But before he could tell him he had nothing to fear, David raised his fists above his head, pumping the air. "Yes!" he cried, leaning forward as far as his seatbelt would allow, putting his hands flat on the dashboard. "Into the water? This is so *awesome!*"

They hit the dock, the wood rattling under the tires, causing them all to jump in their seats, David's head nearly hitting the roof. As the end of the dock approached, Helen picked up speed, the engine wheezing painfully. David raised his arms again as if he were on a roller coaster approaching the first drop.

"*I LOVE BEING ALIVE!*" David bellowed with unrestrained glee as the truck launched off the edge of the dock. A moment of weightlessness, all their rears lifting from their seats. Instead of being swallowed up by the sea, the truck landed with a jarring crash on a hard surface that crackled against the tires.

Arthur looked over to find both David and Linus with their eyes squeezed shut. Linus opened his first. "I'll never get used to that."

"Did we die?" David asked, eyes still firmly closed. "I don't feel dead, but I don't know what that's supposed to feel like."

"You're not," Arthur said. "Look."

David opened his eyes (first the left, then the right) and gasped at the long yellowish-white road that stretched out before them, crusty but solid. Helen turned the windshield wipers on as seawater splashed against the windows.

"What is it?" David asked.

"That's my lady, Zoe," Helen said, the pride evident. "Who you'll meet soon enough. She's an island sprite. Took the salt from the ocean and made a road for you."

"Why?"

"Because she wanted to," Arthur said. How strange the feeling of longing was when the object of such desires was right there in front of him. The island, and all that came with it. "It's her way of welcoming you home."

"Home," David whispered, and laughed as he rolled down the window. Leaning his head out, he closed his eyes, hair trailing behind him as the sea splashed his face.

David grew quieter as salt gave way to sand, the island alive with birdsong in the swaying trees. Eyes wide, he watched everything passing them by, though he didn't speak, not until they crested the hill and the house appeared before them.

"This is where you live?" he asked, sounding unsure.

"It is," Arthur said as Helen pulled the truck to a stop. Right on cue, the front door opened and Zoe appeared.

"That lady has *wings*," David whispered excitedly as Zoe hopped from the top step, fluttering down to the ground. "That's so cool."

Zoe opened Helen's door, helping her lady out. Helen stood on the tips of her toes, kissing Zoe with a loud smack, Zoe brushing a lock of Helen's hair off her forehead.

Arthur stepped out, pulling himself to his full height, stretching his arms above his head. His back cracked deliciously, and he turned to see Linus helping David out of the truck. "Do I need my coat?" David asked him.

"Do you want it?" Linus asked. "You don't have to wear it if you'd prefer not to."

"I can be *naked*? Seriously?"

"Uh," Linus said. "I don't . . . *are* you naked?"

"And?" Zoe asked, arching an eyebrow at Arthur.

"He's perfect," Arthur said, dropping his voice as Linus tried to tell David that it wasn't necessarily considered nudity, but if it made him happy, he could do whatever he wanted. "Where are the others? I would have thought that—ah. How expected."

The children were all gathered at the front windows, hands and faces against glass.

"I told them to stay inside so we didn't overwhelm David," Zoe said. "They've been bouncing off the walls all morning. Literally. Remember when Lucy said he accidentally reversed gravity?"

"Let me guess," Arthur said. "It wasn't an accident."

"It was not," Zoe said.

David, for his part, seemed to revel in his perceived victory of acceptable nudity. He stomped around, arms raised, claws extended, growling and snarling. "And *that*," he said as they rounded the front of the truck, "is how a yeti greets a new place he's never been before."

"Truly?" Linus asked, glancing up and smiling at Zoe before looking back at David. "What a fascinating custom. Do you think I could try?"

Suddenly, Linus leaned forward, fingers crooked like claws, lips pulled back over square teeth, and he let out a surprisingly ferocious growl. It was quite good, better than Arthur expected.

David was just as impressed. "Holy *wow*," he breathed. "Are there such things as hairless yetis? I've never met one, but you've got enough insulation to survive harsh winters, so maybe."

Linus patted his sloping stomach. "My thoughts exactly. We'll have to do it again, and you can teach me how to be a better yeti. David, this is Zoe Chapelwhite. This is her island you stand upon, and it is with her blessing that you are here."

David turned around, and just like that, the boy giving yeti lessons disappeared, replaced by shyness, knuckles popping, a funny little half smile filled with nerves rather than happiness. He looked at the ground, the claws on the tips of his toes digging into the soil. "Hello," he mumbled.

"David," Zoe said warmly, her translucent wings catching sunlight, leaving fractured rainbows on the ground behind her. "We've been waiting to meet you for a long time."

David lifted his head in surprise. "You have?" Without looking, he grabbed Linus's hand, holding it tightly. Linus winced but didn't try to pull away.

"Yes," she said. "I am so very happy that you decided to give us a chance. Would you like to meet the children?"

David hesitated. "Can . . . can Linus and Arthur stay here too? I can do it on my own," he added quickly, "but I think having them here will be better."

"Of course," Linus said. "I doubt I could break your grip even if I wanted to. You are very strong."

"I know," David said. "Pretty much the strongest ever."

When Zoe disappeared back into the house and the children had moved away from the window, David tugged on Linus's hand, pulling him down. "What is it?" Linus asked.

"Nothing," David said stiffly. "Just reminding you I'm here."

"As if we could forget," Arthur said. "I apologize in advance about the noise."

As if to prove his point, the door burst open and a stream of children poured out, all of them speaking at once with Chauncey leading the charge. *The sounds of home,* Arthur thought as Chauncey leapt the entirety of the steps, landed perfectly, and bowed, his eyes bouncing on their stalks.

The rest of the children gathered around Chauncey, each of them—including Sal with Theodore perched on his shoulder—looking as if they were doing their level best to keep from running directly at them. Lucy started to do just that, but Theodore lowered his tail, wrapping it around Lucy's arm, holding him back.

"Oh, come *on*," Lucy said with a groan. "They're right *there*."

"We do what we planned," Sal said. "Who's got it?"

"I do," Phee said, pushing her way from the back. In her hands, she held what looked to be a roll of paper with something written upon it in glittering letters. With Sal's help, she unfolded it, revealing a long banner that stretched across the front of the children, each of them holding part of it up—aside from Theodore, who rested his head on Sal's, eyes blinking slowly as he studied David. He made a strange sound—not unlike the hoot of an owl—that turned up at the end.

"There's no such thing as too much glitter," Chauncey told him. "Except if you eat it."

The banner was torn in places, and perhaps Theodore was right in that there might have been a tad too much glitter—Arthur could only imagine the mess left behind—but in the end, none of that mattered. Because here and now, six extraordinary children held up a sign that read: WELCOME HOME, DAVID! Each letter was written in a different hand, as if the children had all taken turns. In the top right corner, a smiley face with fangs and devil horns.

Partially hidden behind Linus, David peered around him, making a gulping noise when he found all the kids watching him. He ducked behind Linus again.

Considering his options, Arthur made a decision, and hoped it was the right one. Looking back at the children, he called, "Theodore. Would you mind coming here for a moment?"

Theodore didn't hesitate, spreading his wings and lifting up from Sal's shoulder. He crossed the distance in short order, landing on Arthur's, wrapping his long neck around Arthur's front. His reptilian eyes blinked slowly, and he chirped, a low, muttering thing that sounded like grumbling.

"I'm sure it was an accident," Arthur said, stroking his tail. "After all, you didn't know that when you sneezed you'd light the table on fire. No one was hurt?"

Theodore shook his head, followed by a stream of short, pointed clicks.

Linus snorted. "Then it was good Chauncey was there to ink all over the fire and put it out."

David once again made his existence known, leaning around Linus, eyes wide as he stared up at Theodore. "You can *talk* to him?" he asked breathlessly.

"Of course," Linus said. "We all can. It takes a bit to get the hang of it, but if I can learn, you can too. He is what's known as receptively bilingual, meaning he has his own language, and can understand what we say, but doesn't speak the same way."

"Like this?" David asked. He stepped out from behind Linus, arms raised, claws sliding out half an inch. Beginning to growl and snarl, he stomped around them. Theodore's talons dug into Arthur's shoulder as he wiggled from side to side.

"Oh dear," Linus said gravely. "David, what you just said could be interpreted in two different ways, depending upon inflection. You either asked Theodore to be your friend, or you challenged him to a duel on a Wednesday evening using only bananas and a feather boa as weapons."

"I did *what*?" David cried. "But—but it's Wednesday *now*. And the sun is going to be setting soon!"

"And here we are without a banana or feather boa in sight," Arthur said, shaking his head. "However, I think Theodore will agree that having a new friend is better than dueling someone."

Theodore, for his part, said that he would like to do both, if that were possible, explaining that he'd never been in a duel before. When Arthur reminded him that they did not, in fact, have any available bananas, Theodore turned his head toward the others still gathered in front of the house and asked a question.

"Bananas?" Lucy called, brow furrowed. "Hold on." His lifted his hands, face scrunched in concentration. A second later, he held a bushel of yellow fruit in his hands. "Hurray, I did things!"

Talia leaned over to inspect. "Those are plantains, not bananas."

"Crap," Lucy muttered. "Stupid plantains, always looking like bananas." He threw them up in the air, and the fruit winked out of existence.

"What the *what*," David said. "You have magic *banana* powers?"

"Yes," Sal said, eyes alight with mirth. "That's exactly right. Lucy has magic banana powers."

"He's a magic banana boy," Phee agreed. "Can't really do much aside from making sure we have our daily intake of fiber."

"Which helps us poop," Chauncey added.

Lucy's eyes filled with a malevolent red. "I am *not* a magic banana boy! I do not *care* about your poops! I am *Lucifer*." The red in his eyes grew, and the sun seemed to dim, as if a heavy cloud had passed in front of it. "I am the snake in the garden, the personification of dark temptation. I am the night, and all my enemies will bow before me or *perish*!" He cackled evilly, but seeing as how he was only seven, "evil" was, perhaps, a bit of a misnomer. It was more of a squeaky giggle, followed by the stomping of feet.

"You're such a drama queen," Talia muttered, and just like that, the sun's rays burst around them, causing them all to blink.

Before Arthur could admonish Lucy for dimming the sun—*again*—David blurted, "Are you really going to fight Jesus in hand-to-hand combat in the final battle for all our souls, or is that just something someone made up?"

For the first time since Arthur could remember—perhaps the first time *ever*—Lucy was speechless, his mouth hanging open, the red in his eyes fading until all that was left was green. He sputtered nonsensically, and Arthur knew he needed to step in before Lucy recovered. Whatever he might say probably wouldn't help—

Lucy beat him to it. He relaxed, cool as ice. "Yeah, probably," he said, as if it were the easiest thing in the world. "I know karate, so it won't be a fair fight. What's he going to do? Make more fish and bread?" He pressed his hands against his cheeks, eyes wide. "Oh, Jesus, no, *anything* but that. Gasp! Are you turning water into *wine*? Curse you, street magician!"

"Back ten minutes and we're already blaspheming," Linus said, as Helen and Zoe laughed, trying to keep each other upright. "It's good to be home."

"He's not going to fight Jesus," Talia said. "Last night, Lucy stubbed his toe and cried until Zoe kissed it, so all Jesus has to do is wait for that, and the fight is over."

"It was gushing blood," Lucy retorted. "We almost had to amputate, but then Zoe said she already promised Linus we had all of our toes still. I never get to do *anything* fun."

"He's not going to fight Jesus," Linus told David. "Some people make up stories to frighten others. Nothing more than a flight of fancy."

"Can I say something now?" Chauncey demanded. "I've been politely waiting my turn."

"Go ahead," Arthur said.

"Hi!" Chauncey said, waving a tentacle at David. Then he said, "That's it. You may continue."

"That is Chauncey," Linus told David. "He's a bellhop, one of the best there is."

"Hi, Chauncey," David mumbled.

"He knows my *name*," Chauncey whispered excitedly.

"Next to him is Talia," Arthur said. "She's our resident expert in all things garden-related."

Talia waved at him. "I like burying things, like seeds and people who cross me."

"Then there is Phee," Linus said. "A forest sprite responsible for many of the trees you saw on our trip in."

"Hi, David," she said, her wings shimmering in the sunlight. "Do you like the sign?"

David nodded tightly. "No one's ever made something like that for me before."

"We make them all the time," Phee said. "Next time, you can help us, if you want."

"And last but certainly not least," Arthur said, "Sal, one of the most gifted writers I've ever had the pleasure of reading."

Sal smiled a little ruefully. "He likes to talk us up. You'll get used to it. Welcome, David. It feels like we've been waiting to meet you forever."

David stepped away from Linus, dropping his hand. He approached the children, looking up when Theodore's shadow blocked the sun for a brief moment, the wyvern landing once more on Sal's shoulder.

"You've been waiting to meet *me*?" David asked, stopping a few feet away.

"Yep," Chauncey said. "We've never met a yeti before. I *knew* you'd be tall! Also? I really like your hair."

"Thanks," David said, tugging a thick strand. "It can get heavy if it's not taken care of."

"We got you," Sal said. "Zoe does special stuff for my hair, so I bet we can figure yours out too."

Talia stroked her beard. "And I have oils that'll make it soft if you want. There, now that *that's* out of the way, on to something just as important. Presents."

"Talia," Arthur said. "Would you like to try that again?"

She sighed. "Hi."

"Hello."

"How are you?"

"Better now."

"Me too," she said. "Now, about those presents."

"In due time," Arthur said. "First, we have a guest, and we are not rude to guests."

She arched an eyebrow, tugging the end of her beard. "Can we take David inside and show him the house? Notice how I'm being polite and welcoming and not asking about presents again. Isn't that nice of me?"

"You are a saint," Arthur said. "If that's all right with David, you may. Save the surprise until after we've all come in."

"Surprise?" David asked, looking around wildly. "What surprise?"

"Can I touch your arm?" Chauncey asked.

David flinched. "What?"

"I want to grab your arm and lead you where to go," Chauncey explained. "But some people don't like that."

"Oh," David said. "I . . . guess?"

A lime-green tentacle snaked around David's wrist, Chauncey tugging him up the steps, the rest of the children hurrying after them. "Come on! We'll show you where we hide things we don't want Linus or Arthur to know about!"

"Upstairs hall closet with the secret cubby hole in the back?" Linus asked Arthur after the children disappeared inside the house.

"Either that or the one box in the attic they think they're so secretive about."

"They're not very subtle, are they?"

"And so focused on a new guest that we don't even merit a hug? Your children need to learn their manners."

"Oh, they're *my* children when you don't get a hug, but as soon as one of them threatens disembowelment, you're pleased as punch."

"What are you two nattering on about?" Zoe asked, appearing in front of them with her arm through Helen's. They took turns kissing each other's cheeks. "Seemed serious." Then, without waiting for an answer, she said, "What's that on your finger?"

Helen said, "His finger? Did he hurt— *What.*"

Arthur held up his hand, the ring snug, weighted, a presence he could not deny. "Oh, this? I barely remembered it was even there."

"Liar," Linus mumbled as he blushed.

"You *didn't*," Zoe said with an uncharacteristic squeal. She rushed forward, snatching Arthur's hand and bringing the ring an inch from her face. When she looked up at him again, her eyes were watery. She glanced from Arthur to Linus then back again. "Is this real?"

"It is," Linus said. "It may seem a bit fast, but—"

"Silly man," Helen said, her hands clasped under her chin, her smile so wide Arthur was surprised her face hadn't split in half. "There's no such thing as 'a bit fast' when you know it's right." She slapped Linus playfully on the arm. "You *sneak*. Why did you—"

"We have a problem. I think."

They all turned toward the house. Phee stood on the porch, a funny expression on her face.

Arthur took a step toward her. "What is it?"

Phee shrugged. "Did you know that yetis and cats are mortal enemies?"

Calliope stood on the bottom step that led to the second floor, back arched, hair standing on end from tip to tail, which extended in a rigid line behind her. Eyes narrowed, hissing as loudly as a leaking steampipe, Calliope tracked the movement of the yeti standing before her.

Said yeti growled in response, claws extended as he paced back and forth. His lips rippled with every snarl, pulled back over his fearsome fangs. Toenails clicking on the floor, David paced back and forth, never looking away from Calliope.

The others stood off to the side, gazes bouncing between the cat and the yeti. Lucy was near the front, watching with great interest. "I wouldn't try and pet her if I were you," he said with far too much glee. "She'll probably rip your throat out."

"What on *earth* is going on here?" Linus asked, causing all the children to jump. David whirled around, claws receding as he adopted the demeanor of one who had absolutely not been caught doing something they probably shouldn't.

Calliope immediately dropped the act, meowing at Linus. She hopped off the step, gave David a wide berth, and then wound her way between Linus's legs, the picture of innocence.

"Yes, yes," Linus said, reaching down to scratch behind her right ear. "I'm happy to see you too." He stood upright. "David?"

David scowled at him. "You didn't tell me you had a cat."

"Is that an issue?" Arthur asked. "Are you allergic, or do you—"

"I'm not allergic! Cats are *food*."

"Cats are most certainly *not* food," Linus said sternly. "Especially this cat."

"Linus gets upset when we try and eat Calliope," Talia explained as the others nodded around her.

Arthur cleared his throat.

"Also, eating cats is wrong," Talia added. More nodding.

"Much better," Arthur said. "And they're right, David. Calliope is as much a part of this family as anyone else, and we do not eat family members."

"Except when they're pine cones," Chauncey said with a wisdom beyond his years.

"Exactly," Linus said. "Except when they're— Wait, what?"

"I wasn't going to *eat* her," David said. "I was just trying to . . . make her go . . . near my . . . mouth."

"I *knew* he'd be a perfect fit," Helen whispered to Zoe.

"New house rule," Arthur announced. "No one can eat anyone

without their permission, both spoken aloud and written down in a binding contract. Since Calliope is unable to write—given her lack of opposable thumbs—unfortunately, she is not on offer."

"David?" Linus asked. "Can you abide by this rule?"

David glared at Calliope, who had apparently decided his existence did not matter to her in the least as she turned away from him, sat down, and began to clean herself with her paw. "Yeah, yeah, no eating cats."

"Splendid," Arthur said, clapping his hands. "Perhaps now would be the right time to show David his surprise."

"What surprise?" David asked, momentarily forgetting that he had almost lost a war against a most capable feline.

"We'll show you," Sal said, Theodore watching from his shoulder, head cocked. "But you have to close your eyes first."

David looked at each of them in turn, quick glances that swept the entryway. For a moment, Arthur thought it was too much too soon, but then David took a deep breath and closed his eyes. "Like this?"

Trust, Arthur knew, was a treasure effortlessly stolen, often without rhyme or reason. And this particular treasure was a fragile thing, a piece of thin glass easily broken. But here was David, surrounded by strangers in an unfamiliar place, attempting to pick up his pieces and put them back into a recognizable shape. Whatever else he was, David's bravery in the face of seemingly insurmountable odds proved yet again what Arthur had always believed: magic existed in many forms, some extraordinary, some simple acts of goodwill and trust, small though they might be.

"Perfect," Phee said. "We'll help you walk to where you need to go, and I promise we won't make you bump into anything."

"Okay," David whispered, flinching when Talia took his hand, leading him farther into the house. The other children followed along closely—Sal and Theodore bringing up the rear—pointing out obstacles in the way, Lucy running ahead of them to move a chair so Talia and David would have a clear path.

"We'll go see about supper," Zoe said.

Such a funny little thing, showing a boy his new room, and yet Arthur was as excited as the children were. Perhaps it was because he remembered how *he'd* felt the first time coming to the island, scared out of his mind, unsure about everything. If he'd been extended a welcoming hand instead of a raised fist, how might things have turned out differently? Would he even be where he was now?

They found the children in the hallway off the sitting room, gathered in front of a door that had not existed last year. It stood sturdy in its frame, painted a soft blue, with an iron doorknob. Affixed to the middle of the door, a wooden sign with a single word carved into it: DAVID.

"Okay," Talia said, still holding David's hand. "We're going to count backwards from three, and then you can open your eyes. Ready? Three." As the others joined in on the countdown—Linus and Arthur included—Calliope decided she was bored with them and trotted down the hall, tail twitching as she disappeared around the corner.

"Two. One!"

David opened his eyes, blinking rapidly. He stared up at the sight before him and said, "You named a door after me?"

"That's exactly right," Sal said with a solemn nod. "Surprise. You're welcome."

"Oh. Thank . . . you? I've never had anyone name a door after me before." He smiled, but it didn't quite reach his eyes which were once again wary.

"Why don't you open the door?" Arthur suggested. "I have a feeling there's a little more behind it that might help allay any confusion."

David bit the inside of his cheek before nodding. He reached toward the doorknob—slowly, carefully, as if he thought it'd explode. When it did not, in fact, explode, he relaxed slightly and twisted the knob. The door opened silently—a wave of ice-cold air washing over them—revealing a set of stairs that descended into darkness.

Except it wasn't completely dark, was it? No. Because the ceiling shone with an ethereal light, wavy swirls of green and blue and gold and violet. It'd taken time and much effort to get it exactly right. Glow-in-the-dark paint, studying photographs, trying to match it as best they could.

Before Arthur could wonder if David recognized it for what it was, the yeti said, "Is that . . . is that the aurora borealis?"

"Yeah," Sal said, leaning over so he and Theodore could see the fruits of their labor. "Arthur got us a book with pictures of it after we asked what else we could do. We used it as a template to make it look as realistic as possible. All of this is new. The door. The paint. The stairs. We've spent the last couple of months working on it."

"Where do the stairs go?" David asked.

"You should find out," Linus said. "There should be a switch just inside the— Here, hold on." The children moved as he reached through the door. A moment later, warm light shone down on the stairs, the aurora borealis dimming.

"It's cold," David whispered, taking a step toward the stairs. "Like . . ."

"Let's go!" Lucy crowed, and grabbed David's hand, pulling him down the stairs. The others thundered after them.

Linus and Arthur included.

There was a time when coming down to this place would've been nearly impossible, a grim reminder of a past that could not be changed. In all the years since his return to the island (and before they'd learned of David), Arthur had entered the cellar only once: when Linus had discovered the truth, one of Arthur's greatest secrets. But even then, he'd felt the firm grip of panic squeezing his throat, his breath coming out in soft whistles. He'd pushed beyond it by sheer force of will, entering the cellar after a man who, too, was more than he seemed.

When Helen had brought David to their attention, he'd immediately thought of the cellar and wondered if it could be turned into a place of dreams rather than nightmares. Make something new out of something old, and while it couldn't—and ultimately didn't—erase the past, the idea of renovating the cellar into a room for David didn't give him as much pause as he'd expected. He hadn't known what that meant, exactly, the old adage of "time heals all wounds" ringing in his ears. But that wasn't quite true, was it? The passage of time might dull the edges, but it wasn't a cure-all. No, it'd take more than that. So much more.

Like this:

He shivered as he stood with Linus in the doorway, his breath a warm fog that streamed from his mouth with every exhalation. Linus crowded against him, muttering that he was thankful Arthur burned warmer than humans. As they looked on, the children did the same, watching as David moved slowly around the room, taking everything in.

The walls had been painted a soft shade of teal, so much like ice that it felt as if they were standing atop an iceberg drifting through the sea. Any tick marks had been sanded down and painted over, no evidence left that they'd been there at all. Near the ceiling, four vents, one on each wall, blew frozen air from an industrial air-conditioning unit that had been installed at the back of the house. The temperature was set right at freezing, as Arthur had read that yetis preferred to sleep in the cold.

And speaking of sleeping, against the right wall, a queen-sized bed with fluffy pillows and a white comforter, the corner pulled back in invitation. To the left of the bed, a chest of drawers sat beside an old oak wardrobe, the doors open, empty hangers dangling from a metal bar.

On the opposite wall, another set of stairs, lit up by sunlight streaming in through the windows of the newly installed cellar doors. Each door had a circular window in it, portholes to allow daylight to enter in late afternoon as the sun began its descent.

"What is this?" David whispered, standing stock-still in the middle of the room, his toes digging into the oval rug Helen had brought over from her personal storage.

"This is your room," Talia said. "We all have our own. We tried to guess what you'd like, but we didn't want to do too much in case you wanted to change anything."

"It's okay if you do," Chauncey said, black teeth chattering. "You can do whatever you want with it. We won't be mad."

"Except if you make me paint again," Lucy said. "Then, I'll be *very* mad." He cocked his head. "Unless we use blood. That would be all right, I think."

"I don't understand," David said, sounding rather helpless. "What do you mean, *my* room?"

Phee frowned. "It's yours. All of this."

David turned away from them, head bowed. When he spoke, his voice was small, quiet, barely above a whisper. "I've never had my own room before." Then his shoulders began to shake as he sniffled, and a moment later, the most remarkable thing happened.

Arthur wasn't sure what he was witnessing at first. An ice cube, rectangular, about two inches long, fell to the floor and shattered, bits of ice spreading along the floor. It was followed by another. And then another. And then another, and it was then that Arthur remembered something he should've never forgotten in the first place: no matter how much research he did, it wasn't thick tomes that would teach him what he needed to know, at least not fully. Firsthand experience was just as—if not more—important than anything he could read about.

Because the yeti known as David was crying; but instead of tears, ice cubes fell from his eyes, falling to the floor with delicate *plink*s!

Linus, obviously alarmed, started toward David, only to have Sal shake his head. "Let us handle it, okay?" he said in a low voice as more ice cubes fell to the floor. "It'd be better coming from us." He didn't have to say the rest: *Because you don't know what it's like. We do.*

"Of course," Linus said. "I have complete faith in you." Without artifice, without pandering.

Sal turned his head toward Theodore. "What do you think, bud? We got this?"

Theodore clicked his agreement.

"I think so too," Sal said. He looked at the other children. "Give us a second, all right?"

"I don't like it when people cry," Chauncey whispered.

Theodore chirped twice in quick succession, followed by three long growls.

"Theodore's right," Talia said as she glanced at Linus. "Happy tears aren't sad tears, even if they look the same."

Sal and Theodore moved toward David quietly, the yeti trying to keep his sniffles from being too loud. They stopped next to him, looking down.

"Hey," Sal said easily. "Big day, yeah?"

"Yeah," David replied hoarsely. "Big day." Another ice cube fell to the floor. "And I'm not crying. I just have something in my eye. I don't know where the ice cubes are coming from."

Sal shrugged, Theodore rising up and down. "Sure. But it's okay if you *were* crying. I did when I first got here."

David wiped his eyes with his arm. "You did?"

"Oh yeah," Sal said. "It was . . . overwhelming. Not in a bad way, but it's hard to tell the difference when you're in the middle of it. I didn't know where I was, who these other people were, making promises I'd heard before. If they were going to be nice to me, or if they were going to . . ."

"Hurt you," David whispered.

Sal smiled tightly. "So I cried. The first night. The second night. The third. I cried because I was nervous and didn't want to mess anything up. Because I couldn't believe this place was real, that I would get to stay. I'd never had that before. I also cried because I was scared."

"You were scared?" David asked, looking up at Sal and Theodore with wet eyes. "But you don't look like you'd be scared of *anything*."

Theodore chirped, tongue snaking out between his lips.

Sal nodded. "Yeah, what he said. No one here is going to make fun of you, not when we've all been there." Sal hesitated a moment, and Arthur saw a familiar indecision cross his face. His shoulders began to hunch as he turned in on himself. Arthur was about to interrupt when Sal shook his head and pulled himself upright. Theodore spread his wings.

Next to him, Linus whispered, "You got this."

Sal said, "You don't know us, and we don't know you. But things are good here."

"I've heard that before," David said.

"Yeah," Sal said. "I bet you have. Difference is, it's true here. You don't have to trust anything I'm saying." He laughed. "Hell, I wouldn't if I were you. But you'll believe soon enough."

David stared up at Sal and Theodore. He turned his head to look at the rest of them, starting with Lucy, who wiggled his fingers in a wave, and ending on Arthur, who smiled. David then took in the rest of the room: the late afternoon sunlight dappling the floor, the clean walls, the bed, the wardrobe, the drawers, even the rug. "Can I decorate however I want?"

"You can," Arthur said. "This is your space, David. Make it look however you wish."

David nodded and took in his new room in wonder.

It was a little past midnight when the bedroom door creaked open. Linus grumbled as a smallish garden gnome climbed onto the bed, settling between them and smacking her lips.

Ten minutes later, the door opened again, and a forest sprite made her way in. She lay next to Arthur, her head on his pillow.

Four minutes after that, the closet door opened and a devilish voice cried, "You're having a sleepover and you didn't invite me? Oh my heck, what is *wrong* with all of you?" Linus grunted as a little boy jumped on top of him, all knees and elbows.

It wasn't long before a green blob appeared. Flattening himself until he was as thin as a piece of paper, he spread himself on top of them, eye stalks resting on Arthur's chest. It wasn't unpleasant; it felt as if they lay under a blanket made of non-sticky jam.

Of course, that meant no one wanted to be left out, and two more figures appeared: one tall, wearing ratty sleep shorts and a tank top; the other blinked sleepily with reptilian eyes. The tall boy stretched out next to a welcoming cat along the width of the bed, which was big enough to keep his feet from dangling off the edge. The wyvern lay on top of him, head curled against his body. The cat licked the boy's cheek once and closed her eyes.

Arthur was on the cusp of sleep—warm and smothered, a quiet smile on his face—when Talia shot up next to him and yelled, "We didn't get our presents!"

Linus groaned, burying his face in the pillow. "It's time for *quiet*."

"Arthur," Chauncey whispered. "Psst. *Arthur*. Are you sleeping?"

"No, Chauncey."

"Fun! Neither am I. Can I ask you a question?"

"Yes, Chauncey."

"Oh, good. Thank you. Why do you have a ring on your finger?"

No one got much sleep after that.

EIGHT

Two days later—a Friday morning just after ten—Arthur sat in his office, towers of books leaning precariously around him. Before him, paperwork, everything Jason and Byron had on David, though it didn't amount to much: his schooling records (not too far behind where they were on Marsyas, thankfully), and a couple of notes about how inquisitive he was, after he got over his initial reticence. To be fair, Arthur hadn't expected more, given that David had been moved in secrecy.

But it was the old newspaper clipping that captured Arthur's attention. Near the back, attached to a picture of David—blurry, the boy looking frightened—the article was short and without much detail. Three big-game hunters were facing charges after stalking a family of magical creatures for days through a frozen tundra. Given that it was illegal to hunt beings capable of "humanlike thought"—so named in the We Care Law (passed two decades before in a close vote)—the hunters were facing a prison term of up to three years, and fines totaling a thousand pounds. Their crime?

They had killed two adult yetis.

Arthur closed the file, tapping his fingers against the folder.

"Is that about me?" David asked a few minutes later, arriving in Arthur's office right on time. He slumped into the chair on the other side of the desk, arms folded across his chest, his thick hair sleeker than usual. Talia had given him some of her beard soaps as she was of the mind that everyone with body hair should have only the very best.

"It is," Arthur said. "It's one of the reasons I invited you here today. I could make assumptions based upon what I've read, but in my experience, files such as this don't always paint a full picture. I'd rather hear it directly from the source."

"Me," David said, sounding as if he'd rather be anywhere but where he was.

"Precisely," Arthur said, sitting back in his chair. "Yesterday was your first full day here. How did it go?"

David shrugged.

Arthur wasn't to be deterred. "The children took you on a tour of the house. Did you see anything you have questions about?"

David shook his head.

"Good," Arthur said. "Should anything arise, ask."

David sank lower in his seat, to the point where only his head lay against the back of the chair, resting at a sharp angle. Not a puddle, but it could easily go that direction.

"Up, please," Arthur said, wanting to test him just a little. "Posture is important. We do not slump in chairs."

David muttered under his breath as he pushed himself back up, glaring at Arthur. Once he was using the chair for its intended purpose, he said, "No one cares about how I sit in a chair."

"I do," Arthur said. "Thank you. Now, about—"

"I'm not stupid, you know."

Arthur tilted his head in acknowledgment. "The thought has never crossed my mind."

David eyed the papers on Arthur's desk with disdain. "Whatever it says in there, it's not my fault. I tried to do school stuff, but . . ." A fierce glower. "Whatever."

Ah, Arthur thought. "You are a bit behind where we currently are. *But,*" he said as David opened his mouth, "that's to be expected. You have been in upheaval for so long now, of course it would be difficult to keep up with your schooling."

"B helped," David mumbled. "They were good at it."

"I can tell," Arthur said. "Byron included some wonderful notes about your work with them. They wrote how intelligent you are, but that you can sometimes get overwhelmed if given too many tasks. Is that a fair assessment?"

David shrugged again.

Arthur changed tack. "Tomorrow is Saturday. Have the other children told you what happens on Saturdays? It proved to be so popular we decided to make it a weekly thing, unless something else comes up."

David perked up at that before adopting a scowl. "Maybe."

"Wonderful. It's something I look forward to, especially when I'm kept in the dark about what the day will entail. I find that the surprise is almost as good as the adventure itself. Speaking of." Knowing David was watching his every move, Arthur made a show of opening a drawer and pulling out a small desk calendar, showing the months of June and July. "I make it a point to keep track of our days. I've learned that having a set schedule helps keep expectations clear. I'm sure you've seen a similar calendar in the kitchen?"

"I guess."

"Good," Arthur said. "It's there for you to look at, so you know what to expect for each week and where you need to be. We're currently on a short break from our studies, but we'll resume next week. In addition, this schedule also shows what chores you will be responsible for during that week."

"Chores?" David moaned. "Is that why you have so many kids? Free child labor?"

"That's certainly one way of looking at it," Arthur said. "Though I prefer to think of it as everyone contributing to our continued success. You won't be assigned chores during your first week here, but we'll see about adding you next week."

"Yay," he muttered. "All for me? Gee, you shouldn't have."

Arthur chuckled. "Not a fan of rules, I see. That's to be expected. Going someplace new can be taxing, given that you need to learn about the home, the people, the ins and outs. It can take time to get used to how things are done. No one is expecting perfection from you, David. Not only is that unfair to you, it might set a level of expectation that's impossible to achieve." He smiled. "Why don't we start with a question. What do you want to be when you grow up?"

"A monster," David said promptly.

"Fascinating," Arthur said. "I'd like to hear more about that, if you're comfortable with sharing."

David stared at him in disbelief. "Why aren't you scared or mad?"

"Because I have no reason to be, at least not currently. I'll let you know should that change. Continue, if you please."

David hesitated, eyeing him warily. "Everyone thinks monsters are bad and made of nightmares and stuff like that. They say they're *scared* of us, and that they don't like to be scared. But then they pay, like, so much money to go to films with monsters or haunted houses where things scream and jump out at them. They get scared on *purpose*. Why would they do that?"

"An extraordinary conundrum," Arthur agreed.

"*I* think it's because people like to be scared," David said. "The same way they like to be happy. So long as you don't hurt anyone, or eat them, why can't you scare them?"

"A fair question," Arthur said. "I suppose it depends upon intent and consent. Are you scaring them for *them,* or are you doing it for yourself?"

"Both," David said. "And if they already think I'm a monster, why shouldn't I show them how monstrous I can be? Give them what they *really* want." His eyes gleamed as he rubbed his hands together.

"You don't have to be that way," Arthur said. "Not if you don't want to. What some people consider a *monster* isn't what others—"

David shot up in his chair, a fierce glower settling on his face. He gripped the arms of the chair, claws dimpling the leather. "I knew it! You're just like everyone else. Trying to change me into something I don't want to be. What's wrong with wanting to be a monster? It's what we are."

He was right, of course. Even though it was contrary to what Arthur had taught the other children, David was right, in his own way. At the very least, he was speaking *his* truth, and would it really be in his best interest to try to take that away from him? But if Arthur didn't, how would that affect the other children?

"There's nothing wrong with doing what you like," Arthur said carefully. "So long as it doesn't bring harm to others." He paused, considering. "The word 'monster' has many connotations. But it seems to me as if you have decided upon an interesting definition on your own. Here's a thought. What if we worked together to figure out what is required to be a monster, as you see it?"

David relaxed slightly, though his distrust was still evident. "What do you mean?"

Arthur looked through the pages before him, finding David's schooling records. "In my experience, fear can come from many places, not just things that go bump in the night. Take, for example, an accountant. What do you think their biggest fear is? Give me your best shot at tailoring an experience that would frighten someone in such a position."

David eyed him suspiciously. "This isn't, like, a test? You're not going to get mad no matter what I say?"

Arthur chuckled. "You have my word."

David stared at him for a long moment before nodding. He tilted his head back toward the ceiling. "Um . . . I guess that—no, wait. That won't work. I got it! Instead of a spreadsheet, I give them a box of disorganized receipts and tell them they have four hours to make sense of it or I'll roar so loud, the office shakes!"

Once again, the mind of a child knocked Arthur flat. How could anyone think they were capable of harm? "Wonderful," Arthur said. "I appreciate how descriptive that was. Might I offer an alternative?"

David frowned. "Does it involve scaring him?"

"It does!" Arthur said. "Instead of roaring, what if you became so good at maths that you were able to scare the accountant by doing all the calculations on your own, thus rendering his skill set obsolete? Nothing screams fear like the dread of becoming redundant."

David gaped at him.

"But then, of course, you will need to growl at him to prove your point."

"I can do that!"

Of course he could. In the few days Arthur had known him, he could see David wanted to try, wanted to succeed. But it would take time. Nothing was more important than David feeling comfortable. "You can?" Arthur asked. "Wonderful. I've always believed that the more we know, the better we can understand the wider world around us. It's why we take your schooling very seriously. The more we can prepare you, the better off you'll be. It'll help you learn all sorts of things, up to and including better ways to scare people."

"Whoa," David said. "I never thought about school like that. I guess that wouldn't be so bad." His brow furrowed. "Hold on a second. Did you . . . did you just trick me into wanting to go to school?"

"I did," Arthur said. "And funnily enough, I don't feel badly about it in the slightest."

"I'm on to you," David said, pointing a blunt finger at him. "I see *right* through you."

"Delightful," Arthur said. "Given that transparency is paramount, I prefer not to be opaque. And now, I must apologize."

"For what?"

"For not listening as well as I should have. This is the second time you've said you wanted to be a monster, and instead of listening to what you were saying, I told you that you didn't have to be something you obviously like. That was unfair of me, and I apologize without reservation."

David blinked. "Oh. That's . . . okay?"

Arthur shook his head. "It's not. I should have heard you better than I did. So there is no misunderstanding, I shall say this: here, David, in this place, you can be whoever you want to be. A monster?

I will do my best to make sure you have everything you require to see it through. What if you find yourself enamored with cheese and wish to become a *fromager*? I will make that happen. An actor? I don't know how much more I could teach you as you've already proven adept at staging plays on your own, but I will attend every performance, and I will be the first to rise in what I imagine will be a thunderous standing ovation."

"Why?" David asked, wiping his nose as he sniffled, little ice crystals forming at the corners of his eyes. "Why would you do that?"

Arthur leaned forward over his desk. "Because you deserve it, David. That being said, I need your help."

"You do?" David asked. "What can I do?"

"Ah, I'm so glad you asked," Arthur said. "Why don't we start with something simple? We will meet three times a week: Monday, Wednesday, and Friday. On Fridays, like today, I will give you a special mission, one that you can take the weekend to perform. Is that something you might be capable of?"

"A mission?" David asked eagerly, sitting up in his chair. "Like I'm a spy?"

"Exactly like a spy," Arthur said, "if a spy's job is to find out one interesting thing about each of the people in the house. A talent they have, or something they said that you find appealing. Then, next week, you can share with me what you learned."

David nodded. "Got it. You want me to spy on everyone. Find out their secrets, report back so you can use what I learned against them. Diabolical."

"That's not quite what I meant, though I do love where your mind goes. No, this isn't about finding out secrets, but learning about the people you live with. There is a difference, David, much like there is a difference between right and wrong. But I think you know that, given that even though you want to be a monster, you understand that scaring people isn't the same as hurting them."

"So . . . just, like . . . talk to them?"

Arthur beamed. "Exactly. And while the prospect might be scary in and of itself, I think someone as strong and fearsome as a yeti should have no problem seeing it through. What do you think?"

"I can do it," David said, sounding resolute.

"I know you can," Arthur said. "Now, since tomorrow is Saturday, I will give you a brief yet comprehensive outline of adventures past, so that you may have a better grasp on what potentially life-altering and/or life-threatening event you will be participating in. But worry not! We haven't yet lost a single child, so I'm sure you'll be fine."

Saturday adventures were a tried-and-true staple of Marsyas Island, something Arthur had decided to include almost from the very beginning. Initially, it'd been monthly until the children asked if they could do it more often. Arthur and Linus agreed, so once a week, each child took turns planning what that day's adventure would be. Sometimes, there were dangerous expeditions into uncharted territory where anything from cannibals to gigantic snakes awaited (much to Linus's dismay). Other times, they took trips into the village. Just last month, they'd spent the day touring residents' gardens at Talia's request. It had gone extremely well.

(Mostly. Toward the end, she'd discovered a flower bed soaked in chemicals, and had asked for permission to knock on the door so she and the homeowner could, in her words, "have a little talk.")

On a sunny morning in June—thin, wispy clouds stretching from one end of the sky to the other—the responsibility for this particular Saturday adventure fell onto the squishy shoulders of the boy known as Chauncey.

Chauncey, who made his appearance that morning descending the stairs wearing a rather large straw sun hat. The brim was at least a foot in diameter with two holes cut near the top for his eye stalks and was adorned with a massive fake flower with a yellow center and white velvet petals. Over his eyes, a pair of cat-eye sunglasses sat askew, the frames adorned with glittering plastic crystals. He practically floated down the stairs, and when he spoke, his voice took on a posh accent. "*Dahhhlings*," he breathed. "You are all looking *divine*. Perfect day for yachting, wouldn't you agree?"

"I would like to lodge a complaint," Linus said, grimacing as he pulled at the form-fitting wetsuit Chauncey had all but demanded they wear for his day. With Zoe's help, Chauncey had gotten a wetsuit for each of them.

Linus's wetsuit was yellow, almost too bright to look at. Lucy's was red, Talia's brown like the soil she loved so much. Phee's was forest green, Sal's white with polka dots that, if seen from a distance, could have been mistaken for buttons, which explained why Theodore (sans his own wetsuit, saying that he'd prefer to be nude) kept trying to peck at them.

David, too, had a wetsuit—blue, like ice—a rush order that Zoe had put through to make sure he wasn't left out. While it fit, his suit was a little bulky, given his thick strands of hair. But he didn't seem to mind, bouncing on his toes in excitement.

Arthur's own wetsuit was gold in color, and it came complete with a pair of snorkeling goggles that Chauncey insisted they would all need. It was tight-fitting and left little to the imagination, but then Arthur had long accepted that he was knobby in ways that could not be fixed.

Chauncey lowered his sunglasses, revealing his eyes as he looked Linus up and down. "You silly man," he said. "You look brilliant. A *vision*. Yes, that's what you are. Like the sun. The nice, round sun that—"

"Not helping," Linus muttered.

"To the yacht!" Chauncey cried, arms flailing.

"We don't have a yacht," Lucy said. "I would know if we did. I would have crashed it by now."

"We get to *crash boats*?" David asked, impressed. "No one told me that we get to do property damage."

"That's because we don't," Linus said.

"We do," Talia told David. "But only if we pay for it after. And apologize. And promise never to do it again. You can get away with anything once, sometimes twice if you try hard enough."

"*Talia,*" Linus said sternly.

She turned toward him, her eyes unnaturally large. "I'm sorry, Linus. I promise I'll never do anything like that again. You've taught me the error of my ways."

Linus blinked. "Oh, well. Thank you. I'm pleased to hear that—"

"And that's how you get away with it," she told David. "It's quite easy if you can make your eyes big enough."

"Daahhlings," Chauncey said, bringing the attention back to him. "Shall we embark on the adventure of a lifetime? What surprises wait in store? Romance and love? A mystery where someone's priceless hula-hoop is stolen and requires the brain of a green person who is a detective and a bellhop *and* happens to own a watercraft? Anything can happen on Chauncey's Yacht of Dreams!"

"Chauncey," Linus said pleasantly. "It appears that we need to work on your vocabulary lessons. Yachts are defined as sailing or power craft used for cruising, racing, and/or pleasure."

Chauncey lowered his sunglasses slightly, only the tops of his eyes visible. "My good man, that's where you're *wrong*. Everyone knows there is no true definition of a yacht, only that a yacht must have a cabin for overnight stays. And would you look at that! There's a cabin."

There was, though Arthur thought it might not be large enough to accommodate them all, seeing as how it was an old cardboard box barely bigger than Chauncey, placed near the front of the vessel. Inside the box, a sleeping bag, an old pillow, and what appeared to be a pile of seaweed, something that Chauncey considered to be a delicacy.

Which was to say nothing of the rest of the yacht. The reason being, of course, that it wasn't a yacht at all, but a rowboat. And not just any rowboat, no: while large enough to fit them all (even with the "cabin"), the vessel looked as if it belonged on a trash heap rather than on the water. Paint chipped, metal rusted. Small wooden benches. A wooden pole placed in the middle with a thin, limp bedsheet for a sail. Two oars—one of which was broken, the handle mostly gone and leaving only the paddle itself—and orange life jackets for each of them. Next to the box at the front, a cooler and a large palm frond resting against the lip of a bench. The rowboat had been pulled up halfway out of the water, waves lapping gently at its sides.

Like all good water vessels, the rowboat had a name, painted in dripping letters on the side: SEAS THE DAY.

"Isn't she gorgeous?" Chauncey asked, pushing his way through them and moving to either side of the rowboat as if inspecting it. "Got her for a steal from a billionaire who only used her a few times a year."

"Whatever you paid, it was too much," Phee said.

Chauncey ignored her. "Since it's my day to pick the adventure, I get to be in charge. Lucy and Talia, you'll fan me with the palm frond and feed me grapes out of the cooler while paying me compliments."

Lucy shook his head. "I want to be captain."

Talia's hand shot in the air, fingers wiggling.

"Yes, Talia?" Chauncey asked.

"I would also like to be captain."

This, of course, led to each of the children (sans David) extolling their own qualifications for being the captain of the yacht. It devolved into a shouting match where Talia threatened to send Lucy a bouquet of poisonous flowers, and Lucy responded by yelling that he would *love that so much* and that he *double-dog* dared her to.

Chauncey, on the other hand, had a different idea. "It's my day, so I get to decide! Lucy and Talia, fanning and grapes. Phee and Sal are the first mates and the strongest, so that means they get to paddle. Theodore is our figurehead, as all good ships have one. Also, his sense of direction will keep us from getting lost at sea, which is great because if we do, we'd have to draw straws to see who we'd eat to avoid starvation. No pressure."

"But then who's going to be captain?" Lucy asked with a pout. "Linus? He told me he hates being the captain of anything, so you should just let me do it."

"Fibber," Linus muttered under his breath.

"It's going to be the one person who didn't demand it," Chauncey announced. "David."

David looked around wildly. "Are you talking to *me*?"

"Yes!" Chauncey said. "You have the most important job of all. You're going to be captain, which means you're in charge of the yacht. Nothing happens on the ship without your say-so."

"But—I—there's . . ." David slumped inward on himself, shoulders hunched. "Someone else would probably be better." He kicked at the sand, leaving a shallow divot. "I've never been a captain before."

"See?" Lucy said. "That's why it should be me. Besides, what if there's a lava monster rising from a secret cavern on the ocean floor? He won't even know what to do!" Then, perhaps for reasons only known to a seven-year-old boy with a demon in his soul, he raised his hands above his head and shrieked wordlessly at the ocean.

"Lava monster?" David asked in hushed reverence. "There's a *lava monster*?"

"Maybe," Talia said, jumping up the side of the rowboat, hanging off the edge, her little legs kicking as she climbed inside. She immediately began to root around in the cooler. "Eighty percent of the ocean is unexplored, so who knows what's out there waiting to eat us?"

"We're snack size," Lucy said. "Like a little bag of chips." He brightened. "*Cronch, cronch, cronch.*"

"What's this?" Talia asked, lifting an object above her head as she slid off the side of the boat. In her hand, she held a cap: white with a black brim under gold tassels. On the front of the cap, gold yarn in the shape of an anchor.

"That's the official captain's cap," Chauncey said. "When someone wears it, we have to do whatever they say."

Lucy nodded. "Because the hat has magic, and whoever wears it can control anyone they wish. Nice."

Chauncey said. "What? It's just a—"

"That's exactly right, Lucy," Arthur said.

Lucy blinked. "It . . . is?"

"May I?" Arthur asked Chauncey before plucking the hat from him. He turned and moved toward David, who looked either as if he were extremely excited, or wanted to run in the opposite direction. "David, Chauncey has bestowed upon you a gift. Leaders are often called upon in times of great need. And we have need of *you*. Will you answer the call?" He held out the cap.

David looked at it, then at Arthur, then back to the cap. With a trembling hand, he reached out and touched the brim. Knowing David was still feeling things out, Arthur didn't push, letting him making up his own mind.

He was delighted when David took the cap, turned it over in his hands, huffed out a breath, and then lowered it onto his head. It was a little big, sinking on his head until it covered his eyes. Arthur put two fingers under the brim, pushing it back up.

"A fine captain," Arthur said. He snapped to attention, back straight, legs stiff. Making sure David was watching, he offered a snappy salute. "Sir, if I may provide a suggestion. Why don't you give it a go? See how being the captain feels."

"Tell me to do something!" Lucy demanded. "I want to see if it's really magic." Then, under his breath, "Even though *I* wanted to be the one to wear it."

"Um," David said. "Do . . . a . . . cartwheel?"

Lucy groaned. "Boring. Fine. Watch." He ran across the sand at high speed and raised his hands above his head. As neat as you please, Lucy bent forward quickly, hands in the sand, legs kicking up and over his head. However, instead of using the momentum to push himself off the ground, he decided to use his face, and flopped over, spitting out mouthfuls of sand.

"It works!" he cried. "That hat *is* magic!"

"What a special boy he is," Talia said.

They climbed into the rowboat, Linus going first to help the other children up and in. Once they had all boarded the yacht (save for Arthur), Chauncey sat down in his cabin, the stalks on top of his head bent to keep his eyes from rubbing against cardboard. "It's terribly warm," he said, affecting the posh accent from earlier. "Lucy! Talia! I need to be fanned and fed grapes. Wot, wot! Hip hop!"

"I am going to feed him so many grapes they come out his butt," Talia muttered as she wobbled her way over to the box.

Arthur went to the back of the boat. "Ready?" he asked, as Linus helped the children with their life jackets, including attaching a pink floatie around Theodore's neck—at his request—to keep him from sinking should he end up in the water. He could swim quite well, but for some reason, he loved the floatie.

"Ready!" Chauncey called. "Launch the yacht!"

Arthur pushed as hard as he could, feet sinking into the sand, teeth gritting together. The rowboat moved an inch, then two, then it was carving through the water, the sail billowing out as the wind pushed against it. Arthur managed to climb on board (with Linus's help) before the vessel left him behind. He settled on a bench, watching as Lucy fanned Chauncey with the palm frond, Talia throwing grapes at his face that Chauncey missed more than he caught. Beyond them, Theodore sat perched at the front of the vessel, head darting side to side, floatie squeaking every time he moved. Sal and Phee paddled (Phee using the broken oar), but it was the wind that propelled them forward, the blanket sail pulled taut.

"Captain David," Linus said, and David gulped, standing in the middle of the rowboat, swaying side to side. "We are at sea. The ship is yours."

David nodded, looking around the boat, a sea breeze ruffling his hair. He squared his shoulders, puffed out his hairy chest. His gaze was cool, calculating. When he spoke, it was with authority. "Sal, keep watch on the port side. Phee, you've got starboard. I heard these are dangerous waters, and we need to be careful."

"On it, Captain," Phee said, paddling furiously. She didn't provide them with much momentum, but not for lack of trying.

"You got it, Cap," Sal said, the muscles in his arms straining with each stroke.

This appeared to give David more confidence. "Theodore!" he called. "Keep an eye out for enemy ships or icebergs or lava monsters. If you see *anything*, let me know."

Bobbing his head, Theodore chirped his affirmative.

David crawled over one of the bench seats toward Chauncey in his cabin. Talia was peeling grapes with her teeth before tossing naked fruit at Chauncey. Not to be outdone, Lucy swung the palm frond as hard as he could, slapping Chauncey in the face with it.

"Sir," David said, hunkering over to look inside the box. "The trip is underway. Any particular destination in mind?"

"You're a dear," Chauncey simpered, pulling his sunglasses off his eyes and letting them rest on the brim of his sun hat. "Ever since Eduardo left me for a sea cucumber named Leslie, all I've known is this yacht and the call of the open sea."

"I'm sorry for your troubles," David said, patting the top of the box. "I'll make sure today is the first day of the rest of your life."

"Thank you, Captain David," Chauncey said. "Continue on in this direction. I'll let you know when it's time to stop. Now, if you'll excuse me, I need to pretend I have a fainting couch so I can lay upon it and plot revenge against Eduardo and his little trollop."

"We're so weird," Phee said as the rowboat hit a wave, sending a mist of seawater into their faces.

Linus sighed. "That doesn't even begin to cover it."

It proved to be a fantastic day for yachting, even if "yachting" turned out to be a euphemism. The sun was high in the sky, the sea calm, and despite the cramped quarters, Arthur couldn't think of a single place he'd rather be. Though he knew trouble was rising on the horizon like a dark summer storm, it felt distant, almost unimportant, at least for today. He was reminded of a Linus-ism, one of his little nuggets that Arthur cherished beyond measure: *Why is it that I must always worry about tomorrows?*

They sailed (read: paddled) for approximately an hour, Chauncey giving vague directions from his cabin, the island always off the starboard side.

David took to his role as captain as if he were made for it. Always moving from one end of the rowboat to the other, he would pause near each person, complimenting them on their work. When Chauncey complained that the ice had already melted in his cooler, David immediately stepped up and froze the entire cooler into a block of ice. He started to apologize, but Chauncey exclaimed in delight, and that was the end of that.

It was just before noon when Chauncey crawled out from his box and announced that they had arrived. Sal and Phee pulled the oars back in while Linus and Arthur saw to the sail. Once done, Chauncey made them all sit on the bench seats while he stood on top of the box. "Quiet, please! Quiet!"

"No one was talking," Phee said.

"You might be wondering why we've stopped," Chauncey said from his perch. "If you are, kudos! Because my adventure has *two* parts."

"Twist," Lucy breathed, rubbing his hands together.

"I recently found out I possess an undiscovered talent," Chauncey said, pacing on top of the box. "One that will change the very shape of the world as we know it!"

Theodore chirped loudly in excitement.

"You might recall that I can make ink now," Chauncey said. "My nocturnal emissions, as Lucy calls them."

"We need to have a very serious discussion about calling them that," Linus said sternly.

Chauncey wasn't to be deterred. "In addition to my new power of inking, last week I discovered I can do something else." He removed his sun hat carefully, clutching it against his chest as he stared off into the sea. "I . . . can talk to fish."

Silence. Thick, stunned silence, the only sounds coming from the waves against the boat and the seabirds calling from above.

Chauncey grinned. "Did I leave you all speechless? Oh my goodness, I've never done that before. This is so exciting."

"Chauncey," Linus said faintly. "Forgive me, but for a moment, I thought you said you could—"

"Talk to fish!" Chauncey exclaimed. "I don't know how, but when you and Arthur were gone, Zoe took us swimming. There I was, minding my own business and eating barnacles off rocks on the sea floor when a *fish* swam up to me, told me his name, and then told me that *every* fish in the entire ocean has a name."

"Unholy *crap*," Lucy whispered, eyes ringed with red.

"I have to agree," Arthur said. "Why didn't you say anything before?"

Chauncey shrugged. "I wanted it to be a surprise." His wiggled his tentacles. "I also wanted to make sure I hadn't gone insane."

"That was very kind of you, Chauncey," Linus said. "And I've never met a saner person in my life."

Chauncey pouted. "Aw, darn. Can't I be just a little insane?"

"You can talk to fish," Sal said. "So, yeah. Sure. Why not."

"I can tell you want a demonstration," Chauncey said. "Allow me!" He turned toward the front of the boat, Theodore making room on his perch. Chauncey leaned over the side of the boat, sucked in a large breath, and then screamed at the water. "Frank! Hey, *Frank*! You down there? Come on up, friend!"

"The fish's name is Frank," Linus said.

"Fine name," Arthur said. "Means 'free,' or that you are from France."

"Is that right?"

"It is."

"Do you think the fish is from France, then?"

"Eighty percent of the ocean is unexplored," Arthur reminded him. "Could be many French fish named Frank."

"And now we get to meet one. Because he can talk to them."

"*Frank!*" Chauncey bellowed at the water. "You there? *Frank.*"

"Maybe he's in another part of the ocean," Talia said, joining Chauncey to peer over the side of the boat. "It's pretty big, you know."

"I know," Chauncey said, lifting his eyes to look at Talia. "But Frank's school lives around here, and he wouldn't have gone too far. *Fraaaaaaannnnnk!*"

Which was how they found themselves all bent over the side of the boat, shouting "*Frank!*" at the water. Arthur had never yelled at the ocean before and found it to be more soothing than he expected it to be. Out of the corner of his eye, he saw David standing back from the edge of the boat, once more looking unsure. Before Arthur could speak up, Phee made room for him, waving him over. He approached cautiously, standing between Phee and Talia, peering into the water. They reminded him that, as captain, he needed to be louder than everyone else.

David must have taken this to heart, because he lifted his head, pulled his lips back over his fangs, sucked in a deep breath, and then let out the most fearsome snarl that Arthur had ever heard, and he'd once known a griffin named Jessica. The sound carried over the sea, and Arthur wouldn't have been surprised to find out they'd heard it all the way in the village.

"How was that?" David asked, only to find everyone staring at him. He flinched. "I . . . I didn't mean to—"

"That was so *awesome!*" Chauncey screeched, grabbing David by the shoulders and spinning him around. "How did you *do* that?"

"So loud," Talia said with stars in her eyes. "Do you think you could do that when Linus is in the shower?"

"I bet we could line up a row of drinking glasses and he'd be able to break them all by yelling at them," Phee said. "Or all the *windows.*" She tilted her head back to look up at Arthur. "Can we blow out the windows when we get home?"

"We cannot," Arthur said. "As it turns out, windows are important."

"Frank!" Chauncey bellowed in excitement. "I *knew* you'd come!"

They all hurried to the side of the boat, looking over, the rowboat leaning precariously. And there, swimming just underneath the surface, a fish. It was not the most beautiful fish Arthur had ever seen, far from it: it was flat and wide, slightly bigger than Sal was in his shifted form. A beady eye on either side of its head, its scales gray near its top, fading into white toward the bottom. Its mouth opened and closed as it swam.

"Everyone," Chauncey said. "This is Frank. Frank, this is my family that I told you about."

The fish poked its mouth out of the water, opening and closing. As far as Arthur could tell, no sound came out, but Chauncey was nodding along as if deep in conversation. "Right. Right. Yeah. Oh, really? Wow. You don't say. Yeah, I can tell him. Hold on." Chauncey looked over at them. "Frank says Arthur reminds him of a seahorse he once knew called Madam Esmerelda."

"Chauncey," Arthur said, "please extend my gratitude to Frank. As far as I can tell, I've never been told I look like a seahorse *or* like someone called Madam Esmerelda, but I've discovered it tickles my fancy more than expected."

"Ooh," Lucy said. "If you love Madam Esmerelda so much, why don't you marry her?" He slapped his hands against his cheeks. "Oh no! Linus already *asked* you to marry him, so you can't marry a seahorse! Drat! Of all the luck."

"Drat, indeed," Arthur said. "Is this what it feels like to have dreams dashed? More's the pity."

"She can have you," Linus grumbled.

Theodore decided that was the perfect time to ask Chauncey the question everyone had been thinking about for the last three minutes.

"I don't know how I can talk to them," Chauncey said, his face inches from the water, Frank swimming just below the surface. "I think it was kind of like my ink. Just something I can do now." One of his eyes lowered into the water while the other raised over the lip of the boat, turning to look at each of them. "Which brings me to the reason we're here. Since I can talk to Frank, that means I can probably talk to other fish. So I'm sure you'll agree that we can no longer eat seafood of any kind."

"Oh, thank God," Phee said. "Fish is gross."

"*What?*" Lucy yelped. "No! I like crab! And shrimp! And lobster! And those little sardines from the can that I eat in front of Linus with my fingers because it makes him gag."

"But why would you eat something that can talk to you?" Chauncey asked. "Isn't that wrong? Frank says that people who eat seafood are going to Hell."

"Great," Linus said. "Now that I know fish are aware of the concept of Hell, I'm questioning everything."

"What about other animals, then?" Talia asked. "Just because you can talk to fish doesn't mean someone else can't talk to cows or pigs. Doesn't that make it bad too?"

Phee glared at them. "If anyone tries to take bacon from me, I'm going to turn them into a tree. And not a *good* tree. A bad one, like a Bradford pear tree."

They stared at her.

She threw up her hands. "Have I taught you *nothing*? The Bradford pear tree has thorns and the flowers smell like tuna. No one has ever said, oh gee, let me get a good, long sniff of fish flowers."

"We could consider vegetarianism," Arthur mused. "Take meat out of our diet and—"

"I will literally blow up the entire planet if you do that," Lucy growled. "You think meat is bad? Try breathing when you're hurtling through *space*."

"Well, it *is* Chauncey's day," Linus said. "Let's see what he thinks. Chauncey, would you like to explain a little more?"

Chauncey jerked back into the boat, face dripping with water. His eyes darted side to side. "Um. I think we've talked about this enough. We should just go home and—"

"Chauncey," Sal said. "Did you eat Frank?"

"What! Of course not! That goes against everything I stand for! I would *never*—"

"We can see him in your stomach," Phee said.

Sure enough, through Chauncey's translucent green skin, Frank swam in slow circles, little bubbles trailing from his nose. "Oh, that?" Chauncey said. "I can explain. You see, Frank said he's *very* interested in stomach acid, and wanted to see it for himself."

"Wow," David whispered. "This place is *crazy.*"

Linus sighed. "You want to handle this, or should I?"

"Do go right ahead," Arthur said. "You have such a delightfully succinct way of putting things."

Linus clapped his hands loudly to get everyone's attention. "Children. Children! New house rule. No eating anything that has been given a name."

Phee blinked prettily up at them. "I forgot to tell you. I can speak to cauliflower, and I've named them all Peggy. Oh no, I guess that means I can't eat cauliflower anymore."

"Nice try," Linus said. "And don't think we don't see it when you ask Lucy to send your cauliflower to some alternate dimension. Last time, he conjured a black hole."

"Yeah, that sucked," Sal said, and then high-fived Talia without looking at her.

It was about this time that Chauncey yarked over the side of the boat, Frank splashing back into the water. They all waved as Frank flashed them his tail fin before disappearing into the sea.

David tilted his head back to look at Arthur. "You weren't kidding when you said we could be monsters if we wanted to."

"What?" Lucy asked with a frown. "What do you mean we can be monsters? Arthur said that I can't . . ." He trailed off, glancing between David and Arthur with narrowed eyes. "Oh. So *that's* how it's gonna be." He turned away from them, kicking at the cooler and missing before sitting in Chauncey's box and pulling the sleeping bag up and over his head. All Arthur could see in the shadows were Lucy's red-ringed eyes glaring at him.

"What was that about?" Linus asked.

"That's on me," Arthur said quietly. "I don't think I've gone about this as well as I could have."

"You're learning," Linus said, patting his arm. "Even you can't be expected to know everything."

He was right, of course, but that didn't assuage Arthur's guilt. How could he tell one child he could be a thing, but tell another that he couldn't do the same? Granted, David's idea of being a monster wasn't the same as Lucy's, but was it fair to hold one person to a standard and another to something else entirely?

"Guys!" Sal called. "I think we have a problem." When they looked at him, he pointed up at the closed sail. It wasn't moving, hanging limply.

Theodore flew to the pole and gripped it, talons digging into the wood. He plucked at the sail, only to have it flutter back into place. He chirped a question.

"No wind," Talia said. She went to the side of the boat, looking over. "How are we going to get back to the island?" She slid down the side, slumping, pulling her knees up to her chest. "Are we gonna be *boat* people now? I can't grow anything here!"

Linus said, "We could always—" He stopped when Arthur touched his wrist, shaking his head. "What?"

"Children," Arthur said. "You have a new assignment. Without our help, I want you to come up with a way to get back to the island." He glanced at Lucy, whose red eyes narrowed. "The person who comes up with the best idea will get a reward."

A little manipulative? Sure. But even then, it didn't work. Lucy stayed in the box, eyes burning.

"We could paddle," Phee said. "Might take forever, but it would work."

Theodore spread his wings, offering to ferry each person back to the island by carrying them, but then decided that would make him like Merle, and he settled back down, cleaning his scales with a forked tongue.

As the other children gave their ideas ("I have wings," Phee pointed out, "so I could just leave you all here"), Linus bumped

Arthur's shoulder and nodded toward David, who held his captain's hat in front of him, fidgeting nervously.

"David," Arthur called over the noise. "Did you have an idea?"

David cringed, dropping the hat, when everyone turned to look at him. He bent over, picked it up, and said, "Um. I could . . . turn the water into blocks of ice and we could all walk back?"

"That's a good idea," Linus said. "What do you all think?"

Sal and Phee looked at each other and nodded, and then Sal said, "Kids-only meeting. No adults allowed."

"And where are we supposed to go?" Linus asked. "We're in the middle of the ocean."

"Cover your ears and say *la la la* really loud," Talia suggested. "It's what I do when you tell me to do anything."

"We know," Arthur assured her. "Seeing as how you do it right in front of us. Proceed with your meeting. Linus and I will *la la la* with the best of them."

Sal glanced at the angry boy in the box. "Lucy, that means you too. Come on, man. We need you."

Grumbling under his breath, Lucy emerged from the box, stomping over to the others. He stopped next to Phee, arms still folded across his chest.

As the children held their congress, heads close together (with Lucy becoming more involved as it went on), Linus and Arthur covered their ears and shouted, "*LA LA LA.*"

It didn't take long. From what Arthur could tell, everyone had input, including David. Sal made sure of it, giving him a chance to speak before letting the others have their say. Lucy seemed to have forgotten his momentary need to be upset in a box, but Arthur knew it was only a matter of time before Lucy brought it up again, and rightly so. He needed to think hard about what he'd say to Lucy when the time came.

The children reached an agreement, Sal making them all put their hands in the middle. David was last, his white paw on top. That is, until Lucy pulled his hand out from near the bottom and slapped his on top of David's. They stared at each other, Lucy looking smug.

Arthur was about to warn Lucy to play fair, but then David did something unexpected. He lifted his other hand, extended a single claw, and then pressed it gently against Lucy's nose, dimpling his skin. "Boop."

Lucy gaped at him as Linus and Arthur did their best to smother their laughter.

"On three," Sal said. "One. Two. Three!"

"We're not gonna die!" the children all shouted, raising their hands into the sky.

"We figured it out," Sal said as the other children nodded around him. "A way to get us all back that won't be boring."

"I feel like that shouldn't have been part of whatever you considered," Linus said.

"Well, it was," Phee said. "Which is why we've gone with Lucy's idea."

Arthur blinked. "I beg your pardon? David, did you not make the case for your proposal?"

David smiled suddenly, his gaze flicking over Arthur's shoulder. It was an odd smile, a little crooked, with a hint of fangs behind it. "I did. And then Lucy said something that sounded like more fun."

"Oh? And what would that be?"

The sky darkened above them, as if the clouds had hidden the sun away. Before Arthur could look up, the boat began to move slightly away from the island as if getting pulled, the motion causing Linus to grab Arthur to keep from falling. "What the . . ." Linus said, turning to look up at the sun, shielding his eyes. "I do hope that's not a . . . rain . . . cloud. Lucy."

"Yes, Linus?" Said in picture-perfect innocence.

"Question, if I may: Do you know anything about the giant tidal wave heading straight for us?"

Arthur said, "The giant *what*?" He whirled around, and there, towering high in the sky, a massive wave of seawater, at least four stories tall, the top capped with white like the snowy peak of a mountain. It rushed toward them, a roar building to bone-shaking levels, the boat picking up speed from the pull of the wave.

"Hang on, everybody!" Lucy screamed, sounding far too happy at their impending deaths.

Linus moved before Arthur did, grabbing Talia and Lucy in his arms and plunking down in the middle of the rowboat, the front of which was already rising at a low angle as the wave got closer and closer. Sal pulled Theodore from his shoulder, tucking him under his arm as Phee and David dove for the box. Sitting down in front of Linus, Sal held Theodore in his lap, both of them looking up at the wave with bright eyes.

"Chauncey!" Arthur shouted, reaching for him as the boat tilted back and back and *back,* the cooler flipping end over end into the sea.

"I got this!" Chauncey cried. As Arthur looked on in amazement, Chauncey sucked in a deep breath, his chest (or, rather, what *might* be his chest) expanding until he looked like he had swallowed a beach ball. Then he deflated with a forceful exhalation, his entire body (sans eyes) becoming thin as a piece of paper. One tentacle shot out to the front of the rowboat, wrapping around the hull. His other tentacle reached for the rear, latching on tightly. A strong gust of wind hit him square in the chest, and Chauncey giggled as he was lifted up from the rowboat, tentacles stretching, suction cups keeping him from floating away. He rose in the air above them, and it was then that Arthur saw what he was doing: Chauncey had turned himself into a parachute of sorts that cast a green tinge down upon them.

Just when Arthur thought they would tip over, they reached the crest of the wave, water spraying in their faces, blinding them, Lucy shrieking in joy, his hands above his head as Linus tried to keep him from falling overboard. The hurricane around them suddenly stopped as if a switch had flipped, and Arthur opened his eyes and leaned over the side of the rowboat.

They were flying.

They were *flying.*

The sea was at least fifty feet below them, the rowboat slicing through the air as Chauncey rode the tailwind toward the island.

He was still laughing, sounding almost hysterical as the tidal wave collapsed beneath them with a tremendous splash. "Holy freaking *crap!*" he called down. "I didn't think that would work!"

David and Phee poked their heads out of the box. "Are we still alive?" David asked.

"Again!" Lucy cried, bouncing on Linus's lap. "Again!"

"Never again," Linus said, his face doing a remarkable impression of Chauncey's natural color. "I don't think I could survive another—"

They all screamed when the rowboat suddenly dropped ten feet, Arthur's stomach rising to his throat.

"Uh-oh," Chauncey said, stalks shriveling until his eyes rested on top of his head. "The wind is slowing down again. I'm sorry, we're going to crash and probably die horribly. I love you guys."

Theodore chirped and clicked excitedly, head bobbing up and down.

Arthur suddenly grinned. "You're right, Theodore. He *is* porous!"

"Rude!" Chauncey cried as they dropped another five feet. "I'm trying my best!"

Theodore leapt from his perch on Sal, landing on the floor of the rowboat. He turned his head left, then right before wiggling his body as he crouched low, tail flicking behind him. Without hesitation, he shot his head up toward Chauncey, scales flashing with light as he opened his maw, rows of fangs on display as his tongue pulled back. Green fire bloomed from the wyvern, a blinding burst of flame that slammed into Chauncey, inflating him once more.

"Ooh," Chauncey said with a wet giggle. "That *tickles*."

"Well done, you," Arthur said, patting Theodore between the wings on his back as the wyvern continued to breathe fire into his brother.

Linus decided it was time to vomit over the side of the rowboat, Talia rubbing his back, thanking him for feeding Frank and the rest of the fishes. When he sat back down, his face was white and slick with sweat, or possibly seawater. Or both. In a weak voice, he said, "We can't tell the inspector we turned Chauncey into a hot-air balloon and had him fly us home. I shudder to think how *that* would look in a report."

"But you said we could be whatever we wanted," Phee reminded him. "Why would you take this away from Chauncey?"

Linus sighed. "I did say that, didn't I? New house rule. Chauncey can be a hot-air balloon if he wishes, but only in present company, not excluding Zoe."

"Or Helen," David said.

"Or Helen," Linus agreed.

"Or J-Bone," Lucy said. "Because if you think I'm not going to tell him about this the next time I go to the record store, you're out of your damn mind."

Linus closed his eyes and smiled weakly. "Yes. That's something I tell myself constantly."

They landed on the beach, the rowboat hitting the sand with a rattle that caused them all to stumble. Theodore pulled back his fire, and Chauncey withered as he floated toward the beach, dropping the last couple of feet into the sand.

Linus crawled over the side of the rowboat, lying on his back in the sand, pulling piles of sand over to him and hugging them. "Oh, ground. My sweet, sweet ground. I'll never take you for granted again."

"Children," Arthur said as they all picked themselves up. "What did we learn from today's adventure?"

"Grapes aren't very filling," Chauncey said. "Because I'm hungry."

"Too right," Arthur said, sitting on the bench seat as his fiancé continued to extoll the virtues of land. "Next time, we'll pack sandwiches. Phee?"

"I learned that Lucy can make tidal waves," Phee said. "I didn't think he could. I told him as much, so. You know. My bad."

Arthur arched an eyebrow.

"Oh, please," Phee said. "Like we were *actually* about to die."

"Hmm. I'll allow it. Talia, you're up."

She stroked her beard thoughtfully. "I learned that even though fish have thoughts, I'll still eat them because I like how they taste in my mouth."

"Fascinating. I appreciate your candor. Theodore?"

Theodore lay on his back on the bottom of the rowboat, feet kicking in the air. Sal grabbed him by the ankles, lifting him up, letting the wyvern chirp in Arthur's face.

"Wonderful," Arthur said. "Your ingenuity in using your fire undoubtedly saved us all from plummeting toward certain death. I am so very impressed by your thought process. Sal, your turn."

"We figured it out on our own," Sal said with a twinkle in his eye, Theodore on his shoulder, as per usual. "We were in trouble, and we found a way to solve the problem."

"With a *tidal wave*," Linus groused, his legs and hips now completely covered in sand. Then, "Not bad, per se, just one I wouldn't have opted for as I don't like seeing my life flash before my eyes."

"You thought for yourselves," Arthur said. "And not only that, you put a plan into action and as Sal said, saw it through to the end. You are to be commended, even if I question the usefulness of a tidal wave over, say, David's idea for blocks of ice. David, what did you learn?"

"That you're all so weird," David said, panting, eyes wide. "And I *like* it."

"Thank you," Arthur said. "You're also weird, and we like *you*, so it appears we're on the same page. Lucy? I'm curious to find out what you learned."

Lucy scowled at him. "I bet you are. Going to tell me something else I can't do?"

Fair, though it stung. "It seems that you and I need to have a chat."

"Damn right we do," he grumbled. "And I learned another way to make Linus throw up. By my count, that's twelve different ways now that I can—"

"Thirteen," Talia said. "Remember when Sal got a spot, and

you wanted to be like him so you covered your entire face in leaking pimples?"

Linus groaned on the beach.

He knew. The moment he saw Zoe and Helen waiting for them on the porch, he knew. It wasn't the expression on Zoe's face—the worried look that she covered up as soon as she saw them. It wasn't anything Helen did, sitting next to her, her own face carefully blank. No, it wasn't either of those things, though they did add to the feeling of unease that crashed over him, not unlike an errant tidal wave.

It was the white manila folder sitting between them on the step. He'd seen such folders before, when Linus had received his classified instructions from DICOMY. Rowder hadn't wasted any time.

"How'd it go?" Zoe asked with a small smile. "You wouldn't happen to know anything about a giant wave that almost crashed into the island, would you?"

"I have no idea what you're talking about," Lucy muttered, stomping up the stairs and slamming the door shut behind him.

"Uh-oh," Helen said.

"He all right?" Zoe asked.

David wilted, kicking the ground with his hairy feet. "He's mad at me because—I didn't mean to—I was just trying to—"

"Hey, man," Sal said. "You don't need to do that. It's nothing you did. Trust me when I say he'll get over it."

David scowled. "You don't know that."

"But I do," Arthur said. "David, if we felt you had done something wrong, we would've talked to you about it. I know it's easier said than done, but let us worry about Lucy." He glanced at the others. "Why don't you all go inside and change? We'll have an early supper tonight."

"It better not be Frank," Talia muttered, drawing a finger across her throat. She followed the others up the stairs and into the house.

Once Arthur was sure they weren't listening in, he turned back to Zoe and said, "To answer your question, Lucy is in a bit of a snit at the moment, but to be fair, I don't think he can be blamed for it. That rests upon me. I'll see to it shortly." He glanced pointedly down at the folder, only then noticing there were two rather than one. "I assume that's what we've been waiting for?"

"It is," Helen said. "I was also sent a notice."

Linus groaned. "What on earth is DICOMY planning now?"

Helen picked up one of the folders, showing the front to Arthur and Linus. It was addressed to the MAYOR OF MARSYAS. In the top left corner, the official DICOMY stamp: a circle with two hands joined in the middle, one young, one older. Helen pulled out a single sheet of paper and began to read. "Dear Mayor Webb, this letter serves you with notice that an official Department in Charge of Magical Youth investigation will take place beginning the third week of June at Marsyas Island Orphanage. As a duly elected civil servant of the nearest city and/or town, we ask that you disallow any interruption to said investigation. Any and all attempts to keep the DICOMY inspector from completing their assignment will be met with the full force of the law, up to and including fines and incarceration. Have a pleasant day! With sincerity, Jeanine Rowder, Interim Head of the Department in Charge of Magical Youth and the Department in Charge of Magical Adults." She put the letter back in the folder.

"It sounds as if they're expecting trouble," Linus said.

"We figured they would," Helen said. "More and more magical people are finding sanctuary in the village, even if it's only temporary. It was only a matter of time before that got back to the government."

"And the other folder?" Arthur asked.

Zoe shrugged. "Even shorter, if you can believe that. I figured you wouldn't mind if I opened it. Says what you expect. Inspector arriving next week. Wednesday." She made a face. "And that any attempts to deceive the inspector will result in the immediate removal of the children."

"What recourse do we have?" Linus asked, sounding rather helpless. "Are we just supposed to let whoever they send tromp through our home? And can we really trust everyone in the village not to make a mess of things?"

Helen laughed. "I think you'll find help in the unlikeliest places." She leaned forward, elbows on her knees, eyes sparkling. "A gaggle of reporters are in the village, all clamoring to get to the island. Merle didn't make it easier."

Arthur huffed out a laugh. "Upped the prices again, did he? How much is he attempting to charge?"

Helen shook her head. "Not that, Arthur. He told them that he wouldn't take them across. Said—and I quote—'Why the hell would little ones need to talk to reporters? You damned vultures. You'll never step foot on my ferry!'"

"He did *not*," Linus said, sounding just as shocked as Arthur felt.

"He did," Helen said gleefully. "Didn't know the old coot had it in him. Should have seen the looks on the reporters' faces. You'd have thought they'd never been told no before."

"We're not alone," Arthur said, voice strong, sure. "Let them send their inspector. They will find this is not a dark and dangerous place, but a home. And those reporters may yet prove useful, should we require their services. Many things to consider, but for now, I'm feeling a bit peckish. Shall we?"

NINE

The following Monday afternoon—with only two days remaining until the arrival of the inspector—Arthur Parnassus sat in his bedroom in a high-backed chair, one leg folded over the other, his hands in his lap. Through the open window, he could hear Talia muttering to her plants in the garden. Every now and then, the guttural tones of Gnomish changed to singing, a low hum that rose and fell. In the background, the crash of waves and the calls of the birds over the cliffs.

Across from Arthur, in his own chair, Lucy lay upside down, his legs up the back, head hanging off the edge. He hadn't yet spoken, arms folded across his chest, glaring at Arthur with red eyes.

"By my count, this is our sixty-sixth meeting," Arthur said, breaking the heavy silence. "Strange how quickly time passes when you aren't paying attention to it."

Lucy rolled his eyes and said nothing.

"Are we going to sit on the chair as it's meant to be sat upon, or not today?"

Lucy yawned. Not today, it seemed.

"How are the spiders in your brain?"

Lucy shrugged.

"Ah, lost your voice, have you? I do hope you find it. I happen to like it when you talk."

Lucy made a rude sound with his tongue between his teeth.

Arthur tilted his head. "Something on your mind?"

Lucy rolled over, climbing to his knees. He pointed a finger at Arthur and growled, "You *lied* to me."

"That's a very serious accusation," Arthur said.

"You told me I didn't have to be a monster like everyone thought. That I could do *anything* I wanted." He sat back down on his heels, his fierce glower trained on Arthur.

"I did say that, yes. And it's just as true today."

Lucy scoffed. "Then why did you tell David he could be a monster if he wanted? Why should one person get to be one way, and another can't? How is *that* fair?"

"You're right, it's not," Arthur said. "And I apologize for that, Lucy. It presented the notion of a double standard, and that wasn't my intent." He mulled over his own words for a moment. "But none of your ire should be toward David. He's innocent in all of this, and I won't have you—"

"If he's so innocent, then why does he want to scare people? I do, too, but everyone says *I'm* not innocent. Why'd you tell him one thing but told me something else?"

"Fair," Arthur said carefully. "And something I'd like to discuss with you, if you're up for it."

"So you can trick me?" Lucy said with a scowl. "Make me think everything is fine when it's not?"

"Have I ever done that?"

Lucy didn't respond for a long while. Eventually, he slumped farther in his chair and muttered, "First time for everything."

"I'm sorry that I caused you to feel that way," Arthur said. "It was certainly not my intention, but it happened regardless." He folded his hands in front of him on the desk. "I think that out of all of us, David will look to you the most."

Lucy looked over at him. "Really? Why?"

"Because you're kin, in a way. Not by blood, nor am I speaking about brotherhood, though that's part of it. I see you as two sides of the same coin. I think you'll find that David looks to you to see what's right and what is wrong."

"Oh," Lucy said, face scrunching up. "That's... weird. Still doesn't mean I forgive you."

"I didn't think it would," Arthur assured him. "I've done something you think is unreasonable, and you have a point. Which brings me back to the coin. As I said, two sides of the same coin, and yet, you have your differences. David is a yeti. You are not."

"I'm the Antichrist," Lucy said.

"You are," Arthur said. And though it worried him immensely, he didn't stop himself from saying what was necessary. "If you'd like to reclaim that title, you can. We've talked about not using that word, given the connotations behind it, but I would be remiss if I didn't say that regardless of what others think, the title is yours to do with as you wish."

"What's stopping me from changing how others think?"

Gooseflesh sprouted across the back of Arthur's neck, cold and prickly. "Expound."

Lucy sat up once more, his tiny arms waving wildly. "People are scared of us. How we look. What we can do. They hate us because of it. If I wanted to, I could change all their minds just like *that*." He snapped once. "Make them believe like they should, that we're not scary and that we can do whatever we want."

"You could do that?" Arthur asked slowly.

"Think so," Lucy said, tapping his chin. "I think if I really tried, I could do anything I wanted to. Heck, I'm even trying to figure out how to teleport things, like rocks or a full-grown manatee."

"Let's continue with that thought," Arthur said. "Say you do exactly as you described. You force your will upon an unsuspecting populace. You tell yourself it's for the greater good, and it may very well be. Does that make it right?"

Lucy stared at Arthur with ancient eyes. "It'd make things easier."

"Perhaps," Arthur said. "But that doesn't answer my question. Even if your intentions are pure, does eradicating free will to get the end result *you* desire make your actions right?"

Lucy hesitated. "I... don't know?"

"And it's okay not to know," Arthur said. "It comes back to the idea of moral relativism."

Lucy groaned, sounding so much like Linus that Arthur grinned behind his hand.

"Yes, yes, it's terribly inconsiderate of me to spring philosophy on you. I will do better in the future. That being said, humor me. Please remind me what moral relativism is."

"The view that moral judgments are true or false only relative to some particular standpoint," Lucy intoned in a bored voice.

"Correct," Arthur said. "And the argument against?"

"There is no guidance as to what is right or wrong."

"You got it in one." Arthur shifted in his seat, uncrossing his legs. "In this situation, you have people who believe you are something to be feared. On the flip side, you have others who believe you're an intelligent seven-year-old boy with spiders in his brain and a penchant for music. Who is correct?"

"The people who think I'm smart," Lucy said promptly.

"So everyone who believes the opposite is incorrect?"

"Ye-es?" Lucy said, sounding unsure.

"But if we use moral relativism, the argument would be that those who are afraid of you are correct because that's what *they* believe. And that's where it can get tricky. Because if morality is based upon personal desire, how can one find a truly objective moral ground and make the morally right decision?"

Lucy frowned. "So who's right and who's wrong?"

"Excellent question," Arthur said. "And one I don't know there's any single answer to. You told me once you thought humanity was weird, given that when we're not laughing, we're crying or running for our lives because monsters are trying to eat us."

"And they don't even have to be real monsters," Lucy said. "They could be the ones we make up in our heads."

"Precisely. But if you were to take away those monsters—either real or imaginary—by imposing your wants and whims upon those who fear you, what would they have learned?"

"Nothing," Lucy said begrudgingly.

"That's right," Arthur said with a nod. "They wouldn't have learned anything because they were never given the chance. That's why free will is important. It gives us the potential to change minds."

"But why is that up to us?" Lucy asked. "Why do *we* have to be the bigger people and teach them? Shouldn't that be their responsibility?"

"In a perfect world, yes," Arthur said. "They would endeavor to dismantle their prejudices and welcome those who are different with open arms. But we don't live in such a world, and we must do what we can with what we have." He leaned forward. "However, you are correct. It *shouldn't* be up to us to prove we are not a threat. And yet, we find ourselves in the unenviable position of having to do exactly that. Which brings me back to the idea of monsters. Though you may be two sides of that same coin, you and David have your own individual paths to travel. When I told David he could be a monster, it wasn't because he wanted to harm people. It was because he feels that people can find joy in fear, so long as no one gets hurt."

Lucy's eyes flashed. "*I* don't want to hurt people." He paused, considering. "Okay, *some* people, but I don't do it, not all the time."

Arthur held up his hand. "I never said you did. I know you better than that, Lucy. And though I wish it didn't have to be said again, it does, because I apparently haven't done a very good job of explaining. You can be whoever you want, so long as you remember that free will is paramount, even if you don't agree with the choices of others."

Lucy eyed him slyly. "What if I don't become who you want me to be?"

Arthur expected this. Pushing up against perceived boundaries, testing how far they could stretch. All the children did this at one point or another. It went back to what Arthur had said during the hearing, about children being told no and immediately asking why. "I would love you just the same."

Lucy blinked in surprise. "Really? Why?"

"Because every single day, I see the good in you. I see your kindness, your mischievousness. Your wonder at the world around you. Though we may not always agree, nothing you could do would ever make me stop loving you."

Lucy tilted his head back, staring up at the ceiling. "It's hard."

"What is?"

"Being alive."

"It is," Arthur agreed. "But perhaps that's the point: the trials and tribulations of life weigh heavily upon us, but we find people to help lighten the load. It's why I know you'll be good for David. He needs help to carry all that sits upon his shoulders. And I can't think of a better person than you."

For a time, Lucy was silent. He looked out the window, his face bathed in golden light. Finally, he said, "Arthur?"

"Yes?"

"I love you too."

Arthur smiled as fire bloomed in his chest. "I know. Now, I think that's enough for today. I heard a rumor that you acquired a new record in our absence. I would like to hear what you and J-Bone discovered."

Lucy jumped from the chair, wiggling in excitement. "It's Fats Domino! I'll go get it and let you listen to the righteous jam that is 'I'm Walkin'.'"

And they did just that. As the afternoon wore on, Fats Domino wailed about walkin', yes indeed, and I'm talkin' about you and me, I'm hopin' that you'll come back to me.

That night, with all the children tucked safely in bed—Lucy having decided he and David needed to have a sleepover in David's room—Arthur finished his evening routine and found Linus sitting up in bed, resting against the headboard. The comforter was gathered around his lap, Calliope sitting on top and watching Arthur's every step.

"Lucy seems to have had a change of heart." Linus shivered. "I hope that doesn't mean we'll be woken up in the middle of the night because the house is falling down around us."

Arthur climbed up on the bed, scratching Calliope behind the ears and kissing Linus on the cheek before mirroring his position on the bed, their shoulders brushing together. "I don't think it was jealousy, not exactly. More that he felt I was treating David differently."

"By telling him he could be a monster."

"Yes," Arthur said, tapping his head against the headboard. "It was, at the very least, hypocritical of me."

"As much as I hate to admit it, Rowder might have had a point," Linus said, scrubbing a hand over his face. Calliope reached out a paw, laying it on Linus's wrist. Absentmindedly, he resumed stroking her back. "About moral duty. What responsibility do we have?"

"The same as any parent or guardian," Arthur said. "We show David the difference between right and wrong and allow him to grow to make decisions for himself."

"What happens if he makes the wrong one? And what if he has an effect on the other children? I'm not sure telling him that he could be a monster was the right course of action. We should show him how to be a good person rather than giving in to baser instincts, the same as we do with Lucy."

Arthur felt a low rumble of discomfort. He knew what Linus was trying to say, but it sat wrong with him. "Baser instincts? Linus, he is a *yeti*. It's part of who he is. Just because you don't necessarily understand doesn't give you the right to try to take that away from him." It came out sounding rather snappish, and an apology attempted to follow, but he kept it from spilling from his mouth. He couldn't always apologize when things turned slightly uncomfortable—a habit he still found himself struggling to overcome, a by-product of being under the thumb of DICOMY.

"*Me?*" Linus said in a huff as Calliope glared at Arthur. "I thought it was *we*."

"There is a *we*," Arthur said. "Always. But for all that you are and all that you've done, you can never understand what it's like for them, for *us*. You can appreciate the issues and want to help, but you've never had to walk in our shoes."

"Oh dear," Linus said as Calliope tilted her head back to look up at him. "That wasn't my intent. I apologize."

"I know it wasn't. But we must think about *intent* more than most, given our wards. After all, the road to hell is paved with good intentions."

Linus sighed as Calliope rolled onto her back, yawning, her little fangs on full display. "Then how am I supposed to be a good father? How can I help them if I can't relate to them?"

"By being there for them," Arthur said. "And listening. You've proved more than adept at both, but I think it doesn't hurt to have a reminder every now and then. No, you can't know what they—*we've* been through because you haven't experienced it for yourself. And I'm grateful for that. You want to protect them. In that regard, you're no different from me. But I'm reminded of a time when you told me that keeping the children secluded on the island benefited no one."

"I did say that, didn't I?"

"You did," Arthur said. "And you were right, even if it was hard to hear at the time. You showed me that no matter my intent, it was causing more harm than good. That I didn't necessarily need to trust the world outside, but that I needed to trust the *children* because they're stronger than even I gave them credit for."

"And it's part and parcel of being a parent," Linus said slowly, picking up the thread Arthur had started. "To know when it's time to step back and let them make their own decisions."

"Precisely," Arthur said, taking Linus's hand in his, fingers intertwining. "The best we can do is to be there to help them celebrate their victories and to pick them back up when they get knocked down." He laughed quietly. "I'm sure this is a problem faced by most parents since time immemorial. To know when the time is right to let the little birds leave the nest and fly on their own."

"Most parents don't have the children we do," Linus said.

"No, they don't. We're lucky that way, I guess."

"Still. I am sorry."

Arthur lifted Linus's hand, lips brushing against warm skin.

"And I accept, not to avoid further argument but because I know you're still learning, same as me. We have to trust Lucy, like we have to trust all of them. And then we have to do the scariest thing of all: step back and hope for the best."

"Can you do that?" Linus asked without censure. It was simple curiosity born of knowing Arthur better than anyone else, aside from Zoe.

Arthur chuckled. "Time will tell. I hope so, but then I see something that reminds me the world has teeth, and it feels like I'm back at square one." He paused, considering. Then, "Can I tell you a secret?"

Linus squeezed his hand as Calliope began to purr, a low sound that came in fits and starts. "Always."

"Part of me wants to let Lucy do what he said," Arthur admitted. "Allow him to impose his will on everyone. To change their minds, even if they don't want it. It would make things easier."

"It would," Linus said. "But I think you know it'd be a hollow victory, one that we'd have to live with for the rest of our days."

"I know. But despite that, I can't help but think it would be a victory all the same. And what makes it worse is I know DICOMY is trying to do the same: to impose their will upon the populace to get them to fall in line."

"So what do we do?"

"We live," Arthur said.

"And if they try and take our children from us?"

"Then we fight."

On a Tuesday afternoon in summer—the sun high, nary a cloud in the blue, blue sky—the residents of Marsyas Island prepared for war. Or, rather, Linus and Arthur called them all together to attempt to *prevent* war, and grievous bodily harm if possible. Which was why they'd had the children scour their rooms for anything that might be construed as a weapon, or anything dangerous the inspector could use against them.

While they waited in the sitting room—listening to the cacophonous crashes coming from upstairs—Linus paced in front of the fireplace, hair sticking up at odd angles where he'd been running his hands through it. He glanced at Arthur, who sat in a chair, hands folded in his lap. "How are you so calm?" he demanded, hands on his hips. "Were you like this before I arrived?"

"I was a mess," Arthur said. "Frightened more than I'd been in a long time, same as I am now."

Linus blinked. "You didn't act like it."

Arthur tilted his head in acknowledgment. "Just because I didn't let you see it doesn't mean it wasn't there. And it didn't last long. Debating philosophy in the forest while you were in your explorer outfit changed my mind." He waggled his eyebrows. "Seeing you in those brown shorts was quite the distraction."

Linus sniffed. "I do fill them out, don't I? I'm surprised you were able to keep your hands off me."

"It was a monumental struggle," Arthur agreed.

"I suppose if there's hope for me, there is hope for anyone." Linus huffed out a breath. "But that doesn't mean you can flirt with the inspector like you did me. I doubt they'll be swayed by your wiles."

Arthur grinned. "Noted. Especially since the government seems to think I use my wiles to my advantage. To disabuse them of the notion, I will keep said wiles to myself."

"Let's not go *too* far. I happen to enjoy your wiles."

The first two children clomped down the stairs, Phee saying, "And that's why we made this for you. Don't worry about trying to memorize everything right away. Not even Arthur could do that. It'll take time."

David said, "And you're sure this will work?"

"Yeah," Phee said as they reached the bottom of the stairs. "It might seem a little complicated because it's not just about the sounds he makes, but the emotion *behind* the sounds. Thankfully, you have us. We'll all help you learn about different things. Like me with trees. Talia with her plants, Chauncey with the sea, Lucy with scary stuff—"

"What kind of scary stuff?" David asked excitedly as they came into the sitting room. In his hands, David held a ream of paper tied together with colorful yarn. Phee had a bag slung over her shoulder, which she set down near the entryway to the sitting room.

"Like blood and guts," she said. "He's good at all those things. Sal can help with almost everything else because he speaks better wyvern than even Arthur does. That's why they're best friends. When Sal first got here, he didn't talk very much. But Theodore took to him right away. Turns out, some types of wyverns thrive on empathy, and Theodore said Sal shone with it, brighter than almost anything."

David's eyes widened in anticipation. "Thrive on? Like . . . feed?"

Phee snorted. "Not like that, but that's a cool idea. We should tell them so they can act like that's what happens. It's more that they . . . bring the better parts of each other out. And it helped Sal find his voice to learn Theodore's." She paused, frowning. "I wonder if that's why Theodore can breathe fire now."

A pretty thought, and one that Arthur couldn't find fault with. Sal and Theodore rarely went anywhere without each other, and both had blossomed since their arrival on the island. Though Arthur knew he and the others had played a part in it, there was a truth to Phee's words. Theodore had done more for Sal than anyone else.

"What do you have there?" Arthur asked David.

"It's a translation book," David said. "To help me learn wyvern." He flipped through the pages, eyes darting side to side as he read. "Where's the section on curse words?"

Linus crossed his arms. "I doubt they would have put such a thing in—"

"In the back," Phee said. "Last three pages."

David gleefully flipped to the back of the book, smile widening as he read. After a moment, he lifted his head and said, "Click click *rawwwr*, clickety-click."

Linus lifted a hand to his throat. "Well, I *never*. We do *not* use such language in this house."

Phee snorted. "Keep telling yourself that."

"You made this?" Arthur asked Phee.

She shrugged, looking away with a scowl. "*I* didn't. We all did. Thought it would help. It's not a big deal."

"I think it is," Arthur said. "Whose idea was it?"

Phee rolled her eyes. "It was mine."

"I see. That was kind of you, Phee."

She flushed, her wings trembling as David continued to read, his face inches from the pages. A moment later, she leaned over and started pointing out tips and tricks she'd learned in her own quest to understand Theodore.

It wasn't long before they were joined by the rest of the household, each of the children bringing down their own bags, gathering in the entryway as Arthur rose from his chair. Linus joined him as Phee and David stood with the others, all waiting to see what Arthur would say next. Sal stood with his hands behind his back, Theodore perched on his shoulder.

"We've discussed what's going to happen starting tomorrow," Arthur said. "As we did with Linus, we will show our guest kindness and courtesy, and absolutely *no one* will make threats up to and including bodily harm and/or death."

Everyone looked at Lucy and Talia. "What?" Talia asked. "I'm a *gnome*. I'm supposed to be threatening. It's, like, my thing."

"Right there with you, sister from another mister," Lucy said. "Except I'm not a gnome, just the incarnation of evil."

"Be that as it may," Arthur said, "we don't want to run the risk of anything negative going into a report. As such, I expect all of you to be on your best behavior."

"And each of us must play our parts in order to keep David from being discovered," Linus said. "The inspector can't know he's here."

David raised his hand.

Amused, Arthur said, "Yes, David?"

"What if they see me? Will Lucy and Talia kill the inspector and bury them in the garden?"

"Yes," Lucy and Talia said together.

"*No*," Linus said loudly.

Theodore chirped and squeaked, spreading his wings.

"Don't tell me what he said!" David cried. "I want to figure it out on my own." He opened the book once more, flipping through the pages before stopping on one, eyes narrowing. "Hmm," he said. "So, if I've got this right, Theodore just said . . . um. Okay. He said . . . ah! He said that murder is legal, but only if you don't get caught." He squinted at the translation text. "Wait, that can't be right."

"There will be no killing," Linus said sternly. "Or maiming," he added as Lucy opened his mouth. "And David, if you are discovered, we will be right by your side. Though we want to avoid that if we can, we must prepare for any eventuality." He eyed each of the children warily. "It's why we've asked you to bring us anything that might be . . . misconstrued."

"You better not throw anything away," Lucy warned. "If you do, there is nowhere on this earth you could hide that I wouldn't find you."

"That threat worked better on me when I didn't know you liked footie pajamas," Linus said.

"That's because they have a flap for my butt cheeks," Lucy said. "Humanity's finest invention, next to music. If I grow up and decide to enslave the human race, I'll make footie pajamas mandatory for everyone."

"Until then," Arthur said, "we are on our best behavior. Show us what you brought. Theodore, let's start with you."

Theodore flew down from his perch on Sal's shoulder, tugging his bag over to Arthur's feet. Gripping the bottom of the sack, he upended it, spilling out its meager contents on the floor: a few of his baby fangs that had fallen out, a green rock that looked like an oversized arrowhead with a thin line of quartz through the middle, and a familiar brass button with teeth imprinted on it.

Linus bent over, scooping up the button, bouncing it in his hand. "Why is this dangerous?"

Phee translated for David as Theodore explained that if the inspector saw how much he loved the button, she might try to take it away. It had been done before, he said, and he thought that meant the inspector might try to do the same. It wasn't dangerous to *her*, but dangerous to *him* as he didn't want to lose one of his treasures.

Linus reached down and patted Theodore's head, the wyvern leaning into it, eyes fluttering shut. "I don't think they'd take your button, but if you feel strongly about it, I will carry it on my person at all times and return it to you once they leave. Deal?"

Deal, Theodore chirped.

Chauncey went next, deciding that a comprehensive explanation was needed for each of the items he presented, most of which were sharp seashells or sea glass he'd found buried in the sand. There was also a pile of pine cones. "It's not what it looks like," Chauncey said quickly as Arthur arched an eyebrow. "I'm just . . . collecting them. Yes, *collecting* them in order to make . . . a . . . pine cone . . . diorama?"

"Oof," Phee said. "That wasn't even remotely believable."

Chauncey groaned. "I can't even *lie* right." He threw up his tentacles. "Congratulations! You caught me. I eat pine cones after everyone goes to bed, but it's *fine,* I can stop whenever I want!"

"Of course you can," Linus said. "Phee?"

She turned over her own sack, the contents spilling out onto the floor. Her contribution was a bit more involved than Theodore's or Chauncey's, bits of driftwood and spiny leaves, along with an impressive dagger with a jeweled hilt that glittered in the light.

"Where did you get that?" Arthur asked.

"Won it playing cards," Phee said.

"What," Linus said.

She shrugged. "I'm good at Go Fish. You know how it is. J-Bone didn't believe me when I said no one had beaten me at Go Fish, so he bet his dagger. And then I kicked his ass."

"Phee," Linus said.

Theodore gripped the dagger in his claws, rolling over onto his back to bring the blade up to his face to inspect. His tongue snaked out, flicking against the jewels. He chirped three times, and Phee was immediately outraged. "What do you mean they're fake?"

"Talia," Arthur said. "You're up."

"I didn't bring any of my tools," she said, shuffling forward and picking up her bag. "They aren't weapons but implements of my trade. If the inspector has a problem with that, they can die mad about it."

"Noted," Arthur said.

Talia turned her bag over, and Arthur almost wished he could be surprised by what he saw, but he wasn't. At least a dozen glass bottles, small with fat, circular bases where liquid sloshed. Each bottle had the same design drawn onto it: a skull and crossbones.

"Is that poison?" Linus asked, aghast.

"It is," Talia said. "Of my own concoction, and I grew all the ingredients myself. Hemlock, deadly nightshade, white snakeroot, with a pinch of cinnamon for taste. According to my calculations, it should take only thirty seconds before anal leakage starts, quickly followed by leakage from everywhere else."

"Anal leakage?" David asked with wide eyes, hands going back to cover his rear.

"That sounds like the name of a band," Lucy said. "Ladies and gentlemen, presenting . . . Anal Leakage! Guess what kind of music we'd play?"

Linus sighed. "Gospel."

"Nope! Gos—oh. Yeah. That's right."

"Are you stalling, Lucy?" Arthur asked mildly. "I see that it's your turn."

"Ha!" he said. "I have no problem turning anything over, because Linus said if we try, anything can happen."

Linus smiled. "That's exactly right, Lucy. Thank you for—"

"Which means *anything* can be a weapon if you try hard enough." He began to tick off his fingers. "Spoons. A flight of stairs. Sinkholes. Peanut butter. Air."

"*Lucy*," Linus warned.

"What? It's true!"

"Be that as it may, we do *not* use sinkholes or peanut butter as weapons. Funnily enough, we've talked about this very thing. Twice." He shook his head. "At least Sal doesn't have poison or death by spoon on his mind."

Sal fidgeted.

Arthur cleared his throat pointedly.

Sal made a face and then pulled out his hands from behind his back. Arthur almost laughed when Linus started to splutter in shock. "Is that—where did you—*why* did you—is that a *sword*?"

It was. A long, flat blade with a wooden hilt wrapped in red fabric. It looked heavy, but Sal held on to it tightly.

"How?" Linus asked helplessly.

"J-Bone's kind of bad at cards," Sal explained, scratching the back of his neck. "He said he could beat me at Old Maid. Turns out he couldn't."

"Arthur?"

"Yes, Linus?"

"Why is the owner of the record store giving our children weapons?"

"Because he's not very good at cards," Arthur explained. "He should really practice more before making bets against others. Lucy, it's your turn."

Lucy sighed dramatically before scooping up his bag. Without looking away from Linus, he tipped the bag over, spilling out its contents. A small ax. An aerosol spray can with what appeared to be a lighter attached in front of the nozzle. A throwing star. A garrote. Last but certainly not least, three red tubes with black wicks sticking out the top.

"Is that dynamite?" Arthur asked.

Lucy lit up. "I'm so glad you asked! It *is* dynamite. I was saving it for something special, like when we need to get rid of a body but then Talia hurts her hand and can't dig a grave so I suggest blowing it up instead and everyone agrees and then I get to light the dynamite and run and *voilà*! No more body to worry about."

"Wow," Talia said. "That was impressive. I'm on Team Lucy."

"Me too," David said.

"And me!" Chauncey said, jumping up and down. "I want to blow up someone's body!"

"I bet it'll rain organs," Phee said. "Cloudy with a chance of lungs."

"See?" Lucy asked, a picture of perfect innocence. "It's not just me."

"Be that as it may," Arthur said, "we aren't going to be blowing up anyone."

"*Thank* you, Arthur," Linus said, frowning down at Lucy.

"At least not until the inspector has left," Arthur continued. "I don't think I need to impress on any of you how serious this is. As unfair as it can seem, our future rests in the hands of whoever DICOMY will be sending. I expect each of you to be on your best behavior. Lucy, that includes you."

"Why does it sound like you trust the process?" Sal asked.

Arthur blinked in surprise. "Explain, if you please."

Sal shrugged awkwardly, and Theodore muttered in his ear. Sal nodded along with whatever Theodore was saying. By the time the wyvern finished, Sal looked determined. "You're making it seem like we have to bend over backwards for DICOMY. That if we try hard enough, they'll believe us when we say this place is safe and where we want to be."

"Why wouldn't that be the case?" Linus asked.

"Why should we do anything for them?" Sal asked. "If they're so worried about what we're capable of, shouldn't they bend over backwards for *us*? Why is it on our shoulders to prove anything? We're kids."

"You are," Arthur agreed. He looked at each of the children in turn. "I wish I had a better answer. If I could shield you from this, I would."

"But since he can't," Linus said, "it's up to us. We'll show DICOMY they picked the wrong family to trifle with. If push comes to shove, they won't know what hit them." He bent over, scooping up a stick of dynamite, gripping it tightly. "Trust me on that. I'll stick this where the sun doesn't shine."

"Ooh," Lucy whispered. "That made me feel tingly." He rushed forward, wrapping himself around Linus's leg, tilting his head back. "Even though it was my idea, I'll let you be the one to light it."

"A perfect gentleman," Linus said, patting the top of his head.

"So you see, children," Arthur said. "They may have the strength of the government behind them, but we have each other. I think DICOMY will find themselves extremely outmatched. Come, now. Let's clean up this mess and prepare for tomorrow."

For the rest of the day, they scoured the house, looking for anything that could be used against them. Sal and Theodore put plastic plugs into each of the outlets, lest Lucy decide to stick a fork in one again, just to see what would happen. David, Chauncey, and Lucy were tasked with putting soft covers on every sharp corner. Phee and Talia took to their jobs with gusto, growing flowers and leafy vines over the exterior cellar doors to make them appear as if they hadn't been opened in ages, but not so much that David couldn't escape through them should the need arise.

At midday, Zoe called from Helen's shop, speaking with Arthur and letting him know she'd be back on the island the following morning before their guest arrived. "Helen will bring them out."

"Are you sure?" Arthur asked. "Linus or I could do it. Helen doesn't need to make more trouble for herself than she already has."

She chuckled. "Too late for that, don't you think?"

"I'm—"

"If you apologize again, I'm going to scream. Helen offered. I accepted. Simple as that. Get with it, Parnassus. DICOMY doesn't get to decide what a family should look like, or how a home should be. It's high time they remember that, and that we're not afraid of them."

"I am," Arthur admitted. "Very much so."

"Do you trust me?"

"You know I do."

"Good," Zoe said. "Because I have a few tricks up my sleeve, ones they won't see coming. Consider it a last resort should things go south."

"That certainly sounds disturbing. I approve."

That night, after a subdued supper, Linus made a decision. He stood from the table, telling the children to clean up the kitchen, and that he'd be back shortly. Just as Sal and David finished washing the last of the dishes, Linus popped his head back in, ordering them all to change into their pajamas and to meet him at the front door.

Upstairs, Arthur asked, "Just what are you up to?"

Linus looked up from his half-buttoned sleep shirt. "You'll see. It isn't much, but I think it'll be enough to distract them, at least for a little while. Hopefully, they'll sleep through the night."

Arthur snorted as he patted Calliope on the head. She sat on the bed, tail twitching behind her, eyes tracking Linus's every movement. "Have you met them?"

Back downstairs, the children had gathered near the front door, each wearing their striped pajamas, aside from Theodore.

"Ready?" Linus asked, pushing his way through the children to the door.

"Are we going to sleep in the forest?" Lucy asked, tugging on his pant leg. "I've always wanted to see if there were night monsters. I bet they're big with fangs and claws and filled with rage that only subsides when sucking out the marrow from the bones of unsuspecting—"

"There will be no marrow sucking," Linus said sternly.

Lucy hung his head, shoulders slumped. "Yet another thing we can't do with bones. What's the point of even *having* bones if we don't get to play with them?"

"We won't be going into the forest," Linus said. "I have something different in mind. Single file, children! You are responsible for the person in front of you. Should we arrive at our destination with a missing member, the person whose job it was to ensure their safety will be lucky enough to listen to me regale them with stories about— Well, then. I don't think I've *ever* seen you get in line that fast before."

"You know how to threaten with the best of them," Sal told him.

"I do try," Linus said. "Follow me!"

He led the way, crickets chirping loudly as the sun ignited the horizon in shades of red and orange and pink. The first stars had started to shine, and the moon looked like a translucent ghost haunting the western skies.

They followed Linus along the side of the house, heading toward Talia's garden. Ever the courteous gnome, she stopped them every few seconds to discuss the latest trends in horticulture, including a study she'd read in *Gardening Science Monthly* that said plants responded more favorably when sung to.

Talia saw them first: the twinkling fairy lights that had been draped along the railing of the gazebo. The wooden floor was covered in at least a dozen pillows and what appeared to be almost every blanket in the house. In the corner, the small portable Zenith record player, spinning dead-people music in the form of Buddy Holly, singing if you knew Peggy Sue, you'd know why he felt blue without Peggy, his Peggy Sue.

"Is this for us?" David asked, looking around with wide eyes.

"It is," Linus said. "Tonight, I thought we should be together. The next two weeks are going to be busy for all of us, and we should have a night when the only thing we have to worry about is Chauncey's night gas."

"I'm biologically unique!" Chauncey exclaimed to no one in particular.

Talia went to the blankets and pillows first, moving them around until she'd made a perfect nest for herself. Theodore did the same, a bigger one for him and Sal. Lucy decided that Phee needed to be brained with a pillow. Unfortunately for him, Phee proved to be quicker, flying up and over Lucy, landing behind him, and then snatching the pillow from his hands. Before he could turn around, she swung the pillow at the back of his head, sending him sprawling onto the floor.

"Do me!" David cried.

Naturally, Phee obliged.

Which then dissolved into a pillow fight to end all pillow fights. By the time the battle had ended, goose feathers floated around them as Lucy screamed he gave up when Theodore tried to shove a pillow down his throat. Linus lay on his back on the floor of the gazebo, breathing heavily, wiping the sweat from his brow.

"That went well," Arthur said, standing above him and looking down, head cocked.

"Too . . . old . . . to . . . function," Linus wheezed, face red, hair plastered against his forehead.

"Ah, well, you certainly didn't act like it," Arthur said. "I don't think I've ever seen a grown man hurl a pillow at a child with as much force as you did."

"We should tell that to the inspector," Lucy said as he peered over his shoulder, trying to look at the flap on the seat of his pajamas. "I bet they'll find it hysterical without holding it against us."

"Or," Linus said, rolling over onto his stomach, "we don't do that at all and instead attempt to act at least a *little* normal so that we don't make . . . things . . . worse."

"Children," Arthur said, "it's time to settle in. Make sure you . . . David? Is there an issue?"

David stood near the steps to the gazebo, gripping the railing with one hand, the other balled into a fist. He tried to smile, but it came out as a grimace. "I . . . uh." He looked away, gnawing on his bottom lip. "It can be kind of hard for me to sleep when it's not cold. Is it okay if I make some ice for me?"

"Way ahead of you," Linus said, pushing himself up off the floor. "Here, look." He motioned for David to move to the right side of the gazebo, near where Lucy and Talia were sitting. Linus lifted up one of the blankets. There, underneath, were rows of frozen ice packs, each about six inches wide, nearly a foot long. The blanket had a zipper along the side, and when Linus opened it so David could see the interior, more ice packs jutted out.

David reached out and touched the corner of one of the ice packs.

"I know you can make your own ice," Linus said. "But I thought I'd help out a little in case you were tired. If you need something, all you have to do is ask."

"Except if it's a chainsaw," Lucy said, lying on his back, kicking his feet above him.

Arthur said, "Children, that's enough chatter. Settle in, and we'll see whose turn it is to tell a story."

"It's *mine*!" Chauncey yelled, eyes poking up through a pile of blankets he was hidden under. "I didn't get to do it last time because Lucy took too long reenacting his favorite exorcisms."

Arthur shook his head. "By my count, it's actually Phee's turn. Chauncey, last time, you told the devastatingly beautiful story of how you fell in love, only to realize your affections weren't returned because the object of said affections was a rock."

"Rocky Stonesworth," Chauncey said sadly.

"So," Arthur continued, "it's up to Phee to send us off into dreamland. Let's give her our undivided attention, and as a reminder to the more vocal members of the audience, commentary is frowned upon, even if you think it's amusing."

"He's talking about *you*," Talia said, shoving Lucy.

He shoved her back. "He is *not*. I bet I can be quieter longer than you can."

Talia and Lucy settled down with the rest of the children—save Phee, who stood above them, the sun finally dipping below the horizon. Her wings glittered in the semidarkness, her hair hanging loosely on her shoulders. She waited until she had their undivided attention before nodding. "And now," she said in an ominous voice, fingers crooked like claws, "I will tell you a tale most foul. A story that'll haunt your dreams and follow you into your waking hours. A fable of the folly of men, and the lengths they go to in order to escape their own mortality. And every single word of it is *true*."

"Oh no," Chauncey whispered. "True stories are *real*."

"It begins on an unseasonably cool April morning. Our heroine—an amazing forest sprite who is good at pretty much everything she does—wakes up, not knowing that today is the day when everything will change, and all good feelings will be gone from the world as darkness spreads. Because today is the day that Linus Baker decides he wants to grow a mustache."

"Boo!" all the children hissed.

"It was *fine*," Linus retorted. "I happen to think I looked dashing."

"Yeah, like you were dashing right toward us to kidnap us," Lucy said.

Linus ignored him. "I shaved it off after four days. But it was *my* choice and had nothing to do with the fact that Theodore kept asking me if he could sample the worm growing on my face."

"Phee?" Arthur asked. "Is there more to your tale?"

"Oh yes," she said. "I haven't even gotten to the part where the mustache becomes sentient and decides to take over the world. And since Linus is attached to it, he turns into a villain and then we save him with a dull razor, shaving foam, and love."

"On with it, then," Linus said, resigned to his part in Phee's story. "I don't know why it has to be a dull razor, but I must admit to being a tad intrigued."

"There had better be explosions," Talia warned her.

"Of the destructive *and* the emotional kind," Sal said.

"Who do you think you're talking to?" Phee asked, looking moderately offended. "There are going to be at least *six* explosions."

"Real or imaginary?" David asked.

All the children turned toward Linus and Arthur with matching expressions of extraordinarily effective pleading. Arthur glanced at Linus, who shrugged. "One explosion," Arthur decided. "But it cannot cause any damage."

"Hurray!" Lucy cheered as David beamed. "I'll make it happen in the air. Phee, you tell me when it's time, and I'll handle the rest. David, you're gonna love this. Arthur and Linus *never* let us explode things."

"Or people," Arthur said.

"Or people," Lucy said with a grimace.

"I can't believe this place is *real*," David whispered in awe.

Phee nodded and cleared her throat. "Back to the story. There I was, not knowing that everything was about to change because of a line of hair on a man's upper lip. At first, it looked like a smudge of dirt, but before long, it grew to the size of a sickly caterpillar." She leaned forward, wings rustling. "And then . . . it began to *whisper*."

"Ooh," the children breathed, rapt attention on Phee.

"It wasn't *that* bad, was it?" Linus whispered to Arthur as Phee continued.

Arthur chuckled, laying his head against Linus's. "It was not. I happened to find it delightful, but then everything about you is."

Linus rolled his eyes fondly. "Foolish, besotted man."

By the time Phee finished (complete with a single explosion high in the sky which turned into fireworks that rained down streaks of gold and green and red), the children were tucked safely into their makeshift beds, Lucy struggling to stay awake, head lolling then shooting back up. They applauded her—including Linus, who might have clapped harder than the rest of them—and she bowed before sinking into her spot next to Chauncey. Little conversations sprang up between them, each quieter than the last. David laughed over something Talia told him, lying on his side, cold blanket tugged up to his shoulder.

Arthur sat propped up against the side of the gazebo, looking out onto the island beyond the garden, the moonlight causing the shadows of the trees to stretch long. In the distance, the crash of waves against the cliffs below could be heard. There wasn't a cloud in the sky, only a vast field of stars that seemed endless. Linus lay next to him, holding Arthur's hand against his chest, fingers spread wide, the slow, calm beat of Linus's heart a metronome for a song only Arthur could hear.

He was startled from his thoughts—disordered though they were—when someone said his name.

He looked up to find Sal watching him, Theodore tucked in

next to him, his head resting on Sal's stomach as it rose and fell, eyes closed. The other children were asleep, along with Linus who had begun to snore softly. "Yes?"

"We're going to make it."

Arthur swallowed past the lump in his throat. When he spoke again, his voice was rough, soft. "Is that right?"

Sal nodded. "Whatever they throw at us, whatever happens, we're going to make it. We know you're scared." He laughed quietly. "I am, too, I guess."

"Are you?"

"Yeah, but . . ." He looked down at his brothers and sisters. "Worth it. All of it."

Arthur watched his son closely. "Even with . . . ?"

"Worth it," Sal repeated, stroking Theodore's snout with the tip of his finger. "Linus told me something once, and I think about it a lot. He said it's okay to not be okay, so long as it doesn't become all we know."

"He's right," Arthur said.

"Maybe you should remember that sometimes," Sal said. "Might help."

Arthur snorted in surprise. "Is that right?"

"Yes," Sal said before yawning, the back of his wrist against his mouth. "Besides, we have one thing the government doesn't. And it's going to change everything."

"What's that?" Arthur asked as Sal closed his eyes. "What do we have?"

His son whispered two words before drifting off to sleep.

"*Each other.*"

TEN

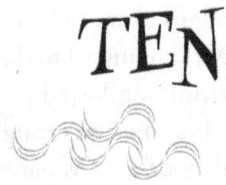

Wednesday dawned warm and clear, the type of summer day when adventure called, to be followed by a well-deserved nap in a swaying hammock attached to palm trees.

Or it would have been, if this Wednesday had occurred anywhere else.

On Marsyas Island, this particular Wednesday meant something else entirely: preparing for war.

"We are *not* preparing for war!" Linus said for what felt like the hundredth time in the last thirty minutes.

"Then why am I wearing a battle helmet?" Chauncey asked.

"That's the colander you nicked from the kitchen," Linus said.

The children had decided to use Linus and Arthur's room as a base of operations, each of them bringing what they considered necessary to face the days ahead. David wanted to wear a cape. Phee helped with it, tying the ends in a knot around his throat. Phee had a crown of flowers in her hair, made up of blooms from Talia's garden. Talia fretted over the state of her beard until Sal brought her one of her creams to help smooth it down while leaving it with a healthy sheen. Theodore hung from the ceiling like a bat, checking in with Linus every five minutes or so to ensure a particular brass button was still hidden on his person. Calliope watched them all coolly from her perch in one of the windows, green eyes bright.

Arthur sat in his high-backed chair, shaking his head each time

Lucy came out of his room with a new idea on how to greet the inspector. The first time he came out, he was over nine feet tall. It'd been disconcerting, seeing as how his body was still that of a child and his legs were now three times longer than they usually were. The second time he came out, he was back to regular size, but wearing a shirt with red lettering that proclaimed him to be DADDY'S LITTLE DEVIL.

"Get it?" he asked quite loudly. "*Get it?*"

"We get it," everyone said, and Lucy beamed.

When he came back out of his room for the third time he asked, "Has anyone seen a scorpion? No worries if not. He's one of the tiny ones, which means he's really poisonous while also being hard to see." Arthur sat upright in his chair, looking toward the open door that led out into the hallway.

A moment later, Zoe appeared, looking grim. She wore tan slacks and a billowy blouse, the sleeves of which hung over the backs of her hands. Arthur rose from his chair. Linus must have seen his movement out of the corner of his eye because he looked at Arthur, arched an eyebrow in a silent question, then followed Arthur's gaze toward the door.

"What is it?" Arthur asked as the children fell silent around them. An unnecessary question because he knew. They all did.

"She's here," Zoe said. "Just got off the train. Helen's picking her up. She's going to take the scenic way around town to give us a bit more time, but it won't be long."

"We're ready," Arthur said, though it felt like a lie. He hated how easy it was to speak untruths when he wanted to protect others. "We're going to stab her with so much kindness, she'll thank us for it."

"Really should work on the phrasing," Linus muttered as he stood up, knees popping. "But I like your spirit. Yes. We're ready."

"I guess I have to hide now," David said, shoulders slumped as he tried to untangle the knot Phee had tied in his cape. "Just let me get this stupid thing off and I'll be quiet. Promise."

"It's not stupid," Chauncey said. "I think you look amazing. I tried to wear a cape once, but it made me look like a superheroic gumdrop."

David laughed, but it faded quickly. He scowled at the knot, claws tearing into the fabric. Arthur stepped forward, pulling David's hands away as he crouched before him. "Do you understand why this is necessary?"

David wouldn't look at him, gaze firmly planted on his bare feet. He shrugged half-heartedly. "Yeah, I guess. I'm not registered, and she could try and use that against me."

Arthur brushed a short string of hair out of David's face. "Exactly. And that's the only reason. We're not ashamed of you. We're not embarrassed by you. You are wonderful, David. And soon enough, everyone will get to learn what we already know."

Then Sal said, "No."

Arthur looked over at him with a frown, still hunkered before David. "What was that?"

Sal stepped forward, looking determined. "Hiding away solves nothing," he said as Theodore nodded from his shoulder. "The only thing it does is make us used to staying in the shadows. That's not fair."

"It isn't," Linus said carefully as Arthur stood. "And you won't hear us trying to argue otherwise. But this is different. Since David is unregistered, he runs the risk of being removed immediately. We can't take that chance, especially since it might affect the rest of you."

"I don't want to be any trouble," David said, sounding like he was starting to panic. "I can hide!" His mouth twisted down as he scuffed a foot against the floor. "And besides, it's not the first time I've had to do it. I'm used to it by now."

Sal shot Arthur a pointed look before moving to stand in front of David, gripping his shoulders. "We don't want that for you. That's why we all talked about it and came to a unanimous decision." His expression softened. "Sorry we didn't tell you about it. We didn't want to make you uncomfortable. But we want to help."

"David doesn't hide," Phee said, crossing her arms and glaring up at Arthur and Linus. "We know it could mess things up for the rest of us, but if *he* can't be seen, then the rest of us won't be either. We'll go on strike."

Chauncey pumped his tentacles in the air. "Strike! Strike! Strike!"

"If she has a problem with David, I'll use her for fertilizer," Talia said.

Lucy nodded. "And *I'll* open up a dimensional doorway in the fabric of reality and send her to a place where even demons fear to tread. What is this evil place, you might be asking? Great question!" He spread his hands wide in a practiced display of showmanship. "It's called . . . Florida."

Arthur studied each of the children in turn and found a united front. Though a trickle of unease wormed its way through his chest toward his heart, it was no match for the fierce pride that burned through him. Without Arthur or Linus, the children had held their own congress and come to a decision on something they perceived to be unreasonable.

"David?" he asked gently. "What do *you* want?"

David jerked his head up, wiping the ice crystals that had formed in the corners of his eyes. He fidgeted, wringing his hands, causing his knuckles to pop loudly. Theodore tittered, spreading his wings and jumping from Sal's shoulders to David's. Calliope—never one to pass up an opportunity—jumped down from the window and brushed against Sal's legs, meowing loudly until he picked her up. She took Theodore's place, tail wrapped around the back of Sal's neck.

David growled at her but subsided when Theodore laid his chin on top of David's head. The yeti froze, eyes rolling up. "Uh. He's . . . what's going on? What do I do? Nothing? Something? Oh my God, tell me!"

"He's showing you that he trusts you," Sal explained. "And that he's got your back. Same as the rest of us." Calliope raised a paw to Sal's chin, forcing him to look down at her. She began to purr loudly as he pressed his nose against hers. "Because we don't hide. Maybe we did, once, but no more. We have the right to exist. Registered or not. If DICOMY has a problem with that, well." He smiled, and in it, Arthur saw his strength, his purpose. "Then maybe it's time we took on the government. Show them what we're *really* capable of."

"Anarchy!" Lucy shrieked, eyes burning red. "Chaos! Buffets with a never-ending supply of macaroni and cheese! Hellfire!"

"David," Linus said, "you haven't answered Arthur's question. What is it you want?"

David looked at the other children, Talia and Phee giving him a thumbs-up. He hesitated. Then, "I don't want to hide. I won't cause trouble, I promise."

"He could stay with me until she leaves," Zoe offered. "No one can find my home unless I invite them to."

Sal shook his head. "We thought about that. It's no different from hiding him here." He took in a deep breath, letting it out slow. "We know it's a lot to ask, but this is important. And it's not as if we didn't think things through."

"We have a plan," Lucy said, clapping gleefully.

"Oh dear," Linus whispered. "Tell us."

At just past noon, the ferry docked at Marsyas Island. Arthur heard the sound of Helen's old truck winding its way up the dirt road toward the house and stepped outside. He was calmer than he expected to be; it was as if every heightened emotion had burned itself out, leaving only a sense of quiet inevitability.

When the truck crested the hill, he stepped off the porch, standing in front of the house, hands folded behind his back. Through the windshield, he could see Helen saying something to the figure sitting next to her, hands gesticulating wildly.

The truck came to a stop, brakes squealing. A moment later, it shut off, the engine ticking like a clock. Helen climbed out of the truck, shutting the door behind her. She glanced at Arthur, rolled her eyes, and then went to the bed of the truck, pulling out a rather large suitcase—black with leather handles, obviously heavy—as she grunted.

The passenger side of the truck opened, and the inspector stepped out, a silver metal briefcase clutched against her chest.

She was tall—at least six feet, which would put her just above Linus and near Arthur's height, and as thin as a whisper. Her brown hair was pulled back into a severe bun, cinched tightly atop her head with nary a hair out of place. Pierced ears with small diamonds. Rings on each finger—gold and silver and what appeared to be onyx, each decorated with colorful jewels, settling against thick knuckles. Her thin, arched eyebrows looked as if they'd been painted on, giving her the appearance of one in a perpetual state of disbelief. She had a beauty mark on her right cheek and her lips were a slash of blood red, causing her gaunt face to take on the appearance of a business-professional skeleton. The inspector wore no-nonsense flats—black in color—along with a gray pleated skirt, the hem resting just below her knees. Given the summer heat, her coat was a strange choice. Cinched tightly at her waist, the red coat was lined with golden buttons up the front—eight in all, four on each side—and a collar that rose dramatically around her head, stiff and lined with fur. She was a sight to behold, and if she hadn't been here as a representative of the government, Arthur might have warned her about the gold buttons and how a certain wyvern might react upon seeing them. But she was, and who was he to ruin what was most likely to be an eye-opening experience?

She shut the door behind her, looking up at the sky with a frown. The sun disappeared behind a cloud as if even it wanted nothing to do with her. That done, she nodded, spun on her heels, and made her way toward Arthur. Her gaze flickered from him to the house behind him, though her face was a blank mask, giving nothing away.

"Mr. Parnassus," she said, her voice deeper than he thought it'd be, sounding like a pair of heavy, ominous doors slowly opening.

She did not extend her hand in greeting, stopping a few feet away from him. Her eyes were flat and narrow, the color of storm clouds. Younger than Arthur and Linus, though not by much. "My name is Harriet Marblemaw. You may refer to me as Miss Marblemaw. I have been tasked with inspecting this orphanage by the Department in Charge of Magical Youth."

Arthur bowed. "Welcome to Marsyas, Miss Marblemaw. I do hope your trip was uneventful. As you're undoubtedly aware, I recently rode the train myself. Fascinating mode of transportation, wouldn't you agree? Though, in my humble opinion, riding the bus was much more pleasurable."

Miss Marblemaw stared at him, unblinking. "I was unaware I came here to discuss public transportation."

"You did not," Arthur agreed. "You are here, as you said, to inspect an orphanage, which puts me at a bit of a loss. You see, this is not an orphanage. This is a home. I hate to think you came all this way with faulty information. That would certainly make your job that much more difficult."

Miss Marblemaw chuckled, shifting her briefcase until it rested against her right forearm. "I was there," she said pleasantly, "for your testimony. It was ... enlightening. And also unfortunate, given how it ended." Before he could respond, she opened the briefcase, looked through DICOMY-stamped files, and pulled out an official-looking document. "This is the order from DICOMY signed by interim DICOMY head Jeanine Rowder allowing me access to the island, the children, and anything else I require during my stay." She held out the page toward him. "I think you'll find that even you won't be able to talk your way out of this."

Arthur ignored the document. "And how is Miss Rowder? Our first—and only—meeting ended with her leaving before we finished. I do hope it was nothing I said."

She glanced over his shoulder. "Where are the children?"

Arthur nodded. "Eager, are we? I don't blame you. I, too, was fit to burst the first time I met them. I'm glad we have that in common."

"That's one way of putting it,". Helen muttered as she approached, setting the suitcase down near the inspector's feet. For her part, Miss Marblemaw barely acknowledged Helen's existence. And she did not tip, which was something Arthur would have to make sure Chauncey was aware of. He would have a few choice words about that, Arthur was sure.

Miss Marblemaw cocked her head, not unlike a bird as she shoved the document back into the briefcase, latching it shut. "Do you think yourself amusing, Mr. Parnassus?"

"I do. Though, as I told one of my young charges, humor is subjective, and it—"

"I thought as much. You seem the sort." She squared her shoulders and smiled. On anyone else, Arthur would have thought it a funny little grin, but with Miss Marblemaw, it seemed as if she thought she was already dealing with a child. In it, everything he despised: smarmy condescension mixed with unearned confidence, all disguised in a candy-apple coating, sticky, sweet. And that made her more dangerous than she'd been even a moment before. Whatever else Rowder was, she wasn't a fool; she'd known exactly who to send to the island. Miss Marblemaw proved that when she spoke again. "I am familiar with your ... history, Mr. Parnassus. Somehow, you've been able to charm yourself into a position of great power ignominiously. You pulled the wool over the eyes of Extremely Upper Management—"

Arthur laughed, trying to keep his anger at bay. The phoenix lifted its head, wings ruffling. "Did I, now?"

"—but I won't fall for your tricks. I am not Charles Werner. I am not Linus Baker. The reason I'm here is to ensure not only that the children are being cared for, but that you aren't filling their heads with propagandic anti-government sentiments."

"Speaking of propaganda," Helen said sweetly, "I remember what happened to all the DICOMY posters you asked about when driving through town. Silly me, I don't know why it took me till just now."

"Good," Miss Marblemaw said, distracted as she moved her briefcase from one hand to the other. She bent over to pick up her suitcase. "Your cooperation will be noted. What happened to them?"

"It appears the salt in the air does not agree with the adhesive provided," Helen said. "And since we did not want to run afoul of the government, we followed their instructions, which said not to use our own, to the letter. Unfortunately, all of the posters blew into the ocean."

Miss Marblemaw stood upright and squinted at Helen. "I absolutely beg your pardon? The adhesive, you say? Noted. I will be sure to inform the appropriate office of the issue. It will be corrected immediately. In the meantime, you have my permission to use tape, or even pushpins."

"Blast it," Helen exclaimed. "We're fresh out of both. I will put in an order posthaste to ensure we have enough tape and pushpins in the future."

"See that you do," Miss Marblemaw said with a sniff. "After all, it is important for any magical person to know their government is watching them, and cares about their well-being."

Helen stepped forward, kissing Arthur on the cheek. Her mouth near his ear, she whispered, "Careful with this one." She pulled away, nodded, and then headed back toward her truck. "Please let us know if you need to head into the village," she called over her shoulder. "Keep in mind that the ferry rates fluctuate, so I can't guarantee the same price as when we crossed. Petrol is expensive, after all, but then, you work for the government, so I'm sure no expense will be spared. Toodles!"

"Would you like to introduce me to the children?" Miss Marblemaw asked as Helen's truck fired up. "Also, while I'm here, I'll need to speak with Zoe Chapelwhite. Since she has contact with the children, she is not exempt from any inquiry. I'm sure you'll be kind enough to facilitate that meeting, won't you? Good man."

Suitcase in hand, she brushed by him without hesitation and walked toward the house.

"Here we go," Arthur whispered, following her inside.

The house was quiet, unnervingly so. Miss Marblemaw stopped inside the entryway, setting her luggage and briefcase near the door. As Arthur closed the door behind them, Miss Marblemaw made a show of opening the briefcase once more, pulling out a clipboard with a red ink pen clipped to the front. She turned and began inspecting . . . the walls? She kicked a baseboard, leaving a small black smudge. Then she ran a finger along the small table near the door, lifting it close to her eyes. "No dust," she muttered. "Odd." She crouched down before an electrical socket, pulling at the plastic plug before shoving it back in and marking something on the clipboard.

Arthur cleared his throat. He expected her to jump. She didn't, only turning her head to glance at him. "Before we go any further."

"Excuses already, Mr. Parnassus? That doesn't bode well."

Arthur waved her off. "Nothing like that. I'm of the mind that if you want something badly enough, you'll find a way. If not, you'll find an excuse."

Her eyebrows rose on her forehead. "Is that an accusation, sir?"

"It was not," Arthur said mildly. "But it would seem as if you're primed to consider most anything suspicious, and I would urge caution against that."

"Would you?" she asked as she stood slowly. "And why would that be?"

"Because if you've convinced yourself there is darkness around every corner, you're conditioned to fear it, especially when it goes hand in hand with a particular narrative."

"The narrative that you, a magical being—one of the strongest known—is attempting to take possession of potentially dangerous children, some of whom have the power to end life as we know it? Is that the particular narrative you speak of?" Coolly amused, as if she were Calliope and he her prey, trying to tire him out before attacking.

"It is," Arthur said. "And one that is extraordinarily problematic. Though I shouldn't have to remind you, I will: regardless of what powers they do or do not have, they are still children. And since you are in our home and they are under *my* care, if at any point I believe you are jeopardizing their well-being—meaning physically, psychologically, or emotionally—I'll do what I must to ensure their safety."

Miss Marblemaw smiled thinly. "I don't know what kind of person you take me for, Mr. Parnassus, but I am offended at even the *suggestion* that I would harm the children in any way. The very idea is preposterous, and I will gladly take an apology, should one be on offer."

"I'm not going to—"

"I see," she said, scribbling something on her clipboard—uncomplimentary, no doubt—before adding, "Let's try a different approach." She looked up, expression bland. "I appreciate the gravity of this situation. I hope you do as well. While I do know quite a bit about you, I am nothing but a stranger to you. Let me share a little about myself." She slid the pen into the top of the clipboard. "I'm not magical. I wouldn't be in this position if I was. However, I do have talents of my own, one of which I think you might find interesting."

"And what would that be?"

Miss Marblemaw said, "I am incapable of experiencing fear. Things that go bump in the night, large snakes with poisonous fangs, mortality, insects, slime, threats from a man who doesn't understand the seriousness of the situation he finds himself in, *nothing* frightens me. It's been that way since I could remember. The sooner you realize that, the better off we'll be."

Arthur paused, mind racing. Then, "I will keep that in mind. Since you are being up front with me, I will do the same with you. As you were sent by Miss Rowder, I assume you have an infestation going on."

Her eyes bulged. "A *what*? How dare you—"

"Bugs," Arthur said. "But not of the insect variety. I am, of course, speaking about listening devices similar to the one deposited in our hotel room before the hearing. If you have brought any with you, and I find that you've planted them in the house, you'll be banished from the island immediately, regardless of whether you've finished your investigation. This is not a threat, it's a fact."

"You can't banish me," she snapped.

He shrugged affably. "Interesting that's what you focused on, rather than a denial. But you're right: I can't banish you. Such powers are beyond me. That beings said, the island belongs to Zoe Chapelwhite, and you are here with her permission. If she does not want you here, you won't be. Simple as that. Do we understand each other?"

The smug expression returned. "You have no proof Rowder or anyone else from DICOMY placed a bug in your room. And since there is no proof, what you're saying constitutes slander. There are legal protections against such things, as I'm sure you're aware."

Arthur chuckled. "That I am. No bugs, Miss Marblemaw. The children are allowed their privacy." He moved by her, stopping momentarily to glance over his shoulder. "Coming? Class is in session. You can meet the children after their lessons have finished."

He almost burst into laughter the moment he walked into the classroom on the first floor, Miss Marblemaw close on his heels, the irritating scratch of her pen a constant reminder. For reasons known only to him, Lucy had changed his clothes again. He now wore dress pants, a button-up shirt, and a little tie half the length of Arthur's forearm. As soon as he saw Miss Marblemaw walking in behind Arthur, his hand immediately shot up, fingers wiggling as he stood on the chair of his desk. The other children looked at Miss Marblemaw with a mixture of worry and interest.

Linus stopped in the middle of his lesson—Wednesday afternoons meant literature discussions—and frowned at Miss Marblemaw before looking at Lucy. "You had a question about the material?"

"I do not," Lucy said loudly. "I just wanted to let you know that I *love* sitting at a desk in the middle of summer so that I can learn rather than play outside."

Linus blinked. "You do? I mean, of course you do. Thank you for saying what we all already know."

Talia's hand rose. "I also would like to say that learning is *so* much fun. In fact, there is nothing I would rather do than learn from you, *Mr. Baker*."

"Why are we calling him that?" Chauncey whispered loudly to Phee, glancing nervously at their new guest.

"Because of the scarecrow standing next to Arthur," Phee whispered back.

Miss Marblemaw grunted and scribbled on her clipboard.

"She's a *scarecrow*?" Chauncey exclaimed. "Oh my goodness. What will they think of next?"

"Children," Linus said, pulling their attention back to him. "Let's focus, please. Just because we have a visitor doesn't mean we can ignore our studies. We should—"

Right then, a yeti sauntered into the room, cool as ice, his cape billowing behind him. He posed for a moment, hands on his hips, before glancing up at Miss Marblemaw and grinning, fangs on full display.

Miss Marblemaw's eyes widened as she took a step back before stopping herself—not frightened, but startled?—mouth twisting. "What is *that*?"

David bowed, almost falling flat on his face, but managing to keep himself upright at the last second. "Greetings, fair lady." He grabbed the back of her hand and slobbered a kiss onto it before she could snatch it away. "I heard tales of an inspector arriving on the island, but I never expected them to be so . . . you. Tell me, does your face normally look like that, or did you do it up special just for me?"

"Another child," Miss Marblemaw whispered, eyes widening.

"We *knew*—" She seemed to remember she was surrounded and her mouth snapped shut with an audible clack of her teeth.

David laughed. "A child? Miss, I am no child. I'm forty-seven years old."

Linus groaned at the front of the classroom. Arthur, on the other hand, was extremely fascinated by this turn of events. When the children had said they had a plan for David, they hadn't shared the particulars. Taking David's acting abilities into consideration was a stroke of mad genius, even if it was more than a little ridiculous.

Miss Marblemaw squinted down at David. "You're . . . what?"

"Nearly half a century," David said cheerfully. "You might be asking yourself, *How can a yeti of that age be so short?* I'm so glad you asked! When I was but a young lad, I found myself between a rock and a hard place. Literally! I was trapped there for seven years until rescued by a traveling carnival, and it stunted my growth. But I don't let it keep me down! After all, I'm an adult."

Miss Marblemaw's face twisted as if an offending odor had filled her nostrils. "You honestly expect me to believe that? If you aren't a child, then why are you here?"

"Arthur and I go way back," David said easily. "Rushed a fraternity together."

"Arthur Parnassus was *never* in a fraternity," she said. "Trust me when I say I've done my research. I know everything there is to know about him."

"Do you?" Arthur asked Miss Marblemaw. "And you're right, of course. I did not rush a fraternity during the time I furthered my education, but only because it was illegal for a magical being to join a human group. That wasn't repealed until well after I'd left."

"By rush, I meant we ran at it," David said. "Because Arthur and I like to run, don't we, old chap?"

"That's exactly right," Arthur said, reminding himself to have a conversation with David later about lying responsibly. "I appreciate you being here, David. Your support during this process means the world to me."

"We're going to have a beer later," David told Miss Marblemaw. "Me and Arthur. Yep, gonna drink some beers and talk about the economy, just like the old days."

"Is that right?" Miss Marblemaw asked. "Strange how that works out. You, here, looking like you do."

David started to shrink in on himself. "I can be here if I want to," he muttered. "I'm *allowed* to—"

"That's right," Sal said sharply. "You *are* allowed to be here." He turned around, raising his hand. When Linus nodded at him, he said, "Before the interruption, we were discussing the negative effects of a totalitarian government, and the dangers language poses, especially when weaponized as propaganda."

"We . . . were?" Linus asked. "I mean, of course we were. That's exactly right. Language can be used for good, but it can also cause suffering."

"To marginalized communities," Sal said, voice clear. He did not turn back to look at the inspector again, but she was looking at him with narrowed eyes. Arthur thought that had been Sal's point: to remove her attention from David. "So, my question is this: If certain language knowingly causes harm, why would a politician use said language in any part of their governance? Does it have a purpose, or is it that they just don't care?"

"Isn't it grand?" Arthur whispered to Miss Marblemaw. "Children having ideas, talking them through, questioning everything."

"We have different definitions of the word 'grand,'" she retorted, continuing to mark up the page on her clipboard.

"Excellent question," Linus said with an approving nod. "Before I provide my own input, does anyone have an insight they want to share?"

"Because they know exactly what they're doing," Phee said. "They know that fear is a powerful motivator, and that many people will believe whatever they're told."

"And why is that?" Linus asked.

Theodore reared back on his own desk, wings spread wide as he chirped excitedly.

"Wonderful, Theodore," Linus said. "You got it in one. The idea of *caring* can be a bit of a minefield. When Sal asked if they—meaning those in power—don't care, is that truly what you think? Because I don't think that's correct."

"Interesting," Miss Marblemaw murmured. "It appears as if your Mr. Baker isn't as brainwashed as you might have hoped."

"Or," Arthur said, "you could let him finish."

"Speaking hypothetically—and only about the book we're discussing—I believe they *do* care, but not in any way that benefits the groups affected. They care about themselves. About control. About manipulation in media, in polling, in the spreading of fear until subservience is not only a relief, but a welcome one at that."

Arthur turned his head slowly to look at Miss Marblemaw, whose face was darkening with barely contained anger. "Do you like to read, madam?"

The skin under her right eye twitched. "There will be discussions on what is and what is not proper for children to learn in their studies. By the end of the week, I'll expect the lesson plans for each child, in addition to a list of all the books you allow them to read. It seems to me that list needs to be culled." She tapped her pen against the clipboard. "For the children's protection, of course."

"But that is enough for today," Linus said. "As you can see, we have a new guest. She is here on loan from the Department in Charge of Magical Youth to make sure you—"

"I can handle my own introductions, thank you very much."

Linus's expression soured momentarily before he nodded. "Of course. The floor is yours."

Miss Marblemaw moved swiftly toward the front of the classroom, the bottom of her coat billowing around her, mere inches from the floor. Instead of asking Linus to move, she crowded against him until he stepped to the side. With that, she turned to look at the children and cleared her throat. "Good morning. I am Miss Marblemaw. You may refer to me by name, or 'ma'am.' Not 'hey.' Not 'you there.' If this concept proves too difficult for any of you to grasp, we will make time for lessons on how to politely address an elder."

Lucy's hand shot up once more, and though Arthur wanted to intervene—*already*—he decided to see what would play out, how the inspector would react to interacting with the children directly for the first time.

Miss Marblemaw took it in stride. "Yes? You have a question?"

"Would you like tea?" Lucy asked sweetly. "We have fresh honey to go with it."

"Good," she said with a nod. "Gentility to government officials is not only proper, it can also be rewarding. Because of your generosity, you shall receive one official courtesy point. Receive fifty points, and you'll be honored with a certificate from DICOMY signed by your favorite politicians."

"Oh, *wow*," Lucy said, tumbling out of his desk. "My *favorite* politicians? But there are so many!"

Miss Marblemaw nodded solemnly as Lucy went to a small table set up on the other side of the room with tea and a tray of biscuits. "That's wonderful to hear. Though many think we should put celebrities on pedestals, I'm of the mind that it's the hard-working people of the government who should be on posters hanging in children's rooms and having their autographs clamored over."

"That's *so* interesting!" Lucy said as he poured the tea carefully. "Gosh, you have really opened my eyes. Thank you for coming here with your face and your words. Sugar? Milk? Or will just the honey be all right?"

"Honey is fine," Miss Marblemaw said. "Now, where was I? Ah, yes. I am an inspector sent by the Department in Charge of Magical Youth. I take my job very seriously, but that doesn't mean we can't be friends." She grimaced, and it took Arthur a moment to realize she was attempting to smile and failing spectacularly. "I want you to think of me like your fun auntie who is here in an official capacity to determine if this house meets all official requirements, or if other options should be considered."

"Your tea, ma'am," Lucy said, holding out the cup toward her with a little bow.

She took it from him with a nod. Sipping from it daintily, she smacked her lips and said, "Quite a bit of honey in that. Next time, about half as much."

"Thank you for the feedback," Lucy said seriously. "I will take that into consideration going forward." Then, he turned to Talia, tapping his chin. "Hey, didn't you tell me about how honey is made? You should share that with Miss Marblemaw so she can see how much we've learned."

Talia smiled and nodded. Waiting until Miss Marblemaw took a long sip, she said, "You think? Not everyone appreciates learning that honey is bee vomit."

Arthur knew Lucy was expecting Miss Marblemaw to spit out the tea in what would most likely be a spectacular explosion. Instead, she swallowed and said, "My grandfather raised honeybees. I am well aware of what I'm consuming, thank you very much."

Lucy frowned up at her, taking a step back. "Uh, that's . . . huh."

She cocked her head at him. "You must have been hoping for a different reaction, then. I see." Pulling out a black handkerchief from the right sleeve of her coat, she dabbed it against her lips. Once done, it disappeared back up her sleeve. She looked down at the tea in the cup, swishing it around a little. When she lifted her head, she was smiling, a real, bright thing that sent a chill down Arthur's spine. "It seems as if we've gotten off on the wrong foot, and for that, you have my deepest regrets. It probably doesn't help that you've had your poor little heads filled with all sorts of nonsense that I can't even begin to imagine. Rest assured, that stops now. From this point forward, I'll show you that your government cares not only for you, but for all magical beings far and wide. We have your best interests in mind and want nothing more than for you to succeed and lead semi-normal lives."

"Well," Phee said. "When you put it *that* way."

"I'm so pleased you agree!" Miss Marblemaw said, a study in obliviousness. "After all, if a mess has been made, it must be cleaned up before it gets worse. Speaking of." She glanced at Sal and held out her teacup toward him. "You there. I'm finished with this. Take it away."

"My name is Sal," he said flatly. "And in this house, we don't tell people to clean up after others, at least not without asking politely."

"He's quite right," Linus said. "As an inspector, shouldn't you lead by example?"

Arthur could almost see the smoke curling from her ears as she scribbled something else on her clipboard. "Delegation teaches responsibility."

"So does self-ownership," Sal said.

"It does," Arthur said, moving to the front of the room, Miss Marblemaw glaring daggers at him. "And Sal is correct, not only about taking responsibility for our actions, but also in that he has a name. Interestingly enough, all of the children do. Perhaps an introduction would be beneficial."

"Fine," Miss Marblemaw said, a version of her sticky-sweet smile returning, setting the teacup on the desk. "When called upon, I will ask that you provide your name, age, species, and one thing you like about living on the island, and one thing you dislike. I expect complete and total honesty. You will not speak until called upon."

Linus scowled at her. "That's not—"

"Tut, tut!" she trilled. "I don't believe I called on Mr. Baker, but here he is, *talking*. You do *not* get a courtesy point."

"Ooh," the children said.

"Species?" Arthur asked, voice hard. "What does that have to do with anything? Surely you've studied whatever DICOMY passes off as files these days."

"Be that as it may," Miss Marblemaw said, "it is better if we hear it directly from the subjects to ensure there are no ... delusions of what is or what isn't. Children, line up in front of me, single file."

No one moved.

"That was not a request!" she said in a maddeningly cheerful voice. "When I ask you to do something, I expect it to be done without hesitation."

Arthur nodded at the children, and they rose from their desks as one, forming a line as Miss Marblemaw had instructed.

Talia was first. She stepped forward, the tip of her cap flopped over. "My name is Talia. I'm two hundred and sixty-four years old. I am a garden gnome, one of the most talented who has ever existed."

"Being braggadocious is unbecoming of a lady," Miss Marblemaw said. "We must show humility, especially when in the company of our elders."

Talia frowned. "But you said we needed to be honest. I *am* one of the most talented garden gnomes. Have you seen my garden?"

"I'm allergic," Miss Marblemaw said dismissively. "Pollen is the bane of my existence. On to the rest. One thing you like, and one thing you dislike. Quickly."

"I love pollen," Talia said, stroking her beard. "And I dislike anyone who doesn't appreciate growth."

"Growth *is* important," Miss Marblemaw said, not quite understanding the minutiae of Gnomish insults. "It's a reward for learning. Next, please!"

Theodore stumbled forward, chirping loudly as he eyed her, head cocked. He spread his wings as he continued to chatter. The children—including David, flipping through his translation text—burst into laughter, and Linus clapped a hand over his mouth, eyes bulging. Arthur kept his expression carefully blank, though he thought, *These children. These remarkable children.*

When Theodore finished (having told Miss Marblemaw that her eyes looked like shiny buttons and that he was planning on taking them for his hoard, and *no*, she absolutely was not invited to see said hoard), Miss Marblemaw appeared bewildered. "What did it say?"

"*He* said he's a wyvern," Sal said coolly. "That he's not quite sure of his age. And that he likes pollen as well, and dislikes people who say one thing to try and win people over, and then stab them in the back."

"Does that happen often here?" said Miss Marblemaw, furiously writing on her clipboard.

Theodore chirped again. *Not until today.*

"Nope," Sal said. "It's hypothetical."

"I'm Chauncey," the boy-blob said, oozing forward. "Ten years young. I seem to be a mixture of octopus, sea cucumber, and probably a bunch of other miracles. But! There's something *much* more important that we should discuss."

Miss Marblemaw leaned forward, eyes dancing. "Yes? Speak plainly, child. You have nothing to worry about because I'm here now. I promise I'll make sure you are safe and—"

"I'm speaking, of course, about a financial investment opportunity." He spread his tentacles wide. "Imagine: me in charge of a sixty-room hotel sitting on the beach complete with all the amenities your heart could desire. Massages! Fine dining! Live music! Your very own Chauncey-approved robe that you get to *keep*! But *wait*. There's more!" His eyes widened dramatically. "Your sixteen-carat diamond necklace was stolen from your hotel room? Have no fear! In addition to being the owner, manager, and bellhop, I will also promise my detective services to help solve any mystery! And this can all be yours if you make a monetary commitment that you will see *tripled* within two years. How much can I put you down for? The more zeroes, the bigger the hero!"

"Nothing," Miss Marblemaw said. "I don't believe in encouraging that which can never be. It's cruel."

"Interesting," Arthur said. "Seeing as how he's already one of the best bellhops in the known universe." He winked at Chauncey. "A great man once said stories of imagination upset those without one. I, for one, can't wait to see the hotel. Find me later, and we'll discuss my own financial contribution." Everyone ignored Miss Marblemaw's pointed *harrumph*.

Sal's turn. He stepped forward, staring at Miss Marblemaw,

barely blinking. Opening his mouth to speak, he paused. Suddenly, he smiled, eyes lighting up.

It did not take Arthur long to see what Sal had: there, crawling on the collar of Miss Marblemaw's coat, a small tan-and-yellow scorpion. He stepped forward, about to warn her, but Miss Marblemaw spoke first. "Are you going to talk?" she asked Sal. "Or just stand there staring at me like you've lost all common sense? I don't have all day."

Sal arched an eyebrow. "You do, though. You have two weeks."

She lowered the clipboard, unaware of the hitchhiker she'd picked up at some point, crawling slowly toward her face, which had taken on a stunned expression that looked practiced. She brought a hand to her throat. "Are you . . ." The hand dropped. "Are you being smart with me?"

Sal nodded. "Yes. Because I *am* smart."

"Or is it that you just don't know any better?" Miss Marblemaw countered. "You are a child, which means you—"

"Beelzebub!" Lucy cried happily. "What are you doing up there, you silly goose?"

"Sacrilege," Miss Marblemaw breathed. Then, in a much louder voice, "Who are you attempting to summon? I *knew* I should have brought holy water to—"

The scorpion's tail reared back, but before it could strike, Miss Marblemaw's hand flashed up, the handkerchief once again clutched in her fist. She covered the scorpion, pulling her hand back as she jerked her head away. As she held up the handkerchief, Arthur could see tiny tan insect legs twitching.

And then Miss Marblemaw closed her fist, crushing the scorpion with an audible crunch.

Silence.

"Island life," Miss Marblemaw said, turning and walking toward the desk in the front. She tilted her handkerchief over the top of the bin. The scorpion's corpse fell inside. It barely made a sound when it hit the bottom. "I suppose you run the risk of encountering . . ." She glanced at her audience. ". . . local wildlife when you're this far from civilization. But that's the trade-off, isn't it? All that fresh air."

"That was my scorpion!" Lucy said, outraged.

Miss Marblemaw glanced at him dismissively. "It *was* your scorpion. Now it's nothing. If you truly cared about it, you would have done whatever you could to ensure its safety. An important lesson on how life works. On to other matters. You must be Lucifer."

He glared up at her, eyes flashing red. "I am. I go by another name too."

Miss Marblemaw chuckled. "I'm well aware. Curious that the scion of the Devil can be so . . . small. Why, you barely reach my waist! If you could, child, same as the others: age, one thing you like, and one thing you dislike."

Lucy rocked back on his heels, smile growing once more. "My body is seven years old, but the demon inhabiting my soul is *much* older than that, so let's say I'm thirty-six. And you know what's weird? I like pollen too! And I dislike when there isn't just piles of it lying around for us to roll in."

Miss Marblemaw bent over until her face was in front of Lucy's. She didn't speak, nor did she blink. For his part, Lucy took a small step back, but didn't look away. Then, Miss Marblemaw snapped upright, made a note on her clipboard, and said, "I won't be intimidated by you. I have God on my side."

Lucy groaned. "Oh, you're one of *those*. Ugh."

Miss Marblemaw ignored him. "Things are going to be different going forward. I will expect you all to be on your best behavior. If, for any reason, you are incapable of doing that, please let me know so that I may cut my visit short and make my recommendations now. Trust me when I say you will not like the results. Are there any questions?" Without waiting for an answer, she continued. "Good. How wonderful it is that we all understand one another explicitly."

Linus recovered first. "Children, I think it's time for your afternoon snack. Why don't we head to the kitchen while Mr. Parnassus shows Miss Marblemaw to the guesthouse."

"That will be just fine," Miss Marblemaw said. "I do hope the accommodations are in better condition than what I've seen so far."

"The bed has been freshly made," Arthur said as he pushed open the door to the guesthouse. Slightly dazed from Miss Marblemaw's introduction, he tried to clear his head and focus on the task at hand. "You will find extra bedding in the hall closet, next to extra towels, should you need them. If you should require turndown service, Chauncey would be more than willing to assist. He likes the practice."

"I highly doubt that will be necessary," she replied as she stepped inside the house. "He seems . . . sticky, and I would prefer not to have the bedding feel the same."

"He's surprisingly not sticky," Arthur said, closing the door behind him. "Unless he wants to be."

Miss Marblemaw stiffened as she reached the entryway to the small sitting room. Arthur saw why when he came up behind her.

Zoe Chapelwhite stood in the sitting room, wings fluttering behind her. She glanced at Arthur over Miss Marblemaw's shoulder before giving the inspector her undivided attention. "Welcome to the island. My name is Zoe Chapelwhite. If there's anything you require during your stay, do let—"

"Zoe Chapelwhite?" Miss Marblemaw repeated. "According to our records, you are an unregistered magical being, which violates—"

Zoe held up her hand and Miss Marblemaw fell silent. After a moment, Zoe dropped her hand and said, "All I want to do is introduce myself. There's no need for immediate hostilities. We have time to answer any questions you might have during your stay."

She glanced at Arthur, forcing a smile. "How did the children take the first meeting?"

"As well as can be expected, given the tremendous circumstances you find yourselves in," Miss Marblemaw said.

"It went fine," Arthur said. "And wouldn't you know, my old friend David decided to stay to help out. You remember David, don't you? The man I knew in my youth?"

"Of course," Zoe said easily. "Wonderful he decided to give us a hand. Haven't seen him in a dog's age."

"Oh, *bollocks*," Miss Marblemaw snapped. "You can't expect me to believe—"

"Of course we do," Zoe said. "Because otherwise, you're calling us liars, and to island sprites, that's one of the greatest insults a human can utter."

Miss Marblemaw blanched but pushed on. "An unregistered magical being interacting with magical children is a recipe for disaster. But since we, the government, care so much, we are willing to let the past stay in the past in exchange for your immediate registration with the Department in Charge of Magical Adults."

Zoe smiled, nose wrinkling. "You are here for two weeks, yes?"

Miss Marblemaw blinked. "Yes."

"Then, as I said, we have time. Let's get you settled in before we start planning the next—"

"You cannot disappear," Miss Marblemaw said. "I know you probably have dozens of hiding places all over this little rock, but if you make me go searching for you, it won't look good in the end."

Zoe laughed, a sound like bells. "Little rock? Appearances can be deceiving. You have no idea about the land upon which you stand with *my* permission, or its history. Greater humans than you have tried to take it from the island sprites, and as the last guardian of this *little rock*, I will defend her with everything I have." The sunlight returned as Zoe's eyes changed back to their normal color. "Welcome to Marsyas! Please enjoy your stay."

With that, she pushed by the inspector, kissed Arthur on the cheek, and swept from the room.

"That went well," Arthur said mildly.

Miss Marblemaw did not agree.

That night, as Miss Marblemaw settled into the guesthouse, Arthur left Linus in the kitchen, putting away the remaining dishes from their supper. The house was quiet, too quiet; seven children and not a single sound?

On any other day, it might not have concerned him right away. But with Miss Marblemaw's arrival, Arthur wasn't taking any chances.

It didn't take him long to find them. Up in the attic, Theodore's room. He heard their voices coming from the open hatch in the ceiling, ladder extended.

Arthur was about to make himself known when he heard Phee's voice.

". . . and how the hell can she not be afraid of anything? How is *that* fair?"

"Maybe she just hasn't met the right person yet," Chauncey said. "Someone who can love her and also scare the crap out of her."

"At least she *looks* scary," David said, and though Arthur wished Marblemaw had never darkened their doorway, he took heart in knowing David felt safe enough to go with the others.

"What do we do?" Talia asked. "If she's not scared of us, how do we stop her?" She sniffled, and Arthur had to swallow past the lump in his throat. When she spoke again, her voice was quieter. "What if she takes us away?"

Theodore chirped and clicked pointedly. Arthur closed his eyes.

"Theodore's right," Sal said. "If we get taken away, we'll find each other again, no matter what. I promise. But we're not going to let it get that far."

"Hell yes," Lucy said. "Don't be sad, Talia. We've got this. Miss Marblemaw says she doesn't have any fear? Then we won't either. See how *she* likes it."

Arthur could hear the smile in Talia's voice when she said, "Thanks, Lucy."

ELEVEN

To say the following days were an exercise in patience would be an understatement, even if patience was something Arthur had in abundance. Linus, too, though a little less so.

The children were another matter entirely.

Take Thursday morning, for example. At exactly half past seven, Miss Marblemaw swept into the house in a cloud of dusky perfume that smelled of wilted flowers mixed with the stench of self-importance. Clipboard firmly in hand, she entered the kitchen to find a group of children (and a forty-seven-year-old yeti) cheering on a wyvern as he attempted to beat his record by swallowing seven whole hardboiled eggs in the space of two minutes.

Unfortunately for Miss Marblemaw, she startled poor Theodore as he worked on his sixth egg, so much so that it shot from his mouth and hit her square in the forehead. Bits of egg and yolk plopped to the floor as Theodore chirped his apologies.

"Wow," Lucy said. "That was eggcellent."

"Eggxemplary," Talia agreed.

"Come on, guys," Phee said. "It's not fair to have an inside yolk when Miss Marblemaw won't get it."

"I want to try egg-based humor too!" Chauncey said. "Okay. Hold on. Give me a second." His face scrunched up as he concentrated.

"Good morning, Miss Marblemaw," Arthur said as she haunted the entryway to the kitchen, plucking egg off her shoulders. "Would you like a cup of tea?"

"Playing . . . with food," Miss Marblemaw muttered, scribbling on her clipboard. "Lack . . . of . . . manners. Of course, I'm not surprised that—"

It was about this time that Calliope decided to introduce herself to Miss Marblemaw. Given that she'd been busy the day before—Linus had found a dead mouse in his favorite pair of loafers that night—she hadn't yet made her acquaintance with their new guest.

She did so by entering the kitchen, tail high above her. With a slow lift of her head, she looked up at Miss Marblemaw.

The two stared at each other for a long moment, both sets of eyes narrowed.

Miss Marblemaw looked away first. "As I was saying, just because you live in . . . this place, doesn't mean you can't show good manners that—"

Calliope began to make low hitching noises, her body quivering.

"What's wrong with it?" Miss Marblemaw said with a grimace. "Does it have mange? Rabies? That won't look good on a report. Surely, you—"

The hairball that Calliope expelled on top of Miss Marblemaw's shoe was extraordinarily impressive in scope. At least three times the size of one of Theodore's buttons, it landed with a wet *plop*, sliding off the side to the floor, leaving a trail of mucus and saliva in its wake.

Having made her introductions, Calliope left Miss Marblemaw behind, rubbing against Sal's legs, meowing her displeasure at the woman who was hopping from one foot to the other, promising swift reprisal against such disgusting felines.

"Good girl," Sal whispered as he patted his lap. Calliope jumped up, bumped her head against Sal's chin, then settled in his lap, her purr a low, broken rumble.

"I got it!" Chauncey cried. "I was having an eggxistential crisis because I couldn't eggxactly think of something to say. After eggstensive eggxamination, I have found the most eggstraordinary egg joke! The reason we all eggsist! Ready? Here goes! Why did the new egg feel so good? Because he just got laid!" He burst into peals of laughter, clutching his sides.

"Ah, yes," David said, for some reason wearing Chauncey's sun hat while shoving pancakes into his mouth at an impressive rate. "Adult humor. I approve, because I'm an adult. Arthur, I have some stock options to review with you. Remind me later."

"Of course," Arthur said, sipping on his tea. "I look forward to it."

"Miss Marblemaw?" Lucy asked. "Did you have a good sleep?"

She blinked as she lifted her head, the wet hairball lying on the floor next to her shoe. "The mattress was too soft, but then most things around here seem to be, so I'm not surprised."

"Oh," Lucy said. "So, nothing crawled out from underneath your bed in the middle of the night and towered above you, but you were frozen in fear as the gaping maw got closer and closer to your face, so much so that you could smell the fetid breath of the monster who wanted to tear out your throat and consume your soul? Nothing like that?"

Miss Marblemaw sniffed. "Even if there was, I would have grabbed it around the neck and disposed of it without hesitation. After all, that is what one does when dealing with interruptions."

Lucy blinked in surprise. "Really? That's... huh. All right, I guess there's always next time. Does anyone wanna bet me how much syrup I can drink before it starts oozing from my tear ducts? Last time, we got up to three bottles—"

"You let him drink three bottles of *syrup*?" Miss Marblemaw demanded.

"Of course not," Arthur said. It had been four bottles. "Miss Marblemaw, why don't we let the children clean up after breakfast, and you and I can discuss the lesson plans you requested while Linus handles the morning classes. I'm sure you're as eggcited as we are to see what we've created. It's really quite impressive, if I do say so myself."

"I'll be the judge of that," she said. And with that, she whirled around and left the kitchen behind.

"Why didn't she have breakfast?" Chauncey asked, one eye turned toward where Miss Marblemaw had been standing, the other on Arthur. "Doesn't she know it's the most important meal of the day? Poor inspector. I bet she'd feel better if she had some pancakes."

"This is a start," Miss Marblemaw admitted begrudgingly an hour later. "That being said, I would be remiss if I didn't say that I have some serious concerns."

"Do you?" Arthur asked, sitting back in his chair. "And what would those be?"

"Where to begin?" Miss Marblemaw flipped through the pages on her clipboard, marked up extensively. "Let's start with what I saw before coming to the island. Are you aware of the reporters in the village?"

"I am," Arthur said.

"Have you spoken with them?"

"I have not."

"Good," Miss Marblemaw said. "A bit of advice: don't. Reporters only cause trouble."

"Is that right? And here I thought they reported."

Miss Marblemaw ignored him. "And that's to say nothing of the village itself. It seems to me to be a hotbed of anti-government sentiments. How often do you take the children there?"

"Whenever they wish," Arthur said. "So long as it doesn't interfere with their schooling."

"And you don't see the problem with that?"

"I do not," Arthur said easily. "After all, they can't learn everything in a classroom on an island. Real-world experience is not only beneficial, but it helps them to adapt."

"Adapt for what?" Miss Marblemaw asked. Then, without waiting for an answer, she continued. "I do hate to think you're giving these children false hope. Regardless of how much Marsyas has devolved given current leadership, that doesn't mean you should continue to—"

"Give the children hope? A sense of community? A place for them to feel comfortable enough to learn and grow and make mistakes, only to learn from them? What should I not be doing, Miss Marblemaw?"

"Lying," Miss Marblemaw snapped. "You shouldn't be *lying* to them, much like you continue to lie to me."

"That's a serious accusation," Arthur said. "I assume you have evidence to support it."

She sniffed. "In due time. First, I don't see any of the approved reading material that DICOMY has listed as being beneficial to a child's development."

"Yes," Arthur said. "I found the list to be lacking in substance."

"Strange. I wasn't aware that your opinion on required material carried much weight." She flipped through two or three pages. Then, "Unfortunately, I'm not seeing in my notes where you were given permission to deviate from DICOMY protocol."

"Be that as it may, you'll notice they seem to be thriving without having to read *Learning Your Place in the World: A Guide to Following the Law* or *A Satyr Discovers the Joys of Obeying*. To be fair, both books have pacing issues, not to mention they're a little dry."

"I didn't know you moonlighted as a literary critic," Miss Marblemaw said, making another note. "You seem to be a man of many hats."

"Parents usually are," Arthur said, steepling his hands under his chin. That word: parent. So simple and yet so excitingly profound.

"Well, not *quite* a parent yet, are we?" She folded her hands on top of her clipboard, pen still clasped between her fingers. "After all, no adoption has been approved. You are, as of this moment, nothing more than the master of an orphanage, employed by the very body you seem to be at odds with." The pen tapped against the clipboard once, twice, three times.

Arthur shrugged. "Love what you do, and you'll never work a day in your life. Isn't that how the saying goes?"

"Things are changing," Miss Marblemaw said airily. "Why, even ten years ago, a single man attempting to adopt children would raise more than a few eyebrows."

"Would it?" Arthur asked. "How curious. I suppose those eyebrows will just have to stay as is, seeing as how I am not single, as you know." He smiled. "In fact, we have wonderful news. Linus proposed, and I said yes." He held out his hand, the ring flashing in the light. He caught himself staring at it every now and then, marveling over how heavy it was for such a small thing, a constant reminder that he was loved.

She blinked in surprise. "Really? You . . ." She shook her head, followed by something Arthur did not expect. "That's . . . congratulations."

He paused. She almost sounded like she meant it. "Thank you. I appreciate your well wishes."

"When is the wedding?"

Arthur chuckled. "We haven't gotten that far yet. Soon, I hope."

She stared at him for a moment, then looked back down at her clipboard, clearing her throat. "You are straying from the required reading. In addition, the lesson plans and individual reports you've provided on each child indicate that while all are excelling—though I question that—you are *not* adhering to the curriculum approved by DICOMY."

"A curriculum that hasn't been updated since *I* was a child," Arthur said. "One of the textbooks DICOMY provides—all twelve hundred pages—has a section devoted to the best practices of subservience to humans. If you cannot see the issue with telling children to be deferential to others simply because of who they are, then there is a problem."

She sighed, shaking her head. "How are we supposed to get anywhere if you won't work with me? All I want to do is my job. To *help*." She smiled at him. "I think you and I can find common ground in that we both want what's best for the children. After all, DICOMY cares."

"So you've said numerous times," Arthur said, settling his hands on the desk. "But forgive me if I don't take your word at face value, given my own experiences with DICOMY."

She hesitated. Then: "I can't speak to that. I wasn't there. But what I *can* speak to are my years of experience as a DICOMY employee. Though you may not see it, DICOMY has changed the face of magical children as we know it. Why is it so difficult for you to make sure the children understand how many people we've assisted through the years?"

"The world is a weird and wonderful place. Why must we explain it all—"

"So that it can be cataloged and studied, and any potential threat neutralized."

He sat forward abruptly. "*Neutralized?* If you think I'm going to sit here and let you—"

"You misunderstand me, Mr. Parnassus," she said. "Perhaps I used too-strong language, but the spirit remains the same. I want to protect as many children as I can. Surely you feel the same."

"I do," Arthur said. "Though I have a feeling we're coming at it from different directions."

"If that is the case," she said, "then why does it matter how we achieve our goals if we're working toward the same thing?"

Arthur sighed. For a moment, he'd thought perhaps Marblemaw might be different. Not Linus—no, no one could ever be him—but something close to him. He'd given Linus the benefit of the doubt, and that had changed their lives forever. Was it too much to think Marblemaw could have been the same?

"I wish I could believe that," he said slowly. "However, I've seen much evidence to the contrary that vehemently shows DICOMY cares not for those under its watch."

"Which is why I think we could all do with a fresh start," she said, smile widening. She was clever. He'd remember that. "After all, I don't see the point of letting the past dictate the future."

The phoenix lifted its head, eyes narrowed. Arthur felt the heat of it, and put it into his voice. "The past of each of the children you come into contact with cannot and should not be ignored. To suggest otherwise is not only dangerous, but cruel. You cannot take it from them. It is *part* of them, warts and all."

Miss Marblemaw pursed her lips. "Being a parent means—"

He cocked his head. "Two minutes ago, I wasn't a parent, but now I am? Please, Miss Marblemaw. Be as consistent as possible."

"*Being a parent means* being ready for any and every eventuality. Have you considered your options if and when, for example, Lucy decides on his own he doesn't like the world as it is? What if he decides to remake it as he sees fit?"

"He's seven years old," Arthur snapped, anger bubbling underneath the surface.

"So was Nero, at one point. Genghis Khan. Ivan the Terrible. While I'm not suggesting he'll do what they did, how can we know for sure? There is so much unknown about who he is and what he is capable of. No matter what you do or how hard you try, even *you* can't say with any certainty that he won't turn toward a path of darkness."

"You've spoken with him once," Arthur reminded her. "That's nowhere near enough time to build a foundation based upon objective evidence. But since you brought it up, it comes down to the idea of nature versus—"

"Nurture," she said. "I know. A false dichotomy. The reality is that nature and nurture do not exist as separate entities. They exist in reciprocity."

"And yet, studies have shown that trauma in the form of abuse changes the physical brain to be hypersensitive to future stress, which can often lead victims of abuse to respond excessively to even the smallest stressors. By doing the exact opposite of nurturing, one runs the risk of creating or exacerbating trauma."

"Which is precisely why I'm here," she said, shifting her weight in her chair. "To determine if you are capable of handling such . . . charges. Mr. Parnassus, surely you can see that my job is to ensure the safety of the children."

"So you say," Arthur demurred. "Objective evidence, and all that."

Miss Marblemaw shook her head as if disappointed. "I am not the enemy. Regardless of what you think of me or what I represent, I hope you understand that. My job is the children, nothing more."

He laughed quietly. "I don't believe that for a moment." He raised his hand as she started to speak. "Whether *you* believe that is another matter entirely, and one I'm not wanting to litigate currently as I doubt we'd reach any consensus. Either you will be who you claim to be, or you won't."

"Are you angry, Mr. Parnassus?" she asked, clutching the clipboard tightly. "Feeling a little hot under the collar?"

Yes, he was, but then he realized what she was doing, and laughed at the absurdity of it all. "Miss Marblemaw, are you trying to make me bring out the phoenix? If you're that curious, all you need to do is ask, and I'd be happy to show you."

She changed tack. "David," she said. "He's not an adult. I don't know how or why you expected me to believe that. Either you think me a fool, or you are nowhere near as intelligent as certain circles seem to think you are."

"Both could easily be true," Arthur said.

"Do you have any proof that David is the age you claim?"

Before Arthur could come up with a semi-believable lie—*to question a yeti's age is to commit a serious faux pas*—a flood of warmth burst under his hand. Without reacting, he moved his hand slightly to the left. There, in a familiar messy scrawl, letters forming in red ink. Four words, followed by a smiley face with devil horns on the top: OPEN YOUR TOP DRAWER!

Arthur cleared his throat and did just that. There, sitting on top of a tray of pens, pencils, and paperclips, a small stack of photographs that hadn't been there only a few minutes before when he'd gone in search of a pen in preparation for the meeting with Miss Marblemaw.

There were four photographs in total—the colors washed out, the edges curled in a sepia-toned haze as if seen through a dream. The first photograph showed a ten-year-old version of Arthur standing in the village near the dock. On either side of him were his friends, the other children in the orphanage, the sun blazing above them. He remembered this moment. They'd gone to town, the master in a rare good mood. The letter and the cellar were three months away. The master had taken the photograph with a boxy Polaroid camera, the picture sliding out the front. He'd given it to Ronnie to shake, and they'd all watched as the image formed as if by magic. They hadn't said as much, of course. That way lay madness.

Two things stuck out at Arthur: the first being that this photograph should not exist. The master had torn it to shreds in a fit of pique after one of the other children had mouthed off about something Arthur couldn't recall.

The second was the fifth figure, standing next to Arthur, hairy arm slung over his shoulders.

David.

The next photo showed Arthur at age fifteen, sitting in a window nook, a book forgotten in his lap. The frozen moment had caught him with his head tilted back, laughing silently. David sat across from him, smiling widely.

The third photograph was Arthur at around thirty or thereabouts. In a pub he'd never been to before, sitting on a stool, a half-empty pint in front of him. Seated next to him, David with five empty pint glasses, head rocked back as he laughed.

The fourth and final picture was of Arthur and Zoe, standing in front of the house. The repairs looked almost finished, and next to Zoe was David, white hair blotted with what looked to be blue paint, the same color Arthur had used on the walls in the upstairs hallway.

"Would you look at that?" he murmured. "Will these do?"

She snapped the photographs from his hand, holding each one an inch or two from her face, turning it this way and that as if she could determine their validity by sight alone. "How did you do this?" she demanded, flipping through the pictures again and again.

"With a camera," Arthur said.

She stood abruptly, chair scraping along the floor. "I have to . . . go do . . . something that requires my immediate attention. I will return in exactly one half hour. I expect to meet with each child individually upon my return."

Curious, this: her reaction was not what Arthur expected. But then, it could be said that trying to understand the motivations of anyone in a government role was an exercise in futility. Still, it was odd. At the hearing, Rowder had successfully gotten Arthur to reveal the phoenix. But not before going on at length about a certain child in particular. Perhaps he should let her in on the event ahead, just to see what she would do.

She had made it to the door when Arthur said, "Saturday."

Miss Marblemaw paused, her hand on the doorknob. She didn't turn around. "What about Saturday?"

"There is to be an adventure. Every Saturday, one of the children gets to decide the outing we'll all take part in."

"Whose turn is it this week?"

He grinned sharply at her back. She claimed not to experience fear. He wondered how true that was. "Lucy."

Her shoulders tightened but she otherwise gave no reaction. "I see. I will be in attendance, of course."

"Of course," Arthur said. "I'm sure it'll be a day you won't soon forget."

True to her word, Miss Marblemaw invited each of the children into Arthur's office, saying they weren't to be interrupted. Arthur, as it happened, did *not* find this to be acceptable. But before he could tell her just that, Talia patted his hand and said, "I've got this."

With that, she followed Miss Marblemaw into the office, shutting the door behind her.

Ten minutes later, the door opened once more, Talia walking out, eyes sparkling. In the office, Arthur heard three ferocious sneezes in quick succession, followed by the wet honking of a nose into a tissue. "She's *really* allergic to pollen," Talia said. "I should've emptied my pockets before going in. Oops."

"Quite," Arthur said as she hugged his leg.

Chauncey went next, bellhop cap firmly in hand, saying he wanted to regale Miss Marblemaw with stories of his journey to become the best bellhop the world has ever known. Whether he succeeded was in the eye of the beholder. Arthur thought he had. Miss Marblemaw, on the other hand, did not seem to appreciate the fact that Chauncey could now make ink.

Next was Theodore, and though Arthur offered to translate, Miss Marblemaw (smears of ink across her chest) declined. Precisely six minutes later, Theodore left the office, head held high, a gold button trapped firmly between his fangs. The button looked suspiciously like the ones that adorned Miss Marblemaw's coat. Arthur stuck his head into the office to ask her if she was ready for Phee, but Miss Marblemaw must not have heard him, glaring down at the loose threads on her coat where a button had been.

Phee's meeting lasted twenty-six minutes. When she came out of the office, she said, "All she did was rant and rave about thieving dragons."

"Strange," Arthur said. "I didn't know we had any dragons."

"That's what *I* told her, but she wouldn't listen."

Lucy went next. The meeting lasted three minutes. When he came out, he shrugged and said, "She didn't want to listen to me talk about sticky buns and Hell. I'm so sad for her."

"Anything else?" Arthur asked.

Lucy looked up at him, a strange light in his eyes. "What else could there be?"

Sal went last, and without a word to Arthur. Instead, he nodded, and then went into the office, shutting the door behind him. Forty minutes later, the door opened and Miss Marblemaw was *smiling*. "Thank you, Sal," she said. "That was an illuminating conversation." Her smile faltered when she saw Arthur standing in the hall, but it was brief. "I appreciate that you take this so seriously. You get one official courtesy point."

"Thank you," Sal said. "I know you only want to help."

After she disappeared back into the office, Arthur fell in step beside Sal as they moved down the hallway. "Are you all right?"

"I am," he said. "Stabbed her with kindness."

"The best kind of stabbing, or so I'm told."

"David?"

"Safe for now," Arthur said as they reached the top of the steps. "You wouldn't happen to know anything about photographs in my desk, would you?"

Sal paused, lips quirking. "How did they get there?"

"As if by magic. I notice you didn't ask what the photographs showed."

"Did they help?"

"They did."

"Huh," he said. "How about that?" He descended the stairs, whistling.

Bright and early Saturday morning, the residents of Marsyas Island piled into a maroon van, their excitement palpable. Adventure called, and those lucky enough to answer did so with a wide-eyed exuberance only found in the young and the young at heart.

And then there was Miss Marblemaw.

"What is she *wearing*?" Phee asked, face plastered against the window as the inspector made her way from the guesthouse toward the van.

For once, Arthur didn't have a ready answer, but only because Miss Marblemaw appeared to have gotten into a ferocious battle with a peacock and somehow emerged victorious. That was the only explanation for the colorful feathers of varying lengths that formed a collar around her neck, the ones at the back of her head rising dramatically above her. The feathers were attached to a long black coat cinched tightly at the waist.

"Is it mating season?" Chauncey asked. "Her plumage is on full display."

"That's one word for it," Linus muttered.

"If she starts dancing toward you as she brings you shiny rocks, run in the other direction," Phee said.

"Who wears a coat in summer?" David asked. "Is she hiding secrets?"

Theodore chirped and clicked, and Sal patted his head. "No, bud. She can't fly."

"She's almost here!" Lucy whisper-shouted. "Everyone act normal!"

Right when Miss Marblemaw opened the sliding door and stuck her head in, Talia said, "And that's the reason I decided to devote myself to the Lord."

"Wow," Chauncey said. "That sure was a neat story, Talia. Miss Marblemaw! We didn't even see you there. Welcome! If any birds attack you, don't worry! It's mating season."

Miss Marblemaw pulled her head out of the van, tilting her face toward the sky. "*Birds* could attack me?"

"Maybe," Lucy said. "But you look like you could hold your own, so I wouldn't be too worried if I were you. And look! I saved you a seat. Isn't that fun?" He patted the space next to him, smiling widely.

Miss Marblemaw looked back into the van, a sour expression on her face. "I don't suppose there's a second vehicle."

"There is not," Linus said pointedly. "If you're coming with us, get in."

She did exactly that, heading for the row in the back where Lucy waited for her. Lucy winked at Arthur in the rearview mirror before exclaiming, "You did it! I knew you could. Sit *right* next to me. There you go. Oh, look! Our legs are touching. Linus, we need travel music. Can you give us some tunes?"

"Any requests?"

"You'll know it when you hear it."

Linus began to flip through the stations and had only turned the knob slightly to the left before a familiar pluck of guitar strings filled the van. A moment later, a rockabilly named Gene Vincent sang about how he's led an evil life, so they say, but he'll hide from the Devil on judgment day.

"Righteous!" Lucy crowed as he began to dance in his seat without a care about where his elbows might land. Before long, everyone (excluding Miss Marblemaw) joined in, singing, *move, hot rod, move me on down the line.*

The village was bustling, crowds of people on the sidewalks in colorful summer wear and large hats, carrying tote bags and coolers filled to the brim with snacks and drinks as they walked toward one of the two public beaches available to those who chose Marsyas as their vacation destination.

Others milled about in front of store windows, *ooh*ing and *ahh*ing about overpriced trinkets made of shells and cloudy sea glass, and row after row of freshly made fudge: peanut butter (delicious!), walnut (exemplary!), mint (toothpaste!), and orange creamsicle (revolting!). Crowds gathered in front of mobile carts, some selling funnel cakes with powdered sugar sprinkled on top, others hawking jerk chicken on wooden skewers. An enterprising young woman stood above a wool blanket spread out on the sidewalk at her feet, shouting that she had *kites for sale, get your kites here!*

No reporters in sight, which was a relief. Though their numbers had dwindled since the aftermath of the hearing, Helen told Arthur and Linus that a few of the more insistent journalists had stuck around, hoping for a sighting of the residents of Marsyas Island, and perhaps a quote or three. Luckily enough, after receiving a tip from an anonymous caller who claimed something cataclysmically magical was occurring two hours to the north, the reporters had piled into their vehicles and sped from the village. The directions were vague enough that the anonymous caller—who could it have been?—did not expect anyone to return until at least early evening.

Arthur pulled the van into the mostly empty lot behind Helen's gardening store, parking next to her truck. The children all tried to leave the van at once, Theodore of the mind that beings with wings got to leave first. Phee agreed. Lucy did not, saying that if he didn't get out of the van first, he was going to bring about the End of Days. As it turned out, most of the travelers in the van were used to such bons mots and didn't pay him any mind.

Miss Marblemaw did, however, furiously scribbling on her clipboard. "Lucy," she asked as he climbed over her, "what did you mean by End of Days?"

Lucy almost fell out of the van, but stopped himself at the doorway. "Why?"

"I'm a detail-oriented person. I want to make sure I understand everything."

"Do you?" He leaned forward, face inches from hers. "You know, they say the devil's in the details. Isn't that funny?" With that, he jumped out of the van.

"Today is going to be exhausting," Linus said as he pushed open the door.

As ever, Lucy was full of surprises.

Standing at the center of attention, he proudly announced that since it was *his* day, he got to decide what everyone was doing. Rather than something horrifying and/or life-threatening, Lucy told his captive audience that today, he'd planned something special for each of them. Phee and Talia would get to see some new (and definitely *not* poisonous) plants that Helen had gotten in.

Chauncey was given the chance to show Linus where he worked at the hotel, and what Chauncey's day-to-day entailed in the exciting role of a bellhop. Chauncey practically shouted at Linus that he couldn't wait to show him the break room where there was a microwave, a refrigerator, and a wall calendar from seventeen years ago that showed goats wearing hats. Miss August, as it turned out, was his favorite as she was brown and white *and* wore a daring pillbox hat that really complimented her snout.

For Sal and Theodore, a trip to the library where both would have access to the rare-book section, to be followed by a visit to the antique store where the proprietor had recently discovered an entire jar filled with buttons in storage, and had set it aside for the wyvern to peruse should there be any treasures hidden within.

"As for me, I'll be hanging out with David and Arthur," Lucy said as Miss Marblemaw frowned. "We're going to have whiskey sours and talk about babes." He suddenly frowned and ran over to Linus, tugging on his shirt. "*Psst. Linus.* What kind of babes do I like?"

"You can like whoever you want," Linus said, patting his head.

Lucy looked relieved as he ran back to the others. "And by babes, I mean anyone who looks awesome. I don't know who it'll be yet, but when I do, you'll all be the first to know."

"Why are we still standing here?" Talia demanded. "I've been promised new plants. You don't want to see what happens when a gnome loses their patience. Last time one did, it led to the Dark Age."

"Is that true?" Linus whispered to Arthur.

"It could be," Arthur murmured. "The fall of Rome *and* upsetting a gnome? It certainly sounds like an age of darkness to me."

"And that leaves Miss Marblemaw," Lucy said, and all the children turned their heads toward her slowly, a practiced move that caused the inspector to take a step back. Lucy seemed to catch on to this, taking a step forward, giggling when the inspector took another step back. "Miss Marblemaw," he said in a singsong voice. "You get to decide who you want to go with. Isn't that exciting? What will it be? Plants with Talia and Phee? Books and buttons with Theodore and Sal? Bellhopping with Linus and Chauncey? *Or,*" he said, taking yet another step toward her, "will you throw caution to the wind and follow me into the depths of despair?"

"Despair!" the children chanted, including David, who joined in, shouting with the best of them. "Despair! Despair!"

Miss Marblemaw huffed out an irritated breath as she glared at Arthur and Linus. "You allow the children to go off on their own?"

"We do," Linus said. "It teaches them responsibility and time management, and gives them the opportunity to interact with our community."

"Which means they mingle," Miss Marblemaw retorted, clipboard clasped against her chest, "with *humans*."

"And?" Arthur asked. "It sounds as if you believe they should be segregated."

"*Bup, bup, bup!*" she trilled loudly. "We don't use that word, given the negative connotations behind it. Rather, DICOMY performed focus group research and came to the conclusion that 'voluntary separation' sounds much better than 'seg'—that other word."

"Your tax dollars hard at work," Linus muttered. Then, in a louder voice: "We will use neither, thank you very much. And as a DICOMY-sanctioned inspector, your role here is to observe and report back to your superiors. Anything above and beyond that is outside of your purview."

She narrowed her eyes, the children's heads on a swivel as they looked back and forth between them. "I do hope none of the children find themselves in a dangerous situation, especially when they don't have adult supervision."

"Let's try this again," Arthur said. "Talia and Phee will be with Helen and Zoe. Chauncey will be with Linus. Lucy will be with David and myself. That leaves Sal and Theodore without supervision. Sal is fifteen years old and both have proven they are more than responsible enough to go out on their own."

"For now," Miss Marblemaw said with a haughty sniff. She looked at the children as if she had discovered a new, perpetually wet insect with a thousand legs. Tapping her pen, she let the silence drag on, even as Arthur knew she'd already made her decision. "I will accompany Mr. Parnassus."

"Lucky us," Arthur said. "Children, we'll meet in front of the ice cream parlor in exactly two hours. Please don't be late. What do we say? Punctuality is not just about being on time. . . ."

"It's also about respecting your commitments," the children said.

"Yeah, that," David said, bouncing on his heels. "Commitment!"
"And we're off!" Arthur cried.

Naturally, Lucy led them directly to Rock and Soul, the record shop owned and operated by one Mr. J-Bone (not his real name; no one—not even J-Bone himself—could remember what it was). On the walk to the shop, Lucy regaled David with stories of visits past, the musical discoveries he and J-Bone had made, and the time a former employee tried to exorcise him in the back room.

"What was that?" Miss Marblemaw asked.

Lucy smiled up at her. "Exercise. We did lunges and jumping jacks."

"Hmm," she said, pen flying across the page.

"Is he nice?" David asked as they approached the record store, speaking for the first time since they'd left the parking lot. "J-Bone, I mean."

Arthur was about to intervene—regardless of the lie they were attempting to pull off, David was still a child, and his comfort was of the utmost importance—but Lucy got there first. He held out his hand, wiggling his digits. David hesitated only a moment before closing his hairy fingers around Lucy's. "He's great," Lucy said. "I wouldn't take you to see someone mean, unless we were getting revenge."

David nodded, looking relieved. "Okay. Thanks. Still trying to get used to all of this."

"*And*," Lucy said, "I told J-Bone that we'd come and visit today, and he promised to set the air conditioning as cold as it will go so you don't get too hot."

"Why?" David asked.

Lucy rolled his eyes. "Because I want you to listen to dead-people music with me, duh. Oh, and one other thing: when we go in, we need to say 'righteous' a lot. That's what J-Bone does, and he knows *everything* that's cool."

"He doesn't know me," David said nervously. "So he doesn't know everything cool."

Lucy gaped at him. "That . . . that meant *two* things! Holy crap, where have you been all my life? Come on, I can't wait for J-Bone to meet you. It's gonna be *righteous*." He tugged David down the sidewalk toward the door.

"How odd," Miss Marblemaw said.

"What is?" Arthur asked, glancing back over his shoulder at her.

"That an adult like David would be so concerned with meeting someone new. One might even say he acted . . . childlike."

"Yes," Arthur said. "I suppose that's what happens when you've lived your entire life being told you're a monster. Strange how that works. Trauma, as you're hopefully aware, manifests itself in different ways—some big, some small—and can extend across a lifetime. The fact that you're trivializing it says more about you than it does about him. Now, if you'll excuse me, I have a desire to hear some dead-people music."

He felt her gaze boring into his back.

"Far *out*!" J-Bone said, suitably impressed at the sight of David's retractable claws. "Like, knives on demand. Bet you never have to worry about finding something to cut your bagels. Talk about a blessed life."

Lucy and David stood in front of J-Bone, a tall and lanky fellow who grinned down at them as he leaned against the counter. For reasons known only to him, J-Bone wore a paisley scarf over a red robe with golden tassels, his long gray-and-black hair pulled back into a braid that rested on his left shoulder. Pink plastic sunglasses sat atop his head, one of the lenses missing.

When Arthur entered the shop, J-Bone lifted the bottom of his robe to reveal orange socks with little red flames on them. "Big Bird!" he cried. "Check out my feet gloves. Thought you'd get a kick out of them."

"I do," Arthur said. He extended his leg, placing his foot next to J-Bone's to show off his purple socks adorned with tiny black records.

"Sock bros!" J-Bone cheered, pulling Arthur into a back-slapping hug that Arthur returned in kind. He was about to pull away when J-Bone stiffened as the door opened, the bell overhead tinkling. "Who's the square?" he whispered as he stepped back.

"That's Miss Marblemaw," Lucy said. "She's here to make sure Arthur and Linus aren't sacrificing us in a blood ritual. She works for the government."

"That right?" J-Bone said, scratching his jaw. "She got a warrant?"

"A warrant?" she asked. "Why would I need a warrant?"

"Uh, no reason," J-Bone said, eyes darting side to side. "If you happen to see certain . . . glassware for sale, it's for tobacco and nothing else." As if he thought he was invisible, he reached back and grabbed a pungent glass pipe, shoving it in his pocket.

"Yes," Miss Marblemaw said. "By your appearance alone, I'd have thought the same thing."

"What's that for?" David whispered to Lucy.

"Grass," Lucy said. "Linus said J-Bone likes lawns."

"Oh. That . . . makes sense. I think?"

"Hey, little devil dude," J-Bone said, bending over, hands on his knees. "You'll never guess what I got in."

Lucy's eyes widened as he began to bounce on the tips of his toes. "You *didn't*."

"Sure did," J-Bone said. "Ella Fitzgerald. Billie Holiday. Live at the Newport Jazz Festival."

"No. *Way*. The one where Ella did 'Air Mail' and—"

"Gave a scat performance to end all scat performances? That would be the one."

Lucy threw up his arms. "Yes! *Yes*. Finally! You know, anytime I want to wipe out the entire universe, I remember that humans made *music* and then I think that maybe, just maybe, you weirdos have something to offer after all."

"Gnarly," J-Bone said. "I'm totally down for saving the universe through music. Like, there you are, this little bundle of rockin' chaos, and then there's me, the savior of all mankind. Take *that*, Dad!"

"Yeah," David said. "Take that, J-Bone's dad!"

"I like the cut of your jib, hairy dude with knife hands," J-Bone said. "To the record player!"

"To the record player!" Lucy cheered, adopting J-Bone's gait, a sort of slide-n-sizzle, more dancing than walking. David attempted admirably to do the same, but ended up skipping instead, following J-Bone and Lucy to the left wall, where three record players had been set up for patrons to listen to music while they shopped. Going to the cabinet underneath the middle record player, J-Bone pulled out a gold-and-brown sleeve, Ella and Billie in profile on either side. "Some other killer jams on here," J-Bone said as he pulled the record out. "Ella covering the Gershwins, Duke Ellington. Billie's got Herbie Nichols on the piano for 'Lady Sings the Blues,' and it's so cool, it's like ice."

"Like me," David said.

J-Bone blinked. Then, "Hell yeah, little hairy dude with knife hands. *Exactly* like you. In fact, you might even be cooler than that. You know, being a yeti and all. Fun fact! Thought I met a yeti once, but it turned out to be a hairy footstool. To be fair, I was extremely high on—"

Arthur cleared his throat pointedly.

"—life and all it has to offer," J-Bone said easily. "So it was an honest mistake."

"Yeah, it happens," David said. "I mean, that's righteous."

J-Bone beamed at him. "Look at you, David! We'll make a hep cat outta you yet, just wait and see. Now, are you ready to be transported to Newport? Trust me when I say your life will never be the same." He set the record on the player and lowered the needle. The record hissed and crackled, and then a moment later, tinny cheers were followed by Ella laughing and saying "Thank you!" as the piano kicked in, along with the *tsst tsst tsst* of the snare and hi-hat.

And Ella began to scat, a brilliant improvisation that caused Arthur's nerves to calm and his heart to swell, especially when Lucy and J-Bone started scatting along with her nonsensically, more sound than rhythm.

At first, David looked unsure, but as soon as the music began, his eyes widened slowly, his mouth hanging open. When J-Bone and Lucy began to scat with Ella, he turned his head toward them, starting to bounce a little. And then Ella threw in, "*When the moon hits your eye like a big pizza pie, that's amore,*" causing David to laugh as he shook his rear in an awkward shimmy, his thick white hair flailing around him.

"That's it!" J-Bone cried. "Feel it! She is a *queen*. Do be do whaaaaaaa."

"Arthur!" Lucy called. "You wanna dance too?"

He did, more than almost anything. Without looking at Miss Marblemaw, Arthur slid one foot out in front of him, the hem of his trousers halfway up his calf. He snapped once, twice, and as Ella brought them toward the big finish, he shouted, "Da da di-dilee dop do *bap*!"

"Aw," Lucy said. "It's so cute when you try. We'll have to practice more. J-Bone, play it again!"

After replaying the song seven more times, Lucy proclaimed Arthur and David to be scat masters, and reminded them that it had nothing to do with feces, which Arthur appreciated. After all, they had enough shit to deal with.

David grew more comfortable the longer they stayed in the shop. Though he kept a careful eye on Lucy and Arthur as if to make sure they wouldn't leave him behind, he started sorting through records, asking J-Bone which ones were his favorites. Lucy sat on the floor next to Arthur, both looking for hidden treasures.

Miss Marblemaw followed J-Bone, attempting to ask him questions about his interactions with Lucy, and if he'd ever felt that his life had been threatened. Politely, J-Bone said, "I'm not a narc, and

I'm assisting a customer. I'll be with you shortly. Thanks for your patience!" With that, he turned back to David, who had picked up a record. "The Clovers? Man, that is *choice*. Most people dig 'Love Potion No. 9,' but don't sleep on 'One Mint Julep.' So smooth, it'll make you feel like you're being spread on toast."

Certain that David was in good hands, Arthur looked back at Lucy, who was studying a record sleeve with a concentration he normally reserved for attempting to create sentient mud men. "Lucy," Arthur said.

Lucy looked up. "I don't think I have this one. How many records can I get today?"

"You already have records at home you haven't listened to yet. How many more do you think you need?"

"Well, when you put it *that* way . . . thirty more should be sufficient."

"Three," Arthur said.

"Twenty-nine and a half."

"Two."

"Three it is!" Lucy said. "I knew you'd see it my way." He pulled out another record, discarding it almost immediately before going after another.

"Lucy," Arthur said again. "Can I ask you a question?"

Attention firmly fixed on the records, Lucy shrugged and said, "Sure."

"Today was your day to pick the adventure."

"Wow, your memory is extraordinary. How *do* you do it?"

"And yet, instead of thinking about what *you* wanted to do, you went and planned a day for each of your brothers and sisters."

"But I am doing what I want to do," Lucy said, looking up at him. "We're at the record shop."

"I get that," Arthur said. "But what I'm asking is *why*?"

"Oh," Lucy said. "That's easy. Remember when we talked about being a monster or being good?"

"I do. You were quite upset with me."

"Maybe," Lucy said, grabbing another record and holding it

close to his face. "But I thought about it. Like, *a lot*. I was still sort of mad at you, but then I thought about what makes *me* happy."

Arthur nodded. "And what did you decide?"

"That I like when other people are happy, and it makes me feel good when I get to be part of it," Lucy explained. But because he was still Lucy, he added, "Not *everyone*, just the people I like. For some reason, it makes the spiders in my head go to sleep. Not forever, but for a little while."

"And why is that, do you think?"

Lucy shrugged. "I dunno, but I like how quiet it is."

"Why did you invite David?"

"Because I knew Miss Marblemaw would follow him, and if David is with us, I can make sure she's not being mean to him."

"You wanted to protect him," Arthur said.

"Sure," Lucy said. "Being new is scary, and having *her* here makes things worse. But if he's with us, then nothing can happen to him."

"You're not upset with him anymore?"

He paused. Then, "Don't think so. And even if I was, he booped me on the nose. You can't be mad at someone who does that. It's, like, the law or something."

"You astonish me," Arthur said. "In all the best ways possible."

"That's because I'm amazing." He pointed a finger at Arthur. "But just because I want to make people happy doesn't mean I can't do other things too."

"Like what?"

Lucy leaned toward him, eyes glinting red. "*Monster* things," he whispered. "Do you think that when Miss Marblemaw finishes her inspection she'll let me have her skull if I ask nicely? It's not like she's using it very much."

"That's certainly one way of putting it," Arthur said. "But why don't we keep that between us?"

"I can do that," Lucy said with a sly smile. "*If* I can get four records."

"Five," Arthur said. "And that is my final offer."

"You're so righteous," Lucy said. "Give me some skin, you cool cat."

Who was Arthur to refuse such an offer?

Later, Arthur would tell himself it was inevitable, that it was always building to *something*. The hearing, David, Miss Marblemaw, the thinly veiled threats from the government: all of it a confluence, creating a perfect storm in broad daylight. The moments in his office—the brief instances where Miss Marblemaw showed proof of her humanity—were a lie, and though he hadn't let himself believe her, he had hoped she'd be different.

Perhaps her admitted absence of fear should have been his first clue: though David's time on the island had been short, the yeti had already taught Arthur that a bit of fear could be healthy. What must it feel like to fear nothing? Wasn't fear a part of the human condition?

He couldn't help the darker thoughts. What if people who lacked fear were despised and tracked like animals? Surely Miss Marblemaw would have a thing or two to say about that. Or, she might even try to hide it from the world. In ways, so alike, and yet now she was about to prove him wrong in the worst possible way.

Arthur was with Lucy, picking out the fifth record he wanted to purchase. J-Bone and David had made it to the rear of the store, though Arthur could still hear David asking question after question, J-Bone never tiring of answering.

Miss Marblemaw—out of sight, out of mind. Arthur hadn't seen her in a while, but then he was distracted by Lucy's constant chatter about how *this* record is a banger, but *this* one is bangeriffic, a marked distinction.

Arthur said, "Is there anything above bangeriffic? That doesn't seem possible—"

A strangled cry, followed by the thudding of feet. Arthur's head jerked up to see J-Bone hurtling down the middle of the record shop, yelling at the top of his lungs. Behind him, waddling monstrously with claws outstretched, David, lips curled up in a ferocious snarl, fangs on full display. J-Bone hit the front door, causing it to fly open, bouncing off the side of the shop. David followed him outside.

"Are they playing tag?" Lucy asked. "I want to play tag!"

"I don't—" Before he could finish, Miss Marblemaw swept through the record shop, coat trailing behind her, a twisted expression on her face, furious.

Arthur shot to his feet as Miss Marblemaw burst outside.

Without hesitating, Arthur bent over, scooping up Lucy in one fluid motion as he ran for the door, blood rushing in his ears. For his part, Lucy rolled with it, climbing around Arthur to his back, arms around his neck, little feet digging into his sides.

The sun blinded him the moment he left the record shop. Blinking rapidly to clear his vision, Lucy's breath hot in his ear, Arthur skidded to a stop, bumping into people who had gathered on the sidewalk, all looking at something in the street. Pushing his way through the crowd, Arthur felt his rage boil over when he saw what everyone was staring at.

Miss Marblemaw, in the street, hand like a vise around David's wrist. She towered above him, coat billowing around her ankles. David struggled against her, but her grip was firm. "How *dare* you chase humans," Miss Marblemaw snapped down at him. "You could have *killed* that poor man!"

"Don't worry," Lucy whispered in his ear. "I've called them. They're coming."

"What? Who are you—"

"Hey!" J-Bone snapped from the other side of the street. "We were playing around! Get your bloody hands off him!"

Miss Marblemaw faltered, but it was brief. "It does not *matter*." She jerked David's arm again, and David whimpered, eyes glassy as he struggled to get away. "This . . . this *thing* is an animal! Animals have *instincts*. You run, their prey drive kicks in, and—"

"Remove your hand from him immediately before I burn it off."

Miss Marblemaw turned toward Arthur slowly, a strand of her hair plastered against her forehead. "Another threat, Mr. Parnassus? Are you sure that's an appropriate response? Especially in front of so many witnesses."

"You're scaring him!" J-Bone yelled.

Miss Marblemaw looked down at David, who dug his feet into the ground, trying to break free. She leaned forward and said, "What childlike fear for one who hasn't been a child in decades." Her grip tightened.

Arthur took a step forward as Lucy slid from his back. People around him gasped as flames began to spread along his shoulders, his arms, his hands, crackling, snapping. The phoenix screamed in his chest, wings spread wide, its eyes a pair of burning stars.

But before the phoenix could erupt, Lucy tugged on Arthur's shirt, making him look down. "This is what she wants, Dad."

Dad, Arthur thought through fire.

A shadow momentarily blotted out the sun, and Miss Marblemaw yelped when a wyvern dove toward her, wings folded at his sides. She ducked, and David jerked free, stumbling back against—

Sal, standing in the street, eyes cold as Theodore alighted upon his shoulder. On his left, Phee and Talia, the former holding David's wrist as ice cubes fell from his eyes and shattered on the concrete, the latter glaring daggers at Miss Marblemaw. On Sal's right, Chauncey and Lucy. Behind them, as furious as Arthur had ever seen him, Linus, who glanced at Arthur, nodded, and then turned his focus back on Miss Marblemaw.

Talia stepped forward as the inspector pulled herself to her full height. She continued walking until she was only a foot away from Miss Marblemaw. The top of Talia's cap barely reached her waist. Talia looked her up and down, and said, "DICOMY is dumb, but I can't believe they'd send someone so stupid. Linus wasn't stupid, so why are you?"

"You do *not* get to speak to me that way," Miss Marblemaw said, face twisted and almost purple. "I am your elder, and therefore your better."

"Actually, I'm older than you," Talia said. "So that makes me *your* elder. As such, a bit of advice: I'd be careful if I were you. Some of us are more powerful than we look."

Miss Marblemaw glowered down at Talia. "The Antichrist is—"

"Oh, not me," Lucy said with a grin. "I mean, not *just* me. She's talking about Phee."

Miss Marblemaw blinked. "The forest sprite? Surely you jest. What is she going to do? Grow a tree?"

"Funny you should mention trees," Phee said, joining her sister in front of Miss Marblemaw. Through his fire, Arthur saw the inspector take an answering step back. "Because the last time people hurt my family, I turned them *all* into trees. Their flesh became bark. Their blood turned into pitch. Arms, branches. Fingers and toes, leaves."

"You wouldn't *dare*," Miss Marblemaw said.

"Uh-oh," Chauncey said. "You really shouldn't have said that."

Phee's wings began to flutter as she lifted off the ground, rising until she was face-to-face with Miss Marblemaw, her hair a crown of fire. Without looking away from the inspector, Phee leaned forward until her nose touched Miss Marblemaw's. "Try me," she said in a flat voice. "Touch *any* of us again, and it'll be the last thing you do before I plant you in the park and let dogs use you as a toilet."

"DICOMY will hear of this," Miss Marblemaw said, the skin under her left eye twitching dangerously. "They'll hear about *all of this*, and not even Arthur Parnassus will be able to talk his way out of this one."

"Good," Linus said coldly. "Because I'll be sure to make everyone aware that you put your hands on someone without their permission. And I don't believe we'll have to go far for witness corroboration."

People began to nod around Arthur, though they gave him a wide berth. He didn't blame them for that; his fire was still running along his arms and hands, under control but only just. But then another figure appeared beside him, unafraid. "They knew," Helen whispered to him. "Talia and Phee. I don't know how, but they knew."

Miss Marblemaw bristled. "I acted because I thought a human was in danger. Anyone would have done the same."

"Except we didn't," J-Bone said. "Because we know them." He glanced at David, expression softening. "Thanks to the little hairy dude with knife hands, I was able to fulfill a lifelong dream of getting chased by a yeti. How many people get to say that? Well, probably more than just me, but still! I got to, and it was even better than I hoped it'd be. Let's hear it for having dreams realized thanks to a yeti named David!" He began to cheer loudly, clapping his hands hard.

The other children joined in. Zoe and Linus too. Then the crowd began to cheer until it was a roar, Helen as loud as anyone. Arthur lent his own voice to the wall of noise as his fire dissipated.

As Miss Marblemaw looked on furiously, David began to smile.

The ride home would have been uncomfortable had Merle not agreed to take her back himself. "Leave it to me, Mr. Parnassus," he grumbled, eyeing Miss Marblemaw with disdain as they stood on the dock, the ferry behind them. "I'll get her over."

"If there were to be an unavoidable delay," Arthur said, "I would completely understand."

"Oh, aye," Merle said with a nod. "It happens. Sea can be fickle." He spat a thick wad into the sea. "Price has gone up, too, wouldn't you know. Summer season, and all that." He tilted his head toward Arthur. His breath smelled faintly of onions and tobacco. "Heard she gave you some trouble in town."

"Rumor mill working overtime, I see."

"That it does," Merle said. "Kids all right?"

"I don't know," Arthur admitted. "I hope so. Children can be remarkably resilient when they need to be. I just wish it didn't have to come to that."

"Why are you letting her go back?" Merle asked. "Seems to me, you should give her the boot. Kids safer that way."

An enigma, Merle was. Caustic, grouchy, and more than a little obtuse. And yet, he'd refused to bring the reporters to the island. He was asking after the children he usually only had the stink-eye for. *It's started,* Arthur thought in wonder. *Change, the voices of the few building to an unending roar.*

"Keep your friends close, keep your enemies closer," Arthur replied. "Believe me when I say Harriet Marblemaw will never find herself in that position again. She has made an enemy of me this day, and I won't soon forget."

Merle nodded. Then, in a lowered voice, he said, "If you need help hiding a body, I'm your man. The sea is very, *very* big."

"Thank you, Merle. Your kindness is not only welcome, but a salve to the soul after the events of today. But worry not; I have plenty of children who know how to hide a body."

Under David's thick hair, the skin of his wrist was bruised, the clear outline of fingers in darkening shades of violet. It didn't hurt very much, he claimed, and since his body was already freezing, there was no need to put an ice pack on it.

That did little to comfort Arthur. David seemed to have bounced back quickly, laughing at something Chauncey said by the time they arrived back on the island. Arthur hadn't lied when speaking of the resiliency of children, but he wished such things were never tested. Trauma had a way of manifesting itself in the unlikeliest circumstances, and Arthur and Linus would keep a close eye on David to make sure any potential triggers were avoided.

Linus and Zoe fed the children an early supper while Arthur stood on the porch, watching the road. As the sun began to set, Miss Marblemaw appeared over the rise, huffing and puffing, her skin slick with sweat, the peacock feathers drooping against her face.

She stopped when she saw him. He didn't call out to her, didn't raise his hand in greeting. He just stared.

She jutted her chin at him, and then went to the guesthouse, slamming the door behind her.

She didn't appear again for the rest of the evening.

That night, no matter how Arthur tossed and turned, sleep remained elusive.

Dad, Lucy had called him, easily and without forethought, as if it weren't the most transformational moment of Arthur's life. *Dad.*

When asked earlier how they'd known David was in trouble, it was Sal who spoke for them before climbing out of the van. "Lucy called for us."

Linus and Arthur had exchanged a perplexed glance, Zoe looking just as confused. "What do you mean, 'called'?" she asked.

"We heard him," Sal had said. "In our heads. He told us David was in trouble."

"Lucy?" Linus asked quietly. "Is that true?"

"Yep," Lucy had replied. "They're my brothers and sisters. Of course they heard me. Why wouldn't they?"

Arthur rose from the bed, smiling at the way Linus snuffled and snorted in his sleep. "Lovely man," he whispered, pulling the comforter up and over Linus's shoulder. Calliope lifted her head, her gaze following him. She leaned into his touch when he scratched behind her ears. He was about to head into his office to catch up on work when something flashed outside the window, a low light that bloomed twice more.

He went to the window, and even though it was a terrible angle, he thought he saw the source of the light coming from the gazebo in the garden.

Pulling on his robe, he first checked Lucy's room. The boy was asleep, snoring loudly, lips flapping. Next to his bed, lying on a slowly melting block of ice, David, little trails of cold fog streaming from his lips. Arthur let them be, closing the door before stepping out into the hall. He checked on each of the children, peeking his head in. Sal was sleeping on his stomach, face down into the pillow.

Theodore slept on his back, head curled into his side. Chauncey floated on saltwater, his tentacles loose around him. Talia slept in her burrow, leaves fluttering with every exhalation.

Phee wasn't in her room.

Refusing to let panic take over, he went downstairs and through the front door, stepping off the porch and turning right. He followed Talia's garden path until he came to the gazebo. There, sitting on one of the benches, Phee, wearing her sleep clothes but apparently wide awake, tongue sticking out between her teeth in concentration. As Arthur looked on, she raised her hands in front of her, palms facing each other, fingers crooked like claws, a tangle of dirty roots floating between. Her forehead grew lines as she strained. A moment later, another flash of light—white, soft. When the light faded, a small sapling hovered between her hands, the roots twisted and dangling. She snatched it out of the air and set it on top of a pile of similar saplings sitting off to her right. On her left, more roots.

Arthur cleared his throat, and Phee jumped, only relaxing when she saw who had interrupted her. "Couldn't sleep?" he asked, climbing the three steps into the gazebo.

She shrugged, looking back at her saplings. "Thinking."

"Is that right? Sounds serious." Given that the air was unseasonably cool, he removed his robe and settled it around her shoulders, fussing over her until she slid her arms through the sleeves. "Can I ask what you're thinking about?"

"Trees," she said dryly.

"And you felt the need to make them in the middle of the night."

"Why not?"

"Why not, indeed. Well, if it's all the same to you, I'd like to watch, if I'm not interrupting."

Phee nodded and got back to work. They sat in silence, the only sound coming from the low fizzy *pop!* each time a tree came into existence. The more she made, the stiffer she got, her shoulders near her ears, the corners of her mouth turning down. Though he desperately wanted to ask, he waited. Phee would come to it, in her own time.

And that proved accurate ten minutes later when she set down a new sapling, looked at Arthur, and said, "I would do it again."

"Do what?"

"Turn people into trees if they try and hurt us."

He swallowed past the lump in his throat. "Would you?"

"Yes," she said, looking down at her hands. "I know that doesn't make me a good person, but—"

"You *are* a good person," Arthur said fiercely. "One of the very best I've ever had the pleasure of knowing. Just because you feel a certain way about those who might try to do you harm doesn't negate any other part of you. If anything, it makes you human."

She made a face. "Well, I wouldn't go *that* far. Rather be a sprite than a human any day."

"I thought as much, and I'm glad to hear it. But even if you're angry, that doesn't give you the right to hurt other people."

"Even if they want to hurt us?"

Arthur hesitated, picking and choosing his words carefully. "I would expect you to protect yourself. Or others, if it came down to it. But I would also ask you to think of the repercussions of your actions." He sighed. "Though, I might not be the best guide in that regard. I doubt Lucy would take too kindly to being told he couldn't threaten murder on a daily basis, even if he doesn't do anything about it."

Phee snorted. "Yeah, let me know how *that* conversation goes." She paused. "Would you do anything differently? If you had to do it again?"

He resisted answering immediately, wanting to give her question the weight it deserved. Eventually, he said, "No. I wouldn't. Even with all I've been through, with all I've seen, I wouldn't want to be anything other than what I am. If I had to do it all over again just to arrive at this very moment, I would. Over and over again."

"Because you love us."

Dad, Lucy had called him. "With everything I have."

She nodded, looking out into the garden. "We know that. All of us do. David is starting to learn that too. It may take him some time, but if you want my opinion, you should talk to him about staying here. Permanently."

"You think he'd accept?"

"I don't know. But neither will you until you ask. And I'm getting really irritated with Linus's birt gift because there's a picture missing. It looks incomplete."

"Maybe both things can be rectified at the same time," Arthur said. "After the inspector leaves, of course. I won't have her anywhere near him again, nor will I allow her to intrude on such a private family moment."

"She's not going to stop," Phee said, looking at him again. "Miss Marblemaw." She cocked her head. "But you know that already, don't you? Especially after she told you she couldn't get scared."

"I do," Arthur admitted. "But I had hoped that she'd . . . It doesn't matter. You shouldn't worry about—"

"Uh, yeah, no. This is *about* me. It's about all of us. We're in this together."

He wrapped an arm around her shoulders, pulling her close, his face in her hair. "Tell me," he whispered to her. "Whatever your heart desires, please, tell me, and I'll do my very best to make it a reality."

She pulled away in a huff. "I don't need anything. That's not how caring works. You don't do something and expect to be rewarded, right?"

He nodded.

"Then why should I be any different? Doing the right thing isn't *about* accolades or recognition."

"Then why do it at all?" he asked, wanting to hear her answer.

She flushed, picking at a loose string on the robe. She was embarrassed, but powered through it. "You do it because maybe someone will see and do the same for another, and then *that* person will help someone else." She lit up, slyly glancing at Arthur. "Like your ripples in a pond."

He slid from the bench to the floor of the gazebo, on his knees before her. Reaching up to cup her face, he said, "You marvelous girl. I am a much better person having known you."

She turned her head, kissing his palm before he pulled his hands away. "I lied. I thought of something I want."

He snorted, sitting back on his heels. "And it shall be yours."

She studied him, looking momentarily nervous, something he rarely saw in her. He waited until she worked her way through it and said, "It's not a big deal. You can say no if you want."

"If it's a big deal to you, then it is to me. Tell me, please."

She took a deep breath, letting it out slowly. "Can . . . can I fly with you?"

He couldn't speak, stunned. Of everything he thought she'd ask for, this hadn't even crossed his mind.

She mistook his shock for reluctance. "It's okay," she said. "You don't have to." She shook her head. "Sorry. We . . . we talked about it. After you told us what you are. But we weren't sure if *you* wanted to talk about it anymore."

"Why would you think that?" he asked gruffly.

"Because you don't let the phoenix out very often," she said. "You keep it hidden away, like a secret. And we get why. After what you went through here"—she said it hurriedly, with a wince—"it must be hard to even think about the phoenix. And after what that nasty woman made you do at the hearing, I guess you don't want to—"

He stood, extending his hand. She took it without hesitation, allowing him to pull her up. Leading her down the gazebo steps, he squeezed her hand and said to his daughter, "It would be my honor."

The fire came, then, the phoenix rising with a piercing cry. Flames overtook Arthur, but they did not burn Phee. They could never. He was hers, and she was his. He would rather die than harm her, or any of them. As he sank into the phoenix, his mind shifted, changed, the troublesome thoughts of humanity falling away. His vision sharpened as he and the phoenix became one, a crystal clarity impossible with human eyes. All told, it took less than ten seconds for the fire to consume him, and he spread his wings, an impressive span of fiery orange and blood red. His tail feathers fanned wide, stretching, reveling in the freedom. Towering above Phee, he lowered his head, snapping his beak at her playfully. Phee gasped, stroking the small golden-red downy feathers between his eyes.

"Holy crap," she breathed. "You're *huge*!"

He snapped at her again, hopping on two black feet, his talons digging into the soil. He circled around her, nudging her back. "Okay, okay," she laughed. "I'm going. We'll race to the sandbar at the back of the island. On three, ready? Three!" And with that, she shot off into the air, her wings buzzing above her cackle.

Arthur crouched low and launched himself into the air, spreading his wings. They caught an updraft, lifting him higher and higher. *Daughter,* he thought in his alien mind as she darted away from him. *My daughter.*

They flew into the night, a sprite and a bird made of fire. At one point, she flew below him on her back, legs crossed, hands folded behind her head. Making sure he was looking down at her, she faked a yawn, stretched, and said, "Huh. I was sure you'd be faster. Must be getting old. Watch this!"

She folded her wings against her and began to fall toward the darkened sea. He followed after her, wind buffeting his face, ruffling his feathers. The moment before Phee hit the water, she twisted around, her wings snapping open. She hurtled forward, leaving a wake in the ocean behind her, small whitecaps that rolled before disappearing.

Not to be outdone, the phoenix—and Arthur, for they were one and the same—burned the air around him, and in a burst of speed shot past Phee, who shouted after him, "That's not fair! Using rockets is *cheating*!"

They hooked around the island, and the sandbar came into view, a long stretch of semi-firm ground. Hearing the buzz of Phee's wings behind him, Arthur pulled back a little, allowing her to pass by him and hit the ground first, leaving divots in the sand behind her as she skidded to a stop. As Arthur landed, Phee jumped up and down, fist pumping in the air. "I won! I won! I *won*!"

Arthur spread his wings, tilting his head back. The scream that tore from his throat was one of pride—in his daughter, in all his children—and Phee yelled along with him, a battle cry of youth.

Later, as the sun rose, Phee sat against him, one wing wrapped around her as she blinked slowly, trying to stay awake. She yawned as the sun crested the horizon, illuminating her hair so that she, too, appeared to be on fire. "You should bring out the phoenix more," she said as her eyes closed. "It's part of you. Why hide it away when we want to see you fly?"

And then she slept, her breaths slow, even.

"Fly," the phoenix said only once, a low, guttural sound lost to the wind coming off the sea.

TWELVE

Breakfast on Sunday morning was always a boisterous affair. Linus had decided that it'd been far too long since he'd made pancakes, and created stack after precarious stack, thick slabs of butter melting across the top. On the record player, Thurston Harris And The Sharps wailed about his little bitty pretty one, come on and talk-a to me, lovey dovey lovely one, come sit down on my knee.

By the time they sat down—still in their pajamas, of course; it was Sunday, after all—Arthur could almost pretend it was a normal weekend morning, and that everything was as it should be.

This was shattered when David winced, reaching for the plate of link sausages Talia was handing over to him. He took it from her gingerly, favoring his wrist.

"David," Arthur said, causing the yeti to jerk his head up and almost drop the plate. "How are you this morning?"

"I'm alive," David said. "Which is good. I had another sleepover with Lucy."

"He doesn't snore," Lucy said, rolling a pancake into a thin tube and trying to suck up syrup to no avail. "So I let him keep all his blood on the inside."

"And for that, we're all grateful," Linus said. "David, how is your wrist?"

Immediate silence. Everyone froze, waiting.

Aside from David, that is. He lifted his arm, bending his wrist back and forth. "Hurts a little," he admitted, gaze down at the table. "She's stronger than she looks."

"So am I," Talia muttered, stabbing a sausage with her fork. "I'd like to see her try and grab *me* without my permission."

As would I, Arthur thought.

"Why did she do that?" Chauncey asked, a pancake attached to each of the suction cups along his arms. He tried to shake them off, but they held tight. "David was just playing with J-Bone."

"I don't know," Arthur said. "But she was wrong. David, I'm sorry that happened. She had no right to—"

"Why do you do that?" David asked, squinting at Arthur.

"Do what?"

"Apologize when it's not your fault. *You* didn't do anything to me, so why are you apologizing?"

"Because someone has to," Arthur said.

"But why is it always you?" Sal asked. "You didn't do anything to David. You didn't do anything to *us* aside from give us a home and let us be happy. Why do you have to be the one to apologize when it's Miss Marblemaw who did something wrong?"

"Yeah," Lucy said. "She should be in here ruining our breakfast with an apology."

Arthur looked to Linus for help, only to be surprised when he said, "I agree with them. While an apology is all well and good, David and Sal make an important point. An apology stems from ownership of an action that can be considered wrong or offensive. You did neither."

"I'm trying to help them survive," Arthur snapped, causing everyone to look at him with wide eyes. "These people are callous, destructive. Cruel because cruelty *is* the point. You think anyone in DICOMY or DICOMA cares about an apology? They *don't.* But if they at least can hear it from me, I think—"

"Then why did you try and get them to apologize to you at the hearing?" Phee asked.

Arthur deflated, his anger returning to a low simmer. It was getting harder to control, and that worried him. "I—"

A sausage bounced off his forehead, landing on the table in front of him. Arthur was about to remind Lucy that they didn't play with their food, but his words lodged in his throat when he saw it wasn't Lucy.

It was Sal. "Stop it," he said as Theodore bobbed his head in agreement next to him. "Stop trying to act like you're doing this alone. You're *not*. You have us. You have Linus. You have Zoe and Helen and almost everyone in the village. You taught us to own up to our mistakes, and we do."

Arthur deflated, head pounding.

"But you also taught us not to take on the mistakes of others as if they're our own," Sal continued. "You said that there are too many people out there who want us to apologize for everything, even existing. So why are you giving them the satisfaction when it wasn't your mistake?"

"It's not like they can hear me," Arthur said, feeling strangely defensive.

"But *we* can," Sal said. "And what does that look like to us? I'll tell you. It looks like you're scared of them. It looks like you're letting them off the hook."

"Sal," Linus said. "We appreciate your thoughts on the matter, but this is more complicated than just that."

"Sal's right," Arthur said, and Linus looked at him with a sad smile. Not pity, just understanding. "All of you are. I think . . ." He shook his head. "I don't know what to think, to be honest. I'm feeling a tad frazzled as of late, but that's no excuse. I shouldn't have snapped when I did. For that, I will apologize."

"I didn't mean to make things hard," David muttered, hands in his lap. "I can . . . go, if it'd be easier." He sniffled, ice forming in the corners of his eyes.

"You didn't," Arthur said. "And that sounded suspiciously like an almost-apology, something I've recently learned isn't always necessary. David, you have done *nothing* wrong. Nothing. You are smart and curious, and I highly doubt I'll ever meet someone with the stage presence you have. Your offer to leave has been received, considered, and denied. No, you will stay here because this is where you belong." He looked at each of his children in turn. "This is where all of you belong. And you're absolutely correct: Miss Marblemaw owes David an apology for her actions yesterday. I will see to it first thing this morning."

"Ooh," Talia whispered into a pancake. "That gave me the *good* shivers. Can I be your backup muscle? I'll bring three different kinds of shovels so she knows we're being serious."

Theodore asked if she was going to hit Miss Marblemaw upside the head with the shovels.

"Nah," David said, only Linus and Arthur realizing he'd understood Theodore without his translation text. "Everyone knows that you have to kneecap someone. Hitting them in the head might kill them. Hit 'em in the knees, and they can't run after you, tickety-boo."

"Wow," Lucy breathed. "I like the way you think."

"Why don't we see how Arthur's talk with Miss Marblemaw goes before we choose violence?" Linus said. "And Talia, I seem to remember you saying I owed you two hours of weed pulling this morning, so why don't we let Arthur handle our guest, and we can see to that."

"Well played, Baker," Talia said. "I don't feel manipulated in the slightest. You're getting better."

"Thank . . . you?"

"Last one to eat all their syrup gets sent to the edge of the universe!" Lucy bellowed, and what followed shan't be described here. Suffice to say it ended with Theodore hanging from the ceiling, Chauncey trying to lick *other* people's syrup, Talia pouring syrup directly into her mouth from the bottle, Phee wielding four sausages as weapons, Sal getting a pancake to the face, David standing on his chair and announcing that this was the best breakfast *ever,* Lucy accusing Linus of cheating (which Linus firmly denied, even though his napkin was suspiciously coated with syrup), and Arthur watching, watching with a light in his soul (and droplets of orange juice in his eyebrows, courtesy of a garden gnome) that burned brighter than any star.

After washing up, Arthur dressed in black slacks and a dress shirt buttoned up to the top. His socks were canary yellow, adorned with little trees. After all, when one prepares for battle, one must look the part.

He left the house behind, smiling as he heard Talia supervising in her garden, telling Linus to put his back into it because the weeds weren't going to pull themselves. Linus's answering grumble was too quiet for Arthur to hear clearly, but he could guess at what was said.

It didn't look as if anyone was home in the guesthouse. The door was shut, blinds drawn across the front windows. He hadn't seen hide nor hair of Miss Marblemaw since she'd trudged up the road after Merle ferried her back to the island. Part of him—a small, foolish part—hoped that after yesterday's events, Miss Marblemaw had packed up her meager belongings and departed for greener pastures. But he knew that even if she had, it wouldn't be the last they'd hear from her.

Arthur Parnassus could be described as many things, but stupid wasn't one of them. He knew deep down no matter what he said, chances weren't in his favor that Miss Marblemaw would respond with anything resembling an apology. He had to keep his anger in check should that prove to be the case. It was what she wanted, same as Rowder during the hearing: to make him lose control, to have evidence that no child should be left in his care for fear of him erupting in fire, laying waste to anything and everything around him.

"Stab her with kindness," he murmured to himself as he approached the house.

Plastering a bland smile on his face, Arthur knocked on the door, and waited.

No response.

He knocked again, a little harder this time.

Nothing.

He tried the doorknob. Locked. To be expected. The set of spare keys was back in the house, but if push came to shove, a measly lock wouldn't stop him. Privacy was important, but Miss Marblemaw had made such courtesy a nonstarter. He knocked again, and when no one answered, stepped off the porch. Considering calling for Zoe to see if she could locate Miss Marblemaw on the island, Arthur first moved around the side of the house. Windows closed, blinds shut here too. The back of the house was set against a small bluff, a rocky trail leading down it into the woods and toward a small beach on the northwest side of the island. They rarely used this beach, seeing as how it was more black rocks than white sand, but it had its charms, otherworldly though they might be. Making a decision, Arthur slid down the trail deftly, leaving a cloud of dirt behind him. At the bottom, he bent over, brushing the dust from his shoes and socks.

It took ten minutes to reach the beach through the trail in the woods. Birds called, insects buzzed, and the warm morning promised an even hotter afternoon. Sunlight dappled the forest floor through the thick canopy, and as Arthur rounded the last bend before the beach, he froze briefly when he heard a voice that should not have been on the island.

"—it's not as if it's difficult, Harriet," Jeanine Rowder said as Arthur moved behind the thick trunk of a palm tree, peering around it out to the beach. "That you're unable to do what I've asked is not only troublesome, it reflects poorly upon you. Perhaps I was wrong to place my faith in you."

Miss Marblemaw was alone on the beach, standing in front of a large gray boulder. On the rock, the metal briefcase she'd brought to the island, but it didn't look as it had before. The interior lining of the lid was pulled down, revealing a screen with a green sheen to it, Rowder's face almost the same color as Chauncey's. Atop the screen, a tiny satellite dish spun in a slow circle, beeping every few seconds.

"I'm *trying*," Miss Marblemaw replied, sounding more than a little pathetic. "You don't know what it's like here. It's nothing like I was told it would be. These children are—"

"Trying," Rowder repeated, the screen rolling with wavy lines. "You're *trying*. I didn't send you there to *try*, Harriet. I sent you there to do what others before you could not. You assured me you were up to the challenge, and yet here you are with evidence to the contrary. You've been there for four days. Time is running short. You're sure you weren't followed?"

Miss Marblemaw turned her head from side to side, Arthur pulling back behind the tree. "No," she said finally. "I wasn't. I don't know why I couldn't do this in the house."

"You know why," Rowder said. "For all we know, the phoenix has taken a tip from us and bugged the hell out of that house. It's what I would've done. And I wouldn't have gotten *caught*."

Miss Marblemaw's expression grew pinched. "How was I to know they'd check the lightbulb? You were the one who told me to put it there in the first place!"

"You should have," Rowder said coldly. "I told you not to underestimate them. Regardless of what else the phoenix is, he's clever, which makes him dangerous. And having the weapons at his disposal means it's up to us to stop him."

"The children," Miss Marblemaw said.

"Yes," Rowder said. "I don't care what else you have to do in order to have the Antichrist removed, but you will do it. I will have him if it's the last thing I do."

Though the sun blazed down upon him, it felt as if Arthur had stepped into David's room again, skin and blood like ice, an electric shiver arcing up and down his spine.

"Are you certain this is the best course of action?" Miss Marblemaw asked, and Arthur's fury lessened. Not by much, but enough to consider her words carefully. She sounded . . . unsure? Or something so close to it that it didn't make a difference. He could work with that. It might take time—not that they had much—but maybe he could convince her that—

"I'm certain," Rowder replied. "More than I've ever been in my life. I have seen what people like them are truly capable of, and I fear for all of our futures. Never before have we been on a precipice like we are now." Her eyes narrowed. "And need I remind you, without me, you wouldn't be an inspector. You'd still be in the mail room, toiling away. I lifted you up, put my faith in you. I *made* you what you are, and this is the thanks I get?" She shook her head. "Maybe I was wrong about you."

"No!" Miss Marblemaw said quickly, leaning forward. "I can do it. I know I can. It's just . . ."

"Spit it out, Harriet. You're wasting precious time."

"What if you're wrong?"

Yes, Arthur thought through fire. *Yes.*

"I'm not," Rowder said flatly. "You were at the hearing. You heard what everyone else did. Arthur Parnassus is a liar, but more than that, he's a *magnetic* liar. Whatever he says, you mustn't believe. An animal backed into a corner will do whatever it can to survive. He is no different. We must ensure the children aren't being brainwashed by whatever he decides is the issue du jour. Are you going to tell me you did everything you could when he unleashes his army upon the world? Could you live with yourself knowing you could have stopped it before it began?"

Miss Marblemaw hesitated.

Arthur breathed in. Arthur breathed out.

She said, "No. I couldn't."

Arthur closed his eyes.

"Good," Rowder said. "Now, about the Antichrist."

"Why can't I just take him in the night?" Miss Marblemaw asked. "Sedate him and remove him while everyone sleeps."

"Are you out of your *mind*?" Rowder asked incredulously. "He'd know immediately, and there wouldn't be enough of you left to bury."

"But if I sedate the child, he won't—"

"I'm not talking about the Antichrist, you bloody fool! Arthur Parnassus would burn you to the ground before you made it three steps from the orphanage. No, we do this by the books. Say whatever you must in your reports to get it done, Harriet. Given the . . . complexities of this situation, I alone have the final decision as to the removal, but mine won't be the only eyes on your reports. Make it count. Legally, of course."

"I will," Miss Marblemaw said. "But—"

"But *what*?" Rowder growled. "Out with it, Harriet. I don't have all day to sit here and listen to you whine on and on. Plans are in motion, and they will not fail because of your ineptitude."

"But, I just . . . I have to ask, Miss Rowder. Why would the Antichrist listen to you at all? Why would he do anything you wanted him to? What's stopping him from killing all of us and returning to the island?"

"That's where the other children come into play," Rowder said, and a print of Arthur's hand burned into the tree, the bark blackened, smoking. "By your account, he's close with them. He considers them his brothers and sisters, as if a monstrous thing could ever understand *family values*." She laughed, a low, throaty thing. "He cannot, as he's a demon hell-bent on destroying everything we hold dear. But on the off chance there's a sliver of light in the rotting carcass of his soul, then he'll do whatever I tell him to keep the other children safe. Imagine having an endless reservoir of magic at the government's command. Why continue to fight the good fight when we can just as easily place our will upon the world with a gentle hand and a well-placed threat to the Devil himself? Never again will we be questioned for our actions, not when every magical being is under government control through the Antichrist."

Lucy had thought the same thing. And yet, as a boy of seven years of age, he was making a different decision. He chose joy. He chose happiness. He chose *others* above himself, even knowing he had the power to do whatever he wished. Why could a child do what adults could not?

"Not everyone will agree with you," Miss Marblemaw said, clearly uncomfortable. "Most of all Arthur Parnassus and Linus

Baker. You saw what Parnassus can do, and I fear that's only scratching the surface."

You're right, Arthur thought coldly. *I've barely begun to show you what I'm capable of.*

"Which is why I entrusted you with this," Rowder snapped. "Removing the children is the first step. The media is already playing their part by continuing to push the photograph of the bird breaking free in Netherwicke. We couldn't have planned it better if we tried. The world knows him for what he is now. And when we announce we've removed the children, everyone will understand that we saw something, we said something, and we *did* something that no one else before us could do: we protected the children who needed us most. You have ten days, Harriet. Do not disappoint me. You know what will happen if you do."

The screen went black. Miss Marblemaw reached up and closed the briefcase.

Arthur left her on the beach.

He did not remember walking back through the woods. He did not remember climbing up the trail, slipping and skinning his palm. He did not remember passing by the shuttered guesthouse. He did not hear Linus and Talia chattering away in the garden. He did not feel the creak of the porch steps beneath his feet. He did not smell the scent of polish—lemon, crisp—that caused wood to gleam. He did not see anything but a narrowed tunnel, the edges as ragged as the harsh breaths he took.

He made it to the bedroom and shut the door, leaning his forehead against it. In his chest, a snarling star of fire, flares snapping like a whip. Rage. Horror. *Fear.* All of it merging, amassing into a misshapen, sentient lump of oily black.

Nearly blind with panic, he turned, and his heart stuttered in his chest.

"Hope," his mother said, standing near the window, "is the

thing with feathers." She faced away from him, her straw-colored hair cascading down her back. She wore a lavender dress, the one he remembered vaguely from his youth because it had pockets. According to her, a good dress always had pockets.

"Anger," she said without looking at him, and he wasn't so far gone that he thought her real rather than memory, but it was a close thing. "It builds on top of old wounds, on scar tissue. It grows and grows until it becomes all you know."

He'd been here before. This conversation was one of the few he could remember, a precious treasure hoarded in the furthest recesses of his mind. He had a part to play, and play it he would. When he spoke, it was not as a man, but as a child. "How do you stop it?"

Though he could not see her face—would he even recognize it if he did?—he knew she was smiling. He could hear it in her voice when she said, "With hope, little bird. With hope, because hope is the thing with feathers."

"*I* have feathers," he said excitedly. And then, "Mother, I—"

But she was gone, gone, gone, *years* gone, *decades* gone, and how he had *grieved* the loss of her, of his father, of the only life he'd ever known, a life with laughter and gazing at the stars and flying higher and higher until he thought he could touch the sky.

With the last of his strength, Arthur stumbled over to his chair, collapsing into it, chest heaving, eyes burning. He raised his hand to his face as his shoulders began to tremble.

He floated through the rest of the day, unable to shake the high-pitched buzzing noise in his ears, a sound that made him feel as if he were being pulled beneath the sea, dragged down to black depths where darkness lived.

The buzzing only grew as the day wore on, Arthur lost to it. There were moments of clarity, brief though they were. Smiling when Talia and Linus came back in the house for lunch, their knees and hands caked with dirt. Nodding when Chauncey explained (in great detail!) how he'd spent his morning with David and Lucy, and that they'd pretended to be gigantic beasts knocking over buildings made of wooden blocks. Praising Sal and Theodore for their cataloguing of the wyvern's hoard with little labels to show why they were important. Exclaiming over a leaf Phee had grown in the shape of Helen, stout, strong, colorful, a perfect representation of its counterpart.

Miss Marblemaw arrived late afternoon, her clipboard clasped firmly in her hands. Appearing no more nervous than she had been the day before, she asked after Zoe, reminding Arthur that she *would* interview the island sprite, and any efforts to keep that from happening would be considered an act of subterfuge.

As she droned on and on, Arthur wondered what she'd think if he lit her on fire right then and there. Would she scream? Would she plead for her life? Would she beg and beg and beg until her vocal cords melted and smoke streamed from her mouth?

It's not as if I'd have issues hiding the body, he thought wildly. *She'd be nothing but ashes.*

"Mr. *Parnassus.*"

The haze parted and he saw Miss Marblemaw glaring at him, obviously having said his name more than once. They were in his office. He couldn't remember coming here.

He forced a smile, hoping it would be enough. "What was that?"

"Are you even listening?" she spat. "I expect you to take this seriously, Mr. Parnassus."

"Oh, I am," he assured her. "You want Zoe. All you have to do is ask. I'm sure she'd be delighted to speak with you."

"As she should be," Miss Marblemaw said with a sniff. "Now, on to other matters. I've noticed that Sal and Theodore are—"

He stood from his chair. "Excuse me, Miss Marblemaw. Something requires my attention. I must see to it immediately."

He walked around the desk, the buzzing sound absolute, his brain a hive of crawling wasps with poison-slick stingers. He had almost made it to the door when Miss Marblemaw grabbed his wrist, her grip firm. "We are in the middle of a discussion," she told him. "Please take a seat until we've finished."

He looked down at her hand on his arm. David, trying to pull away, whimpering as she yelled in his face.

Have you ever hit a kid?

No.

Slapped them?

No.

Put their fingers in a drawer and closed the drawer so hard, it . . . it . . .

He lifted his head and let the phoenix rise behind his eyes. He didn't know what she saw, but instead of being afraid, she looked merely curious, as if a great firebird appeared before her on a daily basis. As he leaned toward her, Arthur could see himself reflected in her eyes. He looked furious. "Remove your hand," he said in a low voice. "And if I *ever* see you touch anyone on this island without their permission again, there is nowhere on this earth you could run that I wouldn't find you."

She pulled her hand back slowly. "Another threat, Mr. Parnassus?"

"It is," he said. "And I mean every word."

She didn't speak again.

No matter what he did, he couldn't stop the fury from growing. It latched on to him, a black shroud wrapped snugly around his shoulders. Sticky. Understanding. Knowing. *Come into the darkness where it's safer,* it whispered. *They think you a monster. Why not give them what they ask for?*

How long? How long had this been part of him? How long had it been building? Since Miss Marblemaw's arrival? No, it was before that. The hearing? The bug in the hotel room? Agreeing to appear in the first place?

Or was it further back than that? Did it start with Linus? After all, he *had* been one of them. Yes, he'd seen the error of his ways, but it'd taken him *years.* Seventeen, to be exact. Years of child after child, of orphanages with masters who understood their jobs, with masters who did not. Why hadn't he done more? Why hadn't he acted sooner?

But then, of course, there were the children. Each of them with their history, their trauma, their stories of abuse and survival as if any child should have intimate knowledge of such things. And he took it from them as best he could, shouldering the weight of it, letting them heal, letting them grow, letting them *live*.

And what of the others? What of all those he helped over the years, all those he couldn't get to in time? Was it *their* fault? Or was it the masters who took him in after testifying? The masters who were scared of him, the masters who thought ignoring him would be beneficial for all?

Was it when he was a scared and lonely child forced to relive each and every terrible day during questioning? Perhaps it was when he was pulled out of the cellar into the sunlight for the first time in six months, blinking against the brightness that had nothing to do with his fire. Or maybe it was the cellar itself, the tick marks on the walls. Maybe it was the first time the master had slapped him across the face for speaking out of turn. Or when he was taken by strangers after his parents died, each of them telling him he had nothing to fear, that he would be cared for by people who understood him. Maybe it was the death of his parents—first his father, then his mother—catastrophic events that ruined him in ways he couldn't expect. Could it have started then?

He thought that might very well be the case.

A lifetime, then. It'd been with him for a lifetime.

He didn't know what that meant. He didn't know what to do. Supper, though he barely touched his food. The children talking, talking. Zoe sitting to his right, her knee bumping against his. Across the table, Linus, quiet, forehead lined, glancing at Arthur every now and then with increasing frequency. Arthur smiled. Linus did not.

After, in the sitting room, David performed his one-yeti play, PI Dirk Dasher on the hunt for the Beast. Costume changes. Linus taking Jason's role. Gasps. Laughter. Applause when David bowed, looking stunned at the cheers being lobbed at him. His wrist seemed fine now, and didn't *that* just beat all? Either David didn't feel it anymore—though that memory was undoubtedly seared into his mind, wasn't it?—or he was trying to push through it. Regardless, Arthur burned.

Sleep. Each of the children in their beds, warm and safe, Chauncey with toothpaste on the corner of his mouth, wiped clean with Arthur's thumb. "Oh, come on! I was saving that for later!" A gentle kiss on his head between his eye stalks, and as Arthur turned to leave, Chauncey said, "Arthur?"

He stopped. Everything stopped. For a moment, he was himself again, free of the fires of rage. "Yes, Chauncey?" he asked without turning around, knowing he was in the eye of the storm.

"Are you all right? You've been quiet today."

He did the one thing he promised he'd never do: he lied to one of his children. "I'm fine. Just thinking my thoughts."

"Good thoughts or bad thoughts?"

Perceptive, but then they all were. "Thoughts," he said, unable to lie again. "Sleep, Chauncey. Tomorrow is another day."

And it *was*, wasn't it? Another day. And then another and then another, where the screws were being tightened, where the shadow of the government stretched long, and he *wanted* to go to Lucy. Wanted to open the door to his room—a closet? A *closet*? Might as well have been a cellar; a master by any other name (*Dad Dad Dad*) was still a master, after all—and say, "You were right. We can't win. Do what you have to. Don't hurt anyone, but take their fear away. Take their anger. Take their hatred, their bigotry, and remake the world as it should be."

It was close—far closer than it should've been. His hand was on the doorknob, hearing the low, sweet tones of dead-people music just inside, Buddy Holly singing that you say you're gonna leave, you know it's a lie, 'cause that'll be the day when I die.

"Arthur?"

He whirled around, the buzzing sound like a great, lumbering machine destroying everything in its wake. Linus stood there, just in the doorway, looking concerned. Unsure. Worried, so worried that Arthur almost *laughed*.

"What is it?"

"These people," Arthur said, wild, peaks and valleys as his voice rose and fell. "These *people*. They take and they take and they *take*. Nothing stops them. Not you. Not me. Not anything we do or say. They will keep coming. There's nothing we can do."

Properly spooked, Linus took a step toward him, hands spread as if gentling a dangerous animal, and oh, was that the wrong move.

"Don't," Arthur said, taking a step back, shaking his head. "I don't want to be touched."

"All right," Linus said, lowering his hands. "Tell me what's happened. Tell me how to help."

Now he did laugh, a harsh, grating sound that was as foreign as it was shocking. "What's happened? Have you not been paying attention? They're trying to take my children from me!"

"They won't," Linus said. "We won't let them."

Arthur scoffed derisively. "And what are *we* going to do if they try? Are you going to pick up arms and defend them? Are you going to give your life so that the children might have a chance to know a world without prejudice? Because that's what I'm willing to do."

"You know I would," Linus said. "I would do anything for them, for you."

"Why?" Arthur demanded. "Why here? Why now? Why none of the other children you encountered? Why did you do nothing to help them?" He shouted: "*Why didn't you save them?*"

Many things happened at once:

fire blooming along his hands, his arms, a pressure building in his chest without end;

and,

Linus, eyes wide, reflecting firelight, taking a step toward him, *without fear*;

and,

music spilling out into the room as Lucy opened the door.

All at once, too much, and the phoenix, the *phoenix* rose up and up, bursting through blood and bone, flesh and memory, until it towered above Linus, Lucy, head bent to keep from scraping against the ceiling . . .

. . . only to find Linus standing in front of Lucy.

To protect him from me, Arthur and the phoenix thought as one.

The pressure intensified, his heart and lungs wrapped in a molten band of metal, and the phoenix screamed, long, loud, before turning and crashing through the window, shards of glass illuminated in orange-red, glittering as he unfurled his wings.

Into the sky, wings pumping, a trail of fire left in his wake. Muscles straining, he rose higher and higher, the stars melting, streaking across a black canvas, and he opened his beak to scream again, only to have white-hot fire pour from his mouth. Higher, higher, the horizon now curved, oxygen thin, causing him to gasp again and again.

An apex, as far as he could climb, and he cried out once more as he was consumed. He detonated in a massive explosion that lit up the night sky as if the sun had arisen anew.

The phoenix blasted apart, feathers and fire shooting off in every direction.

He'd taken to the sky as a bird. He fell toward the ocean as a man.

As fire rained down around him, Arthur plummeted, the island off to his right, the ocean a wall of blue-black rushing to meet him. Movement below, the churn of a vortex, spinning faster and faster. A column of water burst from the sea, hurtling toward Arthur. He sucked in a great breath, ribs creaking, and then he was *surrounded* by water, his descent slowed as he lowered into the ocean. Bubbles flooded around him, making it impossible to see. He didn't know up from down, and time once again became soft, malleable, as he sank into the ocean.

Something bumped against his nose.

He opened his eyes, blinking against the sting of salt.

A fish floated in front of his face. Gray, a black eye on either side of its head. Small fins on either side, and one on the top. Not the biggest fish he'd ever seen, nor the smallest. Strangely, he recognized it—*him*.

Frank, he thought in Chauncey's voice, bellowing at the sea.

Frank's mouth opened and closed, gills working. He bumped Arthur's nose again and pulled back. And then he darted down between Arthur's legs, swirling around the right, then the left. From the depths below, more fish appeared, the same species as Frank. At first a handful, then a dozen, two dozen, *three,* then hundreds of gray fish swimming in a circle around him, faster and faster. The sea around him began to spin in a whirlpool—the fish becoming paint streaks of iridescent gray—but instead of being pulled farther into the depths, he began to rise.

It started out slow at first, then the speed picked up, and Arthur closed his eyes against the saltwater slamming against his face, his lungs screaming for air, lights flashing in the darkness behind his eyelids. As he breached the surface, he attempted to suck in a great, gasping breath, but before he could, he kept *rising,* flipping end over end and landing hard on his back on a beach, nude, sand finding its way into all his nooks and crannies almost immediately.

He sat up in a heady daze, mind still sparking and crackling, the phoenix mewling weakly inside him, ready to lapse into healing unconsciousness.

A fish poked its mouth up from the water, opening and closing.

In a hoarse voice, Arthur said, "Thank you, Frank. I won't forget your kindness."

Frank leapt from the water, moonlight catching his scales. And then he disappeared into the sea.

Arthur began to laugh. He laughed and laughed, arms wrapped around his middle. The first tear was a surprise, the second a warning, and then the floodgates opened: he wept for the children—both known and unknown. He wept for each raised fist. He wept in bittersweet joy, in ferocious heartbreak. He wept at the unknowable mysteries of this universe.

And for the first time, Arthur Franklin Parnassus wept for himself.

Linus found him sitting under a tree, knees drawn up against his chest. The tree—an old, cranky palm that seemed to enjoy dropping coconuts on unsuspecting heads—grew above the beach Frank had brought him to. Off to the right, in the distance, the house on the cliff, lit up like a lighthouse, a warm beacon in the dark.

"There you are," Linus said, huffing as he crested the hill, face red, hair a mess as if he'd been running his hands through it. "You gave me such a fright!"

"Did I hurt you?" Arthur asked in a dull voice.

Linus sighed. "You foolish man. Look at the state of you." He pulled off his robe and kneeled before Arthur, rubbing the water away as best he could. Once finished, he settled the robe on Arthur's shoulders, fussing over it and making Arthur move around until it was cinched around his waist, his rear now protected from spiky grass. "You're going to catch a cold," Linus muttered, rubbing his arms and shoulders. "Where will you be then?"

"You worry too much."

"So I've been told," Linus said. "Still, someone has to."

Arthur flinched, the words a sharp rebuke.

"Oh, stop it," Linus said with a roll of his eyes that reminded Arthur of Phee. "I wasn't talking about you, and you know it. You worry enough for all of us. And no, you did not hurt me. You didn't hurt anyone. Even the window is already fixed."

"Lucy," Arthur whispered.

"Yes," Linus said, grunting as he moved to sit next to Arthur, who, for one whose blood ran with fire, found himself colder than he'd ever been in his life. Linus wrapped an arm around him, pulling him close, Arthur's wet hair pressed against his cheek, his jaw.

Thoughts spun in a violent storm, and it took Arthur a long time before he was able to grab hold of one. It struggled to break free, but he held on with all his might. Above an endless sea and below a sea of stars, Arthur said the one thing he feared above all else. "Perhaps they're right. Maybe I'm not fit to be a father."

Linus didn't answer right away. He stared off into nothing, eyes sad, smile a little sadder. Eventually, he said, "You never got the chance to just . . . be."

"What?"

"Always helping," Linus said. "Always thinking about others. Ever since you were a child, you put the needs of everyone else above yourself. Attempting to mail a letter for someone to come save you and your friends. After, you did your very best to help those in need find a home where they were safe. But you didn't stop there, did you? No. You bought the same bloody house that by rights you should've razed to the ground. You didn't, though. Instead, you did what you always do, and even with these children, these remarkable children, and even with Zoe and Helen and me and the entire world with their damnable, judgmental eyes upon you, you *still* persist. You *still* push on. You help because that's who you are as a person."

"But," Arthur whispered, knowing it was coming.

"*But*," Linus said, jostling him a little, "when do you help yourself?"

Arthur's eyes burned, and he could not speak.

Linus kissed the side of his head. "I see what they say about you, even if you try and hide it from me. I see the good. The horrible. All of it. And no matter what I read or hear, I always think, well, yes, but does that mean they really know him? Of course not. How could they know you need a nightly cup of tea before bed or you can't sleep? How can they know that you sometimes put a flower on my pillow because it reminded you of me? They can't. They can't know that you put your blood, sweat, and tears into an act of unmitigated selflessness in making this house a home. They can't know how you play freeze tag with the children, using the entire island as part of the game. They can't know how you teach them to be proud of themselves, to have a sense of self-worth. They can't know the way Lucy looks at you as if you hung the moon and the stars. The way Phee brightens up whenever you enter the room, even if she denies it. The way Sal is learning to stand on his own as a leader because *you* taught him how. The way Theodore has never felt voiceless, knowing you took the time to learn his language. The way Chauncey continues to be... well, *Chauncey,* sunshine in blobby form. The way Talia knows that no matter what, she will always have someone to exclaim over flowers with. And even David, the way he *talks* about you! *Arthur did* this *and Arthur did* that. They can't know any of it, Arthur. Even with their power, they can't know all that you are. But I do."

Arthur clutched Linus tighter, shoulders shaking.

Softly, Linus said, "You've been strong your entire life. You've had to be. Unfairly. Unjustly. But I think you also believe you're still alone at times, that you have to shoulder everything on your own. You don't. You have me. I can help you carry the weight of it. I can be your rock. I can't do what you lot can, but Lucy once told me there is magic in the ordinary. I must be pretty magical, then, but only because I know when I look over, there you'll be. Fit to be a father? Bah. I've never met anyone in my life more fit than you. Any child would be lucky to have you, and I won't hear anyone saying otherwise, not on my watch, no, sir. You want to have a go at Arthur Parnassus? Well, you're going to have to deal with me first. And though I may not look it, I can be quite scrappy when I need to be."

And that was it. That was all it took. Arthur broke, full-body sobs. But it was different from how it'd been after he was helpfully tossed from the sea with assistance from a fish named Frank. Here, now, surrounded by Linus Baker, Arthur felt warm, safe, loved. As Linus whispered words of calm and peace, Arthur sank into the storm and let it blow him away.

Sunrise broke above the sea, clouds aflame. Seagulls cawed on the wind, black-tipped wings spread wide. Waves crashed, a low, familiar rush. The scent of salt and brine thick.

Arthur said, "The explosion."

Linus startled from a doze, lips smacking. "Beg pardon?"

"The explosion," Arthur said again. "Did you see it?"

"Yes," Linus said with a shiver. "I suspect most people did, or at least the aftermath. It rattled the entire island. The phoenix. Is it . . ." He swallowed thickly. "Gone?"

"Resting," Arthur assured him. "But there's more." He told Linus what he'd heard on the beach, hiding behind a tree. The longer he spoke, the more Linus's mouth twisted down, his eyebrows rising higher and higher. By the time Arthur had finished, Linus was apoplectic, barely able to string together a coherent thought.

"How *dare* she—who does she think she—why, I *never*—ooh, I can't believe—no." He took a deep breath, letting it out slow. "No. No, no, *no*."

"I agree completely. Did she see?"

"Yes. Unfortunately. She was standing in front of the guesthouse when it happened. Heard the window breaking."

"Good," Arthur said. He stood, knees popping. Extending a hand to Linus, he arched an eyebrow. "Coming, dear Linus?"

"Where are we going?" Linus asked, letting himself be pulled up. "It'd better be back to the house for breakfast. I don't know about you, but I've worked up an appetite."

"So have I," Arthur said, surprised. "But that'll have to wait. We have work to do."

"Wait? For *breakfast*? You've lost the plot, my good fellow. No one should have to wait for breakfast. I've changed my mind! Please give the ring back. I'll find someone who respects a good bit of nosh and doesn't think it needs to be skipped."

Arthur kissed him soundly. "No," he said against Linus's lips. "I will marry you, and I won't hear another word to the contrary."

"Oh, good," Linus said. "I doubt I'd be able to stumble upon the loves of my life for a second time, so that's probably for the best."

Hand in hand, they moved toward home.

THIRTEEN

The children waited on the porch, most still dressed in their pajamas. Zoe stood behind them, yellow flowers opening and closing in her hair, her concern evident. Calliope sat on the railing, eyes half-closed, tail swishing over the side.

Chauncey waved, yelling, "Hey! Hi! Good morning! Things *exploded*, and we didn't do it! Isn't that *crazy*?"

"The craziest," Linus called. "We'll head on inside and—"

"Mr. *Parnassus*."

He turned his head to see Harriet Marblemaw marching toward him, dust kicking up around her shoes. For once, she was sans clipboard, her hands in fists at her sides. David growled at her, a low rumble that cut off when Calliope wound her way between his legs. He looked down at her in shock as she stretched up his side, one of her paws touching his hip. *Shhh*, that paw said.

"I say, *Mr. Parnassus*! I'm speaking to you!"

Arthur held up a hand toward her. "Miss Marblemaw, I'll be with you after I've—"

"Was that you?" she demanded, stopping a good distance away from him, panting. "The fire. The sky. Was. That. *You*."

"It was," Arthur said evenly. "Part of being a phoenix means releasing energy every now and then. And I did so, safely away from everyone and everything. No one was hurt, nothing was damaged."

"Tell that to the *window*," she said triumphantly, pointing her finger at the second floor.

They all looked up to find the window intact, the glass free of smudges or streaks.

"I saw it," she snapped. "I saw it with my own two eyes! Glass in the grass! Shards that could pierce and stab! And I have *proof.*" She reached into her pocket. When she pulled it out, she extended it toward Arthur and opened her hand. Upon her palm sat a gold-and-brown shell.

"That's not proof," Chauncey said with sage-like wisdom. "That's a snail's house."

Miss Marblemaw gaped down at the shell before crushing it in her hands. "I know what I saw," she hissed as powdered shell slipped between her fingers. "And I know what you are. You won't be able to hide forever, Mr. Parnassus. By the time I've finished with this place, you'll never—"

"Oh, do be quiet," Zoe said.

"Ooh," the children said.

Miss Marblemaw glowered at Zoe. "And *you*. I don't know who you think you are, but I am a representative of the *government*, which means I have complete and total power here. I won't have an unregistered person telling me what to do. You're lucky you haven't been arrested for—"

Zoe moved past the children, gliding down the steps without touching them. She landed on the ground, and as Miss Marblemaw squared her not-so-inconsiderable shoulders, Zoe's eyes turned completely white, opaque, her voice taking on a deep timbre, wings glittering in the early morning light. "I said, be *quiet.* I'm done hearing you speak to us as if we give a damn about what you say. You are on *my* island, and after your conduct in the village, you're lucky you're still standing of your own volition."

"Threats!" Miss Marblemaw barked in response. "That's all you have. They won't work! You can't—"

"We'll be with you shortly," Zoe said. "Until then, why don't you return to the guesthouse?" She raised her hand toward Marblemaw. Before the inspector could react, Arthur felt the air shift around him—thick, almost corporeal—and then Marblemaw shrieked as she slid backward through the dirt, arms waving wildly. Leaving divots in her wake, Marblemaw hit the porch steps of the guesthouse, the backs of her feet dragging up the wooden steps, her body slanted backward, almost parallel with the porch. The second before she crashed into the door, it opened out, the hinges creaking. Marblemaw regained control the moment she crossed the threshold, rushing toward them, only to have the door shut in her face.

"There," Zoe said. "That should hold her."

"Until she tries to break a window," Linus said.

"I got it!" Lucy said. He scrunched up his face, and then relaxed. "Done and done! Now all the windows are made of plastic ten inches thick! I've never had a hostage before. When do we get to negotiate for a helicopter?"

"Not a hostage," Arthur said. "She's merely enjoying the wonder that is Chauncey's turndown service."

"I left a mint on her pillow," Chauncey said. "I hope she doesn't eat it because I want to."

Before Arthur could reply, Zoe was there, running her hands up and down his arms, his sides, his shoulders. "You're fine," she muttered, eyes returning to their normal color. "You're fine."

"I am," he said gently. "I wouldn't leave you, dear." He kissed her forehead as she clutched him. "But I fear the time we've all prepared for is upon us." Zoe let him go, but she didn't go far, her hand in his, gripping tightly, a welcome touch.

"What happened?" Sal asked.

"Children," Arthur said. "Classes for today have been canceled—"

For the second time in twelve hours, an explosion occurred. Only this time, it was not a thing of fire and feather, but one of extraordinary jubilation. Sal and Theodore grinned while Chauncey wailed in happiness. Talia and Phee pumped their fists in the air as David decided that dancing was an appropriate response to such welcome news, wiggling his hips, eyes bright and cold.

"—but fear not," Arthur continued. "We'll work doubly hard in the coming days to make up for it."

Talia, with her arms still in the air, asked, "Are we happy or mad?"

Phee said, "I . . . I don't know?"

"Your hearts," Arthur said, and the children fell quiet. "Your tremendous hearts. They've carried you far, inexorably linking us together. There is nowhere I'd rather be."

"What is it?" Sal asked. "What's happened?"

"It has come to our attention that a certain inspector has come to our home under false pretenses," Arthur said. "She is not here, as she claimed, to ensure your safety and happiness."

"What a shocking development," Talia said. "Who would've guessed?"

"Not me," Chauncey said. "I thought she just needed a hug."

"I like you," Phee said, patting his shoulder.

"Unfortunately, I don't believe a hug will solve the issue," Arthur said. "No, it's beyond that now."

"Uh-oh," Chauncey whispered, stalks shrinking until his eyes rested atop his head. "We're doomed."

"What does she want?" Sal asked, voice hard.

Arthur shook his head. "I don't want you to concern yourself with—"

"You do that," Sal said, pushing his way to the front of the children. "You *always* do that. You take it all on yourself because you think we can't handle it."

"Sal," Linus said, "it's not that simple. There are things at play here that are complicated even to us."

"I don't care," Sal said, never looking away from Arthur. "If this is about us, then we have the right to know what it is. You can't protect us forever."

His greatest fear laid bare. And didn't he want to push back? Didn't he just want to tell Sal that he was *still* a child, fifteen years old, yes, but not a man? Oh, he did, and it bubbled in his throat, danced along his tongue. He opened his mouth, but before he could speak, Zoe squeezed his hand. "Listen to him," she said quietly. "Trust him."

But Arthur was on the cusp of panicking. "I know I can't protect you forever. But that doesn't mean I won't still *try*. None of you should ever have to know what it feels like to be—"

"Unwanted?" Sal asked. "Unloved? Despised? We *know* what that feels like. We may not have gone through what you did, but that doesn't make our experiences any less important."

"I've never thought as much," Arthur said sharply. "Never. Not once."

Sal nodded, taking a step forward. Behind him, the other children watched, waited. "Good. Because you can't know everything. You can't *be* everything, even if we want you to be."

Arthur cocked his head, squinting at Sal. "Explain, please. Explain why I should consider putting you anywhere remotely close to the crosshairs."

"Because we're already there," Sal said. "We have been for a long time. It may not be about all of us equally"—a knowing look, and once again, Arthur wondered how anyone could have seen Sal as anything but a born leader—"but we're in this together. And even then, we might do things differently."

"Why?" Linus asked.

"Because you can't be everything to us," Sal said. "No matter what you're capable of, the power both of you have, you can't understand certain things. I have to navigate three worlds. Being human. Being magical. Being Black. Can you help with two of those? Yeah, you can. But you know nothing of the last. You *can't*. That's something I need to figure out. Luckily, I don't have to do it alone."

"You don't," Zoe agreed.

"Bigotry comes in all forms," Sal said, "not just against magical people. It wasn't too long ago that you and Linus couldn't get married, and look at you now." And then he broke the world. "You have to trust me. Trust *us*. We may be kids, but we're your kids, Dad. You made us all believe we could do anything. Now you have to trust us to do that."

It was Arthur's turn at incoherence, and he proved to be up there with the best of them. "I—you—how is that—you aren't—oh, dear."

"You've broken him," Linus said. "I never thought I'd see the day when—"

"He's Dad," Talia said. "And you're Papa. We've all decided, so you can't go switching."

"I wanted to call you Pappy, but I was outvoted," Lucy said sadly.

"Oh," Linus whispered as he wiped his eyes over a watery smile. "I see."

"I'm sorry," Arthur told Sal in a hoarse voice. "I should be listening more than I have been. You're . . ." He sighed. "You're right, of course. There are things you'll do and be in life that I won't be part of. That still doesn't mean I won't worry every second of every day."

Sal laughed, shaking his head. "That's because you're our father." His smile faded slightly. "But even then, I have to figure out some things on my own. I need to make mistakes and learn from them. I'm a kid, but I won't be for long." He glanced back at his brothers and sisters. "*We* won't be for long. Isn't it time we showed people what we're made of?"

"The best stuff." Linus sniffled. "That's what you're all made of. The very best."

"Are you sure?" Arthur asked. "I will only ask this once. Are you *sure*?"

Sal didn't hesitate. As the other children nodded behind him, he said, "We're sure."

Arthur looked at Zoe, who smiled. He looked at Linus, who said, "You heard our children. They're sure."

Pride and fear warred within him, but it was a battle Arthur wanted no part of, especially when the victor had yet to be decided. Shoving it down as far as he could, he said, "Harriet Marblemaw is working for Jeanine Rowder, the woman from the hearing. We knew as much but have now come into information that indicates subterfuge."

"My favorite kind of fuge," Lucy breathed. "Next to vermifuge, which is medicine that expels intestinal worms."

Linus burst into tears. "You *were* listening in your vocabulary lessons!"

"Of course I was," Lucy said. "I'm literally a devil. Words are how we bargain for souls, duh."

Lucy didn't try to squirm away when Linus scooped him up into a hug, peppering his face with loud smacks. When Linus tried to set him back down, Lucy clung to him, and Linus switched arms, holding him close. Lucy laid a head on his shoulder.

"She is going to try and take us away," Phee said.

"She is," Arthur said. "But she will not succeed." And though he knew he shouldn't, he added, "You have my word."

"And mine," Zoe said.

"Mine too," Linus said as Lucy blinked slowly against his throat.

"Why?" Sal asked. "What does she want?"

Arthur hesitated. "What people in power always want: more power. Rowder thinks she can use you all to get what she wants. To remake the world until everyone is subservient."

Talia sighed. "It's so hard being this popular all the time. Like, we get it. You're obsessed with us. Calm down."

Theodore leapt from the porch, alighting on Sal's shoulder. He leaned forward, head tilting to the side as he looked at Linus. He chirped a question.

"Yes," Linus said. "Your button is still in my pocket. I will defend it with my life."

Theodore nodded, then turned to Arthur, head tilting the other way, followed by three chirps, two clicks in quick succession, ending with an upturned growl.

The question made Arthur heartsore. "A certified adoption is just a piece of paper. You are my son, and nothing will ever change that."

"Parnassus-Baker or Baker-Parnassus?" Phee asked. "Dad was here first, but I think I like the sound of Phee Baker-Parnassus better. Rolls right off the tongue."

"Chauncey Baker-Parnassus," Chauncey said, trying it on for size. "Yep! That works for me."

"All in favor?" Sal asked.

"Aye!" the children crowed.

Except for one.

"David?" Arthur asked as the yeti ducked his head. "Do you have something to say?"

David shifted his weight from foot to foot, wringing his hands in front of him. "I haven't been here very long."

"You haven't," Arthur agreed. "But you are part of this just as much as the rest of us."

David gnawed on his bottom lip.

Linus stepped forward, still carrying Lucy. Wind swept through his hair, and Arthur was struck by this man, this former stranger who had come to an island and found a home he did not expect.

"We're asking," Linus said, "if you want this to be your home too. To stay with us."

"However," Arthur said, "if you decide your future lies elsewhere, we will do everything we can to make sure you find your place, wherever that may be. I won't lie to you, David. The road ahead will be fraught, but if you choose to stay, we will belong to you just as much as we belong to the others."

David looked up at him with cautious wonder. "You'd be my dad too?"

"Yes," Arthur said. "It would bring me unparalleled joy. I say that not to sway you into making a decision one way or the other, but to remind you that you are loved, here, now, and forever. You will always have a place here with us."

David glanced around at the others, Talia giving him a thumbs-up. When he looked back at Arthur, he frowned. "I can't call you Dad," he said. "Not . . . not yet. I . . ." He sniffled. "I want to, but . . ." He shrugged helplessly.

"You're not ready," Arthur finished for him. "And David, the time may never come when you feel comfortable with that, and no one will think less of you because of it. I can't—and won't—replace your father, or your mother. Though I never had the pleasure of knowing them, I choose to believe they live on in you. How *proud* they must be of you."

A single ice cube fell to the ground. "And I can still call Jason and B whenever I want?"

"Whenever you want," Linus said. "In fact, we'll invite them to the island, if they can get away from their responsibilities for a little while. If not, then Arthur or I can very easily take you back to the city to visit them. All you need to do is ask, and we'll plan a weekend out of it."

"Can they go too?" David asked, tossing a thumb over his shoulder.

Linus paled. "Uh. Yes. Sure. Why not? It's not as if I have nightmares about all of you riding a city bus."

Lucy squished his face. "Aw, Papa dreams about us. That's adorable."

Suddenly dry-eyed, David gave a sly smile that he had undoubtedly learned from Lucy. "And you have to build me a stage so I can perform my plays."

"Absolutely not," Linus said. "*We* will build you a stage. Everyone will help."

"Can we use magic?" Lucy asked.

"Yes," Arthur said. "In fact, from now on, I will insist upon it."

"Hell *yes*," Lucy crowed, causing Linus to wince.

"David?" Sal asked. "What do you think?"

He didn't take long to answer. David, the boy yeti who'd thought he had to perform to be accepted into a magic school, puffed out his chest, hands on his hips. "What are we standing around here for? We have work to do!"

Talia tackled David first, knocking him flat on his face. Lucy wriggled down Linus's side and joined her. Sal and Theodore sank down next to them, both grinning. Phee rolled her eyes, but sat on David's legs. Chauncey—as he was wont to do—lay on top of them, cocooning them in green.

As they laughed and chattered excitedly—David loudest of all—Arthur, Linus, and Zoe looked on. "What are we going to do?" Zoe asked.

It was Linus who answered. "We're going to protect our home. They want a fight? They've got one."

It was Sal's idea, and since he had the backing of the six other children, Arthur, Linus, and Zoe were outvoted.

"We're not going to banish her," Sal told them as they sat in the sitting room, watching him pace back and forth. Behind him was Linus's birt present, still missing a photograph near the bottom. They'd have to see to that as soon as possible. "At least not yet. That'll only trigger a quicker response from DICOMY, and we don't want them to know what we're doing until we're ready."

"But what if they come after us later?" Chauncey asked. "Do I need to get my battle helmet again?"

"Let me worry about that," Zoe said. She held up a hand before Sal could reply. "I'm not trying to keep anything from you. I'm . . . hmm. For now, let's just say I have a plan in mind, but there are a few more things I need to consider because once it's done, it cannot be undone."

A glissando of uneasy excitement trilled up him, toe to tip, a rickety flourish from piano keys made of bone and ice. Zoe spoke of deep magic, something he'd never seen from her before. Though he knew her to be powerful, he'd heard tales of the might of sprites, descended from fairies who had once called this world home. As far as anyone knew, true fairies—tricksters all, or so it was said—had disappeared centuries before. Most thought them extinct, hunted down and murdered until none were left. Others believed they'd left this world for another, moving through the fabric of reality with ease. Phee had already demonstrated her potential, but Zoe, for as long as Arthur had known her, hadn't shown what he thought her capable of. It seemed as if that time was nearly over.

Sal nodded begrudgingly. "I trust you, Zoe. If you need our help with anything, please ask."

"I might take you up on that," she said. "Once I know more, you will too. That's a promise."

"Sal," Linus said. "What are you thinking?"

Sal looked at the other children, who nodded at him encouragingly. "David gave me the idea."

"I did?" David asked.

"Yeah, man," Sal said. "You talked about how you liked being a monster. You don't want to hurt people, just scare them."

"I would never hurt anyone," David said quickly, popping his knuckles. "Honest."

"We know," Sal said. "But with how they've weaponized fear, I think it's time we gave the government a taste of their own medicine, starting with Miss Marblemaw. She says she can't experience fear. I say we put that to the test. They insist we're monsters? Maybe we should show them just how monstrous we can be."

"Are we going to kill her?" Lucy asked, head cocked. Before Arthur could answer—*no*—Lucy continued. "Because I don't think we should."

Arthur and Linus exchanged a glance of surprise. This was a curious turn of events, especially coming from one who advocated death and destruction with the same glee as he did his sticky buns. "While I'm relieved to hear that, may I ask what brought you to that decision?"

Lucy shrugged. "That'd only give the people who hate us reason to hate us more. And besides, I like being nice." His eyes flooded with red, voice deepening. "*Sometimes.*" The red disappeared, and his voice returned to normal. "It makes my spiders sleepier when I do things to help others. I bet this will make them sleep for *weeks*."

"Lucy's right," Linus said. "And while I admit to having concerns about how best to proceed, I think it's high time Miss Marblemaw gets put in her place, without killing or maiming. Agreed?"

"Agreed," everyone said at the same time.

"Stab her with kindness!" Chauncey yelled.

"Tell us," Arthur said. "Leave nothing out."

FOURTEEN

Later that morning, Harriet Marblemaw was released from the guesthouse. The windows turned from plastic to glass, and the front door swung open just as Miss Marblemaw decided that throwing her entire weight against it might do some good. Unfortunately for her, she missed the door completely and nearly fell down the porch steps.

"Ah," Arthur said, standing in front of the house, hands clasped behind his back. "Miss Marblemaw. I wondered where you'd gone."

"You *imprisoned* me," she snarled, spittle flying from her mouth. "That sprite used magic against me without my permission! I will see her *jailed* for this!"

Zoe stepped out from behind Arthur, causing Miss Marblemaw to squeak. "You have my most sincere apologies," she said. "I fear that we've gotten off on the wrong foot. Thankfully, I have something for you to help make up for it."

"I highly doubt anything you could give me will make up for your transgressions," Miss Marblemaw said.

"And here I thought you'd appreciate a demonstration from one of the children, so you can see what they're capable of. If that's not—"

"No, no," Miss Marblemaw said hastily. "You're right. It's important I see what they can do."

Without looking away from the inspector, Arthur raised his voice and called, "Phee! Would you join me for a moment?"

She stepped out of the forest, bouncing an orange in her hand. She cast a cool glance at Miss Marblemaw before joining Arthur and Zoe.

"Why isn't she in class?" Miss Marblemaw asked.

"Since we are nearly six months ahead of schedule with regards to their education," Arthur said, "we've decided to give the children a day off to pursue their own interests."

"I was communing with nature," Phee said. "Listening to the trees."

Miss Marblemaw looked like she didn't believe her, but let it go. "I see. And you have a demonstration for me?"

"I do," Phee said. "You ready?"

Miss Marblemaw snorted derisively. "I doubt all this fuss is necessary. If you're going to do something, then do it. I don't like to be kept waiting, especially when it appears efforts are being made to keep me from doing my job. But *yes*, show me a tree, or whatever it is you do."

Phee smiled, tilting her head. "As you wish."

As if she were bowling, Phee brought her arm back before swinging it in an arc. The orange hit the ground, bouncing and rolling toward Miss Marblemaw. The moment it left Phee's hand and bounced on the earth, the peel split, tiny brown stalks with green leaves bursting through. As it rolled closer to Miss Marblemaw, the stalks became thin branches, scrabbling along the ground like the recently departed scorpion known as Beelzebub. By the time it came to a stop at Miss Marblemaw's feet, the orange was a bundle of leaves and roots.

Miss Marblemaw peered down at it, mouth turned down. She tapped the leaves and roots with her foot. "Is that it? That's what you can—"

The orange exploded outward and upward, the ground quaking beneath their feet. A tree shot up in front of Miss Marblemaw, at least twenty feet tall, the trunk thick and sturdy. The trees' leaves were a deep, shiny green, surrounded by heavy oranges hanging from its branches. It took less than three seconds for the tree to reach its full height, the sound of its creation a loud, thundering roar. Miss Marblemaw was knocked against the porch, sliding down the steps until she landed on her rear on the ground.

"Oh no!" Phee cried, slapping her hands against her cheeks. "*That* certainly wasn't supposed to happen! Are you all right?"

"I'm fine," Miss Marblemaw snapped, pulling herself up, much of her hidden by the branches of the tree. She looked it up and down before plucking a fat orange off it. Using her thumbnail, she pierced the orange, juice squirting out onto her knuckle. She squeezed it tighter until it squished between her fingers, pulp and juice falling to the ground. She dropped the ruined fruit, wiped her hand against her side, and said, "Thank you for that demonstration. You have proven that if the day comes when there is a country-wide shortage of fruit, we now know who will rectify the situation immediately. You get one courtesy point."

"I used a fruit grenade and you gave me a *courtesy* point?" Phee demanded.

"A fruit *what?*"

"Uh," Phee said. "I said fruit *marmalade*. Because everyone knows that fruit can be made into—"

"*Two* courtesy points," Miss Marblemaw said. "And I won't hear another word about it! You earned it, child." She smiled. "Make sure you tell the other children how well you're doing. I bet that'll make them so jealous of you."

"I'll get right on that," Phee said flatly.

"I knew you would! Now, let's go see what everyone else is up to, shall we? After all, we've wasted enough time with this . . . display." She rounded the tree, and without looking at Phee, Zoe, or Arthur, headed for the house.

"It appears Miss Marblemaw has taken a lesson from our own

playbook," Arthur said. "I feel as if I've just been stabbed. Not with kindness, per se, but whatever she considers to be the equivalent."

"Too little, too late," Phee said.

Or so they'd hoped. Unfortunately for the residents of Marsyas Island, Harriet Marblemaw proved to be adept at rolling with the punches. Either that, or she was on to them, and wouldn't give them the satisfaction.

Take, for example, Monday afternoon, when she decided the best use of her time was to convince Theodore that seeing his hoard was not only necessary but could help her colleagues back at DICOMY have a better understanding of wyvern culture. Theodore, for his part, chirped that he'd rather sit on a sea urchin than show her anything and that he was going to spend the afternoon pointing out garbage. Since Miss Marblemaw was not fluent in wyvern, she thought he'd agreed.

As such, she spent the next three hours following Theodore. It took her nearly the entire time to realize he was not, in fact, taking her to his hoard but instead chasing a fly that had found its way inside. She came to this conclusion when the fly landed on her forehead, and Theodore launched himself at it. By the time Miss Marblemaw had stopped yelling in outrage, Theodore had eaten the fly and found a spot in the sun next to Calliope, stretching out and curling his head against her stomach. The thing of evil licked his ears as he closed his eyes, rumbling lowly in his chest.

"*Three* courtesy points!" Miss Marblemaw said in a shrill voice, her hair in disarray. "You've earned them! Make sure to tell everyone you know!"

At Monday's supper, Talia decided that Miss Marblemaw needed to sit right next to her. "I wanted to talk to you," she said, patting the chair.

"Oh, that sounds splendid," Miss Marblemaw said, sounding rather excited for reasons Arthur was sure weren't aboveboard. "As it turns out, I have something I'd like to ask you as well."

"Of course you do," Linus muttered, handing a basket of rolls over to Sal.

Miss Marblemaw took her seat next to Talia, turning to face her. "You are a very pretty girl."

"Tell me something I don't know," Talia said as she shoveled green beans onto her plate.

"I'm so glad you said that, because it turns out I *do* have something to say that you don't know."

"Really?" Talia asked dubiously. "I know a lot."

"You know *some* things," Miss Marblemaw said. "As I said before, it's unseemly for a lady to be braggadocious."

"We're so lucky you're here," Phee said. "Otherwise, how would we know anything?"

"Exactly," Miss Marblemaw said. "Which is why I think Talia should consider shaving off her beard."

Silence, only interrupted by Chauncey whispering, "Uh-oh."

Miss Marblemaw continued as if she hadn't just committed a dangerous faux pas. "After all, a proper lady does not have facial hair, or body hair of any kind. Though the upkeep can be time-consuming, it is important. How else are you going to one day find a husband?"

Talia stared at her. "I'm only two hundred and sixty-four. I'm going to wait until I'm at *least* four hundred before I start thinking about what babes I want to date."

"Be that as it may, best practices start now," Miss Marblemaw said. "Perhaps we can do it together!"

"Or," Talia said, "we don't do that and I pretend that what you said wasn't offensive."

"That's because it wasn't," Miss Marblemaw said with a sniff. "That's the problem with the world today. Everyone is so ready to be offended by just about anything."

"Maybe you shouldn't be the one to decide what is or isn't

offensive to a person in the community you're denigrating," Sal said. "Do you even know why gnomes have beards or what they symbolize?"

Miss Marblemaw flicked her hand at him dismissively. "I highly doubt that a beard on a girl is meant to do much of anything aside from making others uncomfortable."

"And that's somehow Talia's fault?" Phee asked. "Seems to me that instead of getting her to change, you should talk to those other people and tell them to mind their own business. Talia's beard has nothing to do with them."

"That's absolutely correct," Arthur said with a nod. "After all, the length and level of luxuriousness of a garden gnome's beard is directly related to the well-being of their garden. The healthier the garden, the longer and thicker the beard. But then, as an inspector for DICOMY and undoubtedly an expert in all things magical, you don't need us to tell you that." He smiled at Talia. "Have I mentioned how beautiful your beard looks as of late?"

"I know, right?" Talia said. "One hundred brush strokes, every night. Papa's getting really good at it."

"Tonight, *two* hundred brush strokes," Linus said. "Just to make sure."

Miss Marblemaw chuckled, though it had an edge to it. "That's so . . . special. However, I think Talia should consider her future rather than putting all her focus on a garden. Perhaps we could find a nice dress for you to wear. Wouldn't that be wonderful? Something with, oh, I don't know, pink lace, and your hair done up in pigtails. And by shaving your beard, everyone would get to see those chubby cheeks!"

"That would be so *fun*!" Lucy said. "You know what would make it even better? If Miss Marblemaw led by example and shaved her mustache!"

Miss Marblemaw's eyes narrowed. "I don't have a—"

Except she did. Lucy said, "Flora bora slam!" and a long, brown handlebar mustache appeared on Miss Marblemaw's face, neatly trimmed, the ends curled into a little loop. "Now you get to have facial hair too!"

Miss Marblemaw didn't detonate as Arthur expected her to. Instead, she stood slowly from the table, her mustache stiff above her lip as she smiled furiously. "Remove it."

Lucy shrugged. "Okie doke. Satan appease me!"

The mustache wriggled but otherwise remained as is.

"Oops," Lucy said. "So, here's the thing. I'm only seven years old, and still learning. I'm just a little guy!"

"And?" she said, shoulders stiff.

"*And*," Lucy said, drawing out the word for a good five seconds, "that means I sometimes do things I don't mean to. Like giving you permanent facial hair that no matter how much you shave will regrow within six hours, six minutes, and six seconds. My bad!" He blinked innocently at her with wide, angelic eyes. "But good news! You sort of make it work if you squint and tilt your head and look in the opposite direction."

Miss Marblemaw paled. And then she ran from the kitchen. A moment later, they heard the front door thrown open, bouncing off the front of the house.

"Do you think she liked it?" Lucy asked. "Is that creamed corn? Oh my God, I am going to eat *so much of it*."

"Lucy?" Talia said.

"Yeah?"

She threw a roll. It bounced off his head. "Thank you."

"I love your beard," he told her. "It makes you look badass."

They waited for Linus or Arthur to scold them for language. Instead, Linus said, "I agree. It is *very* badass."

"Ooh," Chauncey breathed. "Can I curse now too? I got a good one!"

"You get one," Arthur said.

"Oh my goodness," Chauncey whispered. "I didn't think you'd say yes." He looked around, and then blurted, "Knobby jezebel!" before slapping his tentacles over his mouth.

Lucy fell out of his chair. "Holy *crap*, Chauncey!" he said, pulling himself back up. "That was *devastating*. Good thing Arthur said you could do it, because I think that was the worst thing I've ever heard anyone say about *anyone*."

"I didn't mean it!" Chauncey wailed. "I take it back!"

"Chauncey," David said, "I heard Miss Marblemaw talking. She said bellhops have the easiest job in the world and that anyone with half a brain could do it."

"That *knobby jezebel*," Chauncey hissed.

"I said once, Chauncey," Arthur murmured gravely. "I don't know if my heart could take that again."

"I promise," Chauncey said, tentacle over his heart (which was near the bottom of his body). "I'll never do anything like that again."

"She also said that bellhop caps look bad on everyone," David said as Lucy whispered in his ear.

"Arthur?" Chauncey asked.

"Yes?"

"Can I ink Miss Marblemaw?"

"I would never propose such an action," Arthur said. "However, I am of the firm belief that if one must ink, one must be allowed to do so without interruption."

"She's gonna be so mad when she finds out about my nocturnal emissions," Chauncey said. "I can't *wait*."

Linus sighed.

On Tuesday, two things of note occurred.

First, Miss Marblemaw sat in on the morning's lessons, bits of red-stained tissue paper blotting the area around her mustache. True to Lucy's word, it appeared she'd tried to shave it off, only to have it regrow into the same shape and length it'd been the day before. She didn't mention it, even when Talia greeted her and said she'd be willing to share the soaps she used on her beard.

Instead, Miss Marblemaw took a seat in the rear of the room, her clipboard in hand. She looked at each of them expectantly.

"Are we just going to sit here, or are you actually going to begin the lesson?"

"Before we do," Lucy said, "I mustache you a question. Would you like a cup of tea?"

"No," she said, crossing one leg over the other. "What I want is for you to take your seat and for Mr. Baker to prove that he is fit to educate children. And *David*, since he seems to be interested in child-level knowledge even though he's lived for almost five decades. Forget I'm even here."

"You never stop learning," David said. "That's what I always say." He folded his hands behind his head, leaning back in his chair. He almost tipped over, but acted like he'd done it on purpose. "Careful, kids! Get a question wrong, and Miss Marblemaw might try and assault you like she did me."

"I did not *assault*—"

"I thought you said you wanted us to forget you were here?" Sal asked. "Kind of hard to do that when you keep interrupting our class. Everyone, face forward. Forget Miss Marblemaw exists."

"Who?" Phee said.

Though Arthur had other things to see to—such was life on the island—he didn't dare let Miss Marblemaw out of his sight. Linus was more than capable of handling her on his own, but Arthur thought it wouldn't hurt to remind Miss Marblemaw they were watching her as much as she was watching them.

The lesson proceeded with minimal interruption, usually from Miss Marblemaw coughing pointedly or clearing her throat when Linus or the children said something that she obviously did not approve of. Linus attempted to ignore her, but the longer the lesson went on—going from the wide and mysterious world of mathematics to history—the more Miss Marblemaw made a nuisance of herself, muttering under her breath as she scribbled on her clipboard.

They were reaching the end of the hour—almost time for midmorning break—when Linus said, "History is full of different people making the same mistakes over and over again, never learning from the actions of those who came before them. Time can sometimes prove to be a vicious circle in that regard. People in power attempting to tell others how they should live their lives, but only in the bounds of what *they* consider acceptable. Gatekeepers who believe it is up to them to decide what is morally correct or not. One could argue that—"

"One could argue about *anything*," Miss Marblemaw said loudly. "Some people think their little complaints mean more than the safety of an entire race of people."

"And what race would that be?" Sal asked. "Last I checked, even if we're different, all of us are people." He arched an eyebrow. "Unless you mean the literal definition of the word 'race,' which is a concept used to describe a group of people according to different factors, such as ancestral background, social identity, and visible characteristics . . . such as skin color."

Miss Marblemaw blanched. "That's not what I—I am accepting of *all*—how dare you imply that I—" She stopped, closing her eyes and taking a deep breath. When she opened her eyes again, they were clear above a thin smile. She stood, sweeping her way to the front of the class. "Children, regardless of what you might have heard, the world isn't as dark and cruel as *certain people* want to make it out to be. How could it be, when we have museums and art and music—*music*, Lucy. Don't you love music?"

"Oh, yes," Lucy said. "The deader, the better."

"See?" Miss Marblemaw said, left eye twitching. "It looks as if Lucy and I have found common ground. Who would have thought that possible even three days ago? That's what this is all about. Setting aside our differences and coming together in the spirit of— Where are you going?"

The children had started packing up their books and papers, standing and walking toward the rear door. David led the way, arms above his head as he wiggled his hips, sliding out of the room backward, giving Miss Marblemaw a little wave of his fingers.

Sal was last, Theodore perched on his shoulder. He looked back at Miss Marblemaw and said, "Class was over the moment you started talking." And then he left.

"Linus," Arthur said as Miss Marblemaw spluttered, obviously gearing up for a meltdown. "You look parched. Shall we have our morning tea in the gazebo?"

"That sounds perfect," Linus said. "Perhaps a little cake, if there is any left." He joined Arthur at the rear of the class. Joining hands, they walked toward the door.

"DICOMY will hear of this," Miss Marblemaw called after them.

Arthur paused at the doorway, glancing back at her over his shoulder. "If you need to contact Rowder again with your special briefcase, feel free to use the kitchen rather than lugging it all the way to the beach. While you're here, our home is your home. Now, Linus, I seem to remember I hid some tea cakes away for such an occasion."

"So long as Theodore hasn't sniffed them out," Linus said.

"The nose on our son."

"Indeed."

They grinned at each other and left Miss Marblemaw behind.

The second event of note occurred a short time later. Linus and Arthur sat in the gazebo, sipping peppermint tea, a plate of toasted currant tea cakes stacked in front of them on a tray next to a pewter pot. In the woods beyond, Phee and Chauncey were searching for pine cones ("It's not a problem! Don't look at me when I eat them!"). From an open window upstairs, Frankie Valli wailed that he'd told his girl they had to break up, thought she'd call his bluff, but she said to his surprise, big girls don't cry. Lucy screeched along, David's laughter loud and infectious. They waved to Sal and Theodore, Sal carrying a thick book, Theodore walking beside him, wings flapping, chattering away as they headed for their usual tree on the other side of the house.

Talia was in her garden, coming over every now and then to show them the large pile of weeds she'd pulled, and to remind them that anyone sitting in the gazebo must give compliments to the plants in the garden at random intervals.

"Zoe?" Linus asked quietly as he sipped his tea. Then, raising his voice, "I do love how the roses looked this morning!"

"She's working on something," Arthur said. "Being rather secretive about it. Look at the blooms on those petunias! Fantastic!"

"She'll come to us when she's ready," Linus said. "That being said, I'm curious about what she's doing."

"As am I," Arthur said. "But we will trust her as we've always done."

"Is it terrible of me to say I'd give almost anything to be a fly on the wall if and when she meets with Marblemaw?"

"Certainly not," Arthur said. "For I would like the same. But they can't say I didn't warn them about being woefully outmatched."

"Too right," Linus said. He sipped his tea again, smacking his lips. "Ah, that's the ticket. Nothing like a good cuppa on a pretty afternoon. Oh, look, our guest. And she's . . ." Linus sighed. "Oh dear."

Arthur turned his head to see Miss Marblemaw marching up the garden path. Around her mouth and nose, a pink-and-green scarf, leaving only her eyes and forehead visible. She grimaced at the flowers on either side of her, snatching her hand back when a yellow tulip had the temerity to brush against her.

As such, she was distracted, and did not see Arthur and Linus in the gazebo. They didn't call out in greeting as she stomped by them. Instead, Arthur lifted his cup and took a long drink, throat working. Pulling the cup away, he said, "Should we warn her?"

"Talia? If you think we should—"

"I meant the inspector."

"Oh," Linus said. "No. Here. Have a cake."

Arthur did. He bit into it just as Talia said, "Oh, look who it is! Miss I-Don't-Like-Pollen in a garden practically *made* of pollen."

"I am *allergic*," Miss Marblemaw said. "It is a very serious issue that should not be made light of."

"Oh, my apologies," Talia said, and Arthur chuckled, picturing the sweet, innocent smile on her face. "That must be so awful to be allergic to pretty things. It would make sense if you found yourself allergic to me."

"Speaking of pretty things," Miss Marblemaw said with a sniffle. "I was wondering if you'd given further thought to what we discussed."

"You'll have to remind me what that was," Talia said. "You talk a lot, and I don't always pay attention."

"Really? Do you find yourself struggling to focus?"

"No," Talia said. "Though I can see why you thought that. I was only talking about you."

"I do love peppermint," Linus said. "Reminds me of the holidays. Lights and garlands and good cheer."

"As it should," Arthur said. "I'm fascinated by the idea that senses are tied to memory."

"Your beard," Miss Marblemaw said, sounding as if she were speaking through gritted teeth. She sneezed twice in quick succession. "Giving consideration to shaving it off. I just know there's a beautiful little girl under all that hair."

"Can you hand me the trowel?" Talia asked. "No, the trowel. That's a *spade*. And that's a hose. Do you not know what a trowel is? There seems to be a lot you don't know. I got it. Can you stand back a little? I'm about to dig really fast, and dirt goes everywhere."

True to her word, Talia began to dig, the sound of her trowel striking the soil like music to Arthur's ears. Knowing how quickly she worked, Arthur wasn't surprised when, ten minutes later, she seemed to have finished. "There," she said. "That should do it."

"A hole?" Miss Marblemaw asked. "Why would you dig a hole that large? You already have one over there."

"That's for Papa," Talia said. "In case he goes back on his promise to help me finish weeding the garden."

"An effective threat," Arthur said.

"Quite," Linus replied. "She even put a breathing tube in mine in case I somehow come back to life."

"She thinks of everything," Arthur said.

"What's the other hole for?" Miss Marblemaw asked.

"I'm so glad you asked!" Talia said with a chuckle. Then her voice dropped dangerously. "It's a grave where I'm going to bury you if you *ever* try to tell me to shave off my beard again."

"I beg your pardon?" Miss Marblemaw said in a high-pitched voice.

"Fun fact!" Talia said cheerfully. "You don't get to tell other people how they should or shouldn't look. It's rude. Just because you don't like something doesn't mean others won't appreciate it. I like how I look. And honestly, you'd think with the mustache you have, you'd be a little more accepting of girls with body hair."

"That doesn't give you the right to dig a *grave*," Miss Marblemaw snapped.

"Actually, it does," Talia said. "Now, be a good inspector and climb inside, won't you? Here, let me help."

A moment later, Miss Marblemaw stormed from the garden, her hair in disarray, front covered in dirt.

"Did you enjoy Talia's garden?" Linus asked as she passed by the gazebo.

She stopped, turning slowly to glare at them, mustache wilted as if she'd replaced it with a thick noodle.

"I don't think she did," Arthur murmured, sipping his tea.

"That's unfortunate. Would you share another cake with me?"

"It would be my honor."

"Brilliant."

Miss Marblemaw bellowed, "Courtesy points! Courtesy points for everyone!" And then she stomped her way out of the garden.

On Wednesday afternoon, Chauncey arrived late to supper, loudly proclaiming that he had made a startling discovery that had nothing to do with being able to talk to fish or nocturnal emissions. They turned toward him as he posed in the entryway, tentacles on his hips.

Miss Marblemaw skulked in the shadows, clipboard firmly in hand. She was not in the best mood, seeing as how she'd woken up that morning to find her mustache had turned a sickly shade of yellow, giving her the appearance of having a severe infection.

"What is it?" Sal asked.

Chauncey waited a beat—for drama—and said, "I have become a man."

"Whoa," David said. "That's awesome. How did you do that?"

"There I was!" Chauncey said, oozing around the table, tentacles trailing along the backs of chairs. "Minding my own business, standing in front of the mirror in my room inspecting every inch of my body."

"Ew," Phee said. "Some things should be kept private."

"That's why I was doing it in my room," Chauncey explained, stopping behind Linus's chair. "But this is something that must be shared. Because I found *this*." He lifted his right tentacle above his head. And there, in what served as his armpit, was a single white hair, about half an inch in length, curled at the tip.

Lucy stood on his chair, bent over with his hands flat against the table on either side of his plate. "You got *armpit* hair? That's not fair! I want it too!"

"That's right!" Chauncey crowed. "I have *armpit* hair, which means I'm a man! As such, you might see me carrying a briefcase or getting on important conference calls to talk about business and other adult things. But fear not! I'm still young at heart."

"Careful," Talia warned. "Miss Marblemaw will probably try and make you shave it off."

"No!" Chauncey cried, lowering his tentacle, tucking it against his side. "You can't have it. I grew it all by myself and it's *mine*."

"I can't believe Miss Marblemaw wants to take Chauncey's armpit hair," Phee said.

Miss Marblemaw said, "I *never*—"

"What would she even do with it?" Sal asked.

Theodore was of the mind that she'd use it to stuff a pillow.

"Never!" Chauncey yelled. "That's weird!"

Miss Marblemaw stepped out of the shadows. "If you'd let me finish, I'm trying to tell you that I wouldn't—"

Chauncey shrieked and flailed, running around the table. "She's after me!"

Miss Marblemaw was not, in fact, chasing Chauncey, given that he kept running by her every time he circumnavigated the table. It went on as these things sometimes did, meaning far longer than was necessary. It ended when Miss Marblemaw stepped in front of Chauncey, and said, "If you would just *listen* to me, your armpit hair is—"

Chauncey scream-sneezed quite spectacularly, and Miss Marblemaw was coated from head to toe in dripping black ink. Silence fell in the dining room, the only noticeable sound the *plink, plink, plink* of black droplets on the floor. Behind her on the wall as if flash-fried: a perfect outline of her figure, ink splattered around her. Miss Marblemaw stood there, mouth agape, ink coating her tongue and teeth.

Lucy laughed. "Well, look at me being wrong for the first time in my life. I guess Chauncey was right when he said his nocturnal emissions don't always happen at night. I love learning!"

Miss Marblemaw let out a slow, creaking moan.

"Can I teach you something else?" David asked. "See that spot on the wall where no ink hit but you can still see her shape? That's called negative space. I learned that when I was training to be a private detective. It's how they look at blood splatters."

"And now I've learned something today," Arthur said. "Thank you, David. Miss Marblemaw, would you like a napkin? I have several if you think that would help."

Miss Marblemaw didn't speak. Instead, she squished with every step she took out of the dining room. A moment later, the front door opened and closed.

"Children," Linus said. "This seems like a teachable moment. What did we learn?"

"That you should never try and steal Chauncey's armpit hair," Talia said.

"It's still there," Chauncey said, lifting his arm and showing it off.

"*And* you shouldn't tell a girl she should shave her beard," Lucy said. "Especially when it's none of your business." He glanced at

Linus. "Also, I'm sorry we made fun of your mustache when you grew it. You're not like Miss Marblemaw."

Linus chuckled. "It's not quite the same, but thank you, Lucy. That was very kind of you. Now, who wants dessert? I heard a rumor there's cobbler. Peach, in fact."

"What's a guy gotta do to get a courtesy point around here?" Chauncey harrumphed. "Grow *two* armpit hairs? That's impossible."

On Thursday afternoon—the sky a sheet of clouds that promised a good soaking later on, the sea flat, calm, reflecting the stone gray from above—Sal got his turn. Shortly after lunch, Calliope began meowing loudly, rubbing against his legs in an insistent manner. It did not take one versed in feline to know what she wanted. Calliope, for how evil she could be, loved fiercely, and while Linus was her person, it could be easily argued that extended to Sal as well. The first time he shifted in front of her into his Pomeranian form, she'd frozen, ears flat against her skull as she hissed, tail taut. But then her nose had started twitching, and she'd craned her neck toward him. She'd blinked once, twice, and then pounced on him, cleaning his ears. When she'd finished, she'd climbed off him and nudged him toward the front door. For the next three hours, she'd tried to teach Sal how to hunt, crouched low in the grass as a bird flitted in the low-hanging branches. They didn't get the bird, but that didn't seem to bother Calliope. The entire way back to the house, she'd chattered away, undoubtedly telling Sal he'd do better next time.

After that, barely a week would go by without Calliope wanting Sal to shift. Though she seemed to prefer his human form (after all, a Pomeranian did not have a lap on which she could sit comfortably), Calliope seemed to think Sal was her child, and woe betide anyone who tried to interfere with what she considered hers.

Unfortunately for Miss Marblemaw, she learned this firsthand.

Sal's shifted form was a thing of beauty: small, the size of a decorative throw pillow, with a thick coat of off-white around his head, changing into a rusty orange that extended down his back and legs. His whiskers were black, his eyes dark and intelligent. Discarding his clothes in a pile on the kitchen counter, he began to chase after Calliope. They ran through the house, Arthur grinning at the sound of toenails clicking along the floor as they went up and down the stairs, Sal barking happily.

Their game of tag lasted a good twenty minutes before it ended quite dramatically.

Arthur was putting away the last of the lunch dishes when he heard Miss Marblemaw shout, "Are you *chasing* that poor cat? You there! Leave her alone!"

He hurried from the kitchen, only to find Sal and Calliope sitting on the stairs, six steps up. Miss Marblemaw stood in front of them, glowering. Calliope's head was cocked, eyes narrowed. Sal was panting, little pink tongue hanging out. As Miss Marblemaw reached for Calliope, he began to growl, quivering lips pulled back over sharp teeth. She jerked her hand away. Sal went back to panting, and Arthur thought he might be smiling.

Miss Marblemaw extended her hand again slowly.

Sal growled.

She pulled it back.

He panted and smiled.

Then she made a fatal mistake. Instead of going for Calliope, she went for Sal, saying, "You should be *outside* when you're like this. Dogs in the house! Filthy creatures, their noses always buried in trash or their own behinds. And traumatizing this poor, innocent cat? No, no, *no*."

Arthur said, "I really wouldn't do that if I were—"

Too late. The moment her hands got within six inches of Sal, Calliope proved herself to be the protector Arthur had always thought she was: she launched herself at Miss Marblemaw, claws on all four paws extended. She landed on Miss Marblemaw's front, climbing her way up to the inspector's head. Once Calliope was face-to-face with Miss Marblemaw, she brought a paw back and slapped her, leaving three small scratches on her cheek. Miss Marblemaw's eyes widened as Calliope leaned close, a low and dangerous *mroooowr* crawling from her mouth, teeth on full display.

"Miss Marblemaw," Arthur said in a hushed voice. "Whatever you do, do *not* look like you're challenging her."

Miss Marblemaw nodded tightly. Then she smiled and said, "I'm not challenging you. I just happen to know best when it comes to—"

Wrong thing to say. Calliope's paws were a blur as she attacked, Miss Marblemaw shrieking and spinning around as she tried to pull the cat off her. Despite her best efforts, the inspector proved to be no match against a cat who had taken umbrage at her views on dogs and their place in a home.

For his part, Sal proved to be an exceptional teammate, going to the front door and pulling on a piece of fabric Arthur had tied to the handle for the times when his son wanted to go outside and was in his shifted form. The door swung open, and Calliope battered Miss Marblemaw until she stumbled onto the porch. Mission accomplished, Calliope jumped off her, landing perfectly on the ground. She stepped back inside the house and sat shoulder to shoulder with Sal.

Arthur stood above them in the doorway, looking out to Miss Marblemaw. "Leaving already? I do hope it's nothing we said."

Face scratched up, her mustache missing more than a few hairs, Miss Marblemaw said, "That thing isn't a cat! It's a demon spawn on four legs and I won't—"

"Did someone say demon spawn?"

Miss Marblemaw whirled around to find Lucy standing behind her. She put her hand to her throat. "Where did you come from?"

"Hell," Lucy said. "What happened to your face?" He leaned over, peering around her. "Oh. I see. You messed with Sal. Yeah, you shouldn't do that. Calliope doesn't like it when people do that."

"Rabid!" Miss Marblemaw said. "For all I know, that cat is rabid, and I—"

"Should probably seek medical attention immediately, just to be safe," Arthur said. "Luckily for you, the village has a wonderful health center that treats everyone, regardless of whether they are magical. I've heard the course of injections after a suspected rabies attack is not a pleasant one, so if you must cut your visit short, we'd understand."

"You won't be rid of me quite so easily," she said. "And if I did so, they would come for the cat." She grinned as a trickle of blood slid down her cheek. "Do you know how they test for rabies? They take the head."

"Wow," Lucy said, impressed. "What are you going to do without a head? Walk into stuff? Yeah, I bet you'll walk into stuff. If it helps, I can take your head right now so you won't have to sit in a waiting room. Here, just let me—"

Miss Marblemaw hurried toward the guesthouse, glancing balefully over her shoulder. "You haven't heard the last of this!"

Calliope purred as loudly as Arthur had ever heard her.

It had begun with Lucy; he could see that now. It had never been about Arthur himself, or the other children, not really. Lucy was the ultimate prize: a weapon without equal, a tool and nothing more.

It had begun with Lucy; therefore, it seemed fitting that it ended with him too.

On Friday afternoon—classes over for the week, the weekend brimming with the whispers of adventure—Lucy had his wildest dreams come true.

He got to make sentient mud men.

Arthur sat in his office next to Zoe. Across from them, Miss Marblemaw, finally accorded the meeting she'd seemed so interested in upon introduction to the island's sprite. It was not, in Arthur's approximation, going well for Miss Marblemaw, seeing as how her opening salvo had been to once again stress the importance of registering with DICOMA.

Granted, Arthur wasn't quite paying attention to Miss Marblemaw, though through no fault of his own. Zoe had arrived before the inspector and proceeded to drop a bombshell on Arthur. To say he was stunned would have been inadequate. Zoe's secret—the plan she'd hinted at more than once—did not defy logic; quite the opposite. It made so much sense that Arthur couldn't believe he'd never considered it before. But here, now, sitting next to Zoe, he had to keep himself from laughing hysterically.

"No," she said. "And it'll be no when you ask tomorrow, and the day after that, ad infinitum. You have no jurisdiction here."

"I am an inspector for DICOMY," Miss Marblemaw said. "I think you'll find that my jurisdiction extends further than you imagine. But let's not get hung up on pesky little details. I have questions. First, I understand that you don't reside in the main house. From what I've been able to gather, you have a separate home that the children visit whenever they wish. Is that correct?"

"Yes."

She nodded, making a note. "I'll need to see the residence."

"No."

Miss Marblemaw squinted at Zoe, her mustache frayed and bristly. "No?"

Zoe shrugged. "No."

"You can't say no."

"I just did."

Miss Marblemaw sighed. "Is it too much to ask for the adults in this place to actually *act* like adults? You are being petty, Miss Chapelwhite."

"Or," Arthur said, "she's had centuries of experience with people like you who've made false promises, only to renege when it actually counted."

Miss Marblemaw clucked her tongue. "Pity. I thought you'd listen to reason. It seems I was mistaken. I suppose it would be pointless of me to ask my remaining questions, seeing as how I'll get either stonewalled or lied to."

Zoe smiled, razor sharp. "That might be the smartest thing you've said since your arrival."

"I know you think little of me," Miss Marblemaw said. "Thankfully, likability isn't a requirement for these inspections. My job isn't to come here to make friends. As listed in the *RULES AND*

REGULATIONS, my job is to ensure that the children are being well cared for, and—"

"I can't tell if she truly believes that, or if that's what she's been told to say," Zoe said to Arthur.

"She's no Linus Baker," Arthur agreed, touching the ring on his finger.

Before Miss Marblemaw could retort, they were interrupted when Lucy burst into the room, covered head to toe in mud. He skidded to a stop, mouth hanging open. It snapped closed when he saw Miss Marblemaw. "Uh," he said, eyes darting side to side. "I haven't done anything I wasn't supposed to, and the only reason I came running in here was because I wanted . . . to see . . . how fast . . . I . . . am?" He grinned. "Yep, that's all it is!"

"What have you been *doing*?" Miss Marblemaw said, aghast. "Did you track mud through the entire *house*?"

Lucy looked down at the muddy footprints leading into the office. "Huh. I guess I did. Weird."

"Lucy," Arthur admonished gently. "We're in the middle of a meeting. Please don't be rude. Can you wait?"

"Oh, yeah," Lucy said. "I totally can. Forget I was even—"

From somewhere downstairs, a cry that could only come from a beleaguered Papa: "*LUCIFER BAKER-PARNASSUS.*"

"Uh-oh," Lucy said. "And also, aw. I love that name."

"Lucy," Arthur said.

"Yeah, yeah," he muttered. "I've got some 'splaining ta do." He brightened. "But! I think when you see what I've done, you'll be impressed." He turned toward Miss Marblemaw, smile widening, causing the drying mud to crack on his cheeks. "As will *you*, Miss Marblemaw. I made them especially for you."

"Made what?" Miss Marblemaw asked, face pinched as if she'd just stepped in leavings from a dog.

"Come and see!" he said, giggling as he skipped from the room, footsteps squishy on the floor.

"Shall we?" Arthur asked. "I'm sure Zoe wouldn't mind picking this up at a later time." He didn't flinch when Zoe kicked him underneath the desk.

"This had better not be a distraction," Miss Marblemaw warned. "You're already skating on thin ice, Mr. Parnassus."

"Good thing I can fly," he said, extending his hand to Zoe. She took it, letting herself be pulled up, her wings unfolding. She put her arm through his and they walked around the desk to the door, each of them shaking their head at the little footprints left in the carpet. Stopping in the doorway, Arthur glanced at Miss Marblemaw. "Coming?"

Miss Marblemaw stood slowly. "The child had better not have done anything . . . illegal."

Arthur laughed. "What kind of monsters do you take us for? Don't answer that. We already know."

As they left Miss Marblemaw spluttering behind them, Zoe whispered, "I'd forgotten how much of a bitch you can be when you put your mind to it."

Arthur kissed her hair. "What a lovely thing to say."

To say the mud men were a surprise wouldn't quite be correct; the evidence of their existence was plentiful. First, Lucy had attempted such a thing before. Second, Lucy had entered the office covered in mud.

Your honor, the prosecution rests.

Going outside, Arthur was further unsurprised to find the rest of the children standing next to Linus, his hands on his hips, head cocked as he frowned at the sight before him: Lucy pacing, jabbering away at a mile a minute, hands thrown up as he moved back and forth. It was quite the sight to see, especially when Lucy stopped his explanation to shore up the left leg of one of several six-foot mud men.

"There," he said, pulling his hands away. "That should hold for a little while."

"You made *mud men*?" Linus asked, eyes narrowed.

Miss Marblemaw started coughing roughly when the mud man looked down at Lucy and said, "Muuuuuuud?"

"That's exactly right, Janet," Lucy said. "Papa *is* being rude by not respecting your pronouns." He looked up at Linus, shaking his head. "For shame, Papa. Janet is a mud *woman*. Barry and Turnip are mud men."

"Muuuuuuddddd," Janet said, voice thick and wet.

"Mud mud mud," Barry said.

"I say, chaps," Turnip said, face running with filth. "There I was, lying in my bog minding my own business with the worms and microbes when all of a sudden, I found myself tall and thinking of things I can't quite explain. What is happiness?" A piece of his head sloughed off onto the ground with a wet splat.

"I love you, Turnip," Lucy said, swaying side to side.

"This is unacceptable," Miss Marblemaw snapped, pushing her way through the children. "You can't just give dirt *life*."

"Actually," Talia said, "dirt is teeming with life, so. You can trust me on that because I'm an expert."

"She's right," Phee said. "Everything has life in it." She sneezed. Strangely, it sounded like *except DICOMY inspectors*.

"Semantics," Miss Marblemaw said with a ferocious glower. "I can't believe I have to be the voice of reason here. Can't you see how—how *blasphemous* this is?"

"Your definition of blasphemy is very different from ours," Talia said.

"That's an understatement," Sal said.

"They're just mud," Chauncey said, gazing adoringly up at Barry, who poked his own face, muddy finger sinking all the way in. "There's nothing wrong with mud."

"There is when it's given sentience," Miss Marblemaw retorted. She glared at Arthur. "Are you just going to stand there and let this happen? For someone who claims to want to be a father, you sure are doing everything to keep that from happening."

The fire rose within him again, insistent, furious at the temerity of this person. But it did not burn as fiercely as it had even a few days ago.

Which was why he said, "Madam, I am already a father. Not even one such as you can take that away from me."

"Hello, there!" Turnip called, looking at David. "You seem like a fine fellow. Can you help me? Why is it that a goose can be geese but a moose can't be meese?"

"No one knows," David said. In a lower voice, he whispered, "Turnip *talked* to me. I love this place."

"Can't I?" Miss Marblemaw asked. "Because I thought that's exactly what my position allows." She pulled herself to her full height as the mud men and woman turned toward her. "You think yourself so smart, Mr. Parnassus. And you are, I'll give you that. However, your intelligence has blinded you to the reality of your situation. You see these children as nothing *but* that: children. And while they certainly are young, it is becoming abundantly clear that your control over them is nothing but an illusion. Children running amok without supervision—"

"I'll give her that," Lucy said. "I amok all over the place."

"—and that doesn't even begin to cover what you're teaching them. How could they possibly hope to have any success in life when you fill their heads with fanciful talk of a future that will never be? You are doing them a disservice. You and Miss Chapelwhite and Mr. Baker. You flout DICOMY guidelines as if they don't pertain to you, you insist on including classroom materials and studies that aren't sanctioned. In all ways that matter, you are an employee of the Department in Charge of Magical Youth. Or have you forgotten that?"

"I haven't," Arthur said as Turnip exclaimed over the color of the sky, saying he'd never seen anything so blue. "Thank you for bringing that up. I've been meaning to speak to you about it." Zoe squeezed his arm, a silent gesture of support. "I hereby tender my resignation as master for the Department in Charge of Magical Youth."

Miss Marblemaw gaped at him. "You *what*?"

"He quits," Linus said, marching by her to stop in front of Arthur. "Well played, my love. Let me be the first to congratulate you on such a tremendous decision." He kissed Arthur soundly as the children hooted and hollered.

"I don't like her," Turnip said to Barry and Janet. "She reminds me of that raccoon who won't stop defecating in our swamp."

"Mud?" Barry asked.

"I agree," Turnip said. "She might even *be* that raccoon in disguise. I'm not quite sure if raccoons can take human form. She certainly looks like a raccoon pretending to be human."

"*Mud*," Janet said, punching a fist into her palm.

"You pooped in their swamp?" Chauncey asked Miss Marblemaw. "Can I tell you a secret? I pooped in the ocean and pretended it came from a dolphin, so don't feel too bad."

"I knew it!" Phee yelled.

"You did not!" Chauncey yelled back.

"You can't quit," Miss Marblemaw snapped.

"Funny, then, that I did just that," Arthur replied. "I am not beholden to DICOMY. None of us are."

"And that's where you're wrong," Miss Marblemaw said. She shook her head. "I've seen enough. From the moment I stepped foot on this island, all you've done is lie and obfuscate to hide the truth behind your pretty words."

"Papa?" Talia asked, tugging on his hand. "Why is Miss Marblemaw flirting with Dad? Doesn't she know he loves you almost as much as he loves us?"

"Your dad is quite the catch," Linus said. "It's the socks, you see."

Miss Marblemaw's face was the color of an overripe tomato. "I'm not *flirting*. I'm trying to— No. I won't be pulled into your ridiculous word games again. You can't trick me. None of you can. I see you for what you are. You are an infection spreading unchecked, sullying the hearts and minds of those you claim to care for, filling their heads with ridiculous nonsense. When are you going to tell them the truth? When are you finally going to be honest with the children?"

The phoenix awoke, offended by this woman who continued to breathe their air as if she had any right to. Arthur was in control, but it was close.

But the response did not come from him.

It came from Sal.

"Honest?" he said, stepping forward, Theodore growling on his shoulder. "You're going after him for *honesty*? Who the hell do you think you are?"

Miss Marblemaw turned her head slowly toward him. "Excuse me?"

"Arthur Parnassus was the first person in my life to be honest with me," Sal said. "He was the first person who made me believe that I could be anything I wanted to be."

"And that is a *lie*," Miss Marblemaw retorted. "Bellhops and writers and whatever else you all think you are. Do you believe the world will accept you outside of your little bubble? If so, you are in for an extraordinarily rude awakening. No, you must know the truth. You can't—"

"I'm already a bellhop," Chauncey said.

She blinked. "What?"

"You said whatever we *think* we are," Chauncey said patiently. "But I don't think I'm a bellhop. I *am* one, and at a three-star hotel."

"He's right," Sal said as Theodore nodded. "Chauncey's the best bellhop I've ever seen. Phee is smarter and stronger than the rest of us put together. Talia's gardens have appeared in magazines across the country. Theodore probably has the largest collection of buttons in the entire *world*. Lucy made mud people. *Mud people*. Do you know how awesome that is?"

"Ain't nothin' to it," Lucy said, blowing on his knuckles and rubbing them against his chest.

"And what about David?" Miss Marblemaw asked. "Shouldn't you talk about him? Oh, wait. That's right. He's not a child, but a man! A short man who doesn't act his purported age?"

"Why are you so obsessed with me?" David asked. "I mean, I get it. Look at me: I'm fluffy *and* a world-class actor. But still, you're going a little overboard. I'll have to call my agent and see about a restraining order."

Sal continued to stare at Miss Marblemaw as Theodore snorted. "How many orphanages have I been to?"

Miss Marblemaw blanched as she began to riffle through the pages on her clipboard. "I . . . er, I have it—"

"Five," Sal said. "What does Lucy love most in the world?"

"I . . . don't—"

"Come on, Miss Marblemaw," he said. "You say you know what's best for us, so surely, you'd know *about* us, right? Because knowing what's best implies you know the important things about us. And hell, I'm practically *giving* you this one since Lucy already mentioned it. You know it? No? The answer is dead-people music. What do gnomes call their communities?"

"This is *pointless*—"

"A donzy," Sal said, cool as all get-out. "How many languages can Theodore understand?" Without waiting for an answer, he continued. "Four. English, Gnomish, Wyvern, and Spanish. And how about Chauncey?"

"I have many secrets," Chauncey said.

"How many books did he read about the art of being a bellhop? Sixty-seven. What is Phee's favorite kind of tree? Dragon blood."

"Because they have red pitch, and originally only grew in Yemen and along the Arabian Sea," Phee said. "I'm gonna try and grow one here. They look so creepy, I love it."

"You ever get the feeling you became sentient right in the middle of something?" Turnip whispered to Barry and Janet, who both nodded.

"You don't know the first thing about us," Sal said. "You claim to, but you don't. Even when you first met us, you tried to get us to say something we didn't like about living here. You showed your hand before you even knew the game had started."

"This isn't a *game*," Miss Marblemaw said.

"Then stop treating us like pawns on a chessboard," Sal countered. "You were never going to let us stay here. Admit it. You talk of honesty, but you don't know the first thing about it."

"Oh snap," Lucy said. "Felt that right in my chest."

"I know enough," Miss Marblemaw said. "More than you, to be sure. You are a child, and don't know any better, so it's to be expected."

"Okay," Phee said. "So we're kids. Why have you never asked what *we* want?"

"Because," Miss Marblemaw said, condescending and smug, "you can't know. You are far too young to understand the ramifications of—"

"Being abused?" Sal asked. "Getting locked in a room without food or access to a toilet? Finding a way to sneak out to try and get something to eat, only to be slapped across the face for doing so? *Biting* my attacker because I was *scared*? Being told that I was a monster for spreading my magic? Being forced to stay in my shift and wear a muzzle? Tell me, Miss Marblemaw, tell me what I'm too young to understand. Tell me *exactly* what I'm missing, because all I see is a person trying to take us away from the only place we've ever felt safe."

"Because you don't know any better!" Miss Marblemaw cried. "This place—this *farce* is not the real world. This is nothing but an illusion created by a man with a personal vendetta. What happens when you age out? Do you really think you'll be prepared for what you find in the real world?"

Sal shrugged. "Maybe. Maybe not. Regardless, I know I'll always have a home to come back to. Take us. Right now. See what happens when you try."

Miss Marblemaw took a step back, only to bump into Turnip, who said, "Pardon me, ma'am. Got some of me on your back."

She jumped at least three feet in the air. She craned her neck to see her mud-coated back, spinning in a slow circle. She must have realized she still had an audience, because she whipped back around to face them. "It won't only be me," she said. "Not here. Not now. But soon. That's a promise. And there's nowhere you can run that we won't find you."

"I've had quite enough," Arthur said, stepping forward. "Lucy, be a dear, would you? I'd like all of Miss Marblemaw's possessions brought from the guesthouse. Her time with us has been cut short, and she will be departing immediately."

"I'm not going *anywhere*," she snarled. "I am here until Wednesday, whether you like it or not."

Lucy said, "Ella Fitzgerald skibbidy bip!"

The front door to the guesthouse burst open, and Miss Marblemaw's suitcase and metal briefcase came rolling out, tumbling end over end, kicking up dust and bits of grass. They came to a stop next to the inspector, who ignored them, her gaze trained firmly on Arthur. "This won't end well for you. Surely you see that."

Arthur tilted his head. "So I've been told my entire life, and here I am, still standing." He spread his arms on either side of him. "You want to take from me? See how far you get. I am many things. A man. A phoenix. Pawn. Survivor. Husband-to-be. Former master. Those pale in comparison to the title I hold above all else."

"And what's that?" Miss Marblemaw asked, a nasty curl to her voice.

"A father," Arthur said. "And you have caused my children distress, fear, and pain. I warned you when you arrived what would happen if you didn't abide by my rules. You chose not to listen. Now it's time to reap your just rewards."

"You have no authority over me," Miss Marblemaw said coldly. "Even *if* you somehow force me from Marsyas, I will return in greater numbers, and by hook or by crook, your dream will die the death it should've mercifully received years ago."

"By crook," Linus said. "Honestly."

"It's as if she doesn't hear herself," Arthur replied.

"We certainly heard her, didn't we?"

"That we did."

Zoe glanced at Miss Marblemaw and beyond. "Turnip, would you like to help? It's okay to say no if you don't want to."

"What would you have of me, your majesty?" Turnip asked,

bowing low. Barry and Janet did the same, dripping bits of themselves onto the ground.

"*Majesty?*" Miss Marblemaw exclaimed. "She's nothing but a *sprite.*"

"Harriet Marblemaw has come to our home with nefarious designs," Zoe said. "It's high time she departed. Take her to the docks. Barry, Janet, please grab her belongings and follow me."

Miss Marblemaw didn't have time to escape before Turnip wrapped his arms around her, lifting her off the ground. She bellowed furiously, kicking her legs to no avail. Turnip's hold on her was far stronger than she could ever be. Janet picked up the metal briefcase, and Barry hoisted the suitcase.

"Children," Linus said, "let's go see about your afternoon snack, shall we? Everyone wave goodbye to Miss Marblemaw."

"I'd like Lucy to come with us," Arthur said. "Just in case."

"Yep, yep," Lucy said, rushing past Arthur to catch up with the mud people and Zoe, Miss Marblemaw threatening anything and everything. Arthur nodded at Linus as he herded the other children toward the house, all of them talking excitedly.

The mud people proved to be light on their feet, strides long and sure. However, Arthur noticed that if they got too far ahead of Zoe—not Lucy—they'd slow down, letting her catch up. *Your majesty,* Turnip had said. He knew. Somehow, he knew. Be it the magic of the island itself, or the light that emanated from Zoe Chapelwhite, somehow, Turnip knew what Arthur himself had only learned shortly before.

Miss Marblemaw continued her threats as they made their way down the winding dirt road, Lucy picking up piles of mud that had fallen off his creations and slapping it back on while jogging to keep pace. By the time they reached the docks, the salt road to the mainland had already formed, nearly two miles of solid ground across the sea. As he reached the end of the dock, Turnip carefully set Miss Marblemaw on the road. She reached up to slap him, but he grabbed her wrist midflight, leaning over the dock as he pulled her closer. "I do not like being struck," he said before letting her go. She stumbled onto the road, the salt creaking beneath her feet.

Barry and Janet tossed her belongings after her. They skittered a few feet away onto the road, the briefcase almost falling into the ocean as Arthur and Lucy joined them.

"You have made a grave mistake," Miss Marblemaw said, raising a trembling finger toward Zoe. "People will *suffer* because of your war against decency."

Lucy cocked his head as he looked down at her. "Why do you hate us so much? What did we ever do to you?"

She scoffed. "Hate? *Hate?* It's not about hate. It's about ensuring the future of humanity, something you are destined to destroy." She took a step toward the dock. Lucy didn't blink. "You, boy. Surely you see that. In that withering husk you call a soul, you know as well as I do that it's only a matter of time before you decide to install yourself as the supreme ruler."

Lucy laughed. "Why be supreme when you could *listen* to the Supremes instead?" His shoulders and hips began to wiggle. "*Stop! In the* naaame *of love. Be-fore you* breeeaaak *my heart! Think it oh-oh-ver.*" He bowed.

Zoe and Arthur and the mud people applauded.

Miss Marblemaw did not. She growled and attempted to climb back up onto the dock, only to have Zoe wave her hand, sending her sliding back along the road. She stood with Turnip, Janet, and Barry on either side of her. "Harriet Marblemaw," she said, voice deep. "You are hereby banished from Marsyas Island. No longer will you be able to step foot on our shores." She lifted her hand near Turnip's mouth, wings fluttering. "Spit, please."

Turnip did as asked, spitting a glop of mud into Zoe's hand. She closed her fingers around it, and when she opened her hand once more, a small seashell sat on her palm, orange and white. Bringing her hand to her face, she blew on the shell. The surface rippled before it hurtled from her hand toward Miss Marblemaw. The shell struck the inspector in the forehead, sinking into her skull. She blinked once, twice, three times, dazed, eyes unfocused.

The shell reappeared out the back of her head and disintegrated, the powder blowing away on the wind.

"With that," Zoe said, "you'll be unable to come to our island again. You have forty-five minutes until the salt road collapses back into the sea. If I were you, I'd make use of that time, unless you feel like going for a swim."

Miss Marblemaw did not listen. As if she had all the time in the world, she pulled herself upright, smoothed out her clothes, and then attempted to climb up the side of the dock. The moment she touched a support post, she snatched her hand back as if burned. She tried again. Same result.

Zoe crouched down on the dock above her. "Banished. Permanently. Any attempt to breach the island will result in unimaginable pain. You may think you can push through it, but let me assure you, that wouldn't be in your best interest. You'd be dead before you stood on my sands."

"The *government will*—"

"Forty-three minutes," Zoe said. "Tick, tock."

The last they saw of Miss Marblemaw was when she picked up her luggage and began marching down the road. They waved. Miss Marblemaw did not wave back. Eventually, she was nothing but a smudge on the horizon.

"Lucy," Zoe said, "I think it's time we let the mud people go."

"But *why*?" Lucy said. "I love them!"

"Muuuuud," Janet said, cupping his cheek with one hand.

"And we love you," Turnip said. "In my short albeit eventful life, I have seen things that defy imagination. For example, why is your mud pink and not wet? Do not tell me; I wish to ponder this until I arrive at an answer." He turned toward Zoe and bowed. "Your majesty, the mud has proven its loyalty. We ask that you allow us to live in the forest. Janet, Barry, and I will tend to the bogs and swamps, and they will be the muddiest in the entire world. Our gift to you."

Zoe smiled. "Perfect. I accept, and with my gratitude. I hereby give you and Barry and Janet the titles of the official mud representatives of Marsyas Island. Should you require anything to see your dreams realized, all you must do is ask."

"I think I'll miss you most of all, Barry," Lucy said with a sniff. "You always know the right thing to say."

"Mud mud mud," Barry said.

"See? Like *that*."

"Brother," Turnip said, taking Barry's hand. "Sister." He grabbed Janet's hand. "It's time for the mud people to do what we do best. Create more mud. Onward! Adventure waits for us all!"

The mud people walked down the dock. Hitting the tree line, Turnip glanced over his shoulder. Well, he *tried* to glance over his shoulder, but he missed the mark and his head turned completely around. "Lucy!" he called. "Thank you for never giving up! You will always have a friend amongst the mud people." With that, they disappeared into the thick forest.

"Can I go visit them?" Lucy asked, wiping his eyes.

Arthur ruffled his hair. "Anytime you wish. All you must do is ask. Come. Let us see what the others have gotten up to."

Eyes dry, Lucy shouted, "Hurray! Can I have seven—no, wait, *thirty* biscuits when we get home? The peanut butter kind that Linus makes with the little fork marks on the top."

"I believe that can be arranged. You've earned it."

He took off down the dock, his little feet smacking against the wood. Just when Arthur thought they'd seen the last of him without biscuits in his mouth, he stopped and turned around. "You know," he called to them, "I always hated the word 'master.' Maybe it's time we left it behind?" And with that, he took off once more, visions of warm biscuits undoubtedly on his mind.

Zoe burst out laughing. "Your children."

Arthur smiled. "Aren't they wonderful?" He extended his arm toward her. "Your majesty."

She punched him gently on the biceps. "Shut it, Parnassus. Call me that again, and I'll banish *you*."

"I believe that."

She took his proffered arm.

FIFTEEN

Word spread—and spread quickly—about the banishment of the DICOMY inspector from Marsyas Island. This was not unexpected; Arthur, Linus, and Zoe thought that would be the case. Regardless of the shroud of silence the government believed it acted under, it was not immune to springing a leak. A small one, but in Arthur's estimation, it functioned as a crack in a great stone dam, a weakness that would only grow stronger. He wondered if it'd been Doreen Blodwell's doing, wherever (and *who*ever) she was.

As such, reporters returned to the village with a vengeance, all but demanding access to the island. Per Helen, Merle flat out refused to ferry anyone across, saying the children had had enough interruption.

The Baker-Parnassus family had emerged victorious over Miss Marblemaw, but it was a temporary win. Rowder had shown she was willing to do anything to get her claws on Lucy. She wouldn't let Miss Marblemaw's banishment stop her. With such a thing hanging over them, Arthur thought the mood on the island would be muted, heavy.

It was anything but.

The children. The *children,* bless them, were proud, excited, full of vim and vigor, the likes of which Arthur hadn't seen before. In the days that followed the departure of the inspector, summer-warm mornings and afternoons seemed endless, the children spreading their wings, the pall of the DICOMY inspection falling away. They laughed and ran and learned and played and created and made comments that would cause even the heartiest men to shiver.

Chauncey asked if he could clean the guesthouse as practice for the hotel. Linus volunteered to help, only to have the blobby boy ask if he was *trying* to get him fired? Linus was not, and therefore agreed to let Chauncey handle it on his own.

Theodore nearly wept when Linus returned a familiar brass button. Taking it gently in his claws, he immediately went to his hoard under the couch, tail sticking out and thumping against the floor as he chirped and clicked happily to himself.

Talia, ever the hard worker, decided that the scene on the dock needed to be replicated in shrubbery form. She spent the weekend growing and molding the bushes until she got them exactly as Lucy described. Granted, she only had Lucy's telling to go on, so Arthur was not surprised when she revealed her work, only to have the shrub version of Lucy *eating* Miss Marblemaw, bits of leaves and sticks poking out of his shrubby mouth. It was quite the sight, and everyone agreed it was the best bit of garden art they'd ever had the pleasure to witness.

Phee and Arthur took to the skies, a sprite and phoenix crisscrossing high above the island. Before long, they were joined by Theodore, who alighted upon the phoenix's back, laughing in that lovely way he had. Tilting his head back, he let loose a stream of green fire, and Phee swirled around it, her wings glinting in the sunlight.

Sal had decided he wanted to learn more about the day-to-day operations of the island. Joining Arthur in his office, they pored over records and books, Sal learning about the significant investments Arthur had made over the years with the monies he'd been awarded, and everything else needed to keep the island . . . well, afloat. Sal kept Arthur on his toes with clever questions, and as they worked late into the night, Sal asked if they could keep going for just a *little* longer. Who was Arthur to refuse?

David was as relaxed as Arthur had ever seen him. The few days before the inspector had arrived had only offered them glimpses into the yeti. Now that she was gone, he blossomed even more, an inquisitive boy with a mind like a steel trap. Nothing got by him, and they spent a glorious afternoon watching David carve an ice sculpture with nothing but his claws. Granted, he did so as part of a play he'd written, directed, and starred in, a bittersweet tale of an ice sculptor slash retired master thief who gets involved in One Last Job. The play itself was breathtaking, full of twists and turns (the true villain? *Greed*), and when David finished, thunderous applause followed, none louder than Arthur's.

Lucy was the exception, proving to be quieter than normal. When asked if anything was amiss, he was quick with a smile and an off-color joke, but Arthur—who perhaps knew him best—wasn't fooled. He kept a close eye on Lucy, making sure he was ready and available if and when his son decided to give voice to his thoughts.

It felt like healing, in a way, this, for all of them. None were so foolish as to think they'd heard the last of DICOMY, but in the days following Miss Marblemaw's banishment, a peace returned to the island that had gone missing these last weeks. The suffocating weight of her presence receded like the waves listening to the moon.

Arthur and Linus themselves kept busy, one eye trained on the horizon, watching, waiting. Zoe spent her days navigating the shores of the island from dawn until dusk. When Sal asked what she was doing one evening as she was visiting him in his room, she replied, "Relearning. Listening. Planning."

Arthur stood outside Sal's room, a tea tray in his hands, not yet having made himself known.

"Lucy said Turnip called you 'your majesty,'" Sal said.

Zoe hesitated, but it was brief. "Yes. He did."

Of all the questions Sal could've asked—What? How? Why?—he went in a direction Arthur should have expected, especially from Sal. "Is that what you want?"

Zoe said, "I . . ." Then, "For centuries, I've hidden myself away. I've allowed my anger to define me, to mire me in cynicism. It wasn't until . . ." She chuckled quietly. "It wasn't until your dad came back that I realized I wasn't living. I was in stasis, frozen."

"And he brought the fire," Sal murmured.

"He did," Zoe agreed. "But it was more than that. He brought all of you, and I finally understood what life was supposed to be like. Color, joy. Togetherness. Knowing people are there to have your back even when you're at your darkest."

"You haven't answered my question."

"No, I don't suppose I have. And even yesterday, I don't know what answer I'd have given you. Being forced to hide changes us in ways we don't always realize, but that time is over now. For you. For the other children. For Linus and Arthur. For Helen. And for myself, too. I needed healing the same as you, though our history is different. I don't know that I'm quite there yet—and maybe I'll never be—but that doesn't mean I can't try. And I'm going to because you all have taught me how."

"We had a pretty good teacher," Sal said, and as Zoe laughed, Arthur closed his eyes and smiled.

The end—for it could not be described as anything but—came on an early Sunday afternoon toward the end of June in the tiny seaside village of Marsyas. Deciding they needed a day in town after surviving the previous day's adventure—Talia's turn, and she'd wanted to rehome the group of feral pixies who had been eating their way through her garden—they piled into the van for a day in the village, the children's pockets full of their allowance, waiting to be spent on whatever caught their eyes.

The group of reporters immediately swarmed them as the Baker-Parnassuses' van drove off the salt road onto the beach. Cameras flashed and shuttered, questions shouted, most asking if there was any truth to the rumor that Arthur Parnassus and Linus Baker had defied the will of DICOMY. David slid open the nearest window, leaned his head out, and roared loudly. The reporters scattered as the children laughed hysterically.

"See?" David said. "Scared them but didn't hurt them. It's not *that* hard."

"That you did," Linus said. "Well done, you."

David preened as the others reached over the seat to pat him on the shoulder.

Given the events of the past few weeks, Arthur and Linus didn't let them separate as they normally did. Instead, they parked behind Helen's shop—Zoe and Helen inside, where they'd meet up later for lunch—and moved as a single group, the children leading the way.

The reporters kept their distance, obviously wary, but that didn't stop them from following the family around town, taking picture after picture, Talia and Lucy posing dramatically. Every now and then, one would shout a question, but it always went ignored. They weren't allowed to follow the group into any of the shops, the staff locking the doors behind them, letting the family peruse at their leisure.

It was a good day, a quiet day, a day they all needed without even realizing it. The sun was bright, the sidewalks crowded, people laughing and waving as they shopped or headed for the beach.

Before they headed to J-Bone's shop (he'd apparently found a rare copy of Elvis Presley's first recorded music, a demo with the songs "My Happiness" and "That's When Your Heartache Begins"—Lucy had practically lost his mind when J-Bone called him), Arthur made a stop at the ferryman's dock.

"Ahoy, Merle!" he called, standing next to the ferry, the others gathered behind him. A moment later, Merle appeared over the railing, a scowl on his face.

"I *told* you I wasn't going to take you to the— Mr. Parnassus! Ahoy, there!"

He smiled. "Hello, my good sir. How be the seas?"

"Good and calm," Merle called down. "Need a ride back?" He scowled at the reporters gathered at the end of the dock. "They bothering you? You want me to give 'em the ol' what for?"

"That won't be necessary," Arthur said. "And we're not ready to return quite yet, but when we are, I think I'd like a trip on your ferry, if you have the time."

"For you, I have the time." He peered down at them once more. "And the kiddos? They all well?"

"I made mud people!" Lucy exclaimed. "And now they live in the forest!"

Merle shrugged. "Don't know about all that, but good for you." He frowned. "If you don't need a ride back and you don't want me to deal with the vultures, what can I do for you?"

"I wanted to say thank you," Arthur said. "It's a long time in coming, and you have my most sincere apologies for not seeking you out sooner."

Merle reared back, gripping the railing. "You want to thank *me*? What the hell for?"

"That I do," Arthur said. "I've heard you've been very particular as to whom you give passage to the island. Without you, I fear we might have been overrun. Your kindness has not gone unnoticed, and for that, you have our gratitude."

Merle spat over the railing into the ocean. "Yeah, well, your kids aren't as scary as some people make them out to be. Why, I've never been frightened of them in my life."

"Oh boy," Linus muttered.

"Duly noted," Arthur said. "And with that, we're off! We'll return later this afternoon. Come, children. I expect J-Bone isn't a man who appreciates being kept waiting."

"I doubt he even knows what time it is," Phee whispered to Sal. "Think we can get the machete this time?"

"He said he's the best at Crazy Eights," Sal whispered back. "So, yeah, we're gonna get that machete. Right, bud?"

Theodore spread his wings and agreed the machete was all but theirs.

They walked down the main thoroughfare of the village toward the record shop, David and Lucy leading the way. As they came to a stop at an intersection, a small crowd of vacationers amassed around them, all heading in the same direction. No one whispered about the children, nor did anyone look down upon them with anything but amusement, even as reporters—still keeping a somewhat respectful distance—continued to shout questions, their cameras clicking and flashing. A boxy van filled with frozen treats pulled through the light, tinny music streaming from the speaker attached above the windshield.

"Phee!" one of the reporters shouted as cars moved through the intersection. "Who are you wearing!"

Phee rolled her eyes and said, "What a weird question to ask a kid. I'm wearing clothes from my bedroom. Obviously."

"It's hard being famous," Talia said with a sniff. "Why can't they realize that celebrities are people too? I have dreams and feelings just like everyone else."

"This must be how Jesus felt before they put him on the cross," Lucy said. "Surrounded by paparazzi and sex workers."

"I beg your pardon," Linus said with a frown.

Lucy tilted his head back to look up at Linus. "I didn't make that up! It's in the Bible. Like, for a book about God and trying not to sin, there is a *lot* of stuff in there that makes me look like an angel. For example! Lot's daughter wanted to have a kid of her own, so she got her father drunk and—"

Linus covered Lucy's mouth with his hand as the strangers around them snorted in laughter. "I think that's quite enough. I can't believe I'm going to say this, but we might need to consider removing all Bibles from the island. Too many things in its pages children should not have access to."

Lucy's eyes filled with red as he pulled his head away. "We could have a good old-fashioned book burning."

"Something to consider," Linus agreed. "But we'll talk about it at home. For now, let's focus on— Ah, the light has changed. Onward!"

David stepped off the sidewalk first, glancing back over his shoulder to say something to Lucy. He didn't get far before Lucy's arm shot out, keeping David back.

David almost fell, tripping over the curb as the other vacationers moved on around them. "Why did you do that?"

Lucy ignored him. He took a step down the sidewalk, head cocked. Arthur tried to see what he was looking at, but all he saw was the road leading out of town toward the train station. Dunes of white sand rose like shifting hills, marram grass swaying in the salty breeze. It looked the same as it always did, as far as Arthur could tell.

And then, in the distance, a flash of light, as if the sun had reflected off something metal or glass. A black smudge appeared on the horizon, followed by another, and then another, and then *another*. At least a dozen in all, kicking up a cloud of dirt and dust, giving the appearance of an approaching storm.

"Arthur?" he heard Linus ask from somewhere behind him. "What is it?"

"They're coming," Lucy whispered.

That broke Arthur from his stupor. He scooped up Lucy in his arms, taking a step back. He startled when he bumped into someone, whirling around. Linus stood there, hands on his hips. "What's happened? You look as if you've seen a ghost."

"DICOMY," he said as the rumble of approaching engines grew louder. "They're here."

Linus didn't hesitate. He turned toward the others. "Change of plans," he said quickly. "Back to the van, children! We'll come to the village another day."

"What's going on?" Phee asked, standing on her tiptoes as she tried to see what Lucy and Arthur had. "I thought we were going to the record store."

"We were," Linus said, gently but firmly pushing the children back the way they'd come. "However, something has come up that needs our immediate attention. We'll return to the village another day, you have my—"

And then they were surrounded by a different set of black sedans—ones they hadn't noticed approaching—with large, sharp tailfins and metallic grilles that looked like gaping mouths filled with fangs. They screeched to a halt on the street in front of them, two from the left and two from the right. The doors flew open, and large, burly men climbed out, dressed in black suits with white dress shirts and black ties. Each wore a pair of sunglasses, the lenses mirrored. On their right biceps, a white armband with the word DICOMY printed around it.

Leaving their car doors open, the men didn't approach. Instead, they formed a semicircle around Arthur, Linus, and the children, their arms behind their backs as they stood at parade rest. None of them spoke.

"What are they doing?" Chauncey asked, sounding worried. "Are they going to take us?"

"Let them try," Phee said in a low voice.

"What is the meaning of this?" Linus demanded, stepping in front of the children. "Who are you?"

Silence, only broken by the sound of approaching engines, a persistent buzzing like a hive of furious wasps. In the shops around them, people peered out through the windows. Beyond the men, more people stepped off the sidewalk and stared in their direction, including the gaggle of reporters. They tried to get closer, only to have two of the men break off from the semicircle to stand in front of them, arms folded. The reporters shouted questions, but the men did not answer, nor did they move.

"You there!" Linus snapped, stepping toward the closest man. Arthur could see Linus's reflection in the man's sunglasses, his face stretched as if on the surface of a bubble. "Explain yourselves!"

Rather than answering, the man lifted a finger to his ear, waited a beat, then said, "Yes, ma'am. We have them." He paused. Then, "Understood." He dropped his hand and stared straight ahead.

"Now, see here," Linus said sternly. "I don't know who you think you are, but it's quite rude to appear out of nowhere and harass citizens going about their day. I suggest you remove yourselves immediately."

The man said nothing.

"Bloody gits," Linus muttered, turning around and stomping back to the sidewalk. "Of all the— How *dare* they— We were going to the *record* shop! That's *it*. We've done nothing wrong, and I refuse to allow anyone to suggest otherwise." When he reached Arthur (still holding on to Lucy), he didn't face the men surrounding them. Instead, he stood shoulder to shoulder with Arthur, facing the opposite direction. In a low voice he said, "It's almost time."

"I know," Arthur murmured, the sounds of the engines getting louder and louder. "Still, I'm frightened."

"I am too," Linus said. "But we are not letting them win. We must have hope because—"

"Hope is the thing with feathers," Arthur whispered.

Linus surprised him, then, and Arthur loved him more than he could put into words. "'That perches in the soul and sings the tune without the words, and never stops—at all.' Emily Dickinson. Yes, Arthur. It never stops." He puffed out his chest. "You hear that?" he called to the men around them. "It. Never. *Stops*."

The children gathered closer as the other vehicles approached, and Arthur could barely keep himself from snatching them all up and taking to the sky in a tornado of fire. David hid behind Sal and Theodore, both of them glaring at the men before them. Talia and Phee stood on either side of Chauncey, each holding one of his tentacles. Lucy lifted his head from Arthur's shoulder, frowning. "Do you feel that?" he asked Arthur.

"What?" Arthur asked.

Lucy shook his head. "I don't know. It's . . . empty?"

Before Arthur could ask for clarification, the oncoming vehicles reached the intersection and stopped. At least a dozen in all, the sedans were uniform: black with silver door handles and little flags attached to the front on either side of the hood. Only one car was different: fifth in line, it was white with heavily tinted windows. A man wearing the same suit as the others climbed out of the driver's seat and, without looking at them, went to the rear passenger door. He opened it, and a short, pale leg poked out, the foot wrapped in a sensible heel.

When Jeanine Rowder stood upright, blinking against the bright sunlight, Arthur felt the phoenix lift its head in his chest, eyes narrowed. While still not as strong as it'd been before the explosion above the island, it was champing at the bit to get at her, to blacken her skin until it cracked and broke off. Arthur won out, but barely. Rowder wasn't dressed as if she were on vacation in a tropical paradise: instead, she wore a mauve pantsuit, her coat unbuttoned, revealing a white blouse underneath. Tilting her head toward the driver, she listened intently as he spoke quietly. When he finished, she didn't reply, merely nodding her head.

The other passenger door opened, and Harriet Marblemaw climbed out. It appeared she had somehow freed her upper lip from the mustache Lucy had gifted her. In Arthur's approximation, she'd done herself no favors.

"Booooo!" the children bellowed at the sight of her.

Marblemaw glared at them, her lip twitching into a sneer.

Rowder's heels clicked and clacked against the pavement as she walked down the street past the vehicles. Her steps were careful; she moved as if she had all the time in the world, and the outcome had already been decided.

When she stepped out into the intersection and saw the reporters behind held back by two of her men, Rowder shook her head and sighed. "The press, Mr. Parnassus? Really? I would have thought you'd want nothing to do with them, especially after the coverage you received from the hearing."

"Last I checked," Arthur said evenly, "they're allowed to gather same as anyone else. Unless, of course, the government has decided to interfere with journalistic freedom."

More people came into the streets, pouring from the shops and the restaurants, all of them eyeing the government officials warily. Parents held their children close. Friends whispered behind their hands. Vacationers, residents, human and not, all gathering into a rumbling crowd. He recognized some, but not all: Merle, rubbing his dirty hands with an even dirtier rag. Martin Smythe—Helen's nephew—who had once attempted to exorcise Lucy in a locked room, now glaring at the backs of the officials. Mr. Swanson, Chauncey's boss and idol (a bellhop of great renown), followed by the hotel's cleaning staff: the cooks, the concierge, the managers, the desk attendants, the maintenance workers. J-Bone, wearing a tie-dyed shirt with lettering on the front that proclaimed DON'T PANIC! IT'S ORGANIC. Employees of the businesses: the ice cream parlor, the restaurants, the bookstore, the library. The antique shop owner, the mechanics who'd once worked on the van after Talia accidentally grew flowers through the engine ("It's performance art!"). Magical people: a family of banshees, their hair white as snow; two broonies, short, elf-like creatures with crinkly smiles and wizened eyes; a trio of naiads, water nymphs, towels wrapped around their torsos; a dryad, a slender, tall fellow made of aspen with a crown of yellow leaves that grew from branches not dissimilar to antlers. He carried a metal detector, along with a tote bag that read: BEACH BETTER HAVE MY MONEY.

Rowder eyed them all with barely disguised disdain. "Disperse!" she said loudly. "This is official government business. It does not concern you. Go about your day!"

"We are," J-Bone called out. "This is the time of day when we all come outside and bask in the glory that is the village of Marsyas."

"That's right," Mr. Swanson said, crossing his arms. An older, tall man with sharp eyes and white hair slicked back immaculately, the master bellhop cut an imposing figure. "Coming outside to enjoy everything our home has to offer. Isn't that right, lads?"

His coworkers nodded behind him.

Merle spat on the ground. "And it's our right to peacefully assemble where we see fit. It's the law."

Rowder's eyes narrowed briefly before she smiled a politician's smile: condescending, knowing, and more than a little smarmy. "If that's how it's going to be, fine." Raising her voice so it carried over the crowd, she said, "My name is Jeanine Rowder. I am the interim head of the Departments in Charge of Magical Youth and Adults. I am here to complete the inspection of the Marsyas Island Orphanage. Please do keep in mind that if anyone decides to hinder me, they'll be arrested immediately and charged with whatever I can think of, up to and including interfering with a government official, which carries a hefty fine and potential imprisonment."

Silence, only interrupted by the calls of seabirds.

"Now then," Rowder said, turning back toward Arthur, Linus, and the children. "Mr. Parnassus. Mr. Baker." She tilted her head in an approximation of a bow. "I'll make this as simple as I can." She held out her hand, snapping her fingers. Marblemaw hurried toward her, pulling out a folder from her coat, handing it over. Rowder snatched it from her without acknowledgment. "In my hand, I hold an order. This order, based upon the report from Inspector Harriet Marblemaw and signed by me, mandates that you, upon receipt of said order, remand the children known as Lucifer, Talia, Chauncey, Phee, Theodore, and Sal into the custody of DICOMY."

"No, thank you," Chauncey said.

"If you would like to challenge the validity of the order to the courts," Rowder continued, "you have thirty days to do so in writing. In the meantime, the children will be moved into foster care until permanent accommodations can be made."

Arthur said, "No."

Nonplussed, Rowder replied, "No? Unfortunately, you do not get to say no, Mr. Parnassus. From all I've heard from the inspector, the children are not safe in your hands. Not only is the island apparently run without structure or purpose, you continue to ignore the requirements of someone who is employed by DICOMY."

"I am no longer employed by DICOMY," Arthur said. "Surely you received my letter of resignation sent after Miss Marblemaw left the island?"

"I didn't *leave*," Miss Marblemaw snapped. "I was threatened and then forcibly removed!"

"Actually," Linus said, "you were permanently banished after you declined to follow the rules we have in place at our home. Semantics, to be sure, but as a former employee of DICOMY, I know management can be a stickler for details."

"Be that as it may," Rowder said, speaking *around* them rather than *to* them, "until we can be sure that Arthur Parnassus and Linus Baker aren't harming and/or weaponizing children, we'll do what we must to protect the populace." She smiled down at the children. "There is nothing to be afraid of. We'll be going on a train trip to the city! Won't that be fun?"

"We don't talk to strangers," Chauncey said. "Even if they offer us candy, because Dad and Papa said that's how they'll get ya."

The skin under Rowder's left eye twitched. "But I'm not a stranger. My name is Jeanine Rowder. I work for the government. I'm here to be your friend."

"See something, say something," Arthur said coldly.

Rowder cracked—and though she covered it up quickly, Arthur saw the flash of anger, black and severe. She was on edge, and Arthur thought it had nothing to do with him, or Linus.

When she smiled again, Arthur couldn't stop himself from taking a step back. She looked like a predator on the prowl. "Yes," she said. "Funny you should mention that. Did you ever hear who came up with that particular bon mot?" Without waiting for an answer, she continued. "An intern. An unpaid one, even. Why am I bringing this up now? Let me tell you." She looked at each of the children in turn, then Linus, then Arthur. "Have you ever wondered why *these* children? Why, out of every magical child in the world, you were given these six?"

"Because they needed a home," Arthur said, exactly what he'd said when asked the very same question in the hearing.

"It was a test," Rowder said with no small amount of glee. "An experiment, one in which you were all subjects. The purpose of said experiment was to see if the Antichrist was capable of learning from others, and what that would look like. All of this? Your entire lives? Cooked up by a middle manager during a quarterly meeting upon receipt of your written request. Nothing more, nothing less."

"I *knew* I was famous!" Lucy crowed.

"We're never going to hear the end of this," Talia muttered.

Arthur paused, cocking his head. Then, "Oh. Well. Thank you." Rowder stared at him. "Come again?"

"There appears to have been an unintended result from the experiment. I seem to have found myself with a family. Children, please thank Miss Rowder and the government for bringing us together."

"Thank you, Miss Rowder and the government," the children all said at the same time, neat as you please.

"More games, Mr. Parnassus?" Rowder asked, red spreading across her cheeks. "I should've known you'd—"

"Why do you want me?" Lucy said, and Arthur looked down to find him looking at Rowder.

Rowder flinched, glancing around at the large men standing on either side of her. Once she was certain she wasn't alone, she smiled at Lucy. "You are very special. There is no one like you in all the world."

He shrugged. "There's no other Talia. Or Chauncey. Or David or Sal or Theodore or Phee. Why don't you care about them?"

"I do," Rowder said. "But with you, it's different."

"Why?"

"Because of what you are."

"The Antichrist?"

"Yes," she said as her men shifted uncomfortably, Marblemaw pulling a face, the tip of her tongue sticking out between her teeth.

Lucy nodded slowly, brow furrowed. Though everything in Arthur screamed to stop him, he didn't move when Lucy took a step toward her. Given the hundreds of people standing in the streets, the near silence was extraordinary, only interrupted by the distant crash of waves.

Rowder did her best to appear unafraid, but even she couldn't keep it hidden. Her mouth thinned, her hands trembled before she flattened them against her trousers. Her gaze darted side to side as she bumped shoulders with the men she'd brought with her, men who undoubtedly would grab the children if and when she gave the order.

But she didn't, eyes growing wider and wider as Lucy stared up at her. The silence stretched on for ages.

Then a remarkable thing happened: as Arthur looked on, Lucy bowed his head, sniffling as a single tear tracked down his cheek. When he spoke, it was soft, quiet, barely carrying beyond the semicircle around them.

"I can see things," he said, voice cracking, and it was then Arthur knew this wasn't for show. "I don't mean to. It just . . . happens, I guess. Good things, like knowing my dad was a phoenix before he told us. I knew the first time I saw him, waiting for me on the island. I knew because I saw something magical. Two suns. One in the sky, and one on the beach."

His eyes welled, and he brushed the back of his hand over them. "But sometimes, I see other things. Bad things. Like . . . not the sun. The opposite: darkness. A black hole. Papa taught us about them. You can't see them with the naked eye, but even the smallest of them can suck in all light." He looked up at her once more. "That's what I see in you. Your insides don't have light. It's all dark."

Rowder laughed, but it sounded harsh, forced. She pointed at him, a long red nail at the tip of her finger. "I don't know what game you think you're playing, but it—"

"I'm sorry about what happened to your dad."

Rowder's finger began to tremble. It worked its way to her hand, her arm, her shoulder. It was as if the very muscles under her skin had turned to tectonic plates, rumbling awake after an ancient slumber. It spread through her, and her face turned white as her bottom lip quivered.

"It shouldn't have happened," Lucy told her. "The person who . . . hurt him didn't do it because—no. That's not fair. She had . . . spiders, in her brain. And she couldn't make them sleep. It wasn't him. Your dad. He didn't do anything wrong. It was an accident. She lost control of her magic and . . ." He sighed, a long, breathy thing that sounded like the wind. "You get to be mad. And sad. And anything else because that's what it means to be human. To have—"

Arthur couldn't move in time. For all that he was, he was bound to the seconds and minutes and hours just the same as anyone else. Rowder's hand flew up, viper quick, fingers extended and pressed together. She swung, meaning to slap Lucy across the face.

Only Lucy disappeared into thin air, the momentum spinning her around, causing her to strike the man next to her in the stomach. Lucy reappeared next to Arthur. "Holy *crap*," he breathed. "I can *teleport*?" His arms went up and over his head as he jumped up and down. "Yes. *Yes!* This is the best day ever! I can't wait for puberty. I bet I'll be able to create universes *and* a delicious happy birt breakfast without making a mess of either!"

Arthur felt the fire in him explode. The phoenix spread its wings in his chest and screamed to be let out, to end this once and for all. With all his strength, he kept the bird at bay, not wanting to give Rowder the satisfaction.

"Easy, old boy," Linus murmured, touching the back of his hand. "We're in the end game now."

"Make no mistake, Rowder," Arthur said, his molten fury bubbling just underneath his skin, "that near miss still counts. That is *twice* an employee of the Department in Charge of Magical Youth has abused one of my children in the last week, and I am done with you and your ilk. All of you."

"So David *is* a child!" Marblemaw shrieked. "I knew it! They lied! He's not a forty-seven-year-old whose growth was stunted after being trapped between rocks for seven years!"

A beat of silence, and then everyone in the crowd burst into laughter. "What are you, brand new?" J-Bone called. "Who would ever believe something like that?"

"Right?" Sal said. "What are you even talking about, Miss Marblemaw? David's just a kid."

"Yeah," Phee said. "We told you that a thousand times."

"Remember when I inked on you?" Chauncey called. "That was on purpose! Ha, ha. Okay, no, it wasn't, but I didn't know what else to say, so . . . uh. Ella Fitzgerald, scaddidily doo dippity bip."

"Whoa," Lucy whispered with stars in his eyes. "That was so *righteous*. Look at you, scat man!"

"Enough!" Rowder thundered, a vein throbbing in her forehead.

"Yes," Arthur said. "I quite agree. Enough. Here it is, Rowder, at last. An offer that you should not refuse."

"I will have the children," she snapped. "You have nothing else to give."

He nodded. "See, that's where you're wrong. The children will not be leaving my side, or the side of my husband-to-be. We are a family, you see. The Baker-Parnassuses."

"Bit of a mouthful," Merle said with a sniff. "Still, family discount and all that."

"My offer is this: here, now, we can make a difference. All of us, together. It won't be easy, but you have my word that I will do everything in my not so inconsiderable power to ensure we come together in the spirit of unity and the desire for change. To break that which is already broken counts for naught. It must be rebuilt from the ground up by all of us." He looked at the people around them, the residents, the visitors, both magical and not. And to the reporters, all of whom watched breathlessly, cameras trained in their direction. "As you can see, the world is watching. What will you do, I wonder?"

"You planned this," Rowder whispered. "All of it."

"Did I?" he asked. "Here I was, thinking I was enjoying a day out with my family. Even if I *had* planned this very moment, it should come as no surprise to you. After all, I did warn you that a war against me was one you're not prepared for. Will you except my offer?"

"Never," Rowder spat. "You played your part, Parnassus, and

you played it well. But this fanciful future that you dream of is just that: a dream. *We* live in the real world, where people—"

"Huh," Arthur said, glancing at Linus. "Gave it my all."

"So you did," Linus said with a huff. "Quite impressive, if you ask me."

"You flatter me, my dear. Though, I must admit I really thought I had her with the bit about breaking that which is already broken."

"Delivered with a finesse even the greatest orators in history wouldn't have found fault with. I myself was moved to—"

"Get them," Rowder snarled, and the men started forward. . . .

. . . only to be met with the might of the crowd around them, people moving closer, eyes narrowed, arms folded across their chests. Mr. Swanson and J-Bone moved to either side of Arthur, Linus, and their family. Merle brought up the rear, backed by dozens of people, including Martin Smythe. His aunt, one Helen Webb, appeared at Arthur's side as if by magic. "Say the word," she whispered in his ear. "She's ready."

Arthur nodded as Mr. Swanson said, "You want them, you'll have to go through us."

"Damn right," J-Bone said, people in the crowd nodding along. "You don't get to come in here and break up a family."

"You will *all* be arrested!" Rowder shouted. "If you do not stand aside *now*, I will make it my mission to ensure this village and its inhabitants will never again know a moment's peace, especially when you're harboring monsters—"

"If," Arthur said, "you won't take a proffered hand in good faith, then perhaps you'll bow before royalty."

Rowder gaped at him, and then began to laugh. Before long, her men started to chuckle, and even Marblemaw looked amused. "Royalty?" Rowder said, her mirth evident. "*You?* I know you're a phoenix, Mr. Parnassus, but it would seem being the last of your kind has given you delusions of grandeur."

"Nah, you got it all wrong," Sal said, stepping forward to stand next to Arthur. He leaned his elbow on his father's shoulder, resting comfortably as he crossed one shoe over the other, toe pointed against the ground. But he never looked away from Rowder. "Dad wasn't talking about himself. See, that part's over. You had your chance." Sal grinned, wild and beautiful, and in it, Arthur saw the man he would become. "Now it's *her* turn."

She descended from above in a cascade of shimmering sparks, her wings buzzing ferociously. As her bare feet hit the ground, the pavement cracked, verdant grass shooting up. A tiny daisy sprouted between the toes of her left foot, little white petals resting against brown skin.

Zoe Chapelwhite was a vision: her dress appeared to be a living oil painting, the swirling blue and green and yellow crossing along the fabric, streaking like shooting stars. Her arms and legs—hands and feet still exposed—were covered in thin metal that looked as if it had been fashioned specifically for her. The metal itself was barely visible as dozens of multicolored seashells were stuck to it, each about the size of a button. It took Arthur a moment to see it for what it was: a suit of armor.

And atop her head, white Afro styled around it, a crown. Silver, with dangling chains that hung onto the sides of her head. The top of the crown was dramatic: ten pearl spikes rose across the front, five on either side of a large pink-and-white conch shell that rested in the center of the crown. In the opening of the conch shell lay a glittering cerulean-blue gemstone the size of Lucy's fist.

"Holy freaking *crap*," Phee breathed. "Look at her."

Oh, did he. Arthur remembered the woman in the forest when he was a child, the island sprite who had hidden herself away. The woman who had come for him when he'd returned, unsure, her guilt weighing heavily upon her shoulders. The woman who had picked up a piece of sandpaper and gotten to work building a home out of the remains. The woman who had been with him every step of the way, seeing his plan come to life before his very eyes. His friend—no, his *best* friend, his sister, this extraordinary queen who had welcomed the children to her island with open arms. She'd laughed with them. She'd cried with them. She'd lifted them up, carried them when they could no longer walk, helped them feel *alive* for the first time since they could remember.

And now, here she was, standing tall and proud between her people and those who had deemed themselves superior. She took a step toward Rowder, leaving behind a perfect imprint of grass in the shape of her foot on the street. When she spoke, her voice was clear, crisp. "You are not welcome here."

Rowder recovered first. Looking side to side to confirm her men hadn't fled, she nodded and cleared her throat. "And who might you be?"

"Zoe Chapelwhite," Marblemaw called, still standing away from them as if she knew something the others didn't. "The unregistered island sprite."

Rowder snorted. "Of course she is." Then, "Miss Chapelwhite, as required by law put forth by the Department in Charge of Magical Adults, you are hereby ordered to register with—"

"No," Zoe said.

"Ah!" Rowder said, clapping her hands. "I see where the mistake came from. You thought that was a request. Rest assured, it was not. Stand aside before you do something you'll regret."

"I have many regrets," Zoe said, the colors on her dress swirling brighter and faster, the shells on her armor beginning to spin with a low whir. "But one rises above all the others." She turned in a slow circle, looking at everyone standing around her. At least two hundred, with more coming every minute. "We were happy," she said. "Here. All of us. My friends. My family. I was happy. For thousands of years. And then we were told we were dangerous."

Silence, even from the reporters, all watching with bated breath.

"Lies!" Rowder cried. "Slander! If this were true, there would be documented evidence of—"

Zoe shook her head. "No. You can't deny me my history. I *lived* it."

"I don't know what game you're playing, but it won't work!" Rowder said shrilly. "If what you say happened, then how are you here, standing before us? How is it that *you* out of all the sprites managed to escape unscathed?"

"Unscathed," Zoe repeated. "*Unscathed?* I hid myself under the body of my grandmother. I held my breath when your *government* stood above us, checking for any signs of life. I tasted her blood on my lips. When they were distracted, I fled to the farthest reaches of the forest and closed it off behind me. It was then I made a promise to myself: I would never again concern myself with the horror that is humanity."

"Do you hear that?" Rowder said, raising her voice to the crowd. "*That's* what they think of you. Even though none of us would've been alive when this occurred, we're still supposed to pay the price of those who came before us? Balderdash! Were mistakes made? Yes, of course. But that doesn't mean we're not in the right *now*."

"It's like they can't hear themselves talk," Linus murmured.

"But life found me again," Zoe said. "And though it could be argued I was dragged kicking and screaming into it, my time of hiding away was over. It was then I made a new promise to myself: that no matter what happened, I would do everything I could to ensure the magical people who found my shores were safe. I would do for them what was not done for me: I would give them a chance to live."

"This is all well and good," Rowder said, "but it changes nothing."

"It does," Zoe said. "More than you realize. My grandmother? She was the sprite queen. And since I'm the last one left, that title now falls to me. I am Queen Zoe Chapelwhite." Without looking away from Rowder, she added, "And you are standing upon my land without my permission."

Rowder's eyes bulged. "Your land? Your *land*? Oh, that crown seems to be a little tight on your head. It's making you believe things that certainly aren't true. Here, let me clear this up for you. *This* is the village of Marsyas. You are from the *island* of Marsyas. There is a considerable difference."

"That's where you're wrong," Zoe said. "Have you ever wondered why the village and the island are called by the same name?"

"I don't see what that has to do with anything. You're stalling."

"They are called the same name," Zoe said, "because once, Marsyas was not an island. Once, it was a *peninsula*, a single stretch of land that the sprites called home. In a last-ditch effort to keep the humans from advancing, my grandmother—one of the most powerful sprites the world had ever seen—flooded the peninsula, creating the island. They are one and the same."

"And yet you call yourself an island sprite," Rowder said.

Zoe cocked her head, the chains of her crown dangling next to her ear. "I lied. I am the Sprite of Oceans, the Queen of Marsyas, and I have grown tired of your presence in our home."

"Bollocks!" Marblemaw bawled. "If I'm banished from the island, that would mean I'm banished from—"

"The village, yes," Zoe said. "And you will be." She smiled. "I just need to wake it up." Suddenly, she dropped to her knees, her hands flat against the pavement. She breathed in, she breathed out, a ripple of rainbow crossing her wings.

And then Arthur felt a tsunami of magic crash into him, greater than anything he'd ever felt before. It knocked the breath from his chest as every hair on his arms stood on end. The ground rumbled beneath their feet, people gasping as pavement started to crack apart underneath the queen's hands. But it wasn't destruction Zoe was after: instead of the street breaking completely, a design formed on the road, the rushing lines connecting and creating a large shape that was at least six feet long and three feet wide.

A nautilus seashell, carved into the pavement, curved lines creating the many chambers that made up the interior. As Zoe stood, the cracks filled with blinding white, and balls of blue light began to rise up around her. Her wings buzzed as she rose into the air, the nautilus growing brighter. "I am done hiding," Zoe said, her voice deep, echoing. "I'm done letting others decide who we are allowed to be. You have been warned again and again, but you do not listen. This land is not yours. It belongs to a free people, stewards and caretakers who will ensure that the might of Marsyas will never again falter."

"You don't have the *right*," Rowder snapped.

"I do," Zoe said. "As queen, I do. But perhaps this will help change your mind." She clapped her hands together, palms pressed together. She exhaled and spread her hands.

A space where there had been nothing now held a wrapped scroll, tied off with a string of shells. Zoe snatched it out of the air and flung it toward Rowder. As the scroll flew toward her, the shells disintegrated, the parchment unfurling. It stopped and hovered two feet in front of Rowder's face. She squinted at it. The blood drained from her face. "Is . . . is . . . that . . ."

Zoe chuckled. "A decree from one of your former kings relinquishing all rights to the lands of Marsyas to the sprites, signed in the year 1332? Yes, yes, it is. Not that we needed his legitimacy, but apparently you do. As such, when humans came and destroyed my people centuries later, they went against their own king's ruling. And I will not stand for it any longer." She turned to look at the crowd gathered below her. "The government has come here to take one of our own. Though they claim to be after all the children, there is one in particular they are desperate to get their hands on. This woman wants to use a child to control everyone and everything, and she has threatened the safety of the other children to see her plan through."

Silent, still, as if everyone held their breath, the only sound coming from the distant crashing of waves.

"She has come for Lucy," Zoe thundered. "A seven-year-old *child*. And if she thinks she'll lay a single hand on him, then she is mistaken."

Below her, the shell carved into the street pulsed three times in quick succession.

"Ah, good," Zoe said. "The magic has awoken. Let's see about that banishment, shall we?" Almost quicker than Arthur could follow, she plucked shells from her arms and legs, her hands a blur of movement. It took only the space between heartbeats for a large pile to appear on her extended palm. As her wings wrapped around her, Zoe sucked in a great breath, spinning in a furious circle, blowing on the shells.

They shot out with perfect precision. The men in suits stumbled back as shells passed through their heads and came out the other side before disappearing in a puff of powder. Marblemaw stood frozen, a stunned expression on her face.

A single shell—tiny, cream and white in color—floated in front of Rowder's forehead. She took a step back, raising her hands in front of her face. "Don't. Don't you *dare*."

"I dare," Zoe said, eyes narrowed. "I dare for every child you have hurt. I dare for every adult who was forced to hide their true self because of 'see something, say something.' I dare for all of them. I do this for them, for Helen and Arthur and Linus, for every single person here and around the world who has had *enough*. Jeanine Rowder, you have proven to be an enemy of magical people—my *family*. It is within my rights as Queen of Marsyas to order your head removed from your body."

"Hurray! Then we can find out if she has rabies!" Lucy cried.

"Alas, that would make me no better than you," Zoe said. With that, she flicked her hand dismissively. The shell hurtled through Rowder's head without leaving a mark, shooting out the back and rising in the air above her where it shattered, particles raining down on Rowder.

"Lucy?" Zoe called without looking away from Rowder, who was slapping her forehead repeatedly. "Come here, please."

"The queen has summoned me," Lucy whispered. "Hell *yes*!" Without hesitation, he skipped toward Zoe and Rowder. "At your service, your majesty! What would you ask of me? Are you going to knight me? Or will you give me a country estate where I can let the government people run free in a five-minute head start before I hunt them all down? Either way is good with me!"

Marblemaw looked around wildly as if searching for an opening to flee.

Zoe's lips quirked. "A knight? I do suppose Marsyas will need protection. Yes, that will do just fine. Lucifer Baker-Parnassus, I hereby name you as a knight of Marsyas. If you are ready, I have your first order."

Lucy snapped to attention. "Yes, my queen!"

Zoe nodded, tapping her chin. "Since you are now capable of teleporting, I wonder if that extends to teleporting others. Say, a group of people who have come uninvited and have overstayed their welcome."

"I can do that!" Lucy said, obviously excited. "Where do you want them to go? The moon? Inside an active volcano? Wait! I got it!" His eyes took on an ominous glow, burning coals in endless pits. When he grinned, he seemed to have far more teeth than any other seven-year-old. "I can send them to meet my real dad. I'm sure he'd welcome them with open arms." He giggled as two locks of his hair flipped up, almost like horns. "And when they see his true face, everything that makes them who they are will be *gone*."

"Or," Zoe said, "we can teleport them directly to where Prime Minister Herman Carmine currently is. Let them explain how they have failed, and that the might of Marsyas will rise once again."

"Aw, man," Lucy said, scuffing his shoe against the pavement. "I never get to send anyone to Hell. It's so unfair." He sighed heavily. "Fine. I guess we can do it your way. You're the queen, after all."

"We will return," Rowder snarled, "and in greater numbers. You think this will stop us? You have made a powerful enemy this day, and I will spend every second of the time I have left on this earth making your lives miserable. Remember, *your majesty*, that you were given a chance. From here on, any blood spilled will be on your hands."

Zoe nodded toward the reporters, hanging on every word. "I can't wait to see tomorrow's headlines. Lucy."

"No!" Rowder cried. "Don't! You can't—"

Lucy raised his little hands toward her. "As the great Cab Calloway once said: skeetle-at-de-op-de-day!"

Tiny explosions, little *pops!* that sounded like stomping on bubble wrap. One of the suited men disappeared in a cloud of blue smoke. And then another. And then another. Some tried to run, but they did not make it far. Marblemaw let out an anguished wail before she, too, popped and vanished.

Rowder, now alone, her hair hanging in wisps around her face, panted, mouth hanging open. "This means *war*," she snarled.

Arthur Parnassus stepped forward, moving until he stood next to his son and his queen, who landed on the ground next to him, taking his hand. Lucy did the same on his other side, and Arthur felt as strong as he ever had. Fire and feather, the phoenix lifted its head in Arthur's chest, clacking its beak. "Bring your war," he told her. "Whatever else has happened here, take your banishment knowing this: we will no longer hide. We will not stop. We will remake this world into one it should have been: welcome to all. And since you're not with us, you're against us. Lucy."

Rowder opened her mouth once more, but before she could speak, her forehead began to bulge, then she, too, exploded in a cloud of shimmering dust.

When the cheers started, Arthur wasn't quite sure what was happening. Later, he'd think that Mr. Swanson was the culprit, followed swiftly by the other employees from the hotel. Regardless, it— infectious, unbridled joy—spread quickly, becoming a roar unlike anything Arthur had heard before. He turned in a slow circle, skin buzzing, heart in his throat as the people of the village—human and magical alike—hugged one another, shook hands, jumped up in the air, their fists pumping. Martin Smythe high-fived J-Bone, both of them talking excitedly. And even better—though perhaps a little stranger—Merle, dancing a jig in the street, his ornery smile bright.

Arthur startled when someone took his hand. He looked over. Linus, watching him with a quiet smile. "It's starting," he whispered in awe.

"I am so, so proud of you," Linus said. "You and Zoe and Lucy. The other children. All of you. This, Arthur. This is what you've been working towards. This is what you've been building. Can't you see? *You have changed minds.*"

Linus was right. They had. Perhaps it was on a small scale, and its reverberations might not be felt outside the borders of Marsyas, but, as he'd taught their children, even the smallest things can change the world, if only one is brave enough to try. It wasn't unlike the seeds they'd planted at Linus's former, dreary home. Darkness and shadows, never-ending rain, and yet, color persisted, bursting through and rising, rising toward a blackened sky.

But the queen wasn't yet finished. As Arthur looked on, she walked through the crowd, the people parting in hushed reverence, some bowing. A child—from the cyclops family—performed a neat curtsy, causing Zoe to laugh in delight and squeeze her shoulder as she passed.

It did not take her long to reach her destination. Standing in front of the reporters, their cameras flashing, microphones extended toward her, Zoe raised her hands to quiet their shouted questions. They fell silent. Everyone did.

Except for Zoe. "Thank you for coming to our home. It's not normally this exciting, but we do have many things to offer. Which is why I will say this, and you can quote my every word: as Emma Lazarus wrote, 'Give me your tired, your poor, your huddled masses yearning to breathe free, the wretched refuse of your teeming shore. Send these, the homeless, the tempest-tossed to me, I lift my lamp beside the golden door!'" Her wings spread as cameras clicked and shuttered. "To the world outside our home, know this: Marsyas will be for all magical people who seek shelter, who need a place to rest their heads. We will welcome you with open arms, and help you as best we can, be your stay short or permanent. But," she added, "should anyone attempt to come to our home with despicable intentions, well." Her expression hardened. "I'll remind you I'm a queen, and I'll do what's necessary to protect my kingdom." She blinked. "Oh, that sounded ominous, didn't it? Good thing I have my lady, Helen Webb, who has agreed to continue her role as mayor."

"They're a *power* couple," Phee breathed with stars in her eyes.

"What about the land?" a reporter called. "How can you possibly tell the magical community that they can come here when there isn't enough room?"

"I'm glad you brought that up," Zoe said. "If you would be

so kind as to follow me, I'd be happy to show you what I have in mind." With that, she spun on her heel and walked back toward Arthur, Linus, and the children. Halfway, Helen fell in step beside her, taking her hand and kissing the back with a loud smack. "How'd that feel?" she asked as they approached.

Zoe shook her head. "Strange. Unreal." She paused. "Right."

"Crown wasn't a bad touch."

"Not too much?"

Helen laughed. "Ask me that again later when we're alone. Bring the crown."

"Yes, ma'am."

When the women reached their family, Zoe went to the children first. They gathered around her, all speaking at once, aside from Sal, who stood at the rear, head cocked. Zoe looked at him and said, "This was because of you."

Sal's forehead bunched up. "What do you mean?"

"You," Zoe said gently, "and the strength of your convictions." She looked at each of the other children in turn. "The way you stood up for David, refusing to let us conceal him. The way you have each other's backs, even when the odds are stacked against you. I may be a queen, but it is you who have the true power. Never forget that."

Queen Zoe Chapelwhite bowed before them, the chains from her crown dangling around her face.

It wasn't Arthur who bowed next; no, it was Linus, one hand across his chest, the other behind his back. Then J-Bone. Merle. Helen. Mr. Swanson, the employees from the hotel, the girl who sold kites, the man who owned the antique shop. The new ice cream parlor owner, the librarians, the guys, gals, and nonbinary pals from the bookstore and coffee shop.

It was all of them. Every single being—be they human or something else entirely—bowed for the children.

The wide-eyed, astonished look on each child's face as the village of Marsyas honored them. *This* was hope; the children, love letters to a future that had yet to be decided. Yes, Arthur thought as Sal grinned shyly, hope was the thing with feathers, but it was also in the hearts and minds of those who believed all was not lost, no matter the odds.

Which was why when Zoe said, "I'll need you, I'll need all of you," Arthur wasn't surprised. They had come this far together. It made sense that they would all see this through to the end.

"What are we going to do?" Phee asked as Zoe took her hand.

"Something I should have done a long time ago," Zoe said. "We're going to change our world."

If a visitor had come to Marsyas at that very moment—say, arriving for a pre-planned vacation, the relief palpable as they stepped off the train for the first time, breathing in that warm, salty air—they would have witnessed a most curious sight: hundreds of people following a woman wearing an armor of shells, a crown atop her head. On either side of her, children, all of whom were asking question after question. Two men followed close behind, both a little frazzled. Mixed in the crowd, reporters, shouting, asking if they'd thought this through, *what are you going to do when they come back, are you saying you're at war with the government?*

They were ignored, at least for now. They had seen enough; what they did with what they knew was out of Arthur's hands. Either they'd report the truth, or it'd be spun as it always was. The time for caring about such things was drawing to a close.

Arthur wasn't surprised when Zoe led them to the docks, located in the half-moon bay of the village. Off to their left and right, boats of varying shapes and sizes: small watercrafts, paddleboats for rent, speedboats, and a couple of yachts. At the end of the longest dock, Merle's ferry, waves lapping at its base.

As she stepped onto the ferry dock, Zoe glanced over her shoulder. "Arthur, Linus, please come with us. Merle, you too. The rest of you, stay on the shore. It'll be safer that way."

No one argued with the queen. They gathered at the edge of the dock, people lifting their children onto their shoulders, still others standing on their tiptoes, trying to see what was about to happen.

The wood of the dock creaked under their feet as they walked toward the ferry.

Arthur and Linus, dazed and more than a little tired, held their heads high, moving with barely disguised excitement. When Zoe had come to him to tell him what she had planned, Arthur had tried to grasp it as best he could. "Seeing is believing," she'd said with a spark in her eyes.

When they reached the end of the dock, Zoe crouched above the water. She reached down, cupping saltwater in her hands, letting it drip between her fingers. Without looking at them, she said, "My grandmother understood the ocean. It talked to her in different ways. Almost like Chauncey and Frank. But it wasn't just the ocean. It was all life that called this land home." She turned her right hand, and a single bead of ocean hung from the tip of her pointer finger. It stretched and stretched until it fell, plinking back into the sea, little circles spreading. She closed her hand into a fist. "I am her granddaughter. And I will be the queen she thought I could be." Zoe stood slowly. In the distance, the island. She stared at it for a long moment before turning to face them. "Chauncey, I need your help. Tell the fish, the urchins, the sharks, everything that will hear you. Let them know a seismic shift is coming. The reefs will move, but they will not be harmed. They have my word."

"You can count on me!" Chauncey said, oozing forward to the end of the dock. Bending over the edge, he sucked in a deep breath. Then: "*FRAAAAAAAANNNNNNNNK! YOU THERE, BUD? FRAAAAAAAAAAAAAANNNNK! WE NEED YOU!*"

"While Chauncey is seeing to—"

"*FRAAAAAAAAAANNNNNNNNK!*"

"—the aquatic life, Merle, a word."

Merle wiped his hands on the front of his coveralls, cleared his throat, and then stepped forward, snapping to attention. "Yes, your majesty."

Zoe snorted. "None of that. I will be Zoe to you, and I won't hear otherwise."

Merle's eyes bulged. "Uh. I can do that."

"Good," she said before nodding at the ferry. "How would you feel about being hired on in a more permanent role?"

Merle frowned. "I thought the whole point of this mess was you were going to make it so the island wasn't . . . you know. An island."

"I am, yes. And if I have my way, we will become rather busy in the immediate future. As such, I would like to offer you the position as the official ferryman of Marsyas. Be it by ferry or some other means, you would be the one to bring anyone who seeks shelter to us."

Merle chewed over this for a moment. Then he spat over the side of the dock. "Little ones?"

"I expect so," Zoe said. "And some big ones too. And silly me, I forgot to mention: you will be paid, and paid handsomely."

"Well, why didn't you say so?" Merle grinned. "Sounds like a good deal to me."

"*There* you are, Frank," Chauncey said. And sure enough, Frank leapt from the water, the sunlight catching his scales. "Thanks for coming so quickly. I have a mission for you. The queen has returned, and she's gonna do some *crazy* magic. Tell your school to let everyone in the sea between here and the island know. She's gonna make things how they used to be."

"*We* are," Zoe said as Frank leapt from the water once more before disappearing into the depths. "Because I can't do this alone."

"What do you mean?" Talia asked as Chauncey joined them once more, chest puffed out in pride.

"Magic," Zoe said, "comes from within. It's not just about our gifts." She glanced at David and Phee. "It's about *intent*. What we want from it, what we plan to do with it in the future. My grandmother always said that the earth, the sea, all of it listens to everything we do. It knows those who mean it harm, those who would use it to cause pain and suffering. If we do this, we will be its protectors." She smiled at the children. "You will be its queens and kings, and those who come from somewhere beyond the sea will look to you for guidance, for hope. It is a heavy burden to bear, but one I know you are strong enough to carry, especially since you won't be doing it alone."

"I get to be a knight *and* a queen?" Lucy exclaimed. "It's not even my birt!"

"How do we do it?" Sal asked.

"You're sure?" Zoe asked. "Because I need you to be—"

"You heard our son," Linus said. "We're ready. Isn't that right?"

"Ready!" the children said as one.

"Arthur?" Zoe asked.

Mom, he thought. *If only you could see me now. I'm not alone.*

Arthur Parnassus said, "My queen?"

Zoe sniffled, wiping her eyes. "I told you not to call me that."

"You did," he agreed. "Fortunately, I decided not to listen."

Near sunset on a warm summer evening, the sea calm and aflame in streaks of orange and red. At the end of the dock, a large crowd of people, all standing silently, watching, waiting.

On the dock itself, a family standing in the shape of a *V,* not unlike a flock of birds. At the point of the *V,* a queen, tall and proud, her dress billowing around her ankles, her wings shimmering. She held hands with Lucy, who held hands with Talia, who held hands with David, who held hands with Linus. On Zoe's other side: Phee, then Chauncey, Sal and Theodore, and Arthur, Sal's hand in his, Theodore's tail resting on his shoulder.

Looking out at the island and the sea, Zoe said, "It'll be strong. The pull. Don't fight it. Think of it like standing in the sand and surf. As the waves crash over your feet, you can feel the strength of it, tugging at you even as you sink into it. It's the same, really. Let it wash over you, let it greet you, let it know you for who you truly are, and it will see that our intentions are pure. I'll handle the rest. Whatever you do, *don't let go of each other.*"

The moment the sun touched the horizon, it began. Zoe's eyes filled with a bright white glow, and her wings started to buzz. An ocean wind blew around them—the sting of salt negligible—ruffling the clothes of those who were not avowed nudists. Linus gasped as Zoe lifted from the dock, wind swirling beneath her feet. As she rose higher and higher, Arthur felt it, the pull she'd told them about. It started in his chest, the phoenix lifting its head and calling, calling, its cry so loud, Arthur thought it could be heard miles away. It moved from his chest to his arms, his shoulders, his head, insistent, poking, questioning.

He let it in.

Lucy laughed loudly when he rose from the dock, feet kicking into nothing. Phee did not flap her wings as she, too, was lifted. Then Talia and Chauncey. David and Sal and Theodore, all the children floating three feet above the dock.

Arthur looked over at Linus, who appeared a little green. "I'm not quite sure I'm up to floating," he said. "Some of us like our feet firmly planted on the— *Oh dear!*" He shot up three feet, hair moving slowly around his head as if he were underwater. He started to turn horizontal, and Theodore's tail shot out, wrapping carefully around his neck, pulling him upright once more. "There," Linus said in a quivering voice. "Nothing to it. I'll just . . . float here. Perfectly normal."

Arthur tilted his head back and laughed and laughed as his feet lifted. Unbidden, fire bloomed along his arms. It did not burn as its tendrils spread along Sal and Theodore to Chauncey, where it wrapped around his waist (chest?) like a hula-hoop. Chauncey screamed in delight and wiggled his entire body, the fire dancing around him before it moved on to Zoe. Flames snapped and crackled across her body, the red-orange mixing in with the shifting colors of her dress. It moved on to Lucy and Talia and David, all of whom cackled at the tickling warmth.

And last, it came to Linus. The fire rose above him, taking the outline of a bird. Flames crackling, the phoenix lowered its head to Linus, its beak pressed against his nose.

Linus breathed in and Linus breathed out, and in it, Arthur felt him: scared, worried, but even more, a seemingly endless reservoir of hope and bravery. In it, for a brief moment, Arthur saw what Linus did when he gazed upon the phoenix: love, curiosity, and a staggering amount of pride.

He was the phoenix, and the phoenix was him. It lifted its head once more, and as it took shape—fire giving way to feather—it spread its wings above them, its cry echoing across the sea.

Distantly, he heard Zoe shout, *"Now!"*

He was the phoenix, he was Arthur, blinking, blinking as a white light came from Zoe's chest, forming a small ball in front of her, perhaps two inches in diameter. From Lucy, a devilish red light. From Phee, yellow, like the leaves of a quaking aspen. From Talia, a rough pink, the same shade as her prized begonias. David's was near white, like snow, like ice; Chauncey's as blue as the ocean. Sal and Theodore's wyvern-fire green carrying on it corporeal words in spiky, familiar handwriting that said words like BRITTLE and THIN and SEE ME and I AM FOUND.

And the light that came from Linus was white and red and yellow and pink and blue and green and reddish-orange. He was theirs, they were his, and Arthur thought of the little yellow flower on the steps of the house when he'd first come back, the yellow of Linus's sunflowers, his only piece of color in a monochrome world.

Finally, from Arthur, the orange-red of fire and feather.

The lights from each of them coalesced into a glittering sphere in front of Zoe, the colors mingling, dancing. The sphere broke apart and reformed into the same nautilus shell design that the queen had carved into the street. As it shimmered in front of her, lines of color flashing, Zoe leaned forward and kissed its center.

The shell and the phoenix shot across the ocean toward the island. They reached the halfway point, the phoenix's wings wide as it caught an updraft, rising high into the sky. Below it, the nautilus shell hung suspended, turning until it was parallel with the ocean. The phoenix reached its apex high above the sea, then it fell backward, tucking its wings into its sides as it plummeted toward the shell.

"Hold on!" Zoe cried as the dock started to shake, waves growing larger, water spraying onto their legs, their arms, their faces.

The phoenix struck the shell as Arthur gritted his teeth, the pull enormous, stronger than anything he'd felt before. Time slowed down as the shell shattered, the pieces covering the phoenix across its beak and face and chest and wings.

The bird hit the water, and then Arthur divided in two, split cleanly down the middle. This was the farthest he'd ever been from the phoenix, a division he hadn't even been sure was possible. Every muscle in his body tensed. He was floating above the dock, and he was diving to the darkened depths below, water sizzling around him. Discordant, dizzying, the phoenix pushed itself farther and farther. Ahead, the seabed, wavy lines of seagrass swaying back and forth.

The moment the phoenix's beak touched the bottom of the sea, great cracks appeared in the ocean floor, filling with the same white light as Zoe's eyes. Before it was lost to thousands upon thousands of fizzy bubbles, Arthur swore he saw what appeared to be a massive stone statue bursting through the seabed.

On the dock, Arthur opened his salt-stung eyes.

Land rose from the sea with an earth-shattering rumble. The half-moon bay around them filled with rock and sand and grass and trees and thousands upon thousands of flowers. Boats shifted and groaned as the ocean lifted them up and up—including the ferry—long waterways forming underneath that led into open waters. The boats settled back down, the ferry tipping precariously but managing to stay upright.

In front of them, rocky cliffs formed on either side of a white road inlaid with black shells, creating a cobblestone appearance. Great stone statues—at least twenty feet tall—lined the road, sprites in various poses, holding flowers and saplings and birds and lengthy scrolls.

The road continued forming, stone and bedrock snapping into

place. It raced toward the island, and around their home, the ocean swirled angrily, whitecapped waves crashing onto the shores. For a moment, Arthur thought the island *rose from the sea*, but it was an illusion; the island wasn't rising.

It was growing.

As they looked on, Marsyas grew and grew, and when all was said and done, when the last of the light faded, as the sun dipped below the horizon and they lowered slowly back down to the docks, the island they knew was no longer.

It its place, something both familiar and wondrous. The shape of it was mostly the same as far as Arthur could tell, but it had grown to at least five times its original size. Trees that had never grown on the island before swayed in the breeze, large, as if they'd been growing for decades. Between them, through their canopy, small dwellings, what looked like houses, places that hadn't existed when they'd left the island only hours before.

"Home," Zoe said quietly, a single seagull calling overhead. "How it once was. How it will be from now on." She glanced at them over her shoulder, her eyes having returned to normal. A tear trickled down her cheek as she smiled.

"It's for us?" Phee asked in wonder, taking her hand.

"Yes," Zoe said. "For all of us. A gift from the sea."

"Frank!" Chauncey cried in delight as his friend flipped out of the water. He rushed toward the edge of the dock, looking off the side near the ferry. "Wasn't that *bananas*? I flew and did magic! Everything all right down there? What's that? Wow, really?" Chauncey's eyes turned toward them. "Frank says that as far as he can tell, no sea life was harmed. The starfish aren't happy, but they're called the divas of the ocean for a reason."

Arthur took Linus's hand in his. "Children, shall we see what we've made?"

Lucy looked up at them. "But not just us, right?"

"What do you mean?" Linus asked him.

Lucy pointed back toward the village. They all turned and saw their audience was still there and had, in fact, grown even larger.

Hundreds of people stood watching them with no small amount of awe. Helen stood in the front, wiping her eyes as she laid her head on J-Bone's shoulder. "You said it was for all of us," Lucy explained. "That means them too."

"That it does," Zoe said. She raised her voice. "People of Marsyas! Would you like to see your new kingdom?"

The people cheered and with the children leading them, they found their way home.

EPILOGUE

On a crisp autumn morning, Arthur Parnassus took a stroll. He had no particular destination in mind, knowing he'd do well to avoid the south end of the peninsula due to threat of death. Granted, said threat had come from a rather feisty gnome, and while it wasn't the first time (and undoubtedly wouldn't be the last), Arthur decided not to test her, especially today of all days. She had been looking forward to this for a long time.

Besides, he had other things to occupy his attention this morning, and it kept him from becoming completely frazzled.

It'd taken time for him to become familiar with Marsyas as it was now. It could be argued that only Zoe and the children knew their home better, but even they continued to make new discoveries about it.

The former island—now a peninsula—was still covered in trees, the forest thick. In addition to the main houses and Zoe's home, Marsyas was now dotted with dwellings made of stone and crushed shells, all in warm pastel colors, not unlike the village. Some lay in groves of trees heavy with fruit. Others were built *into* the trees, rope ladders dangling down, wooden bridges connecting the homes above the forest floor. Still others had formed beneath the earth into hillsides, the interiors damp and cool.

And the pathways! Where there had once been worn footpaths, stone walkways now covered Marsyas from end to end, crisscrossing the length and width of the former island. The paths were lined with flora and fauna, ancient statues of sprites covered in moss, leafy vines hanging from stone fingers.

The main road wrapped around the exterior of the peninsula, allowing vehicles to cross, bringing visitors who came to see the new Marsyas. They were the perfect guests: they stayed briefly, spent their money, and then went back home.

Arthur smiled as two children ran by him, their laughter loud and free. As he looked back, one of the children—a girl—disappeared. Her friend—a gap-toothed boy with purple eyes and black, scaly skin—shouted, "No fair! You can't turn invisible. That's cheating!" He turned toward Arthur. "Mr. Parnassus, tell Alice she can't cheat."

A harried-looking woman appeared on the path. When she saw Arthur standing there, she sighed and rolled her eyes. "Billy," she said as the boy groaned. "You know the rules. If Alice wants to use her magic, she can. And Mr. Parnassus has bigger things to focus on today."

Alice reappeared. "Sorry, Billy," she said. "Hi, Mr. Parnassus!"

"Alice," he said, tilting his head. "Billy. You look as if the pair of you have been exploring. Find anything interesting?"

Billy brightened, voice dropping to a conspiratorial whisper. "Sal told me there's treasure hidden somewhere on the island. Alice and me are going to find it."

"Ah," Arthur said. "But what if the real treasure is the friendships you make along the way?"

Billy blew a raspberry. "No, yuck. We're gonna find jewels and coins and—"

"—and then give them all back because they're not ours," Alice finished for him.

"Well, yeah," Billy said. "But we'll get the credit for *finding* the treasure. Come on! Sal told me we have to find a rock that looks like Calliope sleeping in the sun. That's how we'll know we're close."

They ran down the path, disappearing from sight.

The woman—Gayle, mother to Billy—shook her head. "Sorry about that."

Arthur held up his hand. "Absolutely no apology necessary. How are you settling in?"

"As well as can be expected," she told him. Though she still had dark circles under her eyes, they were less noticeable than they'd been upon her arrival. "We both slept through the night for the first time last night." Gayle ducked her head. "I woke up this morning and just . . . breathed. It didn't hurt like it normally did. Then I went to Billy's room, and . . ." She sniffled. "He was still asleep. That hasn't happened for a very long time."

"I'm so glad," Arthur said warmly. "You deserve it. Both of you do. Have you given any thought to what we discussed?"

She nodded, determined. "I have. And if the offer is still open, I'd like to accept." She balked a little. "If that's okay with the queen."

Arthur chuckled. "It was Zoe's idea. Though she is many things, the intricacies of the law escape her. Having a solicitor who understands the complexities will make things that much easier."

"I haven't practiced since Billy was born," Gayle warned him. "It'll take a bit for me to catch up."

"Of course," Arthur said. "And if we can be of any assistance, all you need to do is ask."

"Then I'll do what I can. Could you tell the queen that I'd be happy to meet with her next week?"

"It would be my pleasure," Arthur said. "In addition, we've received word that a psychotherapist has decided to come to Marsyas. A selkie, from what I understand. Once she settles in, she has asked if she can set up a practice here. If at any point you or Billy decide that therapy might be beneficial, we will make it happen. I have requested to be a patient of hers as well, as it's high time I get help to make sense of all I've been through. Same with our children, and for anyone else who might need someone to talk to, especially since she has experience with treating the magical community."

"Because we can't do it alone," Gayle said slowly.

"We can't," Arthur agreed.

Then she asked the one question Arthur had heard time after time, the one question on the minds of anyone and everyone: "What if they try again?"

They, meaning DICOMY and DICOMA, who were currently enjoying an unprecedented blowback of epic proportions. After the confrontation, news had spread and spread quickly of the "Miracle in Marsyas," or so it was called. Splashed across the front page of every newspaper and the top story on every newscast on both radio and television, scenes from an uprising: the Baker-Parnassuses standing surrounded by men in suits, the children looking fearful. Zoe descending from above, the last of her people, a queen. The banishment of the invaders. The return of Marsyas to its former glory.

But there was one image that had burned its way into the minds of almost every single person who gazed upon it: Jeanine Rowder, hand raised, ready to strike. Before her, Lucy, at most half her size, face turned up toward her.

This picture—taken by a visitor on vacation with a birdwatching group—became the indelible image of the battle for magical rights. It was printed in papers, shown on every screen, carried on posterboards during rallies where the magical community demanded equal rights. It was pontificated on by pundits who said it was nothing but anti-government propaganda, that the *real* issue here was that the Antichrist was allowed to run free around a village where anything could happen. "Can't you see what they're doing?" one such blowhard bellowed on a radio news program. "They're going to come after your children, indoctrinate them into thinking being magical is *normal*. It's anything but! It's a *choice*. Now more than ever, our way of life is threatened, and we must protect our children. I can barely even sleep at night thinking of those poor, lost souls. See something, say something!"

Though Arthur would've given much to be a fly on the wall when Rowder, Marblemaw, and the goons in suits had suddenly appeared in the prime minister's office, he had to settle with what came next.

Rowder—as they expected—attempted to spin her banishment by holding a press conference, saying she'd been attacked during what she called "nothing more than an inspection, something to ensure the children weren't being abused." She went on to say that what occurred in Marsyas set a dangerous precedent, and asked what she considered to be the most important question facing humanity today: What happens if another magical person does the same thing?

Unfortunately for her, none of the reporters present seemed interested in following her train of thought. Instead, they shouted questions at her, asking her if she'd ever struck a child in DICOMY's care before, if Marblemaw was facing punishment for harming a yeti child in the street in front of dozens of witnesses, if the government planned on recognizing Marsyas as a country, or if they planned to go to war and invade. If so, one journalist continued, what would keep the Sprite of Oceans from banishing every single person sent? "It's not as if *you* could return to lead the charge," the journalist finished.

Rowder gripped the lectern, knuckles white. She leaned forward, practically swallowing the microphones before her. "I will say this one more time: the boy is the *Antichrist*. He is the *son of the Devil*. How is no one *understanding this*?"

The press conference ended without resolution.

Two weeks later, Prime Minister Herman Carmine held his own press conference in his office. Forgoing his usual pinstripe suit, Carmine instead wore a thick sweater and tan slacks, sitting in an overstuffed chair in front of a crackling fireplace. He smiled, he laughed, he poked fun at some of the journalists. Then, as if a switch had flipped, he turned grave and announced that Jeanine Rowder had decided to retire from public service to spend more time with her family. He had accepted her resignation, he said, in hopes that it would smooth relations with their new neighbor.

"In addition," Carmine continued, "I'm pleased to announce I have picked a new head for the Departments in Charge of Magical Youth and Magical Adults. Although she will need confirmation, I doubt there has ever been someone more qualified for the position. Not only did she previously work with Extremely Upper Management, she's . . . well. I'll let her show you. Doreen, would you join us?"

Doreen Blodwell entered the office. She held herself high, moving gracefully and stopping next to Carmine, her hand resting on the back of his chair. She wore a striking pantsuit—bright yellow and white, with a plunging neckline that left little to the imagination. Carmine smiled at her, and Arthur was reminded of what he and Linus had been told in the elevator before the hearing. What had Larmina said to Linus's question?

How have they not discovered her? Or you?

Because we understand how the minds of men work. Give them a little smile, touch their arm, hang on their every word, and they believe they're God's gift to women. And that's all we are. Pretty girls without a thought in our heads.

"Thank you, Prime Minister Carmine," Doreen said, her voice soft, seductive. "It is an honor to have your backing. After I'm confirmed as the head of DICOMY and DICOMA in the new year, I'll be reviewing any and all protocols that have brought us to where we are now. Change can be a terrifying prospect, but if we continue on as we have for decades, I fear that we'll cross the point of no return." She paused, closing her eyes. No one spoke. Eventually, she opened her eyes and said, "You might be thinking you have no reason to trust me. That I will be just like every person who came before. I hope that this will alleviate any concerns."

She brought her hands to either side of her head, palms pressed flat against her hair. Then her hair *shifted*, first to the left, then to the right, before she lifted the wig from her head. Underneath, her shaved skull, scalp pale. But it wasn't the removal of the wig that would be spoken of for weeks—if not years—to come. No, it was the two bony protuberances that rose from the top of her head. Each was black, two inches wide and an inch high.

As the cameras flashed, Doreen said, "I am a satyr. Half, anyway. When I was four years old, I began to grow horns. My mother took me to a doctor who told her that the horns would only get bigger. He offered a suggestion: disbudding." Doreen's gaze hardened. "The same thing used on livestock. Unlike dehorning, disbudding involves hot irons used to kill the horn-producing cells. It was not without pain. It was not without suffering. They will never grow back." She held up the wig toward the cameras. "This was my armor. This was my defense." She tossed the wig to the floor. "I no longer need it because to hide intimates I have something *to* hide. I do not. Change is coming, and luckily, Prime Minister Carmine has decided to be at the forefront as he understands that nothing can stop it." She dropped a hand on his shoulder, her sunshine-yellow fingernails digging in. "Isn't that right, Prime Minister?"

"Yes, yes," he said hastily. "We'll get it right, this time around."

A week later, a letter arrived via carrier addressed to Mr. and Mr. Baker-Parnassus. Inside, written in bubblegum-pink handwriting, a short note:

It's a start. Give me time.
Don't you wish you were here?
xx

"Do you trust her?" Arthur had asked.

"I want to," Linus had replied. "Time will tell, as it does with all things."

And now, with Gayle waiting for his answer, Arthur gave the only one he could: "If they do come for us again, if after all they've witnessed they *still* try, then they will be met with the might of a queen who doesn't have a single solitary shit left to give."

Gayle burst into laughter, covering her mouth. "Mr. Parnassus!"

He winked at her. "Sometimes, certain words show exactly how we feel. So long as there are no little ears listening in, I might as well let it out every now and then."

Billy shouted from somewhere down the path, and Gayle said goodbye before hurrying after her son and Alice. Arthur waited until she rounded the corner before continuing on.

He found the queen in her clearing, white petals falling from the flowering trees around her home, coating the ground like snow. She sat on an old tree stump, wings bright behind her. Sitting on the thick grass at her feet, a group of new arrivals: three adults and two children, all of whom were væters, beings who communed with nature on a level even beyond Phee and Talia and Zoe. All were small—the tallest of them, the grandfather, was barely half Arthur's size. The children were only a foot high, their eyes twice as large as a human's. One of the children—a girl called Frida—heard Arthur's approach, and touched the forest floor, followed by a low pulse of magic that felt like summer. The white petals swirled around him as if caught in a slow tornado.

Zoe stood, taking the elder væter's hand in hers. "Thank you for your counsel. It's wonderful to have confirmation that the land is happy. Please let me know if that changes at any point, and we'll work together to set things right. Now, if you'll follow the path, the trees will guide you to my representative. Martin has your belongings, and will show you to your new home. Anything you need, ask, and he'll make it happen."

The grandfather bowed before the queen, and then led his family down another path that led to the center of the island.

"How is it going?" Arthur asked as Zoe waved her hand, the stump rolling through her open doorway.

"It's going," she muttered. "My people skills need work. My grandmother told me once that being a queen often meant listening without interrupting. She said you could learn more that way." She huffed out an irritated breath. "It's hard not to interject, especially when I hear everything they went through."

Arthur cocked his head. "I expect many of them are simply looking for a sympathetic ear. It's probably the first time anyone has listened to them."

Zoe waved him off. "I know, it's just . . ." She sighed. "It's not going to get easier, is it?"

"No, I expect not. But the stories we're given, these tales of tragedy and hope, the trust placed upon us to listen to each and every word, it's humbling to be their secret keepers. We hold them here"—he rested his hand over his heart—"and here." He tapped the side of his head.

"How many so far?" she asked, staring off into the woods, white flower petals landing in her hair.

"How many have come to the island? With the væters, we're now up to eighty-four, the majority of whom are magical, including thirty-two children under the age of eighteen."

Zoe snorted. "And how are the classes?"

"Exuberant," Arthur said. "We've been lucky enough to have three teachers among the adults who've come here. They're working with Linus to come up with lesson plans that will ensure every child gets a proper education."

"And there will be more," Zoe said. "If it keeps going like it is, we're going to run out of room at some point."

"I know," Arthur said. "But I won't turn people away. We'll figure it out." Then, because he could, he added, "Your majesty."

She made a face. "Keep it up, Parnassus. Being the Sprite of Oceans has allowed me to tap into power I never had before. You don't want to piss me off."

He grinned. "Noted, dear. Now, on to the reason I'm here. I've been told that I'm not allowed anywhere near the south end of the peninsula. If I attempt to arrive before my time, seven children have promised that my death will be neither pleasant nor swift."

"Lucy?"

"David," Arthur said. "I was very proud to hear such a threat from him. It shows he's adapting quite well."

"I heard David accidentally called Linus Papa last week."

"He did. Right in the middle of supper. Linus burst into tears and scooped David up, and that is now the picture that has completed Linus's birt present. The other children made the frame, and David hung it up himself. Plenty of ice cubes all around after that."

"Good," Zoe said. "I bet he's calling you both Dad and Papa by the holidays."

"The greatest gift," Arthur agreed. "But there is no rush. At least not today."

"Oh?" Zoe asked, blinking innocently. "Is there something else going on today that I should know of?" She tapped her chin. "I can't think of a single thing that—"

He hugged her close, face in her hair. She laughed brightly, wrapping her arms around him, nose at his throat. "Is this real?" he whispered.

"It is," she whispered back fiercely. "Everything. All of it. Today, tomorrow, and every day after."

"I dreamed of such a day," he told her as flower petals danced around them. "And now that it's here, I . . ." He chuckled. "I'm a little nervous, if I'm being honest. More than a little."

Zoe pulled away, gripping his forearms. "Scared?"

He shook his head. "Of this? Never."

"He's with Helen?"

"He is. Told me in no uncertain terms that it was bad luck to see him before the ceremony."

"Kicked you out of your own house, did he?" Zoe asked, amused. "Already started."

"It has," Arthur said. "And I, for one, cannot wait."

"Then it's time to see what your children picked out for you to wear." She pulled him toward her house. "They wanted my input, but I told them that this was from them, and they should do whatever they thought was right. Prepare to be . . . well. You'll see."

"That certainly sounds ominous," Arthur said. "Consider me intrigued."

If one had decided to come to the village of Marsyas on that very day, they would have found a ghost town: no one sold food from mobile carts, no music poured from open doorways that led into shops. Even Rock & Soul, the local record store, had closed for the day, which was odd, seeing as how the proprietor—one Mr. J-Bone—tended to arrive early and didn't leave until late at night. It helped that his home was located right above his shop.

There were people on the sidewalks, but they were few and far between, most of them looking a little spooked given how quiet it was. Every now and then, they'd stop in front of signs that covered the main thoroughfare in the village: on windows and doorways and telephone poles. Short and to the point, the signs read: GONE TO CELEBRATE! RETURN TOMORROW!

"Celebrate?" they murmured to themselves. "What could an entire village be celebrating?"

Why, the event of the season, of course! According to those in the know, everyone who was *anyone* wanted an invitation. And though all who wanted to be invited were, it didn't stop Chauncey and Talia from assigning Merle to be in charge of the guest list. Wearing a rather dapper pinstriped suit with nary a mark on it, Merle stood in front of a grove of trees, demanding that everyone in line be prepared to show their invite, and that he would *not* be accepting bribes if said invite had been forgotten.

Arthur heard this as he approached arm in arm with Zoe. As Merle ushered the last of their guests through the trees, Arthur cleared his throat.

Merle started to turn, saying, "Yeah, yeah, you will wait your turn just like . . . Mr. Parnassus! Zoe! Look at the pair of you. You sure clean up nice."

They had. Zoe wore a smart tailored suit the color of red wine, the coat hanging off her shoulders. The hem of her slacks rose halfway up her calves, her feet bare. In her Afro, white gardenias fresh from Talia's garden. She had forgone the crown, saying it didn't matter in the slightest, at least not for today.

The suit selected for Arthur fit like a dream. While he might not have chosen this particular color for himself, the pale pink slacks and coat hugged his frame as if made for him. Rather than appearing like he was mostly made up of knees and knuckles, he cut an imposing figure; Zoe said he was dashing, and immaculately so. The white button-up dress shirt had nary a wrinkle, but it was his socks that really made the outfit. As per his usual, his slacks were a tad too short, revealing gray socks—a gift from Phee—that had lifelike representations of Arthur and Linus, their foreheads pressed together. He was inordinately pleased with the socks and couldn't wait to show them to everyone whether they asked after them or not.

"You do as well," Arthur said.

Merle looked down at his own suit. "This old thing? Fits better than I remember. Last time I wore it, it was for a funeral that had no food. You're having food, right?"

"We are," Zoe assured him. "It seemed rude to invite people and not feed them."

Merle nodded. "Good. Now, Mr. Parnassus, you probably don't need advice from anyone, seeing as how you're . . . you. But! I know a thing or three about love and want to offer you some advice."

"I'd be delighted to hear whatever wisdom you wish to impart," Arthur said.

Merle lifted his hand and began to tick off his fingers. "Don't lie. Don't cheat. Don't steal."

They waited for the rest.

Merle said, "And that's it."

"How on earth are you still single?" Zoe asked.

Merle sniffed. "I have the sea. Don't need more than that."

"I will not lie, cheat, or steal," Arthur said. "You have my word."

"Fine, fine," Merle said. "But listen to me, jabbering on as if you didn't have somewhere to be. Don't worry about the guests. Ferry's ready to go when you want to kick everyone out."

"Thank you, Merle," Arthur said.

"Can you give us a moment?" Zoe asked him. "Please let them know we'll be in momentarily."

Merle nodded and spun on his heel, pushing through the hanging tree limbs that kept them from seeing down to the beach. Beyond the trees, Arthur could hear the excited chatter of a large crowd waiting for them to begin.

"Are you ready?" Zoe asked him.

Arthur didn't hesitate. He knew. "It's taking everything I have not to run to him."

She reached up and touched his cheek. "If only the boy you were could see you now. What would he think, I wonder?"

He turned his face and kissed her fingers. "That love and fire are one and the same."

When Arthur stepped through the trees, he froze, heart lodged firmly in his throat. It wasn't the King singing, like a river flows, surely to the sea, darling, so it goes, some things are meant to be. It wasn't the soft breeze ruffling the petals of the thousands of flowers that decorated the backs of chairs, the trees, the ground. It wasn't the backdrop of the sea, or the cloudless sky that seemed to stretch on forever. It wasn't the salt in the air, the call of the seabirds from high above.

It was the people. More than five hundred in total, a mixture of magical and not. And as if they had practiced, the moment Arthur and Zoe appeared, they stood as one, turning toward them.

The mud representatives—Janet, Barry, and Turnip—had snapdragons growing from their heads and shoulders. As Arthur and Zoe nodded at them, Janet blew her nose into a pile of moss, Barry's arm around her shoulders, Turnip beaming at them as part of his chest sloughed onto the ground.

Merle stood with Martin Smythe, who apparently found the imminent proceedings so moving, he sobbed into Merle's shoulder, much to the ferryman's dismay. Even then, Merle did little to shove Martin away, grumbling under his breath as he rolled his eyes.

Byron and Jason—having arrived the night before, immediately tackled by David—stood holding hands.

Others, too, so many others, all dressed to the nines. The people from the village. People who could do things that defied imagination and those who believed there was magic in the ordinary. Parents. Grandparents. Aunts and uncles. Cousins, friends, guardians, protectors. While some were crying—it was a wedding, after all—most were smiling, nodding as Arthur and Zoe passed.

And that was to say nothing of the children.

All the children, of course: most looked a little bored, tugging on the clothes of the adults around them, whispering as they asked how much longer this was going to last, and if it was almost time for cake. Many of the kids sighed dreamily as Arthur and Zoe made their way down the petal-covered aisle toward seven children in particular.

To the left of the wooden lattice archway stood Phee and Sal, Theodore sitting on Sal's shoulder, a crown of daisies sitting askew on his head. Phee and Sal wore matching outfits—similar to Arthur's, a pale pink with navy blue ties cinched tightly at their throats. Sal's had polka dots on it, like buttons.

To the right of the archway, Lucy, Chauncey, and Talia. Lucy's suit was in contrast to Sal and Phee's, navy blue with a pink tie. Chauncey wore his bellhop cap, wrapped in pink carnations. Talia was dressed head to toe in her finest Gnomish wear: her black boots gleaming, her blue trousers firmly pressed, her pink vest buttoned up the front, and on her head, her cap, the top tilted slightly to the left.

Underneath the archway, David, standing with Helen at a podium. He looked as dashing as he ever had, his black tuxedo fitted perfectly to his hairy frame, the hair on his face hanging in thin beaded braids woven by Byron and Sal. Helen wore her finest overalls, complete with the brand-new boots that Talia had demanded she order. Sitting on the podium, tail twitching dangerously, Calliope, wearing a lacy yellow collar (courtesy of Sal) and a bored expression, as was her right.

Arthur saw them all.

He saved the best for last.

Linus Allen Baker stood at the front, thinning hair windswept, and he'd missed a button on his coat. Arthur had never seen a more handsome man in his life. Linus's suit fit his roundness perfectly, and though Arthur wanted desperately for Linus to give him a little spin so he could take it all in, he managed to keep that thought to himself.

Because Linus was not wringing his hands. He did not appear nervous. As far as Arthur could tell, he did not say "oh dear" even once as they approached. Instead, Linus was smiling, a soft, gentle thing, a single tear falling from his right eye onto his cheek. He did not reach up to wipe it away.

It hit Arthur then, in this moment: everything he'd done, everything he'd lived for, fought for, all the sleepless nights and miles on the road, the good, the bad, and the ugly, *all* of it had led to this.

Mom, he thought in wonder as his breath hitched in his chest. *Look. Just look.*

Their children did not stand on ceremony, which was why the moment Arthur and Zoe reached the front of the crowd, they launched themselves at him. He stumbled back with an armful of gnome and sprite, their guests laughing loudly. Chauncey wrapped his tentacles around Arthur's right leg as Lucy climbed his back, arms in a loose grip around Arthur's throat. Arthur turned his head into Sal's hair when the boy hugged his side, and chuckled wetly when Theodore's forked tongue flicked against his cheek.

Eventually, they pulled away, returning to where they'd been standing.

The guests took their seats as Zoe stood on her tiptoes, kissing him first on the right cheek, then the left. Her eyes glittered when she said, "This is only the beginning."

"It is," he agreed.

She left him, then, going to Linus. Arthur did not hear what she said to him, but whatever it was, Linus sniffled and then hugged her so quickly, Zoe squawked a bright burst of laughter, her feet lifting from the ground as Linus spun her around. Then, seemingly remembering they had an audience, he set her down, smoothed his suit, and looked at Arthur expectantly.

As Zoe joined Helen and David and Calliope, Arthur took the last steps. Everything else faded away as he stood in front of his beloved, the man who had carved a place for himself in a home on a mysterious island. The man who had come with his cat, his rule book, a misplaced sense of purpose, and little else. The man who had once lived where the rain never ended, and all color had been leached, leaving behind only muted shades of gray in the city. This man, this fussy, endearing man who had learned the world was far more mysterious than he'd ever thought possible, and instead of silencing it, had worked to ensure that no one would be silenced again.

"Hello, Linus," Arthur said softly, as if speaking any louder would wake him from this marvelous dream.

"Hello, Arthur," Linus said, and in Arthur's chest, the phoenix chirped and chittered its pleasure.

"Do I start now?" David whispered to Helen as Calliope batted a thick strand of hair hanging down from his head.

"I hope so," Talia said. "Because if you don't, they're just going to stand there making mushy faces at each other."

"You may begin," Helen told David. "Just like we practiced."

"Right," David said, squinting down at the paper before him on the podium. "Except for all the parts I've decided to ad-lib."

"Wait," Helen said. "Ad-lib? What parts are you going to—"

"*Welcome to the party!*" David roared ferociously, fangs bared, claws digging into the podium as he gripped the sides. "I am your host, David! Before we began, I wanted to mention I'm available for all your scary needs, such as birthday parties, funerals, haunted houses, and book clubs. Tired of just reading books and then talking about them? Well, now you can read *and* run for your lives! All for the low, low cost of—"

"I didn't know weddings had commercials," Lucy said.

"Next time, we'll get sponsors," Talia said.

"*Next* time?" Linus said, aghast. "I beg your pardon."

Talia patted his leg. "Why don't you let me worry about that? You have bigger things to focus on."

Linus sighed as David announced he was pretty sure *he* was at the podium and therefore, no one else could talk. After some debate, everyone agreed that David was absolutely correct, though he should probably wait until after he'd finished to promote his side gigs.

"Can I still make some stuff up?" David asked, tilting his head back to look at Helen and Zoe. "Not *all* of it. Just some. I have something to say."

"I insist upon it," Zoe said. "Have your say, David. We're listening."

David rubbed his hands together in glee, little puffs of cold, crystalline air rising between his fingers. He cleared his throat and began to speak into the salt-tinged quiet. "I didn't want to come here at first. I didn't know who these people were, promising me things I'd heard before." He paused, taking in a breath. "I knew Helen, and she was nice to me. She said there was a place where I . . . where I could be me. Where I wouldn't have to hide." He lifted his head, searching the crowd. Arthur followed his gaze, and saw Jason and Byron raise their hands in a wave. He smiled. "I'm a yeti. I have claws and really neat hair that can get messy if I don't take care of it, and sometimes, I like scaring people. Not to hurt them, but to remind them that fear doesn't have to be bad. It doesn't have to be mean or cruel. It doesn't have to cause harm.

"And that's what I'm learning from my new home. It doesn't matter what we look like, it doesn't matter where we came from, or what we can do. All that matters is that we're here, together, being anything and anyone we want to be." David stared at the crowd in anticipation.

Arthur felt a rush of magic, and behind David, a red neon sign popped into existence, blinking the words YOU BETTER CLAP NOW BEFORE YOU LOSE YOUR HANDS.

Everyone did, and loudly, Jason and Byron on their feet, hooting and hollering.

David beamed as Lucy tilted his head to the side, the sign disappearing. "Thank you! You're such a great audience. My point? This place is different. It really is. And maybe everyone doesn't see it that way quite yet, but they will. It doesn't have to be today, or even tomorrow, but it'll happen. I know it."

Arthur believed him.

"Okay!" David said, clapping his hands once more. "Zoe helped me become an ordained minister according to Marsyasian law. It was difficult work, and I almost lost my life, but in the end, I persevered."

Zoe snorted, shaking her head fondly.

"As such," David continued, "no one here gets married without my say-so." He looked pointedly—first at Arthur, then Linus. "Which means that *if* I think you two aren't ready, we'll reschedule for some time in the next five years after going through my pre-marriage counseling program I'll be creating and you can partake in, all for the low, low price of—"

"David," Helen said, "we discussed the power that comes with being ordained. It does not include fleecing those you serve for all they're worth."

"*Actually,*" Lucy said, "religion does exactly that. I mean, come on. Has there ever been a bigger racket?"

"This is going exactly like I thought it would," Talia said, tugging on the end of her beard. "I approve."

Chauncey pulled on Linus's trousers. "Can you do the vows now?" His eyes widened as his stalks shrank almost completely.

Everyone fell silent as Linus lifted his head to look at him, smile wobbling. With shaking hands, Arthur took Linus's into his own, squeezing tightly. In the distance, the crash of waves, the songs of birds.

"How you move me," Arthur said softly. "Some may look upon you and merely see a man. Their loss, because you are so much more. You are sunlight chasing away the clouds on a rainy day. You are the brightest flower in a garden where color fights to exist. I look upon you and see the man, but I also see life teeming just underneath the surface. You have taught me much since your arrival in our home, but if there's one thing I've learned above all else from you, it's this: there is magic in the ordinary, magic that has the power to change the world. You have shown that in your kindness, in your empathy, in your desire to see our children—and everyone else who finds their way to our shores—thrive and succeed. You told me once that when called upon, you will be my strength. You will be my hope. And, my love, I believe you to be just that. Not just for me, but for all of us. Thank you for choosing us. Thank you for loving us. Thank you for *seeing* us." He raised Linus's hands to his lips. "I am honored to know you, and to be given the gift of your heart. I promise you with everything I have, with everything I am, that I will never let a day go by without telling you just how precious you are to your family. And to me."

Merle pulled out a handkerchief, blowing his nose quite spectacularly into it. He wasn't alone; most of the guests were doing the same or, at the very least, wiping their eyes. Turnip pulled out a clump of moss from his chest and offered it to Janet, who took it and wiped her muddy eyes, Barry laying his head on her shoulder.

Linus opened his mouth once, twice, but no sound came out. He blinked rapidly, looking out into the audience. His gaze moved to the children, lingering on each of them. When he lifted his head once more, Arthur could see the fire burning within, bright as the sun.

Linus said, "I didn't know what living meant, not really. I thought I did. I thought it meant existing in the never-ending rain with only sunflowers and records to keep me company."

Calliope meowed quite loudly.

"Yes, yes," Linus told her. "You too. You and me and not much else, was there? But we found a home even though we weren't looking for one, at least not consciously." He looked back up at Arthur. "Because of you, Arthur. Because of you, the people here can lay their heads down at night and not always have to worry about what tomorrow might bring. Because of you, Sal and Phee and

Chauncey and Talia and David and Lucy and Theodore get to just *be*, which is something so many of us take for granted. Because of you, the world is just a little bit brighter. Because of you, I have hope, I have faith, I have the belief that no matter the odds, we will be happy, we will be free, we will know that because of *you*, things are changing. And I am so bloody honored to be at your side." Tears streamed down his face as he smiled. "Well, old boy, you've gone and done it now. Arthur, I love our children more than I can say. I love our home. I love the life you've let me help build. And I love *you* with every fiber of my being. You are in my every breath, in every beat of my heart, and for the rest of my days, I will be by your side, no matter what."

"David," Arthur said without looking away from Linus, "I have the desire to kiss my future husband within an inch of his life. Do I have permission?"

David grinned as he rested his chin on his hands, blinking slowly at them. "Yeah," he said dreamily. "By the power invested in me, and all that jazz. Dad, kiss Papa so hard!"

Zoe and Helen gasped as Jason and Byron howled their joy into the sky.

Arthur and Linus looked at each other, had a three-second silent conversation, nodded, and kissed. Then, without prompting, both turned as one and hurried around the podium. David squawked as they lifted him up, crushing him between the two of them. "What is *happening*?" David shrieked as Linus kissed the top of his head over and over. "I didn't know weddings meant attacking yetis!"

"One of us!" Chauncey cried. "One of us!"

The other children picked up the chant, and as the roar of the crowd washed over them, Arthur and Linus Baker-Parnassus held on to their son tightly. It wasn't long before the others tackled them with no small amount of tears, and as the sun drifted across the sky above a cerulean sea, a phoenix thought in awe, *Hope is the thing with feathers, yes, and hope is the thing with fire.*

ACKNOWLEDGMENTS

In 2022, I did an event where I got asked a question: "What do you think your legacy will be?" Me being me, I gave a pithy response. "What do I care? I'll be dead."

I still mostly think this way. The idea of a *legacy* makes me weirdly uncomfortable. I want to focus on the here and now, the present, and not worry about how I will be viewed in a hundred years, if I even am at all.

But in writing this sequel, I realized that's not quite true. I *do* want to be remembered as something, and it's very specific: not the Antichrist, but the Anti–J.K. Rowling. I want to be her antithesis, her opposite. I want my stories to fly in the face of everything she believes in. At the end of the day, she has no idea who I am, and that's okay. I'll still be here, chugging away, making sure queer stories are told. And I won't be doing it alone. There are so many queer authors writing stories that matter, important stories that show all the different facets of our lives.

To make it unequivocal: J.K. Rowling's beliefs on trans people are abhorrent and have no place in a modern society. People like her—people who believe trans people are somehow lesser—deserve to be shunned until they disappear into the ether. As Arthur says in the novel, "Hate is loud." He's right. People tend to love quietly and hate loudly. But here's the thing: I don't do *anything* quietly. I'm a loud motherfucker, and I will continue to be, especially when my community is under attack.

To my trans readers: this book is dedicated to you. Without you, there would be no us. You are vital, beautiful, and you deserve everything good in this world. There are so many more of us than there are of them. Yes, they're loud and it can feel like their hate is all we see and hear. And yet, I constantly think about the twelve-year-old boy I met at a small school in West Virginia. After speaking to a group of kids, this boy came up to me and said, "I know all about the gay stuff."

Bewildered, I replied, "What do mean?"

He said, "Last year, I had a girlfriend. He came out as trans, and now he's my boyfriend."

If it is that easy for a child, why is it so hard for adults? I don't have an answer to that, aside from this: the younger generations are smart, worldly, and they *pay attention*. They know what's going on, and they are furious. Between their trans classmates being attacked to books being banned from their libraries, the children know what is being done to them. And when they get old enough, they are going to make this world into what it should have been from the beginning: a place where everyone gets to be free without fear of repercussions because of who they are.

This book would not exist without the help of many people.

First, to Christie, Jenna, Rory, and Justin: thank you for taking the time to speak to me again about the intricacies of social work. As I told you all when I first spoke to you in 2018 and then again in 2022, I can't imagine the level of empathy required to do what you do. Your jobs are so, so important, even if you aren't paid anywhere near enough to do what you do. Thank you for giving a damn about kids, and doing your best to make sure no child is forgotten.

To Dr. Chaudry, I appreciate your insight into the psychology of trauma, and how it can compound. I'm sorry I took up three hours of your time in what was supposed to be a thirty-minute phone call. I apparently had a bunch of questions, and you took the time to answer them all with grace and patience, even when I was getting way off course. Thank you for doing what you do, even when it can feel like you're chipping away at a mountain with a pickaxe.

Before writing *The House in the Cerulean Sea* and again before writing *Somewhere Beyond the Sea*, I also spoke to people who have fostered and/or adopted and people who have been fostered and/or adopted themselves. Thanks go in particular to the Hernandez family, who is, in a way, like a real-life Baker-Parnassus family. They even have a Theodore (a rat terrier named Jester) who likes to hide socks under the couch. Your family—made up of people not related by blood, but by choice—is the reason I believe in the goodness in humanity. Thank you for opening your home to those who need a place to rest their heads.

The following people worked on the novel in various forms. They made the book better than it has any right to be.

Ali Fisher, my editor, continually challenges me with my stories. She makes me think in ways that I don't normally when in the middle of writing a book. Without her guidance, all of my books would be a mess. They are legible because of her. Thanks, Ali.

To Deidre Knight, my agent, and everyone at the Knight Agency, thanks for always championing me, and for always having my back. It's wild to think how far we've come in the last six years, and I'm so grateful to have you in my corner. Any success I might have is because of your tireless efforts on my behalf, and I couldn't ask for better representation.

My beta readers—Lynn, Mia, and Amy—get to see my books in their roughest forms, and yet, they still sometimes tell me I did a good job. Which, to be fair, is a hard thing to do when they get books that are six million pages long and instructions from me that basically boil down to PLEASE HELP MAKE IT SHORTER I DON'T KNOW WHY I LOVE ALL WORDS!!! They tell me when something works, and when something doesn't. Anything good in this book is because of them. Something you didn't like? Blame me. And then remember: it's just a book.

To Dianna Vega, the assistant editor: your job is so involved, I don't know how you do it. Thank you for always keeping me informed, and for your hard work. I think everything would fall apart if you weren't there. Thanks.

Saraceia Fennell is my publicist, the one who sends me out into the world. Publicity is one of the hardest jobs in publishing, and she is one of the—if not *the*—best. I don't think I've met a harder-working person than her, and the fact that she puts up with my particular brand of crazy is a testament to her patience. I think you're the bee's knees.

Becky Yeager handles all the marketing and promotion. The incredible artwork we had commissioned? The blogs, the posts, the playlists? That's all because of Becky. She has so many wonderful ideas for how to promote my work, and I am in constant awe of all the things she comes up with. Thanks, Becky.

If you've read my books over the last few years, chances are you've gazed adoringly at the covers. *The House in the Cerulean Sea. Under the Whispering Door. In the Lives of Puppets.* Green Creek. And now, *Somewhere Beyond the Sea.* These covers are by Chris Sickles with Red Nose Studio. I don't know how he does it. I don't know how he can take the images I have in my head and translate them into something real, something tangible. It's like we have the same brain but with different artistic expressions. I write words, Chris makes magic. I've said it before but it bears repeating: I hope I get to work with Chris for the rest of my career. Thank you, Chris.

In addition to Chris, Katie Klimowicz worked on the cover. She is the jacket designer, and boy howdy, does she always do excellent work. Hell, she creates *fonts* that are specific to a work. Who does that?!?! Katie Klimowicz does that. I think she's very, very rad. Thanks, Katie.

Production was handled by production editor Megan Kiddoo, production manager Steven Bucsok, and designer Heather Saunders. They work on so many little odds and ends and keep the process of getting a novel out into the world as smooth as possible. I think of them like a clock, always keeping time. Thanks to the three of you.

William Hinton is the editorial director, and Devi Pillai is the publisher. I wouldn't be here without them, so thank you for believing in my books, in the power of queer stories. I hope to be a Tor author for many, many years to come.

To my queer community: I write these books for anyone who wants to read them, but in my head and heart, I'm always thinking of you first and foremost. In case no one has told you this today: I'm proud of you. I know it's hard being human. I know that it seems like things are getting more difficult. But please don't forget that while hate may be loud, we are louder. And no one can take that away from us.

The Anti–J.K. Rowling
TJ Klune
March 7, 2024

ABOUT THE AUTHOR

TJ KLUNE is the *New York Times* and *USA Today* bestselling, Lambda Literary Award–winning author of *The House in the Cerulean Sea, Under the Whispering Door, In the Lives of Puppets,* the Green Creek series for adults, the Extraordinaries series for teens, and more. Being queer himself, Klune believes it's important—now more than ever—to have accurate, positive queer representation in stories.

tjklunebooks.com
Instagram: @tjklunebooks